A novel of the Revolutionary War in the South

# FROM CROWN TO GLORY:

*The Journey of a Carolina Family from Loyalty to the King to Revolution*

1730-1780

## THOMAS E. NEEL

Note for Librarians: A cataloguing record for this book is available from Library and Archives Canada at www.collectionscanada.ca/amicus/index-e.html
ISBN 1-4120-6689-1

*Printed in Victoria, BC, Canada. Printed on paper with minimum 30% recycled fibre.*
*Trafford's print shop runs on "green energy" from solar, wind and other environmentally-friendly power sources.*

*Offices in Canada, USA, Ireland and UK*

**Book sales for North America and international:**
Trafford Publishing, 6E–2333 Government St.,
Victoria, BC  V8T 4P4  CANADA
phone 250 383 6864 (toll-free 1 888 232 4444)
fax 250 383 6804; email to orders@trafford.com
**Book sales in Europe:**
Trafford Publishing (UK) Limited, 9 Park End Street, 2nd Floor
Oxford, UK  OX1 1HH  UNITED KINGDOM
phone 44 (0)1865 722 113 (local rate 0845 230 9601)
facsimile 44 (0)1865 722 868; info.uk@trafford.com
**Order online at:**
trafford.com/05-1600

10  9  8  7  6  5  4

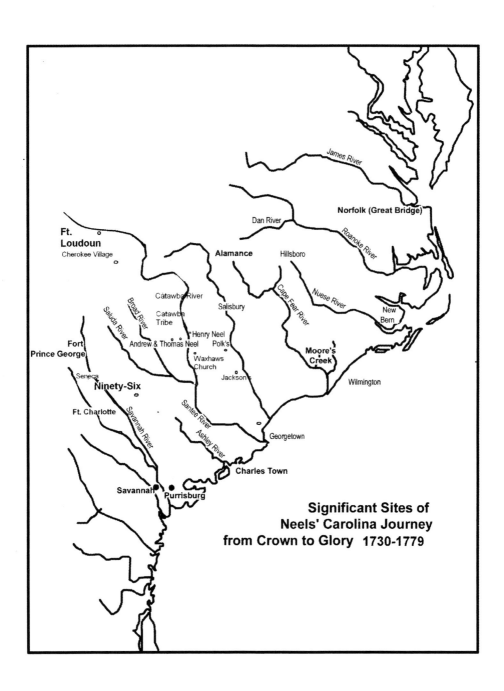

Significant Sites of
Neels' Carolina Journey
from Crown to Glory 1730-1779

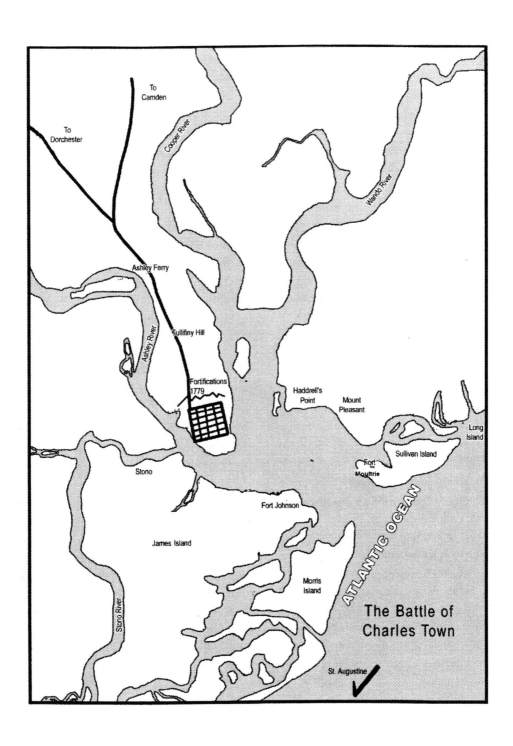

The Battle of Charles Town

# Introduction

This work began with a challenge from my father, Robert E. Neel, on his 95th birthday, to find the ancestors of one Henry Neel born in 1802. With the help of some internet "cousins," Shari Pullon and Jim Neel, I was able to accomplish the task before Bob's passing at age 99.

In the interim I discovered some scarcely recognized heroes of the American Revolution.

This novel is based loosely on the lives and families of Thomas Christopher Neel (DOB 1730), John Henry Neel (DOB 1736) and Andrew Neel (DOB 1746). The genealogists debate the relationship of these scions as to whether they were brothers, cousins, or just happened to have the same surnames. For the purposes of this narrative they are brothers.

I want to thank the research staff of the Carolinian Library, Francis Pettis of the York County Genealogical Society, other discovered cousins and my fellow searchers on the Neel genealogical sites. All of the cousins may not agree with my conclusions, but I could not have finished this work without their assistance.

The research for the work draws heavily from the following works:

McCrady, Edward. The History of South Carolina in the Revolution. New York: Russell & Russell, 1906.

Ramsay, David. History of South Carolina from the First Settlement, 1607 to the Year 1808. Spartanburg, SC Reprint Company 1959.

Buchanan, John. The Road to Guilford Courthouse. The American Revolution in the Carolinas. New York: John Wiley, 1997.

Cochran, David H. The Cherokee Frontier: Conflict and Survival, 1742-1762. University of Oklahoma Press, 1962.

Powell, William S. The War of the Revolution and the Battle of Alamance, May 16, 1771. Raleigh: Division of Archives History North Carolina Department of Cultural Resources, 1975.

Crowe, Jeffrey J. A Chronicle of North Carolina during the American Revolu-

tion: 1768-1789. Raleigh: Division of North Carolina Department of Cultural
Resources.

Lefler, Hugh Talmage. North Carolina History as Told by Its Contemporaries.
Chapel Hill: North Carolina Press.

Pancake, John. The Destructive War: The British Campaign in the Carolinas:
1780-82. University of Alabama Press.

I owe a great deal to my wife, Betty, of some fifty-four years who endured traipsing through battle grounds and grave yards as well as a critical reading of the text. I wish to thank the US and North Carolina Park Service personnel at Alamance, Ninety-Six, Cowpens, Widow Moore's Creek, Guilford Courthouse, and King's Mountain. We also gratefully acknowledge the staff of Bethel Presbyterian Church for the opening of their records. Their assistance was immeasurable. Finally, my thanks to Kadel Laxson for her skillful map work.

One who sets forth on a journey into family history is filled with joy and frustration. Just as you discover one ancestor, you are tempted to find another, ad infinitum. To write about one's own requires a certain dampening of ego. The characters are shown in an unusually favorable light. The hope is that there will be enough fact to allow the story to promote a general spirit of the time.

Thomas E. Neel EdD

# Table of Contents

# List of Characters

An author of a historical novel embellishes the historic record which itself is frequently distorted. The task is to present a believable narrative inventing incidents and characters to fill in the sometimes debated historical record. For example, we were confronted with two historic narratives concerning a scalping- was Jean Neel the wife of Thomas Christopher Neel or was Laurenna Neel, wife of Andrew Neel, the victim?

These are the major characters for which we have some historical record. The date represents the approximate date of birth.

Thomas Neel (1710) migrated from Pennsylvania to Cape Fear and finally the Providence area south of Charlotte. Justice of peace for Providence.

Mary Neel- his wife.

Henry Neel (circa 1720) brother of Thomas and sheriff of Providence.

Colonel Thomas Christopher Neel (1730) son of Thomas (1710) and Mary and father to the twins Andrew and Thomas and other children which are developed in the story.

Captain John Henry Neel (Henry) (1736) perhaps another son of Thomas (1710). Married to Nancy Agnes Reid. They had seven children.

Andrew Neel (1742) brother of John Henry and Thomas married Laureena Smith and produced three children.

Jean Spratt Neel wife of Colonel Thomas.

Thomas Polk- Militiaman and friend of Col. Thomas Neel and neighbor.

Susan Spratt Polk- wife of Thomas Polk, ancestor of President James Polk and sister to Sarah Neel.

Attakullakulla or Little Carpenter- a peace chief of the Cherokees who earned his name by his sharp negotiation skills.

Dragging Canoe- son of Little Carpenter and the war chief of a Cherokee tribe who led several raids.

Flora McDonald- an émigré from Battle of Cullendon and a possible consort of Bonnie Prince Charlie. She spent some time in the Tower of London and was the wife of a British officer.

# Ficticious Characters

Uncle Arthur-slave of the Thomas Neels who acts as a foreman of first Thomas (1710) plantation through two generations.

Zeke Proctor- a trail driver who runs a mule train from Pennsylvania to Charles Town and keeps the Neel plantations advised as to the outside world.

Alexander- huge freedman who acts as Proctor's foil and assists him on his drives.

Running Path-fictitious chief of the Catawba Tribe.

Artimas McGhee- a protagonist who engages in illegal Indian trading with his partner.

Squawman Johnson- a protagonist and partner with Artimas who is constantly opposing the Neels while staying in the good graces of the Crown and some of the Indian tribes.

Christian Huck- Scotch immigrant paroled under the acts following the Battle of Culloden, 1746. He served with the Carolina militia, becomes a close friend of the Neels, but later joins the King's forces against the Rebels. The agonizing decisions of whether to be loyal to the King or join the rebel neighbors represents a typical crisis of the period.

Major Anderson- a British officer and friend to Henry Neel.

---

CHAPTER I

# *Henry Arrives*

## 1736

The peace of the mild but brisk December Carolina afternoon became shattered by the noise of two matched Cherokee bred horses thundering down the roadway toward the Neel plantation. Evergreen sentinels stood along the path and masked the starkness of the hickory, maple, and oak which looked bare as they shed the last of their glorious color. The wheels of the curricle blurred as the large horses driven furiously by their driver shed foam from their mouths. Steam rose from their backs.

At the driveway Uncle Arthur dressed in a rather formal livery of black vest, blouse, pants, hose and shoes, gazed down to see the heads of the two horses coming from a cloud of dust. He turned toward what would later be called a federal house and yelled, "Master Tom and Miz Mary are here."

The horses came to an abrupt stop. Their nostrils flared as they heaved and shook their heads, scattering foam on Uncle Arthur. In disgust he grabbed the bridle and screamed at the young twenty something male as he jumped from the small carriage, "Master Tom, you are killing my babies. I have told you a hundred times, you cannot drive these horses this way. When you was younger I would have whupped you for that."

The six foot red haired man dressed in buckskin smiled at his mentor and added, "How well I remember. I have never killed them yet. Are you glad to see me?"

Arthur turned to his small black son, "Samuel take care of my babies. Rub them down, water them, and then put them away. It will take a week to recover." Arthur then turned to his master and continued condescendingly. "Well, yes, things have been too quiet around here."

They both proceeded to the other side of the two wheeled curricle. Thomas took two month old baby Henry and placed him on one arm and motioned for his wife Mary to take his hand. She slapped it and allowed Uncle Arthur to help her to the ground. She threw back the hood of her full length purple velvet cape, fixed her fiery black eyes on her husband, and turned in rage to Uncle Arthur.

"Uncle Arthur, why didn't you teach this imbecile how to properly drive a carriage?"

1

"Lord, Miz Mary, I tried. I thought you would have tamed him by now," he chuckled.

"He is worse than a wild stallion. Oh look, here comes Thomas."

Young six year old Thomas ran to his dust covered mother and hugged her around the waist, "Mama, Mama, it is so good to see you. Did you see all the soldiers, sailors, and big ships at New Bern?"

"Now, now give your mother a kiss, and we will tell about it later."

He kissed his mother and then his father. Mary, Thomas, and the children moved toward the house to be greeted by Thomas's recently widowed mother and Tom's step brother, John Simpson.

Thomas approached the front door, lifted the latch and went in. The great room with its low exposed beamed ceilings ended with a large fireplace that helped dispel the damp air. Small windows were on each side of the fireplace which furnished most of the light across the room. A small window by the door allowed light but the casement was small enough to allow protection to a potential rifleman in an attack.

After visiting with his mother and his step brother, Thomas went through the dining area and out to the cook house. The smells of a Christmas feast filled the air. On the preparing table pumpkin, mincemeat, and sweet potato pies were laid out. A mix for a cake was standing to the side. Thomas slipped over and stuck his finger into the mixture. A spoon slapped his wrist. "Master Tom, you git yourself out of my kitchen."

He turned to the sixty something black servant, Aunt Sarah, lifted her in the air and gave her a hug. "You spoiled child, put me down!"

"Aunt Sarah, surely you can give your poor starving child something to eat."

"Here take this biscuit and get out of here. We have tomorrow's Christmas dinner to prepare."

Thomas grabbed a piece of pumpkin pie and ran out the door.

He looked out at his father's plantation. It was just six years since his father, Henry, had sold his property in Pennsylvania and moved south with the encouragement of the new Royal Governor, Council, and Assembly of the Colony of North Carolina. The elder Henry accepted land at the confluence of Neil Creek, which he christened, and the Cape Fear River. Their first endeavor was the harvesting of naval stores such as turpentine, pitch, masts, and other lumber for ship construction. These were delivered to the family wharf on the river or, in the case of the masts, floated down to Wilmington. The port of Wilmington was a trial, as sand continually silted the entrance. Raising crops for use on the plantation as well as some cattle complemented the ship stores production. Drovers herded some of the excess livestock to New Bern or Wilmington for market. As the Royal Navy was in constant need of the ship stores, North Carolina became a vital colony for furnishing the stores to support the world's largest navy. Most of the large timber had already been harvested in England, making the goods of North Carolina essential to the welfare of His Majesty's navy. Neel's land was virtually self sufficient by virtue of its harvest, hunting, and livestock. Ship stores produced capital.

To facilitate delivery of ship stores, the Neel heirs built a saw mill by ponding Neil Creek. As the land was cleared, wheat, flax, and a small stock of tobacco were cultivated. Livestock roamed freely with salt and water available each night at the lean-to barns enticing them to return. Soon sizable herds roamed free, and fencing with rickrack became necessary in the barn area. All bonded servants and their families prospered with warm cabins, food, and clothes. Thomas began indenture contracts with those Negroes who seemed able to be independent and to learn a trade. This caused some stir among the neighbors; one simply does not give indentured contracts and eventual freedom to Negro slaves. After his father Henry passed on, Thomas was made the Thane or head of the Neel families. The stepbrother John Simpson gradually became less important in their lives.

The first home for Thomas and Mary on the small farm was a crude affair with a great room, a rod and one-half square. A bedroom was attached as well as an upstairs room. The lodging was made of logs with a thatch roof and chimney at each end. Unusual for a first home was a wood floor. At first a ladder led to the upper floor, later stairs were added. They gradually moved their share of the furniture from the old plantation to the new. The abode was simple compared to the old plantation home of his father, which had many imported furnishings. Servants were still housed in the original plantation. Now thoughts of moving further south occupied conversations.

Most mornings a fog hung over the land when it was not nourished by abundant rain. Not far from the house, fires blazed night and day as the workers burned hickory beneath large kettles preparing pitch for his Majesty's Navy. Others prepared lumber or tapped the pitch pine. All commercial products were hauled or floated to the Cape Fear River, then transshipped to Wilmington.

After a small supper with mother Sussanah and John Simpson, Thomas, Mary, and their two boys retired to their cabin one half mile away. Thomas and Mary contemplated the chance to break away from the plantation of his father and brothers, sisters, and their families. Thomas noticed that Mary was awake. She nursed little Henry.

As he turned to view, he lit a small candle from a taper from the fireplace and remarked, "I love you, Mary. You are even more beautiful."

"Thank you, my handsome husband. You seem restless. What troubles you?"

He turned, placed his hands behind his head, and looked at the raftered ceiling. "I was dreaming of how it would be to strike out on our own in the new lands to the south and west that the Governor Nathaniel Johnston offered us."

Having finished nursing Henry she tucked him in the cradle beside the bed. "Thomas, you restless baboon, I as yet do not share such a dream. I am happy here near my family and the support we enjoyed with Father Henry and our families. Don't you recall the Yamese Indians were subdued here just before we came? The tribes in the south and west are still living like heathen savages."

"Now calm down. I heard the good Lord Cummins had taken some representatives of those western tribes to England and now they are quite content with English rule. Besides I am afraid that His Majesty's bishopric church will soon try to exercise dominion over us. Our treasured rule by local presbyters or elders continues to be illegal. We are concerned that out Presbyterian associations and societies will be crushed. In fact our marriage is illegal since Brother Samuel performed it, and had our little Henry and Thomas not been re-baptized in the bishopric church they would be bastards according to English law."

"I have concern for our souls when I consider that we have a just God when Negroes and Indians are treated so outrageously."

"Now, now my Dear, we can't solve all the problems at once. If it weren't for us their souls would have never heard about the true Christian faith. We are trying to bring the blessings of civilization to both races. I hope someday to avoid the use of indentured and bonded servants and will try to treat the Indians as friends. They need the message of Christ also." Thomas uttered another prayer and blew out the candle. Soon weariness overcame the excitement and they fell into slumber.

At noon the next day the Neel clan gathered at the great house. A massive imported Queen Anne table with curved legs that terminated with a ball at their feet was carefully prepared for more than a dozen. An Irish linen faux damask table cloth graced the top with silver and imported porcelain plates, fancy stem ware, and candelabras at each end. Soon the family gathered around the table and stood back of the caned seated straight backed chairs. At the head of the table was Mother Sussannah, moving down the table were John Simpson, Samuel and Rebecca, Henry Sr., sisters Jane and Elizabeth, Brother Andrew and his wife Alicia, and finally Thomas, little Henry and Mary. As they stood at the table Samuel led a prayer. Sam then lifted his glass of claret and said, "Here is to the new mother Mary the queen of the clan."

The glasses were lifted. Rebecca punched her husband Samuel and blurted, "Queen of the clan? What am I a scullery maid?"

"Well as soon as you make me a father you can be the queen."

"It will not be very soon with your attitude." The table rocked with laughter. There followed a main course of ham, venison, and wild turkey. Vegetables, dressing, and gravy complemented the feast. The family then adjourned to the great room for dessert, brandy and punch.

Andrew stood and remarked, "Now Brother Thomas, you have something to tell us. I don't suppose you went all the way to New Bern solely for a bishopric baptism by those Anglican dandies."

"Correct, Mary and I had quite an adventure. Let me review with you our adventure."

## Thomas's Account of New Bern

Mary and I left young Thomas in the care of Mother and you dear sisters. We departed on an unusually bright December morning and enjoyed good weather all the way to New Bern. Because worship outside the Church of England is forbidden, we Presbyterians as well as Baptists continue to attend "societies" while giving feigned allegiance to the Anglican Church. We must stop this.

Sunday, our small family attended a service of the New Bern Anglican Church as required by law and had Henry baptized. Little Henry frowned and seemed to resent the King's religion. Later, we joined other Presbyterians in the house of a Presbyterian elder/minister Eugene Hodges, and baptized Henry in the Presbyterian faith.

That evening beside a warm fire and after a fine dinner we exchanged the news of the day. Elder Hodges in his well worn waist coat, gators, worn shoes and spectacles cleared his throat and began, "The Test Act is detestable. When we supported King James we thought we would have freedom of religion. Now all people are required to attend the services of the bishopric Church. We are required to pay the wages of their clergy and swear allegiance to that faith. My conscience is not free. I would like to begin tonight's vespers with a reading from the Psalms." He began to read in his deep sonorous voice.

"'Blessed is the man who sitteth not in the council of the ungodly nor standeth in the way of sinners, but his delight is in the Lord and on Him does he meditate day and night.'"

He continued, "I am forced into the counsel of the ungodly. We of the Scottish Church believe, like Elder Knox, that bishops ruling over us are contrary to the teaching of the King James Bible. I feel hypocritical that I must pay for beliefs I do not hold. I am enraged that I cannot legally perform baptisms and marriages in the

King's name. But the day is coming when men will rise up and worship the Lord in spirit and in truth."

Mary then drew back in horror, "Sir, I am indebted to your hospitality; however, what you speak borders on treason. I advise you to be careful with whom you speak or we shall all be punished." (That is just like Mary.)

"There, there, fair madam. We are among friends here. Is that not right, friend Thomas?" replied Elder Hodges.

"Quite right. I am sure my Father's reputation will act as a cloak to protect us. However, I think we should be careful or we shall be drawn and quartered. I go to the governor tomorrow. What hear you?"

"We are not sure how he regards the Presbyterians. I have heard he is a Scot," he responded.

Next morning, having spent the night at the New Bern Inn we called on the Clerk of the Court and registered the birth of Henry. As I was writing the birth notice, the Clerk approached me.

"His Excellency, Governor Johnston, has made inquiries about you. It seems he is looking for a judge of the new area around the newly sparsely settled area, Providence."

"Thank you for the boon, your Grace. Would it be proper to call on him?" asked I. I was mildly puzzled by the requested audience in light of the conversations with Elder Hodges the night before.

"Tuesdays he holds open court for anyone who wishes to address him."

The next day we appeared before the Governor's residence. A captain of the guard was seated on the portico. Two sentries in white gray clay pants, crimson tunics, and regimental headgear stood by with their Brown Bess muskets stiffly at attention.

I stepped forward. "Lieutenant, I am Thomas Neel of Upper Cape Fear and I wish to have an audience with His Grace."

"Please proceed, he is expecting you," he said.

Mary carried young Henry as we entered a hall of the modest two story brick home. The floor was of highly polished oak. The walls contained portraits of the monarchs King William and Mary, Queen Ann, and King George II. A likeness of His Excellency Governor Nathaniel Johnston complemented the pair. Moving down the hall they approached a double door. In front of the door sat a secretary properly wigged and in formal attire. As you recall, there is no established seat of government at this time. The Governor might be in one building with the Council while the Assembly met in a tavern.

"Please state your business."

"I am Thomas Neel, and this is my wife and child. We would address the Governor."

"Oh, yes, Master Neel, he is expecting you."

He then turned and opened the doors to a large carpeted room, with a high ceiling and draped windows from which the sun shone on the Governor seated at a desk. The desk was of the finest workmanship as was his imported James Ranne chair. The furniture contrasted with the bleakness of the rest of Governor's temporary residence.

Bowing from the waist the secretary announced, "Your Lordship, Master Thomas Neel, his wife, and son."

We bowed. I wished I were wigged. I glanced at my travel clothes which consisted of a waist coat, decorated vest, blouse, knee britches, worsted stockings, buckled shoes, and a beaver hat which I removed and held in my hand. Mary wore linen shift with a bodice and cloak. Her hair was encased in a proper bonnet that seemed to draw out her natural crimson lips and dark black eyes. She is as always a striking woman. (Mary blushed and turned away.)

"Please come and join me." He motioned to the chairs by his dais. The Governor wore the uniform of a major of the Fusiliers.

"Thank you, Sir,"

"It grieved me greatly to hear of the death of your father Squire Henry, but I see you have made a glorious addition to the Neels. You have a fine lad there, Madam."

"Thank you, Your Grace. Your kindness is greatly appreciated," replied Mary. I was somewhat concerned at the leering glances the Governor gave Mary.

"How goes it with your family? Are they all well?"

"Yes, Your Grace, my brothers and I are continuing to produce ship stores. We have plentiful mast timber that is much sought after. Our attempts at commodities are somewhat limited because of the paucity of labor and difficulty of transport."

The Governor nodded and sniffed some snuff from his wrist. "I have always been impressed by the industry of the Neel clan. Let me get to my issue at hand. I am anxious to assist Arthur Dobbs and Henry McCullough in developing the land to the south in the rear area called Providence."

He moved to a map and pointed to the area. "The Crown granted these gentlemen over one million acres on the Yadkin, Catawba and Eno rivers. We are to bring in Protestant settlers and need families of the finer sort to keep order there. We are concerned that the Cherokee tribe has run up a great debt with our traders. Further, there are rumors that the French and Spanish are exercising undo enthusiasm for those tribes. We also have Moravians, Quakers, and lowland Scots, like you, coming in from the northwest from the Trading Path. They are without the benefits of the Crown such as justice before the law and systematic exposure to Christian values.

"In addition, I am concerned with the recent slave unrest in the Barbados as well as in South Carolina. If that isn't worry enough, the Crown has granted Lord Oglethorpe a charter for Georgia which will, among other things, prohibit slavery and bring the most abhorred dregs of society to our shores – he wishes to settle his colony with prisoners and debtors. We need to put strong families in the area to strengthen our position and produce some kind of order. I propose to offer 1,000 acres each to you and your brothers to start a settlement in the area. In addition, I propose to make you a captain and constable of the militia as well as Justice of the Peace. As Justice you will also serve as a judge, when I appoint additional justices, and be responsible for the improvements and order in the district. You will have a draw on the armory for any ordnance you and my adjutant feel you may need. What say you?"

"His Lordship is most generous. I would like to take some time for my wife and brothers to think over the offer."

"I understand. As you know you Presbyterians have been shown to be very energetic. Over here we are not concerned about old battles in the Commonwealth. However, the Crown sends us second-rate clergy from which we receive little help. Having loyal subjects of the Presbyterian faith on the frontier would allow you to practice your unusual religion in relative peace as well as establish the values not only among the Indian nations, but also among the banditti who settle in the hinter land without the moderating influence of civilization. My clerk will give you a letter of introduction to Mr. Dobbs." I was abashed to learn that the Governor knew about his rising passion for the purity of the Presbyterian religion.

"Thank you Your Lordship, you have been most gracious. This enterprise will take much thought."

"I hope you will accept. I shall have my clerk draw up an agreement that will be sent to you by the Captain of the Guard. He will be authorized to assist you in any way he can."

We arose, bowed, and walked backward to the door and retraced our steps for home.

"May the Lord be praised," I heard Mary say. "Why, when we are just getting settled in our new home, want to move to that heathen land?"

"We must look to the future, my Dear." I added, "We have an opportunity to live like fat English lords. Anyway we can at least meet with Master Dobbs and see what he has to say."

"I believe His Lordship is a scoundrel. Did you see the way he leered at me? I felt like a common trollop."

"I must get you into the outside world more often. You are a most attractive woman and will have to get used to having men looking at your charming countenance, although they do make me quite jealous."

Mary forced a smile and then hit me with her free hand. "You, like all men are a scoundrel and a cad."

"Ah, the trials of living with the most charming vixen in the colonies," I lamented. (Mary threw a napkin at him.)

We later met with Arthur Dobbs who expressed great pleasure at our interest. He promised tools, seed, surveying, credit, and other means of support for the venture. And now we are back.

***

Around a warm fire in their father's old main grand hall, Thomas ended his narrative and continued.

"I have called you together to discuss an offer from his Lordship Governor Johnston. It appears that there is a need for a militia and strong families to occupy some of the land between the Yadkin and Catawba Rivers. It seems there is a great migration of our mostly lowland Scot brethren down the Warrior Path from Pennsylvania. His Excellency is also concerned about the recent slave insurrections in South Carolina, the threats of the French and Spanish, and, of course, the Cherokees who incurred debts with some less than honest traders. We may need to help the Georgia colony which has recently been given to Lord Oglethorpe. In return for our settlement, he has offered us 1,000 acres each."

Samuel, with much surprise, stated, "I have heard of this Georgia Colony. They will forbid slavery and bring in the vilest rubbish from the slums of London-thieves, prostitutes, and all sorts of base riff raff. Why bring in a colony which forbids slavery when there are threats of insurrections in Barbados and the other Carolina? We would be very close to that vile land."

"His Lordship has given most generous offers. There are some dangers but if enough families take up his offer we should be secure. It wasn't two decades ago that this area was uninhabitable because of the Tuscara and Yamasee Wars. Now those tribes have moved north. Besides, I understand that at least the Catawba tribe out there is quite friendly," added Mary. Thomas looked in surprise at the apparent change of heart.

"What think you, Brother Henry?"

After pausing to light his pipe, blowing a ring of smoke and looking into the air he answered, "It is well to keep on the good side of His Lordship. Also, this is an opportunity to leave a grand legacy to our ancestors. It is indeed a tempting offer. I say we take a trip to look it over."

# CHAPTER 2

# *Providence*

They took a week to pack. Each of the brothers, Thomas, Henry, and Samuel, rode a horse and led a mule with supplies. Each carried two pistols, knife, Pennsylvania rifle, and two hatchets. Some small pots and trading beads were added to the cache and food supplies. They bid good bye to their families and left the operations in the hands of their step brother John Simpson, brother Andrew, their wives, and trusted indentured and bonded servants. The train departed, heading west up the Cape Fear River until they met the warrior trading paths to the south.

On the evening of the third day the brothers were camped near the Warrior Path. They had chosen an area near a stream with a perpendicular cliff at their backs. Soon a full moon appeared. They roasted the hindquarter of a deer and supplemented the kill with some roots. Henry lit his pipe as he leaned against the cliff base. Shadows from the fire danced against the wall. Warm feelings of fellowship permeated. Samuel spoke up.

"Thomas, how has this trail changed since you first saw it?"

"Not much really."

"You know I never heard from you about your first trip here," replied Henry.

## THOMAS'S NARRATIVE OF HIS FIRST TRIP TO THE WAXHAWS

As you have heard the family had settled in Pennsylvania after arriving first at Boston with Roger Williams. After Williams returned to the Puritan faith, we migrated to the middle of Pennsylvania with a group of Presbyterians. We did not feel welcome among the Puritans.

In August of 1728 my family granted me permission to accompany Zeke Proctor on one of his trading trips with the Indians. Zeke usually began his yearly trip at Pennsylvania with ten or twelve mules packed with trade goods.

Zeke hasn't changed much. When I first saw Zeke I was in awe. He was a twenty year old of robust build with a thick black beard, buckskin shirt and pants, beaver hat and trail boots. Zeke, like other traders, rode the Appalachian trails trading with the various Indian tribes. His bronzed face told of his years on the trail. Occasionally, he would do contract service for His Majesty's troops. He rode in the saddle like he was part of his majestic horse, Essau. His train usually consisted of the twelve mules as well as a freedman, Alexander, and occasional roustabouts. Zeke's wit and worldliness made a hit with all the males, but the women feigned shock while being charmed by his romantic nature. Alexander, his black companion, was always an enigma. Extremely tall and mighty in build, he moved freely among white, servant and Indian peoples. He seemed to charm women of all ages and races. But most of all he acted as a foil for Zeke's actions. Alexander liked to remind people that he was a grandson of some African king. There was a constant good-natured banter between the two on this and other assertions, frequently tempered by uncontrolled raucous laughter. Mother was not all that impressed.

In preparation for the journey, I packed a warm woolen blouse, deerskin suit, two sets of moccasins, two sets of socks that Mother made me and a beaver felt hat. Knives, blankets, pistol, horn, lead, and bullet maker were placed in my satchel behind my saddle.

As we were about to leave, Zeke asked, "Thomas, I hear you are handy with iron."

"Yes, sir," I replied.

"Let me see your hands." He examined them. "I can see from your hands arms that you have truly worked as a smithy. I saw you shoeing me animals yesterday. How about smithing on the way south? Sharpening knives for me red brothers will be quite handy."

"If I have the goods, I will serve you well."

Zeke negotiated borrowing a small anvil, bellows, and some tools including a grinding wheel. He did this in exchange for some specie, perhaps Spanish coin, promised on the return. He also added another mule.

Preaching Elder McAntish blessed our entourage. I was given a copy of the *King James Bible* for my saddlebag. Zeke assigned me my horse Jacob – a big cross between a Shire and Arabian approximately fifteen hands high. Samuel Burns joined us that day as we passed their farm. Sam and I would become quite close.

Our duties on the trail consisted of watering all horses and standing one watch of the sand glass per night. We constantly checked all fettered livestock and continually circled the camp.

The first light of morning one I was kicked in the foot by Alexander and told to get some firewood. As we journeyed that day I became more involved with Sam Burns. He was a strong striping lad with a warm smile and an engaging manner. We talked of the old life in Ulster and the challenges which lay ahead. We were both scouting for new land for our families.

The second night we reached the village of York. Earlier, we crossed the Susquehanna by ferry. That was exciting. This Indian trading post was the junction of the Great Trail to the west and the Great Trading Path to the south. Our travel here was rather easy as we were on a crude wagon road. Zeke traded some pots and pans and took a note for picking up either money or hides on the return trip. Zeke explained that the Great Path was a warrior path for southern and northern Indian trade as well as war.

The path meandered the middle ground of Virginia. It was a kind of "No Man's Land" which was used for hunting. The Cherokee in the south and the Shawnee in the north sent occasional war parties against each other. No permanent settlements were in this area for fear of raids. The Iroquois and their confederation in the north were feared by the southern tribes of the Cherokee and Shawnee, so the area became a kind of buffer zone reserved only for hunting.

We continued on the Trading Path. The gentle rolling hills soon gave way to the valley between the Blue Ridge and the Appalachian Mountains, up Uncle Edward Creek. We then cut over to the Shawnee Village of Opequan. I remember much excitement as we came into the village. Dogs barked and little children ran to meet us. Chief Silent Warrior came from his long lodge to greet Zeke. Silent Warrior was six feet tall. His body was strikingly lithe for a man of forty. His small pox marked face, height, and piercing eyes countenanced our attention. Warrior and Zeke linked arms. They were interrupted by a two-year-old Indian lad who came out of a lodge, ran to Zeke, and placed his hands in his belt satchel where he pulled open a deer skin pouch liberating some maple candy. Zeke picked him up and told us that this was his own son, One Who Scampers.

The lodges were of two kinds. The first was an oblong building with a hole in the roof for smoke and an entrance which required one to stoop low in order to enter. There were structures along the log and rickrack walls for sleeping. The second kind of lodge was an open thatched structure used as a summer domicile.

Zeke was an honest trader. As he traded knives and metal hatchets for furs he did not break out the rum until the trading was concluded. That evening as we sat outdoors around the council fire swatting mosquitoes, Chief Silent Warrior told of the origins of the Shawnee people. Co-cum-tha, the great grandmother, who arose from the sea. The word Shawanoes means "water people."

Zeke translated the tale for us. Sam and I were asked about the origins of our people. We told the Genesis account of creation. The Chief was especially pleased with the Noah story and felt that we had copied the tale of the Shawanoes.

Next morning there was much discussion with our troop and the Chief. The talk turned to the summer hunt, crops, concern about the Cherokees, and whether they would be raiding. I set up shop sharpening knives and a few hatchets. The Shawnees' children were most impressed with my sharpening wheel. I made some charcoal for the primitive forge. I then engaged in repairing kettles and fabricating a few broken musket parts. In addition to hunting the people survive on the three "Indian sisters," corn, squash, and pumpkin. This time of year most of the men were hunting and the women were busy curing hides, drying meat and fruits. The village stank of singed animal hair and human excrement. There was a constant buzzing of flies around the hides.

The second night we chose to sleep in the open because of the good case of fleas we received sleeping in the lodge the first night. Sam and I were shocked when a young maiden, assigned to serve us, stripped her buckskin dress in front of us and smeared herself with bear grease as she coyly smiled. As we stood shocked at our first naked female figure. She offered us some bear grease which we refused. We later learned Indians grease to keep the insects away as well as furnish some protection from the cold and the heat. Another explanation of her behavior was perhaps an attempt to tempt us.

Next morning Sam and I dived into the creek and drowned the little critters that used our bodies as a host. As we came out of the water we discovered several young maidens giggling as they gazed on their first naked white men. When they saw us they ran away. Our efforts at getting clean were wasted. That night there was a tremendous thunderstorm, and although we did not sleep in one of the flea infested structures we kept dry under our oilskins.

The next morning we packed. We received corn meal and some deerskin bags as a part of the trade. As the twelve mules and four horse train hit the trail, Zeke related to me that he was worried about the Indian trade. There were renegades coming in and cheating the Indians. Toward evening we set up camp on the Potomac River. We forded the Potomac. As soon as we reached the bank we checked our supplies for water damage and were relieved to find them safe. Alexander and Sam spent an hour hunting and brought in a deer. As we did not have time to process meat, we hunted about every third day.

We continued following the well-worn path along Uncle Edward Creek and visited another Shawnee village. We passed a small band of Tuscalara Indians on the trail heading north. They looked starved and related that they had been robbed by a band of white men. Zeke gave them a couple of quarters of deer. They were a sad group. Zeke also gave them a musket, some powder, and bullets to help them to hunt. The refugees related that some of the tribe had already joined the Delaware and Conestoga. Zeke related that if the great Iroquois Federation heard of his kindness they would be pleased.

The inhabitants of the next village were a mixture of English and French farmer/ traders called "voyagers" who intermarried with the Cherokees. I was impressed with the men. They were of middle stature, of an olive color, their skins stained with gunpowder pricked into pretty figures. The hair of their heads was shaved except for a patch on the hind part. The Cherokees in this village had become quite docile because their ranks had been decimated by smallpox. Some of the women were decidedly comely.

The lodges were made of wood and turf. As we approached the village, Zeke met the Chief Big Buffalo. After an exchange of greeting, the chief looked at me and motioned me toward a young but beautiful girl, probably fifteen. Zeke told me she was to be my companion. I had some questions about this but kept them to myself. Her name was Morning Bird. She had long black hair, a deerskin dress which barely covered her thighs, a comely shape, and winning smile. Her long black hair was turned up and fastened with a silver broach. We had trouble communicating as she spoke only rudimentary English. Most of our communication was by pointing.

The second day Chief Big Buffalo motioned Zeke and me toward him.

"You, young buck. What your name?"

"Thomas," I replied.

"I call you One Who Works with Fire. I watch you. You would be a great boon to our village. Do you have a woman?"

"No," I replied.

"This is my daughter Morning Bird" pointing to his server. "She belong in your lodge. You become my son and part of Buffalo Clan."

I replied, "I am honored, Oh great Chief Big Buffalo, and your daughter is most beautiful; but I have mission to perform for my father who lives in the far north and as a white warrior I vowed to take no woman until I am finished."

Zeke grabbed me by the collar and pulled me aside. "You insulted the chief. It is considered rude to reject his hospitality. Be a man!"

"Sir," I replied, "I am a Christian of the Presbyterian persuasion and consider the sins of fornication to be contrary to the Lord's word."

"You have insulted the chief," he said with a frown, "but I will try to make amends. You know he wants you for a son in law because he needs a blacksmith."

"That is just fine, but where would we get the iron stock? By the way how come there are two chiefs?"

"You ask a lot of questions. The Cherokees really have two chiefs, a war, or red chief and a peace or white chief. Depending on the conditions, the head of the tribe is exchanged. Your friend, happily, is peace chief."

Zeke went back to the chief, apologized, and offered another iron pot and musket. Alexander and Zeke entertained Indian ladies that night. Sam and I spent the night on watch.

As I sharpened knives the next day there erupted much excitement in the village as another pack train arrived. Jeremiah McTavish's group brought out back patting and wrestling; Zeke warned us to be wary of wrestling until we had become more proficient because "no holds barred type" might mean a broken bone, bitten ear, or gouged eye. McTavish broke out a jug which was shared by both trains. Post was exchanged for delivery. McTavish related the concerns of the new colony of Carolina, the wars among the Overhill Cherokees, Catawbas, Creeks, and Watarees. He reported that the tribes were not bothering the traders, but small pox and yellow fever epidemics were about over for those peoples. He had heard that many of the white families in the lower South Carolina areas fled to New Jersey during the yellow fever season.

By September, we reached the Big Lick on the Staunton River and the trading village of Wachovia. Later that week as we stayed west of the Blue Ridge, we made camp at Ingles Ferry. There we were met by a French trader, Pierre Roundeau from the west. He related that the French were concerned about the inroads of the British trade among the Indians. Roundeau stated that the French muskets were not as well received as the English models, particularly the "Bess." Zeke expressed relief that the Pennsylvania rifle has not been introduced among the Indians. In a fight, some Indians stick with the bow and arrow as they can get off five arrows per every shot of a musket and even more than the shots of the slow loading rifle. I left feeling uneasy about the French threat.

Our next stop was Chriswell, followed by the Moravian village of Stalmaker. By this time I was on my third set of moccasins. We then moved toward the east through the Gap heading for Charles Town. We followed the Pee Dee River down a narrow canyon path. Passing through Trading Ford near the tiny settlement of Salisbury, we marveled at the grandeur and beauty of the land there.

At the first of October we arrived at Charles Town. Zeke took his goods to a mercantile house and received credit on a bank in London. He purchased some trade goods and then we turned back. We more or less retraced our steps and returned home by the first of the year. The next year the family, as you will remember, moved down the trail using hogsheads and mules. The trail was still too narrow for a wagon.

Samuel related. "Father never wanted to discuss your Indian betrothal much. My word, you could be a chief by now." They all laughed. Tom threw a small rock at his brother.

"I think Father felt that moving from Pennsylvania was a loss of status," replied Tom.

***

Finally, the brothers reached a spot west of the Pee Dee River. They noticed an occasional settler's structure still in the primitive lean to stage of early settlement. Coming through an Indian old fields clearing, the brothers beheld a cabin. As they approached cautiously, two large dogs charged. Tom grabbed his muskets by the barrel in preparation to swing at them. From the windowless structure a scrawny woman appeared, dressed in a faded shift and cradling a small child in one arm and a musket in the other. "Hail there," cried Thomas, "We wish to parley with you."

"Stay right there or I'll shoot you," she shouted, putting the child down.

Just then the dogs stopped barking and a voice from behind yelled, "Drop your weapons and turn around or I'll put holes in at least two of you." They dismounted and placed their entire ordinance by a tree. Turning they saw a man with a matted beard, tobacco stained leather tunic with a brace of two pistols on him. Tom collected his composure and began.

"My friend, we wish to parley with you. We mean no harm."

"I can see by your clothes and the tack of your mounts that you're not from around here. Everything is too dandy to be from poor folks."

"We are of the Christian faith and bring you greetings from his Lordship Governor Gabriel Johnston."

"I reckoned we be beyond the reaches of His Majesty here. We had enough trouble from him in Pennsylvania and Virginia."

Thomas continued approaching him cautiously and looking up into his grim countenance. "His Lordship has been most generous and is concerned for his subjects. Particularly from the dangers of the slave rebellions, Indian uprisings, and the interference of the papist states of France and Spain. He wants to enlarge his protection over the colony. I am Thomas Neel and these are my brothers Samuel and Henry. What be your name, Sir?"

"Name's Sam Hawthorne."

Thomas offered a twist of tobacco which was accepted. "Can't we parley?"

"If you leave your weapons by the door, I reckon we can." Thomas noticed that his associate seemed less tense.

They trudged toward the cabin. Sam brought their weapons and placed them by the door. The dogs scampered under foot. Entering the dark cabin they found it lit by a fire with some cooking apparatus, including a few pots. The cabin smelled of human sweat, musty clothes and hog fat which must have been rendered in the inside. There were no windows and the floor was the packed earth of a first cabin. Some light shone through holes in the chinking placed there for possible defense with ordnance.

Henry pulled a small leather pouch and offered. "Here is some tea. Could the Madam make us some?"

"This here is my woman, Sally. She doesn't talk much. Sally, make these gents some tea."

"Since we have only two cups, what the hell will they drink it in?" The Neels each quickly pulled tin cups from their belts and handed them to her. She then took the tea and placed it in a small pot on the fire rack.

Thomas continued. "Master Hawthorne, you have begun to develop the land here. How goes it?"

"The land near the river has produced some Indian corn. Mostly we survive on hunting and fishing. At certain times of the year we can scoop them there fish out by the bushel."

"I wonder if you would excuse us for a minute. I would like to talk with my brothers outside."

"That's satisfactural. I took the flints from your firearms."

They went outside the door. Tom began, "We have two choices. We can force this family from our land or we can buy his land and offer him employment. What say you?"

Henry replied, "It is worth a try. White labor has not proven to be very beneficial but they have always been indentured. Perhaps we could try. What think you Samuel?"

"Let us proceed, but I am not ready to claim the land yet. I want to look it over more."

The brothers returned. "We are ready for that tea now, Mistress Hawthorne." She blushed and formed an unaccustomed smile. She reacted as if she had not been treated civilly in a long time.

"She ain't no missus. We ain't never said words over a preacher or a magistrate."

The tea poured, Thomas continued. "We propose to settle here and attempt to produce marketable crops and perhaps ship stores. We would like to purchase your land for a good price and those of any neighbors and give you the choice of moving or working for us."

"You mean you would pay me for my land, allow us to live here, and then offer to pay me to work your land?" A dark scowl came over his grizzled face.

"That is largely it. We might help you build a better cabin."

"What say you woman?" he said turning to the woman.

"A woman's place be with her man," she replied and began openly nursing her small child.

"Well," continued Hawthorne, "I guess we only need to settle on the price."

"We will offer you twenty per centum of any crop you turn in goods, colony currency, or Spanish dollars, in addition to all the meat, produce, and fuel you can take from the land."

"I don't understand this here per centum."

"Well if you harvest 100 bushels of wheat, we will give you twenty bushels as pay."

"Why don't I get 100 bushels?"

"Because we own the land and are giving protection from the Indians, Spanish, French and building you a house and out buildings. In addition we pay for your land and help you improve upon it."

"Why don't I just stay here and sell the stuff to you?"

Thomas asked, "What say you brothers?"

"Let's accept on the following conditions: That we survey ten acres which shall be his and he is not to work any other part of the land. Also, he will be allowed to hunt undeveloped land, must give militia service, and swear allegiance to His Majesty," replied Henry.

"Not on your life. I ain't gonna to swear allegiance to a king with all those taxes and requirements for Anglican Church allegiance."

"As far as we are concerned as Christians of the Presbyterian faith, we need no person to mediate between us and the Christ Jesus. Besides, Brother Samuel here is an elder in the Presbyterian faith. By the way, may we camp here tonight and hold services day after tomorrow, it being the first day of the week and all?"

"Yes, you cain hold services. That will give me time to ponder this over. By the way, we have not had a preacher here ever. I think I will invite some of my neighbors to come."

"Sounds fair."

On a mild January Sabbath, they all assembled at a clearing near the Hawthorne cabin. Amazingly and mysteriously, a half dozen families materialized as if out of the fog and sat on blankets or the wood stumps in the clearing. The men folks were mostly dressed in deerskins, with moccasins or trail packs for shoes. The children were all thinly clad, some with bear skin blankets, and had the look of being freshly cleaned for the first time in ages. The women were clad in flax shifts and blankets. Many of them, occasionally nursing their babies, were tired looking from overwork and an almost yearly addition to the white population of the area. In the back stood a family composed of a man and an Indian woman. Happily the congregants were blessed by a warm winter day.

Hawthorne spoke. "These here folks are from the Cape Fear area and are bringing you a deal from the governor."

A voice from the back yelled back, "We uns hath tried to get away from the government. Why do we want to hear him?"

"One of them is a preacher. At least we can hear him. Brother Samuel, preach it."

Samuel then opened his New Testament and began to read using Romans 13:1-7.

"Let every soul be subject unto the higher powers. For there is no power but of God: the powers that be are ordained of God. Whosoever therefore resisteth the power, resisteth the ordinance of God; and they that resist shall receive to themselves damnation. For rulers are not a terror to good works , but to the evil. Wilt thou then not be afraid of the power? Do that which is good, and thou shalt have praise of the same:

For he is the minister of God to thee for good. But if thou do that which is evil; be afraid; for he beareth not the sword in vain; for his is the minister of God, a revenger to execute wrath upon him that doeth evil.

Wherefore ye must needs be subject, not only for wrath but also for conscience sake.

For this cause pay ye tribute also: for they are God's ministers, attending continually to this very thing."

Sam closed the Bible, looked over the group and began, "Bretheren everyone must submit himself to the governing authorities, for there is no authority except that which God has established. The authorities that exist have been established by God. Consequently, he who rebels against the authority is rebelling against what God had instituted, and those who do so will bring judgment on themselves. For rulers hold no terror for those who do right, but for those who do wrong. Do you want to be free from fear of one in authority? Then do what is right and he will commend you."

Some of the audience grumbled at the passage. Sam continued, "Those of us who are Christians who have been inconvenienced in our faith such as we Presbyterians and Anabaptists, and Quakers, find it hard to follow the leaders of our country especially when they behave in unseemly ways such as wreck rents on our Ulster lands, seizure of our homes, and other reasons that led us to take the dreadful voyage to America. Here in the bosom of a virgin land, God has given us great opportunities. However, King George wants all of his subjects to be happy. We are overjoyed that he is the first of our kings raised in England and actually speaks English. You here on the borders probably have not heard the news that we are now a Royal colony no longer subject to the lord's proprietor. They are more interested in the Spice Islands than us and have allowed us to practice our religion as we see fit. The Lord has decreed that we must all become a member of the

Kingdom of God. Not one of the kingdom of this earth where moth and rust doth corrupt but members of the body of Christ. We must teach our children to read the scriptures so that they can work out their salvation with fear and trembling. As an Elder in the church of Christ I stand ready to assist you in any spiritual need. Shall we pray?"

Sam closed his eyes, turned his head toward the sky and began, "Dear Lord and all wise heavenly Father. These are your children crying in the wilderness for your help and guidance. They are confronted by heathen, and children of the antichrist. We beseech you to touch our hearts that we may all come to repentance and give up the sins we have endured in the past. We ask this in the name of Christ our Savior."

Thomas stepped forward. "This concludes our worship of this day. Any persons here who desire to have their children baptized or wish to have your marriages solemnized we are prepared to do that. I will soon be deputized by his Honor Governor Nathaniel Rice as a judge and captain of the militia for these parts."

"Why do we need His Majesty? His Lords drove us from our lands in Ireland and Scotland. Some of us suffered through indenture in Pennsylvania and others of us traveled with them down the Warrior Path to settle here where we would have the liberty to own our land and live as liberated men," asked a man from the back, Artimas McGhee.

He continued, "We have all suffered from the abuses of primarily the Court parties of England. We have fought for the rights to rule ourselves and practice our religion without papist priests or Anglican Bishops. If we must take the oath of the Test Act we want no part of it."

Samuel answered. "His Lordship Governor Johnston wants us all to live in peace. Since we became a Crown colony, he has no desire to regulate the consciences of the citizens of the British Crown. It was not one decade ago that this area was infested with the hostile Yamese and Tuscaroas who with the evil Spanish were murdering settlers here. How soon we forget the assistance the Crown gave in subduing these tribes."

"I thought we pretty much cleared the heathen out by ourselves," retorted Artimas McGhee. "We did not see many of His Majesty's soldiers around here."

"Did you not know that the Royal Navy chases the Spanish and French from the harbors?"

"Well, we get along pretty well without all of the taxes and bullying we experienced from King James and his henchmen."

Tom continued, "My brothers and I have each been granted lands between the Pee Dee and Broad Rivers. We plan to carve plantations in this wilderness, which will produce ship stores and some food crops and cattle. It is our desire to live at peace with all men including our red brothers. We are also to set up militias for the defense of the area and promote the blessings of a Christian civilization. We will be able to help you yeomen in at least two ways. We can help you develop and sell cash crops and provide employment, if you should like to work with us. Tomorrow we will begin to survey our lands. When they are in conflict with lands you have settled on, we will pay a fair price for your land."

"I want no part of it," replied Artimas. He arose and along with the Squawman and their families departed. Three or four families followed.

Tom turned to Henry, "What think you?"

"We will hear from them again."

Hawthorne approached Henry, "Sir, I would like to throw my lot with you. But first, I would consider it a great blessing if you would say some words which would make a Christian woman out of my woman and also my babies."

"Bless you," replied Henry. Sam then performed a marriage ceremony and baptized his child. He assisted five other families in that endeavor. He also recorded these ceremonies as the first act of the soon to be Presbyterian Society of Providence.

During the next two weeks the Neels recorded observations of the land. They surveyed as best they could and staked their lands. Happily, very few settlements were in the claimed areas. Those occupying areas seemed content with the received thirty acres. They ran into a Catawba hunting party and exchanged gifts with them. Through signing, they promised peace and friendship. The parties enjoyed a feast of buffalo rump and smoked a pipe of peace.

At the end of the month the three brothers returned home to young Thomas, Henry, and their wives. There was much excitement as they described the lands. In February, the brothers traveled to New Bern and reported their actions to Governor Rice. After accepting the Governor's offer they were each granted a patent for a 1,000 acres each as well as a letter of credit for tools needed to start production of ship stores and other objects of commercial value. The land and its description were filed with the surveyor general. The men were also made officers in the militia. Thomas became a Colonel and the brothers Majors. The giddy new miliamen met with the proprietor developers, Arthur Dobbs and Henry McCullough, who were pleased with their commissions and promised them additional land. Their commissions read as follows:

*To all whom these Letters do come.*

*Be it known that Thomas Neel, esq., is hereby made a Justice of the Peace for the areas between the Peewee and Catawba Rivers, the colony of North Carolina on the east and the foot of the mountains on the South, is also granted 1000 acres to be held in perpetuity in such areas as he should establish by survey. He is also commissioned as a Colonel in the North Carolina Militia and is ordered to form companies for the defense and public order of the area. Neel will be called upon from time to time to represent the governor in such business as boundary determination.*

*His Majesty's Servant Gabriel Johnston, Governor, Colony of North Carolina.*

Samuel and Henry received similar commissions. Henry was appointed sheriff of the new district. Young brother Andrew was not old enough to accept commissions.

After receiving their commissions the brothers called a meeting of the families. Here they extolled the advantages of the area and asked for input.

Samuel spoke, "Nancy and I have prayed and thought long and hard about this. Along with our father we developed a fine plantation here. We think we can serve the family by staying here with John Simpson and his family while furnishing support to you as you go to the wilderness. We can give you a note for the purchase of your shares and help finance your ventures."

"What say you, Henry?"

"I reckon that this would be a good plan. We could rely on Samuel as well as John Simpson for support and furnishing supplies. I hope he agrees to my fabulous price!" They all laughed.

"What do the rest of you say?"

Their wives and those of James Simpson Neel agreed. The brothers assigned the lands on the Cape Fear area to Samuel and step brother John and migrated with their families. The grandmother stayed with Samuel and John Simpson at the old estate. Samuel agreed to give the pioneers a per centum of the profits for ten years. They freed some of their slaves who elected to become overseers of the work. Two indentured families also agreed to work for shares on the Neel lands. The families continued to acquire servants as the need expanded. Mary, Tom's wife, continually looked after their needs. She worried about the validity of owning another person. For this reason she saw to it that all family and servants were warm and well fed.

While still living on Neil Creek the brothers constructed dwellings in the Providence area, each of which consisted of a great room, three bedrooms on the top floor and a cooking structure with a covered passageway. Cabins were constructed for servants. The land was in the midst of beech and birch on a hill between the Steele and Sugar Creeks. In an Indian Old Field Tom planted the first crops of wheat and corn. They started to gird trees of the uncleared areas. The trip from Neil Creek was accomplished in shifts. A rude road was constructed large enough to accommodate wagons. Horses and oxen and even an occasional cow were used as draft animals.

Once established in the Province area, the company drilled, using many of the younger sons of the plantations as well as some of the yeomen. Unfortunately, many of the yeomen were undisciplined Scots who did not mesh well with their leaders. Happily, because of the humane treatment of the slaves by the Neels, the South Carolina slave insurrection had no effect.

To the Thomas Neel DOB 1710 family with sons Thomas Christopher 1730 and (John) Henry 1736 were added James in 1743, Andrew 1745, Margaret 1748 (who married William McCullough), Sarah 1749 (who married Samuel Allen),and Elizabeth 1750 (who married a Wilson.) Note dates for the girls are estimates. I do not know the actual dates.

# CHAPTER 3

# War Of Captain Jenkins' Ear

The Providence Company continued the steady settlement and development of their lands. In 1739, Governor Johnson called out the militia to assist the colony of Georgia in the War of Captain Jerkins' Ear. Because of the restrictions on English trade with the Spanish colonies, British merchants resorted to smuggling. In 1735 Robert Jenkins (flourished as a British smuggler 1731-38), in command of the brig *Rebecca*, was seized by the crew of a Spanish coast guard vessel, which compelled him to surrender his cargo and then cut off an ear; an ear which the good captain had pickled and showed to all who would hear his tale in tavern or government gatherings. The incident received little attention at the time, but subsequent outrages against British seamen engendered widespread anti-Spanish sentiment in Great Britain. The affair was hotly debated in Parliament in 1738 after Captain Jenkins appeared with his shriveled ear in hand, and in the following year, confronted by an implacable opposition, the British statesman Sir Robert Walpole was obliged to declare war against Spain.

Thomas received a communication from Governor Johnson asking for the activation of the militia. Thomas sent couriers out, contacting all militia in the vicinity.

Assembly was called on an April morning. Mary remarked that Tom looked quite official in his uniform of the dragoons. The rest were dressed in their usual clothing of shoepack, leather britches, linsey woolsey blouse, and buckskin hunting shirt. Some wore coonskin and beaver hats. Thomas read a notice:

*Here ye all of the King's Subjects in North Carolina.*

*Due to the recent event with the founding of the Colony of Georgia and the possible threats from foreign powers of a Catholic persuasion, all men from fifteen to fifty are hereby deputized as the North Carolina militia. The magistrates of each district are to see that men are drilled in military protocol and are properly armed. magistrate and sheriff of each district will be responsible for setting up a roll of able-bodied citizens. A yearly roll will be taken and presented to the Royal Governor on the first of each year. Quartermasters of each regiment shall submit lists of armament available to His Majesty's Treasurer.*

*Signed: Gabriel Johnston, Royal Governor of North Carolina*

As you recall Governor Johnston, the previous governor, had appointed Thomas as the Colonel of the Neel militia and brother Henry was appointed Sheriff, even though there was no organized county. Once a month, on Saturdays, the Neel Company drilled and practiced with muskets and rifles. The militia consisted of every able bodied man between fifteen and fifty. They were required to furnish themselves with flintlock and bayonet or sword (when the bayonet did not fit a musket), tomahawk, and priming brush. The militia began to make powder with saltpeter and charcoal and began mining lead for use as bullets. Samuel had formed a similar company back on Cape Fear. Most of the neighbors reacted well to the drills, especially since they could draw rations, rifles, gunpowder, and lead from His Majesty's treasurer. However, Artimas McGhee and Squawman Johnson failed to appear for any of the musters. Shortly after the commissions were given, an Indian trader, the always-welcome Zeke Proctor, appeared at the plantation. Zeke, like other traders, rode the Appalachian trails trading with the various Indian tribes. His bronzed brazened face told of his years on the trail. Occasionally, he would do contract service for His Majesty's troops. He rode in the saddle like he was part of his majestic horse, Esau. His train usually consisted of twelve mules as well as a freedman, Alexander, and occasional roustabouts.

After placing his mules in the barn enclosure and his crew consuming a feast of turkey and buffalo, Zeke brought the news.

"The French and Spanish are beginning to enthuse some of the tribes. The Catawbas are still friendly. Lord Oglethorpe is continuing to develop Georgia under the very noses of the papist French and Spanish. If he doesn't watch out there will be a war. The Cherokees seem less friendly as do the small Shawnee tribe they adopted. The slave rebellion a few years ago in South Carolina as well as the West Indies rebellion keeps them on guard. The Spanish have provided a haven down there for slaves and renegade Indians."

Thomas asked, "Didn't you once tell us the Cherokee nation was in His Majesty's service?"

"Yes, I was under bond to His Majesty's ambassador back in 1730 when we had a mission to the Cherokees on the Keowe River."

"Tell us about it."

"Lord Chatworth was given a commission to parley with the Cherokees in the upper mountains, make one of the chiefs an emperor, and establish trade compacts with them before the French or Spanish delivered their dastardly agreements. I had a contract for supplying the trip from Charles Town to Keowe, the village. I was nearly scared out of me wits when his Lordship burst into one of the chief's lodges and threatened to burn it down if the savages failed to salute the health of the King.

I thought longingly of my scalp I felt I was sure to donate. Strangely enough the usually warlike Cherokees submitted. Little Carpenter, whose Cherokee name was Attakullakulla, was appointed Emperor of the Upper Cherokees and was given, along with some of his braves, a trip to visit the King. Little Carpenter is very friendly to the British but some of the younger braves romance with the Spanish. The Spanish are rumored to have sent a papist priest to be among them.

"Artimas McGhee has been trading with some of the Upper Cherokees and trades inferior goods. This has had a bad effect on us."

"Aha, I remember him from our meeting with the Hawthornes. So, that is how he makes a living. I have never seen him work his land," he replied.

Thomas asked, "How do the Cherokees feel about us now?"

"The Chatsworth trip to England helped. However, the French are vigorously engaged in trade with them. Some of our traders have cheated them. Virginians sold some of the braves into slavery when they were not paid by the Carolinas for the help in the old Yamasee war some twenty years ago."

"Just think, Thomas," said Zeke, "Remember what the old chief offered you when you were with me on the trail? If you had not been so persnickety, you could be a Shawnee chief by now."

"It is best you not bring up that offer of the peace chief for Singing Bird in front of my wife. By the way, how is my former betrothed?"

"She married a minor chief and has a young son who looks like you," offered Zeke with a chuckle and a wink at Alexander.

"Impossible. You are a scoundrel," responded Mary.

With that Zeke and Alexander left for their lodgings in the barn. Zeke and his entourage left the next morning headed for the Warrior Path. Thomas noticed some of the young female slaves lingered around Alexander before he left. There was much giggling and laughing. Mary scolded them and suggested they go about their tasks. Tom had noticed that Rachel watched demurely from the kitchen building as Alexander departed. Alexander dipped his trail hat in her direction and smiled.

After the visit with Zeke, the troop began a more intense monthly muster of the company training for defense of the Carolinas. The Neel estates straddled both provinces. After six months of training they were called to muster.

"Troop Attention," Thomas began. "By the authority of His Honor Sir Gabriel Johnston, Governor of the Colony of North Carolina, we organize for possible war with the Spanish in Florida and assist the Colony of South Carolina. The Spanish have insulted His Britannic Majesty, have impressed our seamen, incited the Indians, assisted in the theft of certain bonded property, and threatened His Majesty's colony of Georgia. Now each of you will draw four days ration and we will head for Charles Town. The militia company has been commissioned as Neel's Rangers and leave tomorrow at first light. Major Henry, dismiss the men."

Before the troop was dismissed, a cry lifted from the ranks. "Huzzah for the Neel Rangers, Huzzah for Col. Neel." Thomas lifted his hat and rode away.

The brothers were relieved to see that Artimas and Squawman Johnson decided to join them. Hawthorne did not seem too happy to see Squawman and his friend, Artimas. The rumor was that there would be free land available after the campaign. This helped strengthen the militia's recruitment.

---

CHAPTER 4

# *On to Florida*

They lay in bed that night and Thomas reviewed with his Mary the plans for planting for the year. He was especially worried because she was again with child. "I try to be brave," she sobbed softly, "but I cannot lose a husband and father. Why must you go?"

"My love, we must protect ourselves from the French, Spanish, and renegade tribes. It was not twenty years ago that the Yamasee tribes ravaged this place and it became necessary for the militia to defend the homes. If I don't go we will not be able to bring the King's order and peace to the region."

"How well I know. My family lost uncles, aunts and cousins in that war. But, I am still afraid and melancholy about it." She clung tightly to him.

At shortly before sunrise in the compound he awakened. He kissed young Thomas, Henry, and Mary good-bye, grabbed his rifle, musket, tomahawk, two knives, two pistols, powder horn, cartridges, bullets, lead, flint, lead mold, and a packet of food. He threw on a buffalo robe, another change of clothes, and blanket on the back of his horse and proceeded to the assembly.

"Drummer," he called to one of the young lads, "Beat to assembly."

Soon the company stood before Henry and Thomas. The newly commissioned Henry Neel was demonstrating the manual of arms.

"Now men, I don't have to tell you all how to shoot. You people with Pennsylvania rifles will find you cannot shoot as fast with your rifles as the Brown Bass musket. However, there will be some times when we cannot fight Indian fashion but will fight in formation. When that time comes you will be asked to dress in lines of two. We will then fire on command. The first commands are: 'prime, reload.' When you hear this command, take the paper cartridge in your teeth and bite off the ball. Hold the ball in your mouth and fill the pan. Pour the remainder in the barrel, take the ball from your mouth and the paper of the cartridge and ram it down the barrel. I know some of you are used to using the powder horn and at some times will need to. As long as we have cartridges, you can load much faster. Then the first rank will kneel. They will then hear 'Poise firelock. Cock firelock. Take aim. Fire.' The second rank will then advance and kneel while the first rank stands and reloads. This is the way we will advance across the field. You people who brought rifles will stand as a separate squad whose job is to use your greater range to discourage the officers. At times we will give the company an order to fire at will.

"At that time you may join the musket formations. Now sergeants, begin your practice. Each man shall be allowed five rounds for this purpose."

A bearded disheveled militiaman shouted. "Major Henry, why don't you all put up a few squirrels to shoot at? That is what we are used to shooting."

"Now, Benjamin, we are going to be shooting Spaniards. They are so big even you can't miss. Besides we want to look good in front of those dandies in the Royal troops."

"Shoot. This won't be as much fun as a squirrel hunt."

Henry was observing the practice. He was temporarily deaf and blinded by the black powder, smoke, and noise and did not see Thomas ride up.

"How do they look?" Thomas inquired.

"These men are Indian fighters; they don't take kindly to close order."

"I am sure they will do us proud. Although we certainly look ragged, I hear that some Scotch regiments have been brought over from Gibraltar. I pray we can get along with them. Let's assemble."

A young bugler blew a feeble attempt at assembly. The drummers then began. Finally, the bewildered frontiersmen turned from their firing practice and faced the direction of the officers.

Sergeants began trying to dress the company. One of the men yelled, "Squire Neel, what in the hell are we doing?"

Thomas stood up in his stirrups and looked over the group. "Isaiah Moore, strange that you should ask. Here is the answer, men of the Neel Company; today we march to Georgia to defend our homes and His Majesty's lands. Sergeants, prepare your companies."

To the beat of the drum, the music of the fife, the troop headed south following the Warrior Path and the Catawba River. Except for the officers and sergeants who wore the King's uniforms, the troops were dressed in irregular frontier dress. Generally the dress consisted of a flax or woolen blouse, covered by buckskin shirt, buckskin pants, and moccasins or trail boots. Some of the company were mounted but most were on foot. The luscious green of the up country soon gave way to the piedmont and then the lowlands. They were joined by a dozen Catawba braves who had been persuaded to join by the Indian agent. Thomas noticed some mumbling and pointing as Artimas and Squawman passed them. On approximately every second day the troop came upon a commissary cache, which equipped them with fodder and provisions, usually consisting of jerky and cornmeal.

The Neel regiment was ordered to Charles Town for assembly. It was invigorating to be on the trail with men of good humor and support. On the fifth day the troop entered Charles Town to the waving of banners, drum beats, and a general good time. Thomas and Henry smiled as they rode in front of the men. A thrill came to Thomas, as he had never seen such a sight in his few visits to the seaport. The Neel Rangers assembled near the waterfront and bivouacked there. It was a salubrious time with dancing, fiddle playing, wrestling, bonfires and spirits. The Neel Rangers were separated from His Majesty's troops as were other militia. Good natured insults were traded among the North and South Carolinians and the troops of His Majesty's Dragoons, newly transported from Fortress Gibralter. At day break all were awakened to the beat of assembly. Governor Oglethorpe had been appointed General and Commander in Chief of all military forces in Georgia and South Carolina. Colonel Jones, a representative from Lord Oglethorpe, and Colonel Alexander Vanderussen addressed them.

"To His Majesty's subjects of the colonies of Carolina. As you are aware we have been threatened by the papist states in Florida. Our homes and our families are in danger. We are to march through Georgia to the province of Florida. There we will endeavor to recover our property, our runaways, as well as punish the papist Spaniards for their insult to His Christian Majesty. Captains, you will draw four days rations and begin the march to Georgia. All company commanders will report to me. The first unit will be the King's Foot and Cherokee scouts followed by the Carolina volunteer Rangers, and militia from the northern colonies. Regimental commanders, dismiss your men and be ready to move at first light."

The next morning the Rangers awoke to the beating of drums. Ranks formed and started marching to Florida. The forty-two Regiment of Foot in the red blouses, white bandoliers, ammunition pouches, Bess muskets, and clay white pants of the regulars led marching to the beat of drums and the playing of the fife and pipes. The 200 Carolina rangers of which the Neels were a part trailed behind. Three thousand six hundred Northern colonial troops and 1,000 Indians followed. The Indians who were not scouting meandered all over the group. The Catawba, Cherokees and Creeks had been enticed into assisting Lord Oglethorpe by treaties and gifts. They seemed to be in a contented state as they accompanied us.

The Cherokees were taller than the Creek Indians. They wore breech cloths with sashes which hung down to their thighs. Some were decorated with gunpowder tattoos which described their exploits as warriors. Some had ornaments from their earlobes. Hair was generally absent except for a long braid at the crown of the scalp. They were covered heavily with bear oil which helped keep them warm. They also had an animal skin, usually buffalo, to be used as a blanket or as a coat.

The Catawbas were dressed similarly but were even taller and frightfully painted with a white bull's eye painted on one eye and a black circle around it. They made a most terrifying appearance.

In Berkeley County, South Carolina, a group of slaves escaped and murdered twenty white people. On the way south to Florida, the command looked for these runaways. Spain was encouraging the slaves to revolt. Any slave arriving in Florida was promised freedom by the Spanish. However, many slaves were surprised when the Spanish transported them to Cuba for resale. Governor Oglethorpe had forbidden slavery in Georgia at this time; however, he needed the support of the Carolinians and agreed to help round up any identified slaves.

As the Rangers headed to Frederica where they awaited reinforcements, the oppressive heat began to take its toll. Men began to drop behind. The wet nights in rain, the diet of jerky and the bad water were a constant discomfort. After the first night on the ground, their blankets never ceased to be wet. Gnats, flies, mosquitoes, and dysentery constantly irritated them as the troop skirted swamp lands. Night's sleep was fitful because of the occasional rain and continual damp ground.

The Spanish fleet sailed from Havana with three thousand men under the command of Don Manuel deMonteano, landing south of St. Augustine. At length the troops arrived at the first of a string of small forts, really outposts that had been constructed by Lord Oglethorpe. A group of Catawaba braves led by Running Bear began to spend a great deal of time with them. They camped near them around a small camp fire. It was there they told the legend of the Catwba origins. We then told them about the Christian origins, the Garden of Eden. They became much impressed with their stories and wanted to know more.

1740. After leaving Ft. Savannah, the forces crossed the Savannah River on a ferry and proceeded to St. Augustine, subduing some smaller forts on the way. Most of the assaults were made by regular troops. The Neel Rangers worked as scouts with the Catawbas and occasionally the Cherokees. Meanwhile Governor Manuel de Montiano of Spanish Florida heard of the advance and reinforced St. Augustine with 3,000 troops from Florida and Cuba.

General Oglethorpe was constantly tormented by misfortune. He intended to form an assault against the forts, but the British navy refused a bombardment because of the presence of Spanish half-galleons with complements of guns. Also, the late arriving South Carolina militia began to desert.

After much discussion, the General decided that a frontal assault would be unwise and chose to lay siege. He was assisted occasionally by some of the armed barks of the fleet. However, the fleet sailed away as the hurricane season approached, weakening the siege. The rangers resorted to eating alligators and horses for subsistence. Water was always bad and many became overcome with dysentery.

With the arrival of more Spanish troops, Lord Oglethorpe, after appealing to Carolina and Virginia for more troops, withdrew to Sullivan Island near Charles Town. Shortly the Spanish landed. Skirmishes followed and the Carolinians were gradually hemmed in to one fortified area. Lord Oglethorpe then engaged in a supreme act of deception. He composed a letter, allegedly from troops headed from Virginia, signifying that troops were on the way. Next he released a prisoner. The letter was found on his person and this caused the Spanish to withdraw in fear.

# Chapter 5

# Government Business

In July 1740 the Rangers were dismissed and were returned to their homes. It was a time of joy and sadness. Thomas lamented the loss of many of the regiment to disease, desertion, and death. However, it was good to be headed home. That year a peace was concluded, and the border between Georgia and Florida was defined. Some men had been in correspondence with their wives but were delighted to return home. Wearily, Tom rode up to the house. He had ridden with the militia as they were released from service at Charles Town. Smoke rose from the chimney. He dismounted and Uncle Arthur, one of the servants, greeted him.

"Oh, Col. Thomas, it is so good to see you."

"Thank you, Arthur. How is your family? What news do you have?"

"Well we have gotten along tolerably well. But the big news is in the house, Sir."

He bounded to the door. He heard a click of the latch and a sweet voice, "Who goes there?"

"A weary soldier looking for a good wife to feed and comfort him."

"Well, I'll take any soldier. Mine has deserted me." He heard the lever lifted and the latch opened to behold his beautiful Mary holding a lad of about three years old. Another nine year old hid by her skirts with his thumb in his mouth.

"Oh, Thomas, I am so glad you are home," she sobbed as they embraced.

Looking down at the child in her arms, he remarked, "Is this the much heard about Henry Neel, lately deserted by his father?"

"And who is this handsome lad. Can you speak to your Father?" Thomas hid behind his mother.

"For boys that are attentive to their father I have something. Would you like to see it?"

Grudgingly, little Thomas and Henry moved toward Tom. He took from his pack a miniature tomahawk, a Spanish hunting knife and some maple candy for each of them. Thomas looked in wonder and replied, "Thank you, Sir. I hope you can show me how to use them." The family embraced warmly.

"I hope you never have to use them in anger."

The next Lord's Day brother Samuel conducted a service of thanksgiving. This was followed by a feast in front of the house with all of the family and servants participating.

As a reward for their actions, the officers and men of the Carolina Rangers were allowed to apply for patents on South Carolina land. Tom received 500 additional acres in the Providence region. The family now had a broken string of properties from Cape Fear to the Catawba and Broad Rivers. Artimas McGhee and Squawman Johnson were thanked for their service, even though their presence was rather scarce during some of the military action. They immediately offered their patent land for sale and took the proceeds to Charles Town to exchange for trade goods, such as muskets, blankets, knives, and cookware.

After applying and receiving patents on the land from the governor, the Neels began to develop the land. Because of the slave revolt and subsequent hanging of fifty slaves in Charles Town, Mary began to worry about their safety and those of her children.

One afternoon while at dinner Mary brought up the matter of slavery.

"Why is it that we have bondsmen who are never released from their indenture?"

"The Negroes are not free because we purchase them."

Mary opened her Bible to Deuteronomy 15:12 and read:

"If a fellow Hebrew, a man or a woman, sells himself to you and serves six years, in the seventh year you must let him go free. And when you release him, do not send him away empty-handed. Supply him liberally from your flock, your threshing floor and your winepress. Give to him as the Lord your God redeemed you."

She closed her book and with her winsome eyes inquired. "Why do we keep slaves?"

"My love, the first part of what you read was when a member of one's race sells himself to do such things as pay off a large debt. The Negroes did not sell themselves. When they were captured in Africa and forced to come to Cuba, they became slaves and when we purchased them they became our property."

"Yes, but we have freed Uncle Arthur and others."

"I treat my Negroes as apprentices. As soon as they demonstrate Christian values and have a means of independent living, such as blacksmithing, I free them. The problem is some of them have no place to go. Uncle Arthur can leave anytime he wants to. His daughter Rachel knows no other home. His son Isaiah works at the mill and at the blacksmith shop. When he has served an apprenticeship of seven years, he is but twelve now, I shall ask him if he would like to be free. My concern is that if they would all turned out they will be considered contraband and re-indentured to some cruel master."

"I would like to free his sister Rachel if she wants to go."

"If she wants to go, I would have no objection. However, we should have concern about what she would do. There are people who would like to place the light skinned in brothels. We must be sure she has a place to go."

"Have you ever noticed how Zeke's partner, Alexander, hangs around her? Perhaps they might become a family."

"I feel like a father to that girl. Wild Alexander would have to settle down. I know he has at least one Shawnee child and maybe others. He frequently takes guest privileges in those villages."

"Perhaps he is old enough to consider settling down."

"I have never seen persons with more wanderlust than those two trail men. But, let's give a try."

"Fine, I will watch her and bring the matter of freedom up to her; however, we will see if a romance develops."

Neel's treatment of the servants was somewhat salubrious, because he never sold an individual. He freed those servants who seemed to be able to make it on their own, and none of the Negroes seemed to be that dissatisfied. Indeed, the freed slaves seldom left the plantation. Instead they began to develop land given them on their off hours and took part in either the prosperity or lack of it on the Neel land.

Thomas as the justice of the peace and Henry as the sheriff began to hold court once a month. Since they also served along with James Polk as elders of the Presbyterian society, moral problems of a carnal nature were conducted in a meeting before the elders. Legal and property manners were handled by the court. The same panel of adjudicators effected justice. The usual fare was disagreements over land and occasional assaults. It was difficult to distinguish what was church discipline and what was a civil matter. As the colonies of North and South Carolina wanted settlers on the frontier, few assessments other than militia service were required. Taxes were on the whole trifling and paid by the fruits of the frontiersman's industry. Incursion into Indian lands began to be a problem. These were usually sent on to the governor after warnings to the offending settlers. After the Florida Campaign they had the problem of twenty-five widows and their orphans from the Neel Regiment. Voluntary assessments were collected for their relief.

Both the church and the court worked to place orphaned with families. Because of the high mortality of women due to hardship and birthrate, families were usually able to be combined in a few years. Frequently relatives would shelter the survivors. This made the frontier realize the horror of war.

Because the plantation of Thomas and Mary was on the Great Trading path from

Pennsylvania to Charles Town, many of the commercial traders like Zeke visited the plantation for supplies. Although the Village of Salisbury to the north was more popular, Thomas and Henry's plantation, and later brother Samuel's, became a minor trading post. Catawba Indians and Cherokees and an occasional Creek tribe would camp near them and bargain with the traders or other tribes coming over the mountains. The Neels began to order trade goods from Charles Town and soon had quite a business sending farm goods to Charles Town in exchange for trade goods which were traded for hides. There was talk of a road to Charles Town as traffic widened the Indian trails.

In 1743 the Spanish and French instituted a series of raids against the colony of Georgia from their bases in Florida. In response, the Carolina Rangers were called out again. Because Mary was with child, Thomas stayed behind but Henry led the Neel Regiment for the short successful harassment of the settlement at St. Augustine.

In 1745 the Neels began to receive reports from Lord Stuart, the Indian agent, as well as some of the Catawba and Cherokee headmen that they were being mistreated by some of the traders. This was confirmed one evening when Zeke Proctor and his mule train arrived on his fall tour. The quiet morning was disturbed by the jingle of bear bells, and then over the hill came Zeke and Alexander, his roustabout, and an additional helper. As usual they were arguing. Upon seeing Thomas near his barn, the bickering ended.

"Greetings, your Grace. Can a weary traveler spend the night here?"

"Do you trail bums ever stop wrangling? Since when is an old friend to be addressed as 'Your Grace?" queried Thomas.

"It would appear that as chief magistrate of the area you should be treated with some respect."

"To receive respect from a rascal like you is a real comfort. Come in and enjoy our repast."

Young Henry and Thomas came up. "Well, look at them. In another year I will have to have them be roustabouts and travel to Pennsylvania."

"You will have to fight his mother on that one. She wants Thomas to be a preacher like his uncle."

"Alexander, put away the animals and stay out of the servants' quarters."

"Zeke, what I do on my own time is none of your business," he replied with a wink. "Besides I have friends here."

"Think you may have more than friends soon. I am available for marriage ceremonies for a fee such as a draught of whiskey," commented Thomas.

"I think we may do business; however, the African marriage ceremony may do me just fine." With a hearty laugh all around they made for the house.

After a meal of turkey and wild boar, the party settled by the fire with Zeke, Mary, and the children. Mary was quietly nursing the latest Jane when Tom began.

"How goes the Indian trade?" he asked.

"Curious things are happening," replied Zeke as he lit his pipe. "I suspect some French traders goods in the northern Cherokee settlements. I also notice some resentment when we go to a new village. One of the minor chiefs in the upper Cherokees felt someone named McGhee was very rude and yelled at them a lot. He also was quite free with the fire water before he parleys. This fellow gives us all a bad name. I only break out the firewater when the parley is finished. Some of my competitors, George Groghan, Conrad Wieser and Thomas Lee are venturing into the French Country of the Ohio. This could prove interesting."

"I know this McGhee. Perhaps we better have a talk with him. How are things up north?"

"We continue to see more of your Presbyterian friends coming down the trail to the northern part of the colony. Several Moravians have come down too. They settle west of Salisbury. There is a rumor down from Philadelphia that the Spanish and French are warring against His Majesty. Perhaps the fighting will stay in Europe and the Spice Islands. They seem to be more interested in the Spice Islands than the continent of America. Those fur traders' posts in the Ohio territory cannot help but make the French and Indians mad. I am not going into that area any more."

"I am obliged for the news. Take anything you need for your tour."

The next morning Zeke and his group were gone. Tom noticed Rachel hung around Alexander a long time. He had a wonderful smile on his face. Alexander observed Tom's glance and he winked at Tom as he went by. Tom decided he must have Mary make sure Rachel is aware of the Christian virtues they espouse.

At about mid morning brother Henry dropped by.

"Greetings, Sheriff. To what do we owe this honor?" asked Tom.

"I just returned from Charles Town with the Rangers."

"I hope everyone was safe."

"Our presence in Georgia was enough to drive the Spanish out. I think those borders will be safe for a while. And thanks be to God, we all came back alive except for a few cases of malaria. By the way, here is some post. While in Charles Town the judge there told me that Lord Stuart wants your friend and mine, Artimas McGhee, brought in to discuss some complaints by the Cherokees on their treatment. Seems he is cheating them in his trades. Also, the Hawthornes have complained that a horse is missing and they suspect some of their livestock have been stolen. I am going to meet old Artimas and Squawman Johnson to ask them some questions."

"I think I better give you some help. Let's take two or three of my men with us."

"I would be obliged."

By noon they had assembled two of the men who were former indentures and proceeded west. They came upon the Hawthorne farm. Hawthorne was much more hospitable than during their last visit.

"My good man," Henry began, "we are here to consider certain wrongs done you. I understand that you are missing some livestock."

"That is right, your grace, I suspect McGhee and Squawman Johnson. They were through here last week and had a couple of lame horses. The next morning I found one of my horses missing and later in the woods found this lame animal. Also, as I was planting salt for my hogs, I found the remains of one my hogs that had been butchered. I ran into Running Bear of the Catawbas and he related that he had seen the two while they were hunting. He stated that they were very rude to him. He talked to some of his brothers in the Middle Cherokee tribe and they were concerned at the way McGhee had treated them."

"Would you mind coming with us and showing us where they were?" Henry asked.

"I would be obliged. Why don't you camp here tonight and we will start tomorrow."

Hawthorne's hospitality was driven by the fact that the cabin was small and that he felt his slightly more aristocratic friends would not care for his comforts.

"We would be indebted indeed."

Hawthorne's wife prepared a dinner of squirrel stew and cornbread. She smiled and asked, "Squire Thomas, did thou bring any tea?"

Thomas excused myself and went to his saddle bags and brought her a half pound of tea. He thought that Mrs. Hawthorne looked a great deal happier than she did before. She seemed to smile more and her dress even looked clean. The earth floor was packed and clean. The children seemed to be more alert, especially when Henry slipped them some maple candy.

"Thank you. I remember your tea from the last time. I wonder if you could read some from the Bible tonight."

Thus they spent the evening. The next morning they arose just before sunup and began to follow the trail in the direction that Hawthorne described.

"I thought McGhee sold out and moved out of here."

"He did and sold his property to some Highland Scot. I think he is squatting on Cherokee land," replied Hawthorne.

They ceased talking and moved their horses quietly through the woods. The woods were noisy, which was a good sign. Most of the time the searchers were dismounted looking for trail signs. Suddenly the woods grew quiet. They stopped and moved from the trail into the woods. Soon a deer ran toward them, stopped, and fell with an arrow through its ribs. As they moved to examine it, two Catawbas warriors came up well mounted. The party held their rifles above their heads in a motion of peace. Thomas and Henry were not particularly concerned about danger because they were in the shared hunting grounds of the Cherokees and Catawbas.

One of the braves dismounted and in rather astounding English said, "I am Running Bear. What brings you to the land of the Catawbas, my brother?"

Raising his hand, Thomas dismounted and move toward Running Bear.

"It is good to see you again, my brother. I have missed our long talks around the fire when we were on the trail to St. Augustine. This is my brother Henry Neel, Sheriff, and our neighbor Hawthorne. Those two men back there are with us. We are privileged to meet such a great warrior again. We have heard many great deeds about you. We have come to look for some horses stolen and, at the order of Lord Stuart, check for an Indian trader who has not gained His Lordship's permission. I understand this is the common hunting ground of the Cherokee, Shawnee, and Catawba."

"You speak with wisdom; it is good that we are at peace with our brothers. Walking Bird," he called to his companion in his native tongue, "Dress this animal and take it back to camp. I am going with my white brothers." His companion grunted and turned his horse back to the carcass. Running Bear joined the party. His countenance was typical Catawba. He had his head shaved except for a panel running across the top. An eagle feather was affixed to the top knot. His ears had trinkets hanging from them. He had a deerskin blouse, loin flap as well as deer skin leggings and moccasins. He was smeared with bear grease to keep out the cold. His paint pony was smaller than those of the Neels.

As they rode along, Running Bear continued. "This McGhee and his companion Johnson have caused us much trouble. They come to our villages and get our braves drunk and then trade us bad goods. They speak harsh words. Our village is wise and strong and they dare not cheat us. However, some of our brothers have been severely treated and perhaps murdered by them."

"Do you know where they camp?"

"I will lead you there."

They followed Running Bear all that day and camped that night. He shot another deer with his bow and arrow so as to not alert anyone. The party camped near a stream under some hickory and oak trees. While at supper of a deer quarter before the small fire, Running Bear pulled out his ceremonial pipe. Thomas spoke, "My Brother, let me furnish the tobacco of friendship. I have some fine Virginia tobacco which has a richness that we do not as yet have down here."

Running Bear grunted, took the tobacco, ceremoniously lit his pipe, performed a ritual with his arms and then handed it first to Thomas and next to the entire party. This was followed by some swigs of rum from the jug brought by Henry.

Hawthorne asked, "I have heard that braves are given their names because of some great deed they did. Is that true?"

Running Bear, the Catawba, grunted. "Not always so brave. When I was of the children's clan, I was practicing shooting my arrows. Suddenly a small bear came toward where our horses were grazing. I shot at the bear but missed. The horses were becoming disturbed. I ran at the bear beating with my arrow quiver. I was only ten winters at the time. The braves who were watching thought that this was very funny. When I told my story at the council fire, they named me One Who Runs After Bears. If I were smart it should be One Who Runs from Bears."

He then smiled slightly as the remainder of his companions laughed outrageously.

Next day the party traveled southwest all day until mid afternoon. In the midst of tall pine, beech, hickory and oak, the bramble framed trail was almost non existent at times as it wound near streams and rivers. The warrior motioned the party to leave their horses and follow him on foot. They were so silent that the forest stayed noisy – a good sign. After about an hour they came upon a camp. Cautiously, Running Bear crept to the edge. He returned to their place of concealment and reported that the camp was made of four lean-tos. He said he saw Johnson and McGhee and one other. Their horses were hobbled in the field.

They then held council and decided to confront McGhee but keep an ambuscade alive. The body surrounded the camp but stayed back of the tree line. Each man had two pistols and a musket loaded.

As the sun was setting, Henry approached from the west and called, "I am Sheriff by the pleasure of His Grace Lord Johnston and desire to talk with you."

"We don't need any law here and we ain't done anything wrong, but you are welcome."

Henry approached mounted and rode up to McGhee. "Before I go further I want to inform you that I am not alone. This compound is surrounded."

The unkempt bearded man with his supper staining his deer skin blouse and beard squinted at Henry. Through his sour countenance he asked. "What be your business bothering one of the King's militia who fought at your side against the Spanish."

"I remember well your contribution," Henry replied as he looked on the eyes of three small children who cowered behind the skirts of three women. He could not find Johnson or any other male.

Henry continued, "I recall that you and your friend were one of the first to desert whenever a battle started. Let me state my business. You have been accused of trading with the Catawba and Cherokee without a license from the Governor. Also, Yeoman Hawthorne claims you stole a bay and a roan similar to those staked over there. What say you?"

"They all are damned liars. I am just trying to scrub a living by hunting this area."

"This does appear to be a hunting camp, where is your main home?"

"We live on the Wateree in the province of South Carolina."

"What did you do with the land given by your service in the militia?"

"We traded it for the land down south with some Highland Scot."

"I heard you used the boon to trade for trade goods and cheated the Indians. I have a proposition for you. You must give back the livestock you stole, return to South Carolina, and give up your trade with the Indians."

"It looks like Sheriff, that you ain't got any right to treat us this way. Our families will starve. Besides you are outgunned." Just then Squawman Johnson and another of McGhee's group appeared with guns drawn. At Henry's signal four guns went off concealed from four points of the compass.

"Drop your weapons," Henry commanded. "You are surrounded." All three backed off with their guns drawn.

"Take your damned horses and leave us alone."

"I will do that. I order you to appear before Magistrate Thomas Neel at his plantation seven days hence to face these charges."

"What charges?"

"Charges of trading without a license, failure to patent land, and stealing livestock."

"Son," McGhee commanded to one of his boys, "untie those horses we found wandering in the woods and give them to the Sheriff."

"How can we be sure of a fair trial with your brother as a judge?"

"It is best that you do not malign a King's officer." He then took the lead rope of four animals which he led from the clearing.

With relief, Tom greeted his brother. "That was a brave and foolish thing you did. Do you think he will appear at court?"

"I doubt it. We probably have not heard the last of him."

"You certainly had me sweating. I thought there were going to be more orphans in the Providence."

Running Bear added, "When we adopt you to the tribe you shall be called, One Who Tricks the Thieves." This brought a twinkle in his eyes, a smile on his face and a laugh from all of them.

As the party separated from Running Bear, Henry asked, "Where did you learn to speak the King's tongue?"

"During the Yamasee War, when the Virginians were not paid, they sold some of their allies, namely us, and our families into slavery. Me, Running Bear, being an orphan, was adopted by a Quaker family where I lived until I was about fifteen. During that time I mastered the King's tongue."

After bidding Running Bear good bye they returned home. Thomas held court on the first Monday of the month with only minor business such as forwarding patents and making reports. Sheriff Brother Henry appeared with a writ charging the McGhee's and Johnson's with illegal trade and theft of certain property. Thomas noted the defendant's lack of attendance and posted the writ and report to the Colonial Court in New Bern.

CHAPTER 6

# A Visit to the Catawba Indian Village

Henry and Thomas continued to develop their plantations. They transported turpentine and hemp to Charles Town but were unable to get ship masts to market when the rivers were low. Their patent required furnishing naval stores to the Royal Navy. The brothers experimented with tobacco and cotton. Corn, peas, wheat, and beans for their own use were their main effort. Small amounts of beer and whiskey were manufactured from the surplus grain. Cattle and hogs were driven to the Charles Town market at least once a year. Wilmington was too far for such an economic endeavor. Trade goods were exchanged for iron. The Neels developed a forge and blacksmith shop to fabricate the iron into useful objects.

There began to be problems with the Governor and lower House. His subsistence was by "presents" from the Assembly. In 1746 he wrote the Board of Trade in England that he had not received any salary in eight years. Governor Johnston, like other governors, made a good deal of his fortune by land speculation.

Problems also emerged with the boundary between North and South Carolina. Governor Johnston of North Carolina met with Governor Johnson of South Carolina to try to resolve this issue.

The lower Yadkin and Catawba rivers greatly facilitated trade with Charles Town seaport of the South Carolina Province. Tom began to complain about the heavy tax placed on North Carolina goods. As a precaution, the Neels registered their disputed lands near the border with the government of South Carolina and paid the poll tax as citizens.

All during the 1740's the privateers from Spain and pirates attacked ships between Charles Town, Norfolk, and points north. Governor Johnston, sanctioned by the King, issued letters of Marque and Reprisal, but only a few ships were fitted out for the patrols. However, the family used this opportunity to establish a saw mill on the Steele Creek for production of lumber for ship and house building in Charles Town as well as the growing rice plantations in the lower areas.

The Highland Scots began to migrate to the Carolinas in the 1740's. A great influx began after 1746 when the Scots invaded England in an attempt to place "Bonnie Prince Charlie" on the throne. They were defeated at the Battle of Culloden in 1746 by the forces of Lord Cumberland. Many atrocities were committed mainly by the English forces after defeating the Scots. "Quarter" was not given.

By 1743 Squire Tom's family consisted of John Henry born 1736; Thomas Christopher, 1730, and Andrew, 1740; Jane, 1741; and James, 1743.

Mary was again with child. Tom began to be concerned about her children's education and those of Tom's brother. On a trip to Charles Town he inquired concerning an indentured servant of letters to instruct his children in reading, mathematics, Latin, Greek, and the new double entry bookkeeping method. In November, the brothers received word that three scholars were available. Henry, Samuel, and Tom journeyed by horseback with a spare horse in tow. They interviewed the three scholar candidates and chose John Dalton who agreed to work for two years in exchange for his passage bill, room and board, and a severance allowance of land, clothes, and tools at the end of the term.

Mary and Rebecca, brother Samuel's wife, were delighted to meet the young man and the prospect of the improvements a scholar portended.

Through the 1740's the clan continued to prosper. The mill continued to process forest goods for building and ship building in Charles Town. There was a great need for tall oak. Strong trees for ship masts were pulled to Camden and floated down the rivers when the water level was right.

Thomas continued as the Justice of the Peace, squire, and representative to the assembly then meeting in Bath. However, he sometimes missed the assembly with the heavy demands.

The family increased with the addition of Andrew, Margaret, Elizabeth, David and Joseph. As scions Henry, Thomas, and Andrew approached manhood, Mary and Tom spent many hours pondering the fate of their children. Son Henry seemed to be inclined toward the work of the plantations. His mind was fixed upon finance. He had also picked up the blacksmith trade. Thomas and Andrew, on the other hand, loved to spend time in the woods hunting and established some great relationships with the Catawba tribe. Thomas flourished under the tutelage of John Dalton, the resident scholar.

It was a crisp fall day in 1745. The maples had taken on their yellow brilliance. Some elder trees were turning their stunning red. Some more advanced had fallen to the earth. It was a good time. The corn had been put away in the crib. Hogs had been killed and smoked and cured. It was a good day to be alive. Sitting by the fire together, Mary turned and asked.

"Didn't Henry and Tom go hunting today and aren't they due back?"

"My dear, they are old enough to take care of themselves. I don't expect them until Saturday. They are hunting with the Catawbas. Besides Arthur is with them."

"I am not sure that is a good idea. They are only fifteen and eleven."

"The Catawbas pride themselves in being our friends. Besides Uncle Arthur will watch out for them."

"I hope you are right. We are so fortunate to have a good man like Arthur working for us. But I hate for them to miss their lessons with Master Carlton."

"The woods are good teachers, too."

On Saturday afternoon the boys rode in accompanied by Arthur, the older servant. Their parents met them on the porch and noticed two deer dressed and strung across the saddles of two of the horses. Henry jumped from his horse and cried.

"Father and Mother, we had a great adventure."

"First you must have Arthur there take care of the animals and deer. Then come in and we will have some supper. Arthur as soon as you hang the animals and put up the horses, please join us for supper."

After supper, Henry began.

## YOUNG HENRY'S STORY

While we were hunting we met your friend Running Bear who led us to his home in the one of the Catawba Villages. Crying Cloud, the medicine man, motioned us to his lodge to spend the night. It was a birch covered lodge with a small opening for a door and a hole in the roof for the fire.

"Come in me White brother," said the Medicine Man. He was Running Path's aged uncle.

"It is an honor to be in your lodge, Uncle," I said imitating Running Path. Path began translating for us.

"I understand that you have been on the Great Warrior Path and the land of the Shawnee, Cherokees, and Creek brothers."

"We have not but our trader friend Zeke Proctor has."

"I know this Proctor. He is a good man. Is the path still used for war for the brothers of the south when they raid the brothers of the north?"

"He says he ran into very little trouble as most tribes were friendly. However, there has been a terrible outbreak of the pox which has weakened the Cherokees. The recent war between the colony of South Carolina and the Tuscaroas has led the tribe to move north."

Young Henry continued relaying the words of Running Bear. Running Bear said, "I talked with our Tucarora brothers. After being driven from their homes many moons ago they were adopted by the Conestoga tribe. We are more worried about the British than about the French. We Catawba peoples learned to live with our white brothers and under the protection of our Great White Father. Commissioner Stuart has helped us. We learned much from each other about farming. However, we have a sad heart as Brother Wolf, Brother Bear, and Brother Beaver are fleeing to the west make us feel hunger in our lodges. We ponder these things. Our brothers the Shawnee have left their homes to go west because their hunting grounds are gone. Our neighbors the Cherokee seem restless. We wonder about this too. Do you Presbyterians hope to be friends with us like the Quakers?"

"Uncle, I cannot speak for me elders. However, we have heard of some of the villages of the Cherokee, the Catawba, and the Shawnee. Some prosper and some do not. Zeke Proctor, the trader, also saw the fear in the eyes of the Tuscaroas he passed on the trail. I hope we can all live happily."

"The coming of the White man gives me a troubled heart. I don't understand their ways. To the White man war is not the supreme heart-stirring test of manhood. It is only for material advantage. His greatest passion is acquiring personal wealth. He makes himself a slave. He sweats year after year to raise one hundred fold what he can use. His color is unhealthy; he lives in filth with no regard for the purification which keeps a man pure in spirit and body. Wherever he goes there is drunkenness, disease, and death.

"From dawn to dusk our children know freedom whether the young warrior builds a canoe, hunts a bear, seeks a woman, or joins a war party. We do not wish for wealth. We only want to be at one with mother earth. The earth was a gift from her to be allowed to be used freely, not cut up into little spaces for the sake of one man and his family. The earth is ours to hunt and protect.

My nephew learned ways of the white man. He reads the skins that talk. He works on the shiny rocks and makes many iron goods for us. I hope, Running Path, that you will remember the ways of your fathers as you go to old age. I pray to the Great Spirit to help us in the ages to come. I like you Nail (Henry's Indian name) and hope you will visit us often. What I said may hurt, but it is the truth. I hope that someday you will consider being adopted by the Catawba tribe."

"I consider it an honor to be your friend, Uncle." With this I turned for home very troubled over what Crying Cloud had said.

"Well, Henry my young explorer and trader," his father Tom began, "it looks like you had quite an adventure."

"Yes, the visiting with the tribe is a great adventure. Uncle Arthur knows the forest and was a good friend of the chiefs."

***

In the late summer 1746 Zeke Proctor stopped by on the way to Charles Town with skins he had traded with the Cherokees.

That night after supper he and Alexander joined Mary and Tom on the porch of the main house. They burned a tar fire to discourage the insects while they sat hoping for an evening breeze in the stifling heat.

Thomas addressed Zeke, "I hear you have a license to trade with the Cherokee. What have you heard about their temperament?"

"When I was with Lord Cummins in 1730, he set up Moytoy of the Keowee as Emperor of the Cherokees. Since Keowee is a lower Cherokee town, the king or Uku of the Chota, or sacred town, did not recognize the emperor as the principal chief of the confederation was supposed to be from Chota. This made Connecorte, or Old Hop as he was known, angry that he was not chosen. He began to make overtures both to the French and Virginia. He hoped to end the monopoly on trade with the Carolinians. In 1741 old Moytoy was killed in a fight with the Choctaws. Governor Glen then chose his thirteen year old son, Ammonscottee, as the new emperor.

This so angered Old Hop of Chota that he sent his second man, the one we call The Raven, both to the Virginians and French asking for them to trade with them. Old Hop was from the Over the Mountain Cherokees. Chota was the traditional home of the Great Chief of the Cherokee federation. Amonscottie was a lower Cherokee.

"Even though some trade was started with the French, it backfired on Old Hop because the French trade goods were not as abundant and not of the same quality as the English. The French had problems getting their goods through the English fleet. The French relied on errant commercial sea captains who could slip through the slight blockade and place the goods on the docks of New Orleans.

The Indians love our pots, steel hatchets, knives, guns, powder and bullets. The beautiful Cherokee maidens are beginning to hide their lovely charms in calico. The old chiefs are being pressured to move toward the English. In times of trouble, we steer clear of the upper Cherokee as well as the Choctaw. In fact, I only trade with the Catawbas and Cherokees and have never asked for a license for anything else. I don't like the Shawnee. The Cherokees allowed a small Shawnee tribe to settle north of the land as a buffer from the Catawbas and the settlements of you gentlemen.

By the way before I forget it. I am obliged to you for taking away the license of McGhee and Johnson. What did they do?"

Thomas replied, "That was some time ago. We received many reports of their cheating the Indians and they stole some property from the settlers including

Master Hawthorne's livestock and horses. By the way, I didn't take away a license, they never had one. Have you heard from them?"

"Last I heard they had been adopted by the Creeks and had turned Indian. I hear they don't care for your company."

"Yes, after my brother and I visited with them they seem to have disappeared. It could be they have heard about the warrant we have for their arrest for failure to appear in court. If I could obtain proof that they were trading with the Creeks without a license that could be added to the charges. A few more complaints and McGhee and Johnson will swing from a tree."

Zeke continued, "Is the Assembly going to give the Governor any money for the militia in case there is trouble?"

"If the Indians threaten he will probably be asked to embargo goods rather than try to fight them."

"I was afraid of that. There are some traders who give the short yard for skins and a short pound for corn and powder. They rely a great deal on rum to arrive at an agreement. I don't want to sound too pious but fair trading has gotten me a long way."

"His Excellency the South Carolina Governor speaks well of you. What else have you heard?"

Zeke replied, "The Governor treads a narrow path between the need for Indian allies and the customs and complaints of angry Creeks, Catawbas, and the Carolina Frontier."

Thomas answered, "Yes, the Charles Town Rice Kings only care about their slaves and their effete ways. They only want the Indians as a buffer so they can live like English lords. The town is already the most pretentious in North America. It even surpasses some of the Spice Islands. They are encouraging people to occupy the land like we do for the same reason—a buffer against warring tribes and the French."

"Don't spring those French words on me. What means effete?"

"A worthless dandy who never gets his hands dirty and looks down on those who do, a would-be gentleman. They aspire to be gentlemen but don't possess the quality."

"I always thought you was one of them, Tom. A gentleman I mean."

"A man who works the forge, serves in the militia, serves His Majesty and two governors can never qualify for one of those pompous asses."

"Your land has been coming along. I also like your forge. You make the best horseshoes in the Carolinas. Is that right Alex?"

Startled Alex looked up having just returned from the servants' area. "I suppose," said Zeke with a wink, "that you have been spending all of your time dressing the animals."

Alexander retorted. "Usually I spend my time with the folks. They are having a dance down there. Master Tom, you sure do have great parties and such lovely young ladies. It is so dull up here with you."

"I am glad I can oblige. I just hope I don't have another mouth to feed in nine months."

Startled Alex smiled and said, "Why, Your Grace, Tom, don't you know I am a Christian? However, when I decide to leave the trail I'll be back to look around."

They all chuckled. Thomas said, "Have some sack punch, Alex, and cool off."

After recounting many stories and finally retiring, Mary began, "I don't appreciate your attitude toward Alexander's recreation. I think it is unchristian to encourage him in sinful practices."

"My dear, men of the trail cannot afford to settle down. Raising a family would be impossible. In the Indian villages, men consider it an honor to share their wives with strangers. Why do you think we have so many mixed bloods among the Cherokee?"

Mary frowned, "Perhaps it is not a good idea to let our boys wander among the Catawbas."

"Fear not, fair maiden. The Presbyterian ethic is strong and the Running Bear will be looking after them as well as that medicine man."

# CHAPTER 7

# A Visit from the Magistrate

## 1749

The October court day broke sunny and warm at the Neel settlement. Justice Neel greeted one of the North Carolina Circuit judges, who was to observe and then hear some of the cases. Justice Matthews sat on a just constructed dais on the porch of the Neel settlement in his robe, wig, and collar.

Sheriff Henry rose, "Hear ye, Hear ye, Hear ye. Come before His Honor Justice James Mathews of His Majesty's court of North Carolina all ye that have business with the Crown. Justice Matthews.

"Thank you, Your Honor Sheriff Neel. First, I bring you some news. There is some concern about the fact that the issue of the Albemarle representatives to the Assembly still fail to appear because they desire to have the legislature meet in Edington while the Governor has assembled the legislature at New Bern on most occasions. There is great concern that the Governor, being a Scot, failed to celebrate the victory of the English at Culloden Moor in April, 1746. He further has encouraged Highland Scots to migrate here in spite of many of them being declared Rebels. I have a copy of the pledge of the Disarming Act which has been applied to all of the Highland Scots, which has been posted here. The oath taken reads:

> *I do swear, as I shall answer to God on the great day of Judgment, I shall not, nor shall I have in my possession a gun, sword, pistol or arm whatsoever, and never use tartan, plaid or any part of the Highland garb; and if I do so may I be cursed in my undertakings, family and property-may I never see my wife and children, father, mother or relations- may I be killed in battle as a coward, and lie buried without burial in a strange land, far from the graves of my forefathers and kindred; may all this come across me if I break my oath.*

The forces of Lord Cumberland thwarted the attempt by the Scots to place Prince Charles Stewart on the throne at the Battle of Culloden Moor. Many atrocities were committed. Many of the Highland Scots are migrating here because of the King's decree banishing them to the colonies for seven years and others are coming voluntarily.

I also bring you news from the governors of North and South Carolina. There is a distressing report that the French are building forts on the Ohio River and seek control of the entire river. However, we are at peace with our French neighbors because word has reached us that last October the French and our beloved King signed a treaty of peace. Be it known that there will now be a tax on exported indigo. His Lordship, Governor Glen, of South Carolina has been concerned about traders without a license. He is also concerned with the cheating by traders of Indians. He has implored the justices of neighboring colonies to strictly monitor Indian trade. The Governors of both colonies as well as the Lord Granville are most appreciative of the bravery and industry of the Providence province. Hail to the King."

There was an answering response and then Justice Matthews heard cases involving land disputes, horse thievery, property disputes including slavery, and trading complaints. He also recognized patents which he, Mathews, would take back to Bern. Since some of the claims were probably in the disputed area of South Carolina, these would be forwarded to Charles Town from New Bern by ship.

Sometimes the traveling magistrate would choose to travel overland to Charles Town and take a ship back to Bern, the capital of North Carolina. The court days were always exciting as people would come from the area to see the trials and punishments ranging from stocks, to confinement, to hanging. Indians, barterers, and traders—licensed and unlicensed, as well as an occasional troop of the King's own were present.

At the conclusion of the day's business, Thomas asked His Honor James Matthews to spend the second night with him; his escort was quartered on the grounds. After a supper of venison, corn pudding, pork roast, and wild greens, Thomas and his wife, Mary, Henry, James sat around the fireplace with a glass of sack.

"What further news, Sir James?" asked Henry.

"There is great unrest among the Cherokees, Choctaws and their enemy the Creeks. Governor Glen of South Carolina has arranged a peace between the two peoples and has set up a boundary which he hopes will bring peace. There have been incidents where the peace has been broken and this has caused the good Governor Glen to approach his assembly for construction of possible forts. As you know the Cherokee nations is really a federation of three loose tribes: the Overhills at Chute, the Valley, and the Lower Cherokees at Kiowa, those being the principal villages. There are rumors that the Cherokees are trying to break their 1730 compact with Sir Cummings and start trading with the French and Virginia. Virginia has offered to build a Fort on the Long Island of the Holston for the purpose of promoting the Cherokee trade. Both Carolina Governors are opposed to this. Governor Glen has threatened to embargo all goods unless the Virginia and French negotiations cease. This will anger the Cherokees."

Mary chimed in, "Thank goodness we have the friendly Catawbas and the Shawnees between the Cherokees and us."

His Honor replied, "I pray it will thus always be. On another matter, the Governor is considering licensing your rebel Presbyterian ministers as clergy. I think it is about time. Some of our short sighted lords claim that any children of an Irish Presbyterian marriage are bastards. What a pity. I don't know what will happen when these Scots with their Church of Scotland like litany join the religious mix here. The Crown does not send enough clergy and rebels when the people provide their own. It is as if the colonies have become separate countries from England."

"That is correct, Sire," added Henry. "With all of the new settlers coming down from Pennsylvania and Virginia by the Warrior and Trading Paths, there is a real need for not only clergy but sheriffs to keep the King's law. And don't forget those Highlanders settling in the Cape Fear region. We have personally heard people here denounce the King, especially, when his Council insists on specie for the payment of quitrents rather than commodities. I need not tell ye how scarce currency is in these parts."

"What say you to all of these Scots coming because of the recent rebellion in Scotland?"

"The Highlanders are coming over here like lemmings fleeing to the ocean. The Assembly passed a law giving them land and ten years free of taxes. South Carolina, also, gives them land and bounty to start a new life. The colonies are way ahead of civilizing influences."

The next morning they wished His Honor godspeed and looked forward to his return at the next circuit. He mounted his steed and gave the captain of the escort a nod and they were away.

# CHAPTER 8

# A Mission to the Cherokees

In the spring of the year 1749, after much discussion, Thomas moved his family and patented new lands on the Catawba River near the disputed border between the two Carolina colonies. There he began a new plantation. This was part of the land grant given as a result of service in the Georgia expedition.

One of his neighbors was William Hill who was later to establish an iron works some ten miles from the new Neel plantation. The principal source of ore was nearby Nanny Mountain. The abundant hardwood forests furnished wood for charcoal necessary for processing the ore into pig iron. Just as the mill began to produce, the Parliament passed the Iron Act which forbade the construction of rolling and sheet mills, steel furnaces, and tilt hammer forges in the American colonies. Hill decided not to file for a permit but instead would concentrate on serving the local population with kettles, plows, horse shoes, and various hardware, hoping he would not be discovered. Henry, being the sheriff, decided to look the other way. The borders of the county extended from Providence south, but Sheriff Henry was not sure how far west his jurisdiction lay. The Iron Act, along with the Test Act, would serve as an irritant which would plant the idea of more local control. In fact, in 1754 Benjamin Franklin of Pennsylvania was to put forth what was to become the Albany Plan of Union for giving the colonies more control over their affairs thus avoiding the serious time lag waiting for communications from London.

In the spring of 1751, Thomas and Henry were called to Charles Town by Governor Glen. The letter arrived expressing interest in discussing the boundaries of the two colonies. Squire Tom and Sheriff Henry arrived at the Owl Inn near the harbor. The next morning a British Major called on them while they were at breakfast. He approached their table. The Neels rose.

With a bow, the major began, "Do I have the pleasure of addressing Masters Henry and Thomas Neel of the Catawbas?"

"You do, sir. May we be of service to you?"

"I am Major Buford of the Royal Lancers and an adjutant to His Excellency Christopher Glen. My commission is to act as your escort to the Governor who wishes the pleasure of your company and counsel."

"It is a pleasure to be of service."

"Excellent, may I send a coach within the hour?"

They agreed and at the nine o'clock hour a coach and four arrived and the Catawbans were taken to the palace. As they gained the long driveway to the Governor's palace, Tom remarked, "There is certainly a contrast in the elegance of the South Carolina Governor's home and the digs we have in North Carolina."

"Agreed," answered Henry, "New Bern and Wilmington were never like this."

"I know, but the Governor of North Carolina is considering making an even grander palace."

After the usual protocol, the frontiersmen were shown to the chambers of his Excellency Christopher Glen. They approached his desk, and the wigged Governor dressed in the uniform of a Colonel of the Dragoons bid them to sit down. The Neels bowed and were suddenly aware of their primitive frontier dress of buckskin blouse, trousers, and shoe packs.

"Thank you, I am indebted to you for responding to my call. Your fine reputations herald your arrival. First, the request for help on the border is but a ruse. We will be asking you for this input but I need some good men to work on a clandestine mission. What I am relating must be held in strictest confidence. May I have your word and trust?"

"What you say will be held in trust; however, we would like to hear the mission."

"You may have heard that we are having some success in bringing peace between the Choctaws and Cherokees. This effort has been greatly strained when a hunting party of the Cherokees was allegedly robbed by some white settlers. His Majesty's Justice James Francis at Ninety-Six is alleged to have protected the settlers who claimed the Choctaws did the deed and not them. It is His Majesty's policy to be a friend of the Cherokees who are constantly courted by the French. My request to you is to go to the fort at Ninety-Six and conduct an examination of the facts there and report back to me. It is far-fetched but I want you to pose as part of a boundary commission to establish boundaries among the Cherokee, Choctaws, and Creeks."

"Your Excellency, we are honored to be of service; however, we have plantations and government responsibilities which auger for time to place our homes in order. Thomas, can we be ready in a month?"

"Henry, I concur. We should be able to leave in a month."

The Neel brothers took to their horses, stowed their commission papers, and returned home. After saying good-bye to their families, they trudged the Trading Path for the fort at Ninety-Six, named so because the village was ninety-six miles from the Cherokee village of Keowee.

April first brought them to the outskirts of Ninety-Six. The area had been cleared around the settlement of most of its vegetation. There were no palisades or exterior walls of any kind. A series of pens and huts surrounded a slightly finer house and a tavern. A common barn was attached to the tavern. Traders, some not licensed, mingled freely with the Indians of the Choctaw, Creek, and Cherokee tribes. There was an uneasy calm among the tribes as Governor Glen attempted to bring peace among them. Henry and Thomas's dress blended fairly well with the costumes of the traders—buckskin pants, trail moccasins, checkered blouse and buckskin jacket. Each of the brothers carried two pistols attached to his upper body as well as Pennsylvania rifles in their saddles. The two horses they rode were large stallions which were accompanied by two pack mules with supplies.

They stopped at the Bull Horn Tavern, tied their horses and pack animals and went inside. The room was dark and smelled of rum, roasted beef, pork, and human sweat. The hearth supported an animal being roasted as well as two large kettles. The odor of freshly cooked bread also added to the harmony of smells. Two serving wenches scurried among the tables serving meat on pewter plates as well as rum and occasionally whiskey and warm beer. After an inquiry concerning care of their animals and lodging, they took the animals to an open barn and then trudged to the lodging of a local trader. This landlord managed to give them one bed, which they shared with another, rotating turns so they could get some decent sleep.

The next morning Henry and Thomas made their way to the court of Justice James Francis which was housed in his domicile. They approached the door of the house and knocked. A female servant answered the door.

Henry began, "I am Sheriff Henry Neel of the Providence area of North Carolina, and this gentlemen is my brother, Justice Thomas Neel of the same area. We are on a special mission for His Excellency Governor Christopher Glen."

"Wait here, sirs, and I will announce you." She then turned back into the house. Soon a rather rotund man appeared. He was short and bald, wore square spectacles, had a careless red beard, and had a floral vest which had been stained by careless eating. He wore silver buckles on his waist and shoes, and linen breeches.

"Welcome my countrymen please come in and sit down. Molly, bring these gentlemen some tea. What news do you bring?"

Tom replied, "We have brought you the post from the Charleston area as well as a commission to study possible boundaries between the Creek and Cherokee tribes."

"I hope the boundaries will work. There is a great deal of unrest out here.

Henry asked, "Could you tell us about it."

Justice James motioned them to sit down by the fire. He took a small stick, stuck it in the fire and lit his pipe. As the smoke drifted to the ceiling he began. "About a month ago, a hunting party of the lower Cherokee towns was ambushed by a party of Choctaws who took their skins and brought them here for trade. A Cherokee Chief of the Lower Towns, Little Carpenter, appealed to me to bring two traders they think they saw trading the same skins that were stolen. They claim that these two traders had stolen the skins and horses. When I had the trial and found them not guilty, the Cherokee chief, Little Carpenter, stomped in anger and broke an arrow shaft. He claimed that the treaty had been broken like the arrow."

Tom added, "I know this Little Carpenter. He served with us in Georgia. Who were these traders?"

"One is known as Squawman Johnson and the other is Artimas McGhee."

"McGhee! So that is where he went," exclaimed Henry. "We have an outstanding warrant for him in North Carolina."

James continued, "I find that hard to believe, Sir. These are both fine men who never fail to return my hospitality. They are devoted men who add much to the pleasure of an evening with their delightful tales."

"Do they have a South Carolina Trading license?" asked Tom.

"Gentlemen do not ask other gentlemen such questions about other colonies."

"I would hardly call them gentlemen. Scoundrels and robbers would be better. Anyway we shall begin our surveys of a boundary between Creek and Cherokee lands. If we can be of further service let us know." With that the brothers bid good-bye and proceeded to the warehouse and tavern.

"I don't believe my colleague is overly endowed with Christian virtues," said Tom.

"It is unbelievable that he could arrive at such a fine opinion of McGhee and Johnson. They are the very looks of evil."

They went into the store to scout for news. As they came in, a group of traders were gathered around the clerk and stopped talking the minute the Neels walked in. Tom began looking at blankets and tack. Henry walked up to the counter and asked for a twist of tobacco. After Henry gave the proprietor some English coins, the proprietor commented, "We don't receive such fine currency here very often. What brings you gentlemen to these parts?"

"We are here on behalf of His Excellency Governor Glen who wishes us to establish a line which will bring peace among the Cherokees and Creeks."

A bearded hunter, dirty and looking like he just came from the trail, put down his decorated Indian Musket and hatchet on the table and after ordering a drink looked at Henry and said, "You ain't welcome here. We don't need anybody taking away our hunting and trading rights."

"I will not be abused, sir. I am an officer of the King and Governor on a mission.

What I have to do has nothing to do with your hunting. We come to bring peace. Now if you will excuse us we will bid you good day." Thus ended Tom's speech and first acquaintance with the patrons of Ninety- Six.

As the pair strolled slowly outside they felt the hostile eyes of the tavern watching. They returned to the home of Justice James and after a greeting related to him what had happened to them in the tavern. He expressed shock at how they had been treated. It did not sound sincere.

"Just how often do Johnson and McGhee come here?" asked Henry.

"They make a round of the Creek territory about every two months."

"I know you said that you don't check their licenses, but what have you done about the complaint from His Excellency that you have not dealt justly in this case."

"I resent, Sir, your implication. I heard the case and dealt fairly. It is clear to me that the Choctaws stole those skins."

"How do you account for the fact that one of the Indian ponies was in possession of McGhee."

"He told me he traded for it from a Choctaw."

As they were speaking a trader burst into the room and breathlessly related, "Your Grace, Your Grace. You must come quickly there has been an Indian raid; Senacas as well as a few Cherokees have raided settlements, burned houses, and killed a trader at his store and killed two Chickasaws."

Justice James ran to the tavern, rang the alarm bell and gave the news. He called for the local militia and prepared to march the next day. Tom and Henry approached the Justice and suggested that they be allowed to conduct the King's business, and if while the militia be used to guard Ninety-Six, Tom and Henry could meet with the Indians concerning the boundaries. With some grumbling Justice James agreed.

The next morning Tom and Henry, having provisioned themselves, started north toward Keowee, a lower Cherokee village. As they began the trail, they made a habit to zigzag every fifteen minutes as a gesture of peace. The third day they were about a mile from Keowee when two Cherokee braves on beautiful chargers blocked the trail. Tom and Henry raised their rifles above their heads. Then Tom, dropping one hand, motioned with his hand to his mouth that he wished to talk. He continued with the sign of a head man. The taller Indian motioned them to follow. One of them traveled in back while the other led. Henry felt a little uncomfortable about this.

They soon arrived at a break in the forest and came to the Keowee village. Situated near a stream, it was a beautiful village among the pine and hardwood trees.

There was a garden plot laid out in preparation for planting. Women were tanning hides, children playing games. Their homes were solid structures made of posts with earth covering. The smell of tanning and human waste was overwhelming. They were motioned toward a large council house. They dismounted and proceeded toward the lodge. The Indian who met them was of small stature. He wore a bone decorated vest, buckskin leggings, decorated breech cloth, and linen shirt. His head was bare except for the usual topknot. Large earrings were in his earlobes. The Neels were in the presence of Little Carpenter, Right Hand man of the Chota Uka, or supreme chief. Thomas recognized him, and knew he spoke English.

"Greetings, my brother, I am Colonel Thomas Neel. We marched together in Georgia many seasons ago."

For a moment Little Carpenter stood by with a half dozen braves and only stared with piercing eyes. Finally he spoke.

"I remember my White Brother. Do you come in peace?"

"We have come at the request of His Lordship Governor Giles."

"I thought His Lordship had become blind and deaf and could not see the plight of his Cherokee children. I would go to the Great Father King George and tell him of this blindness."

"The Governor has sent me to hear your troubles and try to correct them."

"We have heard of your justice, Captain Neel, from our Catawba kinsmen. They tell me your justice is strong medicine. The Justice of James is filled with evil. We complain to him about the traders and they go unpunished. My young braves grow weary of his actions and long to take matters into their own hands. But come let us have council together."

As they approached the lodge of Little Carpenter, Thomas asked, "I am honored, my Brother, to work for peace with you. Great Attakullakulla, if I may ask, how did you get the name Little Carpenter?"

"It is the name that Lord Cummins gave on my trip to see the King. He thought I spoke so well at treaty time that I built a good treaty, a good builder or carpenter. Makes us laugh."

As they continued toward the council house, Tom turned to the chief and asked, "Why are you a second man of the Sacred Village Cheota of the Overhills down in the Lower Cherokees?"

"The Beloved Man which you call Old Hop has sent me to the lower villages."

Ducking through the skin covered door they entered a large room. There they found a dozen warriors sitting on the ground around the common fire. The roof had a hole for the smoke, but smoke was still evident.

Joined by a half dozen other chiefs, they sat down. The ceremonial pipe was passed. When it returned to Little Carpenter he motioned the ritual – first pointing the pipe to the north, then to the south and finally the east and west. All set motionless for many minutes.

Finally, Little Carpenter rose to speak in Cherokee. "Brothers, His Excellency has heard our words and sent one of his finest warriors to hear our grievances. Let us hear him. Speak my brother." As he spoke, Little Carpenter translated.

"Our great father King George thinks you have been wronged. The men who robbed you go free. The Governor has asked me to bring the traders Johnson and McGhee to justice. He also pleads for you to try to live with your neighbors the Chickasaws and Creeks. We ask you to return your captives from your recent raid and live at peace with your brothers. We shall now leave the council while you consider."

As they started to the door, one of the chiefs asked, "Why does His Excellency allow the traders to cheat us? Why does he refuse to give us guns and ammunition to fight our enemy the Creeks? How does he expect us to hunt without guns?"

"My brother poses a hard question. His Excellency received bad medicine from his headmen when he stopped selling you guns and ammunition. We are here to bring peace and try to get the Governor to open fair trade."

There was much grunting in response. Tom and Henry had difficulty telling how they felt. Tom and Henry left the Council and were standing outside when Morning Woman, wife of Little Carpenter, came up and offered meat to them. While pulling at the buffalo meat and squaw bread, two young Cherokee women came and motioned the brothers to accompany them. Aware of the custom of shared beds for strangers, they motioned that they wished to stay outside. They found a spot between two houses, put down their bedrolls and went to sleep.

The travelers were awakened by the chickens. Soon Little Carpenter came to them. He squatted near them as they sat up in their bed rolls.

"Our council has heard of many troubles. We have heard that the Iroquois plan to strike us this spring. We have heard that a thousand whites are about to march on our lower towns. The crops have been bad the past two trips of the earth, there is bad hunting, and the traders are cheating us. We grow weary of fighting and worry. Something must be done."

"Perhaps if we could bring some of the cheating traders to justice, we could calm some of the fears of your people. I will speak well of your people before the Governor. I would also like to take your captives back to the Chickasaws with an apology so you may become brothers again. I would also like your help in finding the traders McGhee and Johnson."

"Good. Let us leave for the Chickasaw Nation within the hour."

The brothers with Little Carpenter then headed south to the Chickasaws. There they met with Squirrel King, chief of a Chickasaw Village. Little Carpenter gave his apology to the Squirrel King for the capture of some of his braves, and was delighted he did not demand a hostage. The captured Chickasaws were brought forward. This caused much tears and wailing as the braves were reunited with their families. Little Carpenter brought forward five head of cattle as tribute. Tom threw in a kettle to cement the agreements.

Squirrel King related that McGhee and Johnson had been through there two days before and made some of the younger braves drunk and then stole some of the hides rather than paying for them. The chief sent out scouting parties but they had not reported back yet. After spending the night in the Chickasaw village, the Cherokee warrior and the Neels were dismissed for home.

They began searching for McGhee and Johnson. Squirrel King had suggested that the traders had headed further south after the Cherokee raid in which the Chickasaws were taken prisoner. The party left accompanied by two trackers from the Chickasaws.

As the party progressed further and further away from the land of the Cherokees and into the lands of Georgia, the Neel brothers were concerned about the limits of their authority. Tom asked, "Are we trailing for personal gratification or are we on the King's mission?"

Henry growled, "You ask too many questions."

On the second day, one of the trackers picked up the trail of four horses with shoes typical of the smith at Ninety-Six. Little Carpenter pointed to the trail and said, "This trail leads to a village of the Senecas. We soon will be discovered by their braves. We must make a noise like we are careless. They are friendly to our people. Perhaps we can parley with them."

As they traveled the trail began to widen and the forest became more trampled. It also became quieter. Suddenly, two Seneca braves in war paint blocked the trail. Following Little Carpenter's lead they began to zigzag and place their rifles high in the air. Little Carpenter signaled with his fingers and lips that he wished to parley. He then left the Neel party and zigzagged toward the Senecas where he parleyed with them. In a few moments he returned and said they could follow them to the village. Upon arriving, they found the village in a high degree of excitement. Two white men were tied to stakes in the center and old women were beating them. The housing structures were very similar to those of the Cherokees. The group dismounted and cautiously walked to the chief lodge. Tom noticed the burned remains of a log cabin structure. Many goods were strewn on the ground.

The visitors were taken to the council house where they were entertained by the head man. He related that the men on the posts were cheating traders who were caught stealing their skins and had sold them muskets which were of low quality. They also related that all of their trade goods were of French origin. The young braves had grown angry and stormed their store house and commenced to torture the traders. Through Little Carpenter, Henry asked their names. He said they were known Black Heart and Little John. Their English names were McGhee and Johnson. The noise and excitement was beginning to grow. The young children were dancing around the hostages. Suddenly McGhee looked up and catching Tom's eye shouted. "Squire Tom, save our Christian souls. They are about to kill us."

Tom turned to Little Carpenter, "I am tempted to let this happen. However, what would it take to free them?"

"The Senecas do not feel they are of King George's people. They are strongly influenced by the French and Spanish. Perhaps an offer of trade goods would help," replied Little Carpenter.

"Let us talk to the Head Man and see if we can convince him that we would like to punish McGhee and Johnson for what they have done to your people. Also, I think we have enough proof to have His Excellency take some action against our friend the Justice. I wonder if the good chief would like one of our Pennsylvania rifles?"

Tom asked Little Carpenter to challenge the chief to a shooting contest. If he could shoot an ax at 200 paces, he would give him two Pennsylvania rifles and ammunition in exchange for the prisoners.

Little Carpenter then went to the Head Man and parleyed. The chief agreed to the contest. Like most of his tribe he liked wagers. Henry took one of his steel hatchets and stuck it on a stump at about 200 paces. Tom then invited a brave, the best one chosen by the head man, to shoot one of his trade muskets. The brave did and missed. The crowd roared in laughter. Tom loaded his rifle, sighted and the hatchet spun off with a ringing as the bullet made its mark.

Tom then took his hat and put it on the head of McGhee. McGhee, sensing what was about to happen begged him for mercy. Tom backed off 200 paces and fired at the hat knocking it off McGhee's head but grazing his scalp. Blood poured down his face as he cursed loudly. There were "oohs" and "ahs" among the crowd.

The Seneca Chief agreed to release the prisoners and return two of the captive horses in return for the two rifles, bullets, and ammunition. Through Little Carpenter, Tom agreed to the terms, but wanted two muskets so that they would not be completely unarmed on the trail. The chief agreed. Little Carpenter and the chief spent a few minutes in private conversation.

Henry sauntered over to McGhee and Johnson. "Well, gents it appears you will live a little while longer. Get your fill of food and water while you are here because ye're next stop will be Ninety-Six. There will be a break for making water three times a day. The rest of the time you will be tied to your horse."

"We are obliged for saving our lives, Squire. However, we have done nothing wrong."

"Well, for one thing you failed to appear before a lawful magistrate. Of course, we could turn you over to the Chickasaws here."

"Your Grace's point is well taken." said McGhee.

Because the party lacked adequate saddles the prisoners were thrown face down over the back of their beasts and a rope run underneath the horse to secure them. They resembled game after it was shot. Every two hours the prisoners were allowed water and could walk two hours if they wished to avoid the constraints.

Thus began their journey back to Ninety-Six. The first night they arrived at the Savannah River after spending half the day looking for a place to ford. After crossing with the water up to the horse's stomach, the party dismounted. The prisoner's bonds were checked and then tied back to back with their hands free and legs bound. A stew was prepared from the jerky they had brought. As the group met around the campfire, and after posting the guard detail, Tom sat down with Little Carpenter.

"My brother," began Little Carpenter, "what do you intend to do with these bad fellows."

"I suggest that we take them to Charles Town and there turn them over to His Excellency Governor Giles. I want to avoid Ninety-Six because these fellows have too many friends."

"I am with heavy heart. While in the village of the Seneca brothers, I heard of a plan of the small tribe of the Iroquois who came here several seasons ago. They are joining their brothers from the north in a plan to chasten the Cherokees. We have heard also that some of the whites were ready to strike against us. It is not a good time for our people. We have just finished a war with the Creeks, the hunting has been bad, and there is much trouble among the various towns of the Cherokee people. Our young men desire coup. Our elders trouble over the condition of the people."

"Has the King's agent, Stuart, been aware of these things?"

"He longs for the comfort of Charles Town. He does not seem to remember that the French have a fort on the Hiawasee and have visited our villages."

Tom gave Little Carpenter a gold coin with the likeness of King George. "With this coin I pledge to you that I shall put your case before the Governor and tell him of your concerns."

"I place my trust in the white brothers. I would like to take the prisoners back to my village Keowee. We can keep them as hostages until His Excellency is ready to try them."

"The First Man of Keowee has a good plan. You must pledge them no harm."

Tom then motioned for Henry. He explained the plan and then the Indians and the whites enjoyed a pipe ceremony. Henry passed around a small jug of rum. Except for the rotation of two guards throughout the night, they all slept except for the prisoners who were very uncomfortable in their bonds. They did not take part in the ceremony nor the libations with the rum.

At sunrise after a breakfast of coffee and jerky, Tom approached McGhee and Johnson.

"Well my friends, you are now going to be the guests of Little Carpenter and his friends in Keowee. They have pledged you no harm and are taking you to Keowee until they can meet with His Lordship. I suggest you be on your best behavior because they do not take too kindly to certain robberies they have experienced."

"They will torture and murder us."

"I have their pledge."

"You can't trust an Indian."

"I suppose I can trust you? Wait, I don't have to worry. They are your hosts. Good day, my friends."

Tom and Henry started for home. They wrote the Governor of South Carolina about their activities and asked for reimbursement for the Pennsylvania rifles.

# CHAPTER 9

# Thomas Christopher Neel and Henry Find Mates

A return to the Providence settlement brought life back to normal for the Neels. Thomas (1710) sent a report of the trip with Little Carpenter to Governor Giles of South Carolina as well as another report to Johnston the Governor of North Carolina. He suggested that the nefarious traders be retried at some place other than Ninety-Six, and that among the charges, failure to appear and trading without a license be added. He defended his action of turning the prisoners over to Little Carpenter because of the problems of bringing them such a long way with only two personnel.

Spring crops were planted on the plantations. Much needed maintenance and supervision were effected. During one Sunday afternoon after services, the three older Neels were enjoying a smoke on the front portico. They were joined by John Dalton, a former tutor of their children who had arrived the night before.

Henry asked, "What news do you bring? What have you done for yourself since you left our service some years ago?"

"First I bring you the sad news that his Lordship Governor Johnson has died and it is rumored that Sir Arthur Dobbs will be appointed Governor of South Carolina."

Henry interjected, "We must lower the flag and send our condolences. He has been mostly a good governor and has tried to serve our interests well. He never could control those rascals from Albemarle. However, he tried. But, continue."

"Sir, using the money advanced after my service with you, I journeyed to New Jersey and attended the college there and am now ordained as a minister of the Presbyterian Church."

"Here, here," the brothers replied in unison.

Mary added, "Oh, Master John we are so proud of you. You did so much for our children."

Thomas added, "Yes, we have heard that our Philadelphia brethren are quite anxious to establish a learned clergy. I know I am tired of hearing the same sermons from the brothers."

"The reason he does not preach is that when he tries, the snoring makes it hard for the women to hear," retorted Henry.

John Dalton replied, "I see things have not changed much."

Henry continued, "But what of the news?"

"It seems that those of our like precious faith have had some problems concerning the road to salvation. All of us believe that some are predestined to be saved while others are not. We prove our salvation by our actions, piety, helping the poor, studying the word, and other good works. At Princeton College some people feel there should be an outward sign of inward grace. When we are moved by the Holy Spirit we should have some recognition of it. Those of us who believe this are the 'New Lights'; those who believe that there is no need for such testimony are the 'Old Lights.' Many people are being added to the Lord's church by the New Lights. Recently the Synod of Philadelphia recognized both. Now the five churches in Charles Town continue to reject the New Lights even though there is a great interest in the people of the New Light."

Thomas commented, "That is well and good but what have you heard about the Indian troubles."

"I understand that Governor Gooch of Virginia is tired of the Quakers in Pennsylvania not doing anything about the French encroaching on the Ohio country and is considering sending the Virginia Militia under a young colonel named Washington to ask them to leave. However, on my voyage down here, there seemed to be very little concern. I attended church in Charles Town and found the brethren were more enthused about the Cherokee question. I was encouraged to come and see if the settlements here were ready for a congregation of the saints."

The five elders—Thomas, Henry, James, Sam, and James Polk—were in attendance. James Polk spoke. "It is my feeling that we have an earnest need for a genuine kirk. John can preach the gospel, improve the morals, and purify the faith. We all know John, and I suggest we immediately notify the Presbytery or our intention. And, further, I offer the Old fields near the river as a site."

Henry added, "Since the congregation here has gathered for the afternoon preaching, let's put it to a vote. Do I hear a move that we accept the plan of Brother James Dalton?"

Thomas added. "For the sake of our children, heavenly days yes!"

John preached the afternoon sermon. Some ten families were in attendance. The men voted unanimously to approve the new congregation. Thus began the Presbyterian Church of the Waxhaw.

After the decision to start a new kirk, the families gathered for a feast on the grounds of Uncle Henry's home. No sooner had Thomas Christopher sat down on the blanket than he stood up again, as did brother Henry. A family with a lovely daughter approached them.

Mary stood with the help of her husband Justice Thomas. "Why, Sally Spratt how good to see you! Henry and Thomas Neel, may I present Squire and Mistress Spratt and their daughters Jean and Susan from Ft. Mill."

Greetings were exchanged. The Spratts were at the Waxhaw for communion Sunday. Mary implored, "Jean please join us."

Jean's eyes met the intense eyes of Thomas and noticed his wonderful smile and rugged frame. He then noticed her calico cotton dress, slightly hooped pannier and a white scooped bodice which barely stayed in the realm of modesty covering her snow white bosom. He stood spellbound.

"Mother and Father, do you care if I join the Neels?"

"What I have heard of that gallant young officer, you will be in good hands," replied her father.

The smile on Thomas's face grew brighter.

"Thomas," began Mother Mary, "Jean and Susan are from Ft. Mill. Her father owns a plantation there and enjoys good relations with the Indians. In fact the Indians built the fort where they live. It is called Fort Mill because of the mill the Spratts built there."

Thomas had trouble limiting his gaze to an appropriate interval. Here was Jean, a black haired fair skinned beauty with the cheek bones of an Indian, dark eyes, and naturally colored lips. She had an aura of confidence and feigned modesty. Tall Thomas suddenly felt clumsy as she turned to him.

"Master Neel, we have heard of the many adventures of the Neel Rangers. What exciting things did you see?"

"I,I,I," he stammered, "saw things too terrible for your tender ears. But I saw valleys, meadows, and forests of great beauty. I hope the wars are over. I long for peace and the privilege of developing the patent that was given me for my service."

"Oh really, where is this land?"

"It lies along the south side of the Catawba just east of the reservation."

"It must be difficult to clear land by oneself. Lieutenant is that stallion yours over there?"

"You mean the gray one?"

"Why yes. I would like to examine it more closely. I am partial to big strong stallions. Would you excuse us Squire and Mistress Neel?"

She stretched out her hand. Thomas helped her to her feet. She had taken off her bonnet and let her long black tresses cascade down her back. It was then that Thomas realized even more what a beauty she was. As they walked toward the horse, Jean tripped, grabbed his arm and left it there much to his pleasure.

"Tis a fine animal, Lieutenant. However, my horse Victory is faster."

"When he is rested this horse is a champion. By the way, that is his name."

"How clever. I would like to see him race. Why don't you come to Ft. Mill, and we will see who has the better horse."

Thomas Jr. was shocked. He had never seen such a spirited and forward girl. He was so spellbound by her beauty he could not but stutter.

"I, I, I would be delighted to call and see what your horse can do."

"Splendid. Let us return to my family and we can discuss the race further."

She took his arm as they returned to the picnic area. There they found Squire Thomas Neel and Squire Spratt talking.

Thomas Sr. turned and said, "Oh, there you are Mistress Spratt and son Thomas. I was just telling Squire Spratt about your thousand acre patent here across the Catawba."

"Yes, he tells me you plan to start clearing the land."

"It is a fine land, sir."

"Yes," interrupted Jean, "and he will not be far away from our home so we can race our horses."

"What on earth are you talking about, Daughter?"

"Lieutenant Neel has challenged me to a horse race with Victory and his stallion, Champion."

"It is more like I accepted a challenge."

"Fine, I shall expect you to be ready to race at Ft. Mill next noon day."

"Come, Daughter, it is getting late. Good day, Sir. Thank you for an enjoyable afternoon."

Thomas Senior answered, "The pleasure has been mine." He then winked at Squire Spratt, "We may be seeing each other more often. I think my young man is smitten."

"He may be a great soldier, but he seems to be too easily captured." Both fathers had a hearty laugh.

The next Saturday noon Thomas arrived for the race. News of the race spread from Ft. Mill to the Waxhaw village. Henry and James had accompanied him. The Royal Road to Charles Town had been completed to Ft. Mill, allowing wagons and carriages to traverse easily in contrast to the narrow trails to the north and west. They rode into the Spratt complex and were met with fine looking hounds as they traversed the tree lined drive way. The Neel boys dismounted and were met by the young men of the Spratt family. The Neels had silken vests over white shirts, breeches with white hose and buckled shoes. They wore waist coats and three cornered hats. The Spratts dressed in an identical manner.

Servants took their horses to the barn. Sam Spratt suggested they go inside. After the usual formalities they sat down to dinner. Jean and Thomas sat together. After the meal, Jean turned to Thomas and asked, "Master Neel, are you ready to race?"

"If your filly is as beautiful as you are charming, I shall be continually stumbling."

"Flattery will not serve as forfeiture for the race. Shall we go to the barn?"

Jean had quickly changed to a riding ensemble consisting of a wide man's broad brimmed hat, a shocking special split skirt which showed her figure well, a blouse, riding boots, and a riding jacket. As they approached the barn, people who had gathered for the race gasped. Soon the grooms led out both Jean's mare, Victory, and Thomas's stallion, Champion.

Thomas was impressed with the musculature of her horse. Though only a few hands high it had the look of a thoroughbred. If it had been born a century later it would be called a quarter horse. It was called a warm blooded animal from its Arabic origins. As Victory stood by Champion, it became apparent that Victory was much faster. Champion on the other hand had been procured from the Cherokees who were great breeders. He was a "hard" horse built for the hardship of campaign and trail. He had strains of Andalusia blood probably from the Spanish as well as a mix of stronger breeds. His European origins called his strain to be a "cold blood." He stood almost sixteen hands high, Victory but fourteen.

The horses were snorting as if ready for a race. Victory rubbed Champion's neck with her nose. He seemed pleased.

"'Tis a fine horse, Madam. I believe the horses get along quite well."

"Yes, if we could get the loan of your stallion we could start a fine breed."

Thomas was somewhat shocked. However, he was even more shocked when the grooms helped Jean on the horse and he glanced at her slim booted ankle. The new style split skirt advanced to her calf revealing a shapely leg.

James, Henry, their parents, and the crowd followed the couple to the quarter mile race track. Their mounts snorted as they heard the crowd which lined the hill. Old Champion seemed to be quite interested in his new stable mate. Once Victory tried to bite him. He didn't seem to mind.

"Now Master Neel," began Jean with a smile, "Our first race will be to complete this quarter mile track. The second will be a cross country race. But we have not discussed the wager. I will wager the opportunity to court me against your horse if you lose."

"Does that mean that if I lose I lose my horse and the opportunity to court you?" he asked smilingly.

"It means that you have lost your queue as well as your horse and will have to wait for the others." She had grown more coquettish. Strange excitement was troubling Thomas. His heart seemed to pound in ways it had never done when he was in danger.

They approached the starting line. Tom's horse towered over the filly. Squire Spratt called out. "When I drop my hat the race will begin." And then he did just that.

The filly shot ahead. Old Champion at first seemed puzzled and then he felt a heel in his flanks and began to stretch out. Victory was about three lengths ahead at the first turn. Soon old Champion realized what he was supposed to do and began his fabled stride. By the time they came out of the far turn he was gaining. However, the combination of a heavy stallion war horse and a 200 pound rider could not match the quarter horse speed of the 120 pound Jean and the spirited filly. To the cheering of the crowd Jean won. She ran past the finish line and turned, "Well, Lieutenant Thomas, I guess you will be walking home, and I will be building up my horse line."

"I believe you said there was to be an overland course." Thomas said dejectedly.

"Oh yes, I believe I did. We will race to the Waxhaw church site and return."

As they turned back to the crowd the Neel and Spratt boys were laughing. Brother Henry shouted, "Tom, I guess you need some more riding lessons."

"You better hope I win or we will be riding double saddle back home."

Jean took off. Victory gained her usual early advantage while Champion, known for stamina, trailed behind. The path was barely wide enough for one horse. This meant that passing would be difficult. Trees and a dense forest lay on both sides. Tom had to duck under an occasional low limb. After about twenty minutes they reached the church yard. Jean drew up her panting horse to the small stream and said, "Truce. We water our horses."

"No," Tom grumbled, "My old war horse doesn't need water." With an even start they both raced back. This time Tom soon gained the front and gave no quarter. He didn't need to; he could hear Victory becoming winded. After a few minutes they broke back into the clear to the cheering crowd. Tom finished about twenty lengths ahead of the exhausted Victory. He brought his heaving, lathered stallion to a gradual halt. He dismounted and walked the horse to cool it down.

Jean galloped up, dismounted and started walking Victory. "Well, how are we to decide? You won one race and I won the other."

"I suggest that you get the horse, and I will be allowed to court on one condition."

"I don't think I like this. What is that condition?"

"That I be allowed to kiss you in front of all these people. That way I shall discourage the other suitors."

She took off her hat and shook her head back. Her long black hair broke free. "Well, what are you waiting for?"

The crowd cheered as Thomas gave her a kiss on the cheek. She turned his face and made him kiss her on the lips. The crowd cheered more.

Elder Thomas jokingly turned to Squire Spratt and said, "Shall we discuss a dowry."

"We might as well. What did you have in mind?"

"How about a return of a certain stallion?"

"I believe that stallion will be as busy as its masters. Can't spare it. Come let's have a spot of rum."

At the next communion Sunday, Thomas Christopher Neel and Jean Spratt were married.

***

Rumors began to trickle in concerning the unrest of the upper towns of the Cherokee. Stetco among the northern towns had many of its younger braves accompany some of the northern tribes as they raided the Catawba Indians. Traders were fleeing for their lives as their stores were burned and goods stolen from them. Traders fled to Augusta and Ninety-Six for safety.

The long awaited Cherokee uprising urged by the northern tribes and the French appeared to be beginning. An outbreak was avoided when one of the northern principal chiefs, The Raven of Hiawassee, marched to the Stetcos villages and ordered his brethren to stop their raid on the Catawbas and the English.

Meanwhile, Little Carpenter had journeyed to Charles Town and was given an audience by the Governor. He was disappointed that he did not receive the same attention he received in 1730 when Lord Cummings took him and a half dozen other warriors to London. The Governor thanked Little Carpenter for the prisoners, Squawman and Artimas, and promised justice. The little chief also returned some of the goods which had been taken by the Northern Cherokees. He received some gifts including guns, ammunition, and cooking ware. Trade had become an essential part of the Indian life as they had not mastered the arts of iron work.

Governor Giles of South Carolina now faced a hostile Assembly who had the ear of the traders and northern settlers. The Commons read a petition from Justice Francis of Ninety-Six complaining that the northern settlers had not been served. Governor Giles then presented his evidence against the traders including the theft of the deerskins. He was further defeated when the Commons ordered that McGhee and Johnson be released. The Governor removed Justice Francis from his office and command of the militia. The Commons answered with a continued embargo on all trade with the Cherokees.

With reluctance, the Governor wrote the principal chief of the Raven of the Hiawasee thanking him for his efforts but alerting him to the fact that an embargo was in effect. He also demanded that some of the warriors accused of wounding or killing whites as well as Little Carpenter who was rumored to have met with the French appear before him. He declared that if these conditions were not met, he would use force against his red brothers.

There then began a civil war among the lower, middle, and upper Cherokees. The pro-English faction from Hiawasee Tellico wanted to force the main sacred village, Chota, to their belief. They immediately went to the Mississippi and collected the scalps of two Frenchmen in hopes of provoking retaliation.

Old Hop Uka of the Cherokees and principal chief of all Cherokees sent from his village of Chota Little Carpenter and others to negotiate a trade agreement with Virginia.

Thomas had just finished the court day and walked onto the porch for a smoke. Sons Thomas, Henry, and James were expected soon; they had come to help their father in fortifying the block house. He was startled to see the three running their horses at a gallop.

"Father," yelled Thomas Christopher, "There is a party of Indians coming."

"Go into the house." The boys handed their father a rifle and went into the house and shut the shutters. He was concerned that the Cherokee civil war may have drifted down from the east.

Soon the band appeared. The head man began to zigzag slowly toward Tom. He stood up with his rifle above his head. The Indian on a large charger, not the usual Indian pony, came forward and stopped about twenty paces. Tom recognized the dress. The brave wore a bone decorated vest, buckskin leggings, decorated breech cloth, and linen shirt. His head was bare except for the usual topknot. Large earrings were in his ear lobes. He recognized the man as Little Carpenter. The Indian dismounted and they grasped each other by a forearm grasp.

"Welcome my Cherokee brother. Do you come in peace?"

"I am always at peace with my white brother, Thomas, who stands for peace."

"I would consider it a great honor to allow me to return the hospitality shown me."

"Our horses need rest and fodder. May we turn them into your meadow and camp here?"

"Only if you will allow my blacksmith to check their hooves and allow us to prepare a feast."

"My brother is very kind. We have not shod our horses as the white man but this would help us on our great journey. I will tell you of it later."

Henry's family came that evening to be joined by most of the servants and families of both plantations. A feast was prepared of corn pudding and roast pork under a tree in the yard. The six Indians that accompanied Little Carpenter ate without plates, cutting away pieces of meat and dipping their hands into the pudding. They "oowed" and "aahed" at the small cakes that were passed among them.

Little Carpenter lingered behind after the braves had gone to the barn for the night. He joined Henry and Tom around the camp fire.

Tom asked, "What brings you so close to the land of the Catawbas?"

"First, we sent a peace belt to our brothers and told them of our desire to pass through some of their lands. We are on a mission to the colony of Virginia. The Governor Giles has not allowed us to trade guns and ammunition. We have had Frenchmen come to the northern villages and offer to trade with us. We want to remain loyal to King George. Since the Carolina Governor will not honor the treaty we made with King George, we are going to Virginia and see if we can get a trade agreement with Governor Dinwiddie."

"I understand that the Governor wants to help you but his Assembly doesn't."

"My brother speaks with great wisdom. However, I must take my rest."

"Let us know what supplies you will need."

"My brother is most kind."

All of the Neel men stayed in the house with their arms ready. There was a night patrol to see if the Cherokees were not intent on mischief. Later we heard that Little Carpenter had to caution his braves that there were not to be female privileges among the servants as was the custom of the Indians for guests in their own villages.

By an hour after sunup the Indians were gone on the Warrior Trade Path to the north. Mary stood by Thomas as the troop left the compound. "I was concerned," she said. "But the way Little Carpenter looked at us and the kindness and courtesy he showed made me feel at ease. His eyes are so penetrating and that smile is so disarming. I wish there were more like him."

"Aye, but I hear that South Carolina Governor Giles wanted him to turn over some braves for taking part in some raids on his neighbors. It is a good thing we live in North Carolina and only help the South Carolinians when we feel the need."

The rumors of alignment of the northern towns of the Cherokees with the French continued to grow. Trade continued to be a powerful tie between the whites and the Cherokees. The Cherokees and other Indians had grown accustomed to the iron ware and fire arms available from the Europeans. Virginia and the French continued to offer competition to the trade with the Cherokees, Creeks, and Chickasaws. Thomas heard of a delegation led by Little Carpenter which in July 1753 met with Governor Glen. In order to convince him of their loyalty, he and his party killed eight people who were French and brought two prisoners. As the conference began, Little Carpenter grew belligerent when the Governor seemed reluctant to restore trade and ammunition. Little Carpenter maintained that the Governor had violated the Treaty of 1730 by refusing to restore trade. Finally Glen lifted the embargo and agreed to restore trade.

The heat of mid summer complemented the sound of katydids and whippoor-wills, as everyone found a convenient tree to lounge under one Lord's Day. Five or six families from the area had come to the Neels where John Dalton delivered an address and communion was given. The talk was of war and the news from the North that a young Virginia Colonel named Washington was turned away from the new French Fort Duquesne. There was a rumor that an attack on the French fort was imminent mainly by the Virginia militia and led probably by Governor Dinwiddie of that state.

The Neel home was coming to be known as a place of hospitality as it was located on a minor trail of the Great Warrior Path. The defeat of the Highland Scots at the Battle of Culloden in 1746 led many Scots to migrate, first to Charles Town and then up to the west. This had finally led the Cherokees to cede their abandoned lower towns to the Government of South Carolina. The Neel planta-tions were scattered from the borders of Anson County south. The formation of Anson County made Thomas Neel's judicial responsibilities on the northern end more extensive. He increasingly turned the management of the plantation over to his sons. The compound now included a saw mill, blacksmith shop, and mill. Approximately 5,000 acres were under control with about 400 under cultivation. Quarterly meetings with other judges in the district rounded out a full life.

Thomas sat on the porch having bid good-bye to some of his neighbors as well as his brother Henry. Suddenly he heard the dogs and glancing to the west he saw a bearded trail tired figure accompanied by a large smiling Negro.

"Welcome my friend," said Tom. "You are lucky we still have food for the stomach which was left over from the food we had for the soul. How goes it, Zeke?"

"I gave my soul to the forest, but I wouldn't mind some for my stomach."

Alexander took charge of the animals and returned.

"What has been your mission this time?"

"Mainly staying away from all the settlers coming in. Forage is getting harder and harder to find. The game has been run over the mountains and my red brothers are getting agitated over the sharing of their sacred hunting grounds. But more directly, I have been supplying some Virginia forts and trading for skins among the Shawnee. My Shawnee son is growing up. He hardly recognizes me. Alexander has a beautiful Shawnee daughter. Things are heating up with the French. Everywhere you go you see French trade goods. Some of the tribes who are not usually on my route are a little surly."

They were joined by little Andrew, Henry, and their mother as she brought some cold venison, corn pudding, and raspberry tea. Tom continued, "Do you think there will be a war?"

"Governor Glen is trying to bring the Cherokees to his side. He is fighting the Assembly which is not too anxious to give him any money. By the way, I think I will have some dispatches for Governor Dinwiddie of Virginia. How about taking that young buck Henry on a trip to the north?"

"Oh Father. May I?"

"Let's wait to decide. That would be a two month trip. When will you be back, Zeke?"

"I'll be back within the month."

That night Henry spent a restless night. The next morning he began to groom his horse more often and began planning his trip.

Later, elder Thomas and Mary were alone. Mary spoke. "Why is it that our son must go north with those ruffians?"

Thomas sat back on his chair, lit his pipe and looked at the ceiling. "We Ulster Scots have always been restless and liked action. The lad will be a leader of this colony someday and should have a look at someplace other than the borderlands. I think it will be a good thing."

"Won't he be subject to danger?"

"I doubt it. He will be under the protection of Zeke who is well liked by all the Indian tribes. In fact, he is the only man I know who gets along with the Shawnee and the Cherokees."

The first week in August Zeke arrived. After spending the night, the family bid farewell to the entourage which now included a message to Governor Dinwiddie. Henry was euphoric with the thought of hitting the trail. He had a broad hat, linen shirt, deerskin blouse, deerskin pants, and trail boots, as well as oilskins and a bed roll. His armament consisted of a Pennsylvania rifle, two pistols, knife, powder horn, flints, trail knife, and steel tomahawk. As he was about to leave, his mother ran up and placed a Bible in his saddle bags.

The first snow fell in late November. There had been reports from a trader who had proceeded up the Warrior Path to Virginia of the families coming down the Wagon Road. However, for the last month they had heard nothing. Mary was concerned about her son.

Late one afternoon the dogs began barking. Into the clearing came the sound of bear bells and harness. Soon in the red of the setting sun came a string of six mules and three riders. One of them had a red beard, a broad smile. He jumped from the saddle and ran and picked up Mary, his mother, and spun her around. "Mama your little boy is home."

"Henry Neel put me down. You have frightened ten years off my life with worry. Oh I have prayed for your return."

Thomas advanced toward him and embraced his son. "Come we must have something to eat and drink and hear all about your adventure. Zeke and Alexander, you will join us and thank you for taking such good care of him."

After dinner Thomas turned to Zeke, "What is the news?"

"The French are building forts on the Ohio and Mississippi Rivers. The old peace treaty is about over. The Iroquois up North are pretty much with His Majesty. The Mohawks and Shawnees are kind of iffy. We met with one of His Lordship Dinwiddie's deputies and he has given me a message for Governor Glen. Apparently they have buried the hatchet about trade, and Virginia has offered to build forts with the Carolina boys. We leave at first light. Oh! By the by, I think your friends McGhee and Johnson are up to their old tricks. We were threatened one night on the trail but drove off some bushwhackers. Later the Shawnees told us of two people coming in and stealing skins that were ready for trade. From their description, I would say they are your favorite skin robbers."

"Too bad they have so many friends in the South Carolina Assembly."

"Now, young man, tell us what you have done."

"Father it has been a glorious adventure."

Zeke piped up, "Glorious, you should have seen him sparking my Shawnee daughter."

"She was a very nice girl and beautiful too."

"Yes, he was bathing in the river, and Shawna and her friend stole his clothes. He had to run bare naked after them. I don't know what happened when he ran into Shawna's uncle's lodge after them."

With a twinkle Henry replied, "You will never find out by me."

Zeke asked, "Are you a man yet?"

"That is enough, Zeke Proctor. Go on with your story, son," added Mary in disgust.

Henry began. "It was a great adventure. I love the woods. We departed and stayed on the Warrior and Trading Paths until we reached the trading ford at Salisbury. We then followed the Pee Dee River to the mountains. There were beautiful meadows, stands of chestnut, and wild berries and grapes to eat. About every third day we would have fresh game, sometimes only a squirrel or rabbit. Zeke doesn't like to kill more than we can eat. So a deer's hind quarters would only last about three days. We went into the path between the great mountains and turned north reaching the Moravian village of Stahlmakers where we spent a few days. I attended a service at their meeting house. Outside of Draper's Meadow we spent the night with some Shawnees. We were well received by Shawna and her friends including Alexander's daughter." Young Henry winked at Alexander.

"At the village of Frederick, we were met by a courier from Colonel Dinwiddie. The Courier was worried about the Shawnee but thought the northern tribes were loyal. He told of Little Carpenter's trip a year before and that the little chief was rather disappointed. The courier told us that Virginia would help the Carolinas if they wished to build forts. He understood that the Cherokees were willing to help in any war with the French if there were forts to protect their families from the marauding French Indians, such as the Creeks.

"We then turned back south and again spent some time with the Shawnees. However, they seemed to be quite friendly with me. I went hunting with some of the young braves. Shawna fixed me a great meal from the deer I brought in."

"Yes, and he received a name among the Shawnees, One Who Runs Without Clothes," jibed Alexander. Zeke and Thomas roared in laughter.

"Stop it," cried his mother, "I can't bear to hear about such things."

Zeke asked, "Which bear do you mean—bear like carry or bare like no clothes?"

"Zeke Proctor you grow more evil every year." Her smile betrayed her real feelings.

"Oh, nothing happened. We then left and while we were camping near Draper's meadow we heard some noise near our mounts. I went to check and found two figures lurking near my horse trying to untie his hobble. I shouted and Zeke came up and fired in their direction. Later when we appeared at another Shawnee village they described two men who tried to get their braves drunk and steal some skins. They were run off. Zeke heard the description and is sure that they are McGhee and Johnson drifting further north. The rest of the trip was rather uneventful except for the number of people we saw on the trail moving toward the Carolinas from Pennsylvania. We frequently would leave but parallel the trail for several miles in order to have enough forage and game. Anyway it is good to be home."

On the Lord's Day several families assembled at the Thomas Neel's for Sunday service as the new Waxhaw structure was not completed. Young Henry gave a small report of his adventures. He told of the proposal of Governor Dinwiddie to help the Carolinas build forts. He told also of the expedition that Colonel Washington organized to go to demand that the French abandon forts on the Ohio River. He related that there was a feeling of war and that the northern Iroquois seemed to be friendly to the English. There was a communion, a lesson and then sermon by John Dalton, followed by a dinner on the grounds.

Henry's mother, Mary, approached him as the dinner was being prepared on the grounds. "Henry, I would like to introduce you to Master and Mistress Reid and their daughter Nancy Agnes."

Henry shook hands and mumbled something like I am glad to meet you. However, he was awe struck at the vision before him. Here was a black haired, peaches and cream skinned beauty, looking at him with beautiful blue eyes. She was rather tall and of good figure. Her countenance was intense and bespoke a woman who knew her beauty and used it to control her suitors.

"I enjoyed your report of your adventures, Master Henry." She continued, "What can you tell me about Philadelphia and Williamsburg."

"Thank you," replied Henry blushing and shifting on his feet. "We never made it to those cities. I have never been anywhere but Charles Town."

"You must go to the city more often. I am enchanted with the life there. Did you know that there are theatre programs and libraries there? I do adore reading literature and plays. Do you, Master Neel?"

"I enjoy reading but I haven't had the time to explore the theatre."

Just then Tom Polk came by. Tom was Henry's age, both tall and commanding. The Polk farm was about five miles from the Neel compound. He began, "Hello, Neel, glad to see you back. Why Miss Agnes how good to see you. I was wondering if you would like to see my new stallion?"

"I would be delighted. Would you excuse us, Master Neel?" And the couple was off leaving Henry agitated, confused, flushed, and determined to know this vision of loveliness better.

# CHAPTER 10

# Cherokees Go to War Against the French

The Cherokees seemed to be getting along quite well with their English neighbors in 1754. Governor Glen completed Ft. Prince George among the lower Cherokees near the village of Keowee. Glen made the journey to emphasize its importance. The fort was poorly built and at first was not heavily garrisoned.

1755. The Governor of North Carolina, Arthur Dobbs, asked Justice Thomas to be his representative to a meeting called by Governor Glenn of South Carolina and the Cherokees. On his way to the meeting, Governor Arthur Dobbs toured the southern provinces. He stopped at the village of Salisbury and met with judges of the district. They discussed the problems of tax collection, Indians, the spread of vermin among the produce, and the need for churches and education. Thomas spent a great deal of time with the new Governor discussing the surveys of the county and His Lordship's lands being done by Matthew Rowan. Arthur Dobbs was the original partner with Selwyn and McCullough in the purchase of 400,000 acres which made up the Providence district and some of the surrounding areas.

Governor Glen invited Old Hop, principal chief or Beloved Man of the Chota of the Cherokees to the conference. Glen had proposed to Old Hop his ceding some Cherokee land holdings in South Carolina which had been abandoned by the tribes. Because of his age and difficulty traveling, he asked Attakullakulla or Little Carpenter to speak for him. Five hundred and six Cherokee chiefs, headmen, and warriors met near Saluda on July 2, 1755. Little Carpenter, responding to a question from Glen, said that the Cherokees would go to war against the French if their families could be protected from the French Indians by yet another fort in the west and that they would be furnished guns and ammunition.

As a result of the treaty, almost immediately The Great Warrior of the Cherokees, Ocanostota, led a warring campaign against the French and Indians in the Illinois Wabash country. He returned with French prisoners whom he turned over to the South Carolinians. Later, in 1755, Ocanostota would lead a raid against the Creeks and drive them into Georgia.

On a cold January 1756 evening Thomas was surprised to see an entourage of a dozen mounted troops pull up to his porch.

"I am William Byrd, a commissioner from His Excellency Governor Dinwiddie and this is my fellow commissioner Master Peter Randolph. Do I have the pleasure of addressing Master Thomas Neel?"

"You do indeed. How may I be of service?"

"We seek subsistence and shelter for the night for which we will pay."

"It will be an honor. Our facilities are limited. However, it will be a privilege and honor to have you accept our hospitality. We have a room for you two gentlemen and the troop may have the privileges of the grounds. If they need supplies or shoeing my man here will assist them."

William Byrd told of the boundary study he completed defining North Carolina and Virginia. Henry and Thomas exchanged information on the subject as there were similar problems between North and South Carolina. Byrd was particularly chagrined at the loathsome lazy nature of the back country settlers on the north western borders of North Carolina. He described them as lazy, unchristian and possessed with slothfulness. He also gave news of the war in Virginia, including the defeat of General Braddock. He had funds to share with South Carolina Governor Glen to build the fort required by the Cherokees.

Next morning Byrd and his entourage left. It was reported later that the commissioners met with Little Carpenter. Byrd brought beads of wampum, offered to build a school for Cherokee boys, and would use these young men in settling future disputes. Little Carpenter expressed dismay that the fort promised had not been built. He further said that their hatchets against the French would remain silent until there was another fort in the upper regions to defend their families while they pursued the French and their Indian allies. Little Carpenter let it be known that when serving with the Virginia troops, Cherokee troops had been killed and scalped by the white settlers, who sold their scalps to the Virginians for those of French. Angry relatives of the dead men rose up and threatened the commissioners. Little Carpenter ordered the commissioners to stay in their tents while he extended apologies and made gifts in their behalf.

After taking time to go to the sacred town of Chaota to confer with the Beloved and Chief Warrior, Old Hop, Little Carpenter agreed to the terms. The terms were that the Cherokees would furnish 400 warriors after the fort was built. The Cherokees toasted the King's health and left, happy that they had secured the fort and opened up a trading path with Virginia.

Thomas was left in a quandary. As he saw it the Carolinians saw the Cherokees as protection against an attack on their states by the French and their allies. The Virginians wanted the Cherokees to assist in an offensive against the French and their Indian allies in the Ohio Country. The governors Dinwiddie and Glen quarreled by dispatches.

Thomas was pleased to see Zeke as a rather large mule train entered the yard. "Well, look at the prosperity of the King's trader. What are you doing bringing half of Charles Town west like this?"

"I be bringin' supplies for the Fort Prince George and Ft. Loudoun," Zeke replied.

"What news do you bring?"

"First of all I suppose you heard that His Excellency Governor Glen has been replaced by Governor Lyttelton. Rumor has it that Governor Glen was surprised as he was on his way to Ninety-Six and on to Fort St. George with workers and soldiers. He went home. Your friend Squire Byrd nearly lost his hair at Chaota Town, and if Little Carpenter had not intervened he probably would have his hair on a pole. It seems that when he went to negotiate with Little Carpenter for the fort, he was met with the families of some of the braves who were murdered by the Virginians while they were on the way to fight the French. Since the good Commissioner came from Virginia, he had to be placed under the protection of Little Carpenter. By the way he is probably the strongest chief, but he is having a challenge from the Tellico villages that either want neutrality or more relations with the French. The good news is the French cannot get many trade goods in. Little Carpenter traveled plum from Chaota to meet the new Governor. He was greeted with a salute worthy of a head of state. I understand the meeting lasted several days. At the end Little Carpenter won a promise for the end to the corrupt practices of traders, particularly McGhee and Squawman Johnson. The new Governor acknowledged the supremacy of Chaota over all Cherokee villages and gave our little chief some presents to send to the Tellicos who were flirting with the French. I hear that Little Carpenter as part of the agreement raided French settlements on the Mississippi. While he was away our friend, trader McGhee, tried to undermine the Chaota chief's authority and enhance the rival Ostenaco of the Tellicos. When he returned, Little Carpenter had the trader's scales seized and sent to Lyttleton. Even though they were found in error, because of McGhee's influence with the Assembly, he managed to keep on trading.

"I leave in the morning for Fort Prince George. If I were you, I would get cozy with those Catawba. I don't know how long the Cherokees will be on our side. By the way I hear your friend McGhee is irritating the Cherokees again."

In 1756 in spite of continuing arguments between the Governors of South Carolina and Virginia, the work began on the second fort, Ft. Loudoun, among the western or upper Cherokees. Lyttelton badgered the Assembly to appropriate more money and called up 200 troops and regulars under command of Captain Demere and the temperamental engineer William Gerard De Brahm. Virginia had sent a force of sixty mostly laborers to help.

As the work progressed, the French and their Creek allies began to sew dissension among the Tellico or northern band of the Cherokees, telling them that the Fort was not for their protection, but for control over them. The individual villages began to go their own way and did not always respect the wishes of the Beloved Man of the Chota, Old Hop. Unscrupulous Indian traders such as McGhee continued to cheat the Indians with the short yard and short scales. False debts were assessed against the tribes.

Things were not going too well when a Tellico murdered the pregnant wife of a Ft Loudon man. In an effort to placate the British, Old Hop of Chaota, beloved man and chief of all Cherokees, ordered all the overhill headmen including the village of Tellico to come to Ft. Loudoun and pledge their loyalty to the Crown.

To further bolster the relations with the British, Little Carpenter organized five war parties to go against the French and their Indian allies where a fort was being built on the Ohio. As a further bond of friendship, a force of Cherokees was dispatched north to help Colonel Washington. Their use was less than satisfactory as the braves were hard to control and again some of them were scalped for bounty by the Virginians. Governor Fauquier of Virginia berated the Cherokees for their refusal to fight the Shawnee and had them escorted home.

While passing through the Catawba Valley, Little Carpenter and his band camped at the Neels'. Here Thomas and Henry heard of the problems with the Virginians. Thomas warned him of a threat on his life by some of the Virginians as well as the Tellico band of the Cherokees. Little Carpenter was off to placate Governor Lyttleton.

---

CHAPTER II

# Sadness and a Tripvisit to New Bern

It was a cold day in January 1759. Mother Susannah, wife of Henry (1683) who came to Cape Fear in the 1730's had been confined to bed for four days. Her breathing became harder. Uncle Henry bled her, but she grew steadily weaker. Uncle Samuel arrived from Cape Fear as well as most of the family. Finally, she breathed her last. Samuel performed the last rites, and she was buried under an elm tree in the back area of the plantation house grounds.

Two weeks later, Henry was awakened by his father while it was still dark. "There is something bothering the dogs," cautioned his father Thomas. "Get your piece, get dressed, and let's get outside."

In rode Running Path of the Catawbas with two braves. They were dressed in war costume with a white bulls eye painted over their right eye which was surrounded with a black circle. Their heads were shaved except for the topknot and they were armed with lance, bows and arrows, hatchet and musket.

Thomas and Henry his son walked from the houses toward the riders. Recognizing Running Path, Thomas held his Pennsylvania rifle at his side and addressed his friend, "Greeting my brother. Alight so that we may counsel, eat a meal, and tell of our times."

"Thank you, Brother Neel. We must hurry to bring all our clans to our holy village. The Settico band of the Cherokees has begun raiding the area toward the setting sun."

"What have you heard?"

"Many of the white farms have been burned more than all the fingers. They have carried off captives. You must excuse us. We have warnings to do."

"Thank you my brothers. Henry, ring the bell, light a signal on the hill, and send runners to assemble the militia."

Young Henry did as told as well as sending couriers to alert the outlying militia members. The next morning Sheriff Henry and Squire Thomas assembled Henry's company of the militia.

"Men, we have heard that the Overhill Cherokees have raided some settlements and have taken captives. Prepare for one week's rations and report here tomorrow with full fighting gear."

From the back one grizzled man with a front tooth missing yelled, "Does this mean we can get us'ens some Cherokee scalps?"

"I am quite certain that this is a rogue band. We are not to harm any villages unless we can determine they are involved. We must be careful because we will have Catawba braves as scouts. Don't shoot your friends. Sergeants dismiss your men and draw rations and ammunition."

That night the families of James, Thomas and Sheriff Henry assembled. Thomas led a prayer and then began.

"We are going on an expedition to find out what has happened to some of the settlers to the north. We are particularly worried about the Hawthornes. We know that God will protect us in what we are about to do. Young Henry, you will be on your first campaign. I want you to stay with Running Path if he returns in time and scout for us. See you all in the morning."

That night as they lay in bed, Mary turned to Thomas, "Tom, I hope you will take care of thine self as well as Thomas and young Henry. They are so young."

"Madam, you can be proud of Henry as well as Thomas. Henry gets along so well with everyone and is especially liked by the Catawba."

"I would hope so. He spends much time down on their reservation. I have even heard he has been keeping company with a young Catawba maiden."

"Well, he is almost twenty. Let's say our vespers and get some sleep."

Thomas did not sleep. All night long he considered the problems that Little Carpenter must be having with Moytoy, one of the chiefs who probably led the raids. He hoped that Little Carpenter might be innocent of any of these supposed atrocities, as he seemed to be working for peace.

At sunrise, there was a beating to assembly by young James who was the drummer for the Neel regiment. Approximately thirty militia mustered. Col. Thomas addressed them.

"Men of His Majesty's Neel Rangers. Today we march west to determine the damage done to the person and property of the King's subjects. It is rumored that a renegade band of the Cherokees has raided some settlements in there. You will draw your rations as directed by Major Sheriff Henry and his nephew Sergeant Henry Neel. We ask you to ride single file but about twenty paces behind the visible scouts. Do not fire unless you have a definite target and do not fire unless ordered all day today and tomorrow. We order this because we will be in the country of the friendly Catawbas. Besides our out rider scouts are Catawbas and they may sometime look like Cherokee. Do not fire unless ordered by an officer. His Majesty's Governor Johnston would like to express his appreciation for your service. Drummer beat to assembly and march. Follow me."

Thomas mounted a splendid white charger. He wore buckskin vest, buckskin trousers, linen shirt, brimmed beaver hat, and trail boots. To the jangle of harness, canteens, and powder pouches, the troop moved westward.

The first day was without incident, and the company covered thirty miles. They mainly kept to the banks of the Catawba River. The second day they veered southwest toward the Pee Dee River. As Thomas and his brother Sheriff Henry were attempting to negotiate the rough trail, they were surprised by Running Path.

"Colonel Thomas. We see smoke over the hill. Our braves are scouting ahead. We would like to take young Henry with us in case we must talk to the whites."

"You may proceed." Then turning he commanded, "Squad halt and take cover."

Within an hour young Henry returned weeping, his horse lathered and wheezing, "Father, it is beyond imagination."

"Easy son. We will go see." Thomas spurred his horse and galloped toward the hill. Sheriff Henry came after. When they broke through the woods and into a clearing they saw Running Path and one of his braves. There they saw the remains of a clay chimney, a silent sentinel above the charred remains of what once was a cabin. Strung upside down from a tree was the body of James Hawthorne with a pool of blood still dripping from his scalpless head. A dozen arrows were in his body. His clothes had been stripped and he had been mutilated. Nearby was the body of a small boy. No animals were in the shed. Remains of a hog were in the embers of the fire. Half of it was gone.

Squire Thomas jumped from his horse and wretched on the ground. Running Path stood motionless by his horse. At length Thomas said, "Who do you think did this, my friend?"

"The death is symbolic. The body upside down is a curse on your Christian idea of a cross. There is a double hand of arrows less one in the body, which would indicate a blood lust for braves to be avenged. Their arrows are usually retrieved. These were left there for a purpose."

"What was that purpose?"

"The feathers on the shaft and the shape of the arrows are the mark of the Saticoy of the Tellico Cherokee. My belief is that it is the clan of Moyjoy."

"Isn't that the clan that went north to assist against the French and lost some braves?"

"That is as I heard."

Elder Henry rode up. "Henry, how many braves were killed by the Virginians when the Cherokees were helping Governor Faquifer?"

"I heard the number as the same number of arrows. My God this is most terrible. Have you found all the bodies?"

"No, the young boy and his mother are missing."

"They were taken as trophies," added Running Path.

Sheriff Henry spoke. "I'll get a couple of men to bury the bodies. Do you think we should camp here?"

"I think we could control their rage. But I think it might be a good idea to let the troops see it. See if you can get someone to get some game for tonight."

The night did not go well. Sentry duty took on new meaning. Thomas ordered a round of rum to ease the despair. After a supper of a young roasted deer, Thomas rose and uttered a prayer for the departed and then addressed the company.

"My friends, it is easy to be overcome with rage over what you have seen. Easy to forget that God's creatures are white, red, and black. It is our feeling that this killing is in revenge for something the Virginians did. It is not excusable. This was the work of the Tellico band under Moytoy. We must remember that the Chaota Cherokees probably had no part in it. Tomorrow we will scout the area to determine the number of families that have been harmed."

After a week the company turned toward home. They could not find survivors but did find nineteen settlers' homes destroyed along with their crops. No livestock were found. At each site a prayer was said and evidence was gathered to determine the names of the martyred. As these people had worked hard to avoid the tax rolls, their names were not readily available. Sometimes a burned Bible was available or a brand on dead livestock. The men screamed for revenge. Thomas felt that they did not have the resources to pursue the renegades but promised to petition both governors for aid.

After returning to the plantation, Sheriff Henry made an inventory of all armaments available. Dismissing the militia, Thomas composed a report to both governors on what he had seen. Thomas chose his son Henry to deliver the reports first to Governor Lyttelton in Charles Town and then to the North Carolina Governor at New Bern.

As young Henry waited for a sloop in Charles Town, he toured the city and was entertained by the governor, including his presence at a ball in honor of the governor's niece.

Upon hearing the massacre report, South Carolina Governor Lyttleton called a meeting of his Council. As the Council was meeting, a message arrived from Col. Coytmeyour with essentially the same message that a band of Cherokees had attacked some settlers.

Young Henry set sail for New Bern to deliver his report to the new Governor Dobbs of North Carolina. This was quite an adventure as Henry had never been at sea before. Henry was concerned as the sloop made its way north and finally docked at New Bern. He was startled at the contrast of the two capitals – North Carolina had far less developed capitol buildings than South Carolina, Charles Town. He found a room at an inn and the next morning approached the Governor's residence, which was far from the elegance of the one in Charles Town.

Clad in his traveling clothes, he wore a waistcoat of imported brocade, with a neck scarf on a linen shirt, knee britches with hose closed with buckles, and to cover this he wore a large turnback coat. His ensemble was enhanced with a handsome pair of shoes. He was wigless but wore a tricornered hat.

He approached the residence compound and was confronted by the guardhouse. Two grenadiers with white clayed trousers, white bandoleers, crimson tunic, black tri-cornered hats, and black calf boots stood at attention. A sergeant appeared from the small structure. "Please state your business, Sir." He slurred as he looked over Henry's attire.

"My good fellow," Henry said condescendingly, "I bring dispatches from His Excellency Lyttelton, Governor of South Carolina and His Honor Squire Thomas Neel of Catawba concerning the state of the affairs. Here is my letter from Governor Lyttelton."

"Thank you, sir." He replied with much more courtesy. "Corporal of the Guard, escort Master Neel to the residence."

"Aye, sir. This way, sir."

They passed through a pleasant English garden and mounted the steps of a rather plain brick building. There on the porch the Captain of the Guard arose.

"Sir, this gentleman is Master Henry Neel with dispatches from His Majesty's militia and His Excellency Governor Lyttleton of South Carolina."

"Thank you sergeant. This way, Sir."

They entered a great hall. Portraits of William and Mary and King George graced the walls as well as likenesses of past governors reaching all the way back to the proprietary days. A secretary rose from his desk as they approached. The secretary went through the great doors to confer with the Governor.

"Sir," asked the captain of young Henry as they waited. "How goes it on the frontier?"

"The Overhill Cherokee from the Tellico have performed a blood coup on the western settlements. Numerous people have been killed or captured and much property destroyed."

"What has the militia done?"

"We mustered and surveyed the areas. Some Cherokees are loyal to the Crown. We did not take any offensive action, merely assessed the damage."

"The war improves in the Ohio country, but I do hope the Cherokees will stay with us."

"One of the chiefs we call Little Carpenter is a great friend of my father. Perhaps he will be able to prevent further blood shed."

The secretary appeared and escorted Henry through the double doors and into a high ceiling room with draped windows. After bowing, being introduced, and invited to tea, Henry joined the Governor at a small serving table.

"Master Henry, what news do you bring?"

Henry sat stiffly in his chair as the cup shook in his hands and replied, "Sire, I have dispatches from my father Colonel Thomas Neel, of the Providence Militia as well as correspondence from His Excellency Governor Lyttleton."

"Oh yes, I am anxious to meet the new governor. We have been sending some troops and resources along with Virginia to fortify the frontier. Now please enjoy your tea while I peruse these documents."

As he read Henry reflected on what it must have been like twenty years ago when his parents had brought him here as a baby. He admired the elegant furnishings and decor as different from the frontier but not nearly as exquisite as that of the South Carolina mansion.

"My, my. What is the Militia's next move?" asked the Governor looking up over his square reading glasses.

"We await your orders, Sir. We continue to cooperate with the South Carolinians as well as the Virginians. However, the Overhill area is a very dangerous area for settlers. The settlers constantly invade Cherokee hunting grounds without permission. Some of the traders are constantly cheating the Indians. However, the good news is that one of the principal chiefs, Little Carpenter, is very loyal to the English."

"That is news. We had heard there was a warrant out for his arrest."

"Little Carpenter is not afraid to speak his mind and has run some traders out of some of the villages who have cheated. One named McGhee, Father brought to Charles Town for trial but the court and assembly refused to indict. He is one of the causes of Cherokee unrest. In all due respect, Sir, we hope Governor Lyttleton has more influence over the Assembly than did his Excellency Governor Glen."

"Thank you. I must insist that you attend a meeting of my Council this afternoon to apprise them of the conditions on the southwestern provinces. We are continuing to marvel at the growth of the western areas of the colony. So many of your Irish and Germans have come down the Warrior and Trading Paths that they have made a virtual road. Some wagons are now coming through. This and the war with the French and their allies have placed a heavy burden on the treasury of this colony. We are indeed fortunate to have such justices as Squire Thomas, your father, to administer these frontier areas. I have heard of his good work from the Chief Justice Matthew."

"Thank you sir, but I would like to sail on tomorrow's tide."

"I believe you are acquainted with the trader Master Zeke Proctor."

"Why yes."

"He leaves in the morning for Ft. Prince George with supplies and post for your father and Charles Town. May I suggest you go with him?"

"I would be delighted."

Summoning all his courage, Henry met with the Council and gave his view of the situation. The next morning he joined Zeke and Alexander. As usual they were fussing at one another about whatever small irritation they had at the time. The Governor had given Henry a standard cavalry horse and a packet of dispatches to be delivered to the south. The journey of about a week brought them to the Thomas Neel compound.

They arrived on a Saturday. There was much excitement as Henry told of his meeting with the governors, his voyage, and return with Zeke.

The next morning Zeke left to avoid attending the Lord's Day Service conducted by Uncle Andrew. Six families attended including the Polks and the Reids. Henry was spellbound to see Nancy Agnes Reid again sitting with her family. He nodded as he sat on a bench in the great room. After the sermon and communion the congregation heard the account of Henry's trip to the New Bern.

A dinner of meat pie, corn, queen's cake, and tea followed the church service. Henry could not keep his eyes off Nancy Agnes during church. Summoning up his now frequently used courage after being kicked by his brother Tom, he approached Nancy with his trenchant of meat pie and a spoon. "Mistress Nancy, may I join you." She was dressed in calico dress with white trim and a bonnet.

"Well, of course. Tell me of your visit to Charles Town and that dreadful town of New Bern."

"I was rather busy in Charles Town; however, I was able to attend a Governor's Ball. It was a rather gay affair with many of the Rice Kings, the King's officers, and, of course, young ladies."

"How utterly interesting. Was there any particular young lady?"

"The Governor assigned me to escort his niece who was visiting, Her Ladyship Eleanor Lyttleton."

"Oh tell me more." Her beautiful blue eyes squinted at him. Her ruby lips grew thin as she stared directly at him. It was hard for him to take his eyes off the usually, but not quite at this time, angelic face.

"Well the Madeira was most refreshing. The tureens of soup were elegant. The roast suckling pig was outstanding. The jams, preserves, breads and cakes were the most delicious."

"And the dances?"

"There was a five piece string orchestra with a harpsichord. They played minuets and some reels."

"And?" Her eyes shined excitedly.

"Oh yes. I attempted two reels and then this handsome British officer noticed my distress as Her Ladyship and I sat out two minuets and took her off my hands. She seemed to be shocked at some of the things I told her of the frontier. Seeing her well taken care of, I excused myself, paid my respects to the Governor, and went to my quarters to prepare for the going home next day."

"You mean you did not attend the grand promenade, the presentations?"

"I did do two reels. I never learned those French dances."

"Did you get to attend the theatre?"

"I did attend a presentation of *The Merchant of Venice*. Which reminds me; I have something for you. Will you excuse me? I shall go get it."

Henry briskly left the room and got his package and brought it back only to see Nancy talking to Tom Polk.

"Oh Henry, I was just telling Tom about your trip to Charles Town. He has never been. Excuse us, Tom," she related with a mischievous twinkle in her eye.

"Good to see you Thomas. How is your stallion?" Henry asked with a sly smile. He remembered that at their last meeting Thomas Polk had stolen Nancy from his presence in order to display his new horse.

Henry took Nancy Agnes's arm and led her to a bench under a large oak tree. "Here. I have something for you."

He handed her the paper bound package. She opened it and found a silk scarf and a copy of *A Midsummer's Night Dream*. An eager smile broke on her lovely face; her eyes brightened.

"Oh, Master Henry. How thoughtful. I can't think of anything I would like more." She squeezed his hand.

"If you don't mind Mistress Reid, I would like to approach your father for permission to court."

"I would be honored. But from what I have heard from him he will probably say it was about time."

And indeed Squire Reid did wonder why it took so long. In fact he confided the request almost immediately with Squire Thomas. They both had a hearty laugh. After a month of extensive courting with at least two bundlings they were married.

## CHAPTER 12

# Rangers Go to War

Squire Thomas (1710) called Sheriff Henry, Uncle James, young Henry and others together. "I have just read the dispatch from His Excellency Governor Dobbs. It seems young Henry here has made quite an impression on him. He has been ordered to form a company of rangers to be called Second Neel's Rangers to proceed to Fort Prince George and assist in whatever capacity the Governor of South Carolina wishes. We have received a dispatch from the new Governor Lyttleton requesting a militia assembly at the Congarees instead of Fort George for the purpose of bringing the lawless Cherokees into submission. By the way, you will leave in four days. So get your men together."

The parties began to go home. Henry asked Polk and his own brother Thomas to assist him. In two days a company of twenty rangers was organized. Henry was commissioned a brevet captain by the squire and head of the militia. Polk and Thomas kept their commissions as lieutenants. There was some grumbling at having Henry temporarily outranking them. Nancy Reid Neel was there as they left. She waved and Sam and Thomas saluted smartly. They were dressed in the green colors of a dragoon which had been furnished by the Council of North Carolina. Each of the mounted troop had been issued a green tunic, linsey woolsy britches, bandoleer, black tri-colored hat, and high topped boots. The North Carolinians wanted to make an impression on their brothers to the south. However, since their rifles were not muskets they carried no bayonets. The men of the outback preferred hatchets and knives to the bayonet. It was better to club someone with the end of a rifle than to see his stomach opened with a bayonet. Hitting the enemy in the head seemed more humane. Henry expressed some concern that the rifles, while of greater range and accuracy, were more difficult to load than the muskets favored by His Majesty's troops. All the rangers were mounted on their own horses. Each carried a cutlass in a scabbard, cartridge boxes with cartridges, as well as powder horns as an alternate source for powder.

After three days they topped a small rise and looked into the valley drained by the Reedy and Saluda Rivers. This was the Congarees. Tents were erected around the floor of the valley. One particularly elegant tent flew the flag of the southern colony and the Union Jack. Henry's squad threaded their way through the tents. Various huzzahs arose from the South Carolinians to see help from the neighboring colony. He approached the tent and was met by a Captain in the dress of the Gold stream guards.

Henry dismounted and saluted. "I am Brevet Captain Henry Neel of the Neel's Rangers from the province of North Carolina. I bring greetings from His Excellency Governor Dobbs."

The Captain drew his hand to his tri-corner hat in a salute. "Sir, the General has not yet arrived. However, I shall announce you to Major Anderson." At the sound of the name Henry had a start.

In a very short time the Captain returned and announced that the Major would see him. Henry entered the tent, took off his hat, placed it under his arm and stood at attention. The Major, dressed in the uniform of a grenadier, rose from his desk, advanced to Henry and shook his hand.

"Can this be Captain Neel of the Waxhaw and Catawbas? How pleasant to see you."

"And you, Major Anderson, I shall forever be indebted to you for taking away the threat of dancing the awful minuet. Even though I envied the loss of such a lovely partner."

Anderson laughed heartily, "Ah but you are too late, my friend. Her ladyship and I are now engaged."

"My heartiest congratulations. I am sure she will be very happy."

"What news do you bring?"

"On a personal matter, I am now a married man having taken a bride of the family Reid of the Catawbas. Second, I have been temporarily commissioned to form a company of rangers to assist the colony of South Carolina in subduing the renegade Cherokees who have ravaged our lands along the Catawba River."

"My congratulations to you, Sir. I guess this gives me a free hand to court her ladyship. I understand the Governor is not sure to which colony the upper lands belong, but I welcome your assistance. I accept your orders and commission. Lieutenant Moss will give you your assignments."

As they left Henry turned, "Thank you Major, and congratulations again. I don't think I could have ever mastered that Minuet."

"Thank goodness, Captain. She was quite taken with you. What would have happened should you have mastered the minuet? We must share some cups soon."

Neel's Rangers were assigned tents and began to drill with the South Carolina militia. The Governor sent the Assistant Indian superintendent, Captain John Stuart, and seventy troops to reinforce Ft. Loudon in the Overhill country.

Henry heard from Zeke, as he passed through after supplying Fort Loudoun and Fort Prince Henry, that there was unrest among the Cherokees. It seems that the commander of Fort Prince Henry, Henry Cotymore, and two of his officers had been accused of raping two Cherokee women of the neighboring village twice. Tistoe, headman of the Keowee village appeared before the Fort and asked for ammunition to hunt. He was refused. He and some thirty other chiefs journeyed to Charles Town for the purpose of bringing about peace among the whites and Cherokees. The chiefs were headed by Oconostota, War Chief.

The new Governor Lyttelton was about to leave for the Congaress area when he learned of the delegation of chiefs. The Cherokees were somewhat puzzled that they did not receive the usual extravagant reception as was customary. They appeared before the Governor who interrupted them in the middle of their presentation. He pontificated that he was well acquainted with all the acts of hostility of which the Cherokee people had been guilty. He would soon be in their country where he would let them know his demands and the satisfaction he required, which he would certainly take if they refused. As they had come to Charles Town to treat him as friend, not a hair on their heads would be touched, but as he had many warriors in arms, in different parts of the province, he could not be answerable for what might happen to them unless they marched with his army.

After the speech, Ocanostota the great warrior tried to speak. But the Governor silenced him and demanded that the twenty-four braves responsible for the raids on the Catawba River be brought before him for execution. The Governor's Council would not allow him to continue negotiations because the Overhill Cherokees (alleged perpetrators of the raids) were not represented. Four of the Council, including Lieutenant Governor Bull, wanted to detain the chiefs as hostages until final satisfaction of the colony's demands. The Governor overruled the Council and promised the Cherokee chiefs that he would protect them. So that they would be protected from the irate citizens he would personally escort them to Prince George with his militia there to await the hand over of the twenty-four braves responsible for the Catawba massacres. It soon became apparent to the chiefs that they were not being escorted for their protection but had become hostages. Four of the chiefs escaped. Among them was Round O who proceeded to warn the tribe. The chiefs were then placed under a captain's guard which caused much resentment.

Upon reaching Ft. Prince George, the chiefs were placed in a room originally meant for six soldiers and kept under guard. As the militia was poorly trained and with the onset of smallpox, the Governor decided not to proceed with his plan to go to the upper villages. He summoned Henry Neel. Henry approached the Governor's tent (His Lordship was concerned about smallpox in the fort and had erected his standard outside) and stood at attention. "At ease, Captain Neel. I understand from Major Anderson that you are acquainted with the Cherokee chief Little Carpenter."

"He has visited our plantation on occasion."

"I would like for you to find him and bring him here so that we may resolve our problem with our guests."

"May I speak frankly, Sir?"

"Proceed."

"There appears to be a great deal of resentment among your so called guests. They came as peace makers and now they are hostages. My friends the Catawbas tell me that French agents are instilling malignant thoughts into the minds of the Tellico Cherokees. Those that escaped will surely be fomenting anger among all the towns."

"Enough! Coddling is not the way to subdue these savages. I order you to find Little Carpenter."

"As you wish, Sir. I will be under way immediately."

Henry found his brother Thomas and began their trip north to the village of Chaota to find the little chief. On the second day they were surprised to see a party of Cherokees headed south. Henry performed the usual zigzag meeting. Thomas held his rifle above his head in a sign of peace. It was Little Carpenter who recognized Henry.

The head man zigzagged toward the two and then exclaimed, "It is the young brave of my brother Thomas Neel! What brings you in the uniform of the northern militia?"

"I have been asked by Governor Lyttleton to escort you to Fort Prince George for a conference."

"We go for that purpose. We have heard bad things about the new governor. How he holds the chiefs. It is a bad time for us. Our chief whom you call Old Hop has died, and Standing Turkey is the new, as you would say, emperor."

"It grieves me to hear this. May we walk with you?"

"As I trust the medicine of your family we walk in peace."

The next day the party appeared before Governor Lyttelton. The Governor had set up a table with chairs for himself and Lt. Governor Bull. Little Carpenter and his band sat cross-legged on the ground. Henry introduced the Governor to Little Carpenter.

"I am Attakullakulla, friend of King George. With Lord Cummins, I crossed the great sea in 1730. When visiting King George, he promised to protect us from the Creeks and other enemies and would always give us trade goods. Now we have been deprived of goods and must defend ourselves from our enemies. You have refused us ammunition and take powder for the hunt and we are unable to bring pelts for trade. Our peace delegation has been imprisoned at this fort. Our braves were badly treated in the service of the King in Virginia. Nineteen of them were murdered by the people there. Our young braves were angry and wished for a blood coup. I do not understand this need for hostages. Several years ago some white settlers were killed by the Choctaws and no hostages were asked by the English. Are we no longer the King's friend? I wish to go to see King George again as I did in your year 1730 about the treaty we signed with Lord Cummings and the way we have been treated."

Henry was shocked. The Governor's council grew grim. Soldiers on the perimeter seemed to tense, particularly since Little Carpenter spoke elegant English.

"There is no need to see King George, I represent him. The great King will not suffer his people to be destroyed without satisfaction and he seeks to let you know that the people of this province want peace and are determined to have it. What I say is merciful in intention. If I make war with you, you will suffer for your rashness; your men will be destroyed and your women and children carried into captivity; what few necessaries you now have will be soon be exhausted and you get no more. But if you give the satisfaction I shall ask, trade will be opened and all things done right. I have twice given you a list of murderers. I will now tell you there are twenty-six men of your nation whom I demand be delivered up to me to be put to death or otherwise disposed as I shall see fit. Your people have killed that number of ours and more; therefore, that is the least I will accept." The Governor then gave them twenty-four hours.

The next morning Little Carpenter delivered two of the supposed murderers and the Governor agreed to release Ocanostota, chief man of Koewee town and the head warrior of Etatoe. The two surrendered Indians were put in irons. When this happened some of Little Carpenter's party fled so that the remaining exchange could not be effected. The little chief went after them. When the Governor became aware of Little Carpenter's departure, he dispatched Henry and Thomas after him. When he returned a peace treaty was concluded. It was agreed that the twenty-four remaining chiefs would be confined until the twenty-six guilty were exchanged. Little Carpenter maintained it would take some time to find the guilty because they were out hunting. Another guilty Indian was surrendered. Three were taken to Charles Town where they died in confinement. Little Carpenter then headed north.

Young Captain Henry turned to his brother, Thomas. "It seems to me that the Governor has broken his promise about 'not harming a hair on their head.'"

Thomas replied, "This could be the beginning of trouble. Little Carpenter is a friend of the English. I hope his son Standing Turkey, the new Beloved Man of the Chaota is too."

The spread of small pox began to have its effect on the militia. They began to drift away. The Governor returned to Charles Town in triumph, believing he had accomplished his ends without a drop of blood being spilled. Henry, Thomas, and Tom Polk headed for home.

Henry and Nancy made many trips to the home of her parents. They frequently met Nancy's family weekly at the church meetings. Henry, Thomas, and James drove one herd of cows to Charles Town and picked up the news that Lyttleton was regarded as a hero. This caused a great deal of worry.

In the spring one evening they heard the familiar sound of a bear bell, yelling, fussing, and name calling—Alexander and Zeke entered the yard. Squire Thomas made his customary gestures of hospitality which were accepted and then he asked for the news.

"Well I just returned from a re-supply at Ft. Loudoun. Things are pretty quiet up there but no one knows how Standing Turkey feels about the English. The French traders are getting bold again and telling the folks that the English want to enslave them and that is why the forts were built. The Cherokees seem to forget that they asked for the forts. Anyway, with the imprisonment of the chiefs at Ft. Prince George, the northern towns are beginning to believe that the French were right. However, the English goods are much in demand and they hate to give them up. I am not going that far north any more. Ft. Prince George was fully surrounded by angry Cherokees after the militia left. The Cherokees killed fourteen white men within a mile of the fort. Ocanostota is livid with anger toward the commander, Major Coytmore, both for his behavior among the Cherokee women and the fact that the twenty four chiefs are still hostage. Things are not good."

Squire Thomas drew from his pipe and commented. "I think we better strengthen the stockade here. There may soon be trouble. Thomas and Henry take some men and begin that in the morning."

The next morning Running Path of the Catawbas rode up and gave some distressing news. He had heard that the Cherokee chiefs in the fort had been slaughtered in retaliation for the ambush of the commander Coytmore. There were few men among the Cherokee who had not been affected by the slaughter and the war belt had been passed among all of the Cherokee towns. He added that principal chief Ocanostota was now an enemy of the English. Work on a blockhouse was continued in earnest. A detachment of the Governor's commissary came through the area requisitioning corn, fodder, horses and wagons for the anticipated war with the Cherokees. The Neels supplied a wagon filled with corn as well as a team and slave driver.

A courier brought a dispatch signed by Governor Bull informing all that Governor Lyttelton had been appointed Governor of Jamaica. He further requested that the Neel Rangers immediately be pressed into service to aid the English regulars. They were to meet at the Congarees again. The courier brought news of Cherokees killing twenty settlers near Long Cane Creek, and on March 3 a group of warriors attacked Guy's fort at Ninety-Six but were driven off with many casualties.

Leaving seventeen year old brother James to complete the family fort, Tom Polk, Thomas, Henry and the Company of Rangers began their trip to the Congarees to meet with the Governor. When they arrived they were met by Major Anderson. He related the events at Ft. Prince George. It seems that once the chiefs were confined there, Ocanostota surrounded the fort with his people. One morning an Indian woman who was always welcome at the fort came to see Captain Coytmore. It was rumored that she might have been his mistress. She related that Ocanostota wanted to speak to him near the river. Accompanied by Lieutenants Bell and Foster, the Captain moved forcefully to meet the chief. He had a bridle in his hand and related that he wished to catch a horse to go to Charles Town to appeal to the Governor to release the prisoners. Coytmore replied that he should have a white guard to go with him. At that point the chief made a signal with his bridle and fire sounded from ambush. The captain was mortally wounded but taken back into the fort by the lieutenants. The soldiers then went to the prisoners to place them in irons. Upon entering the room of the hostages, they were attacked by the Indians who somehow had received knives. The soldiers then massacred them all.

Major Anderson assigned the Neel Rangers to Major (later Colonel) Middleton.

Henry, Thomas, and Tom Polk were invited to supper with Major Anderson. After the meal Major Anderson began.

"Things are not well. We hope to have a regiment of His Majesty's troops soon. However, we have two tasks. The first is to try to bring peace to the middle towns and then to relieve Ft. Loudoun which is under siege. I hope I can rely on you men to temper the urge for revenge among your troops. Also, because of your close relations with the Catawbas, I am placing you with the scouts. You will use them for reconnaissance before the main body. Lieutenant Polk, I am placing you in command of that part of the Neel's rangers not used for scouting."

The 1760 May morning's silence was broken by the beat to quarters. The militia and rangers formed ranks. To their surprise came a regiment of Fusiliers under command of Colonel Montgomery, lately of New York. The King finding the northern hostilities under control had sent aid to the south. The troops looked splendid in the crimson tunics, bayoneted muskets, boots, and high hats. They marched smartly to the parade ground and on orders turned to face the assembled militia in perfect order.

Major Anderson addressed the militia. "Rangers and militias of the King's province of the Carolinas. We are privileged to welcome the King's Regiment of Fusiliers lately of New York. Their purpose is to assist us in crushing the renegade Indians. We have also received correspondence from the Provincial Assembly to wit that twenty-five pounds will be awarded for each Cherokee male scalp and that all prisoners shall become the property of the soldier capturing and will be sent to the Barbados as slaves. Colonel Montgomery, welcome to the Congarees. I now surrender command to you."

"Thank you Major Anderson. Men of His Majesty's regiments. It is our task to march against the renegade tribes and wipe out their means to make war. We plan to burn their crops, and otherwise eliminate their ability to make war. We will march tomorrow morning. Each man will carry one week's supply of rations and armament. There will be only minimum baggage. We plan to live off the land. Major Anderson you may dismiss your men."

Some one then led some "huzzahs." The troops were then dismissed.

As they walked back to their tent, Henry turned to his brother Thomas. "Do you believe in an eye for an eye?"

"I can't think that cracking the heads of lower Cherokees when the upper Cherokees are having the problem is right."

"Well, you remember what those of the tribe of Moytoy did to poor Hawthorne. We cannot let a group like that continue. After all they were only two days march from our plantation. And yet the scriptures seem to indicate that it may not be entirely right. I am thankful we are assigned to scouting with the Catawba tribe." Just then they saw Running Path of the Catawbas. He was crouched by one of his brave companions as they were applying the classic bull's-eye on the right eye as well as other war paint.

"Greetings my brother," greeted Henry. "How goes your preparation?"

"We go to avenge a raid on our village and scout for His Majesty."

"But what if these villages we raid are not the ones who raided you?"

"It is a blood oath. Our people as your people must be avenged. We join at sunrise, my brother."

"Sleep well my friend."

Henry did not sleep well that night. He felt that Governor Lyttleton had handled the whole affair badly and that the murdering of the chiefs at Fort Prince George was sheer doom to peace. The treacherous act of holding chiefs who had traveled 200 miles to make peace was a sure catalyst for war. After much struggle, he decided that his fate was in the hands of God and King George. He just could not feel good about making slaves of his enemy and being paid for scalp. He knew some of the men and knew how bloodthirsty they were. They would not be entirely driven by King and country. Sleep finally came when he turned his attention to fair Nancy. He smelled her fragrance and saw her vision as he drifted away.

Drums rolled, muster was taken, and the column began to march southwest. Henry and Thomas and ten of their chosen men were assigned to scout with Running Path and six of his warriors. They sometimes broke into small squads of three. After the muster the scouts disappeared into the woods.

The Rangers found a camping spot on the Twelve Mile River and guided the main troop to it. The next morning Montgomery's troop surprised the small lower Cherokee village of Koewee. Colonel Montgomery gave the order and the entire company charged the village. Every adult male was put to the sword. Henry and Thomas had not been a part of the assault as they were scouting the next village. Soon the troops drew up and surrounded the larger village of Estatoe. It was abandoned but the troops burned over two hundred structures and destroyed or confiscated all livestock and crops. Soon all of the lower Cherokee towns were in flames.

Edmund Likens, the local Indian agent, sent two chiefs to the middle towns informing them that by suing for peace they might avoid the savage slaughter. Colonel Montgomery, upon finding that the tribe had no desire to negotiate, proceeded with his plans to punish as he marched to relieve Ft. Prince George. As he advanced toward Etched, the nearest town in the middle settlement, he found a low valley completely covered with brush and trees so thick that vision was hindered beyond three feet. This was a natural "ambuscade" for the Indians.

The Rangers were dispatched ahead. The path was so narrow and the cane brush so high and overgrown that single-file was the required travel. Captain Morrison's company was first followed by the Neel Rangers. Suddenly Captain Morris yelled as fire broke out on all sides. It was as if Braddock's defeat was being re-enacted. The light infantry and the grenadiers advanced and charged into the thicket. The soldiers could only reply to the flashes of guns. Since a flash pan on a musket took about one second to ignite, the target was frequently gone by the time a militia gun fired. The woods resounded with war-whoops and yelling. The carnage lasted an hour with twenty killed and seventy-six wounded. The number of Indian wounded and killed was uncertain for they drug both kinds of casualties away.

The army was so reduced that they decided to retreat back to Fort Prince George. There was no further attempt to reinforce Fort Loudoun on the west. In August Colonel Montgomery left for New York, leaving four companies to assist in guarding the frontier.

CHAPTER 13

# *Action at the Forts*

In July the Rangers were released from Fort Prince George and headed for home where a grand celebration began. Henry spent a good deal of time with Nancy Agnes and their new family. In September the boys drove a herd of cattle to Fort Prince George and again conferred with Major Anderson. He related that there would probably be another call because of the fear for Fort Loudoun in the Upper Cherokees. The Virginians who had promised to reinforce the garrison there had turned back. The expedition of Colonel Montgomery failed to get through because of the ambush at Twenty Six Mile creek and the loss of most of his militia to pox and desertion. There was much concern for the garrison there.

Upon returning home in August, Henry decided to go to the Catawba villages for news of any further problems with the Cherokees. He saddled his horse and took some bread and beads as symbols of friendship. About noon he arrived at the village. It stank of tanned skins and human waste and sweat. Women were curing skins. A few braves were in the village, while many of the women and children were in the fields with the corn.

As Henry approached, dogs began to bark and little children ran to him. Soon he reached the lodge of Crying Cloud. As he drew near, the old medicine man arose from his lodge and leaning on a pole raised his hand in greeting. Henry, knowing a little Catawba, acknowledged him.

"Greetings Uncle. It has been a long time since we have counseled together. How goes it with you?"

"Welcome son of Thomas Neel. My dim eyes dance at the sight of you. Your deeds as a warrior precede you. I hear you performed many deeds against our enemies the Cherokees and have much coup."

"The legends boast of more than I did. People confuse the deeds of your nephew Running Bear with mine."

"You and Running Bear are brothers. I meditated about adopting you to the tribe but you are like the running elk. You never stand still long enough. In fact why is it that you have not claimed a woman like Running Bear?"

"Uncle, I have found a woman almost as beautiful as Little Doe, Running Bear's woman."

99

"I trick you. I hear you have a woman from the clan of Reid," the old man chuckled.

"The winds tell too much of my life. Have you seen Running Bear?"

"He is on a hunt to the west and should be back anytime."

Just then dogs began to bark. From the west came Running Bear with a pack horse containing four carcasses, trailed by a white man and three braves. They dismounted in front of the Medicine lodge.

"Greetings my uncle and you, my brother. I bring some good news and bad news from the west. This is Captain James Stuart who has been a captive of Little Carpenter. We would like to council with my brother."

Henry moved forward. "It is a pleasure to see you, Sir. I heard you had taken some troops to Fort Loudoun. How goes it?"

Stuart was dressed in a combination of Indian clothing and remains of a captain's uniform. His face was drawn, his eyes sunken, and a shaggy beard graced an unsmiling face. Stuart stood up straight and was silent for a minute and then began, "It is a good boon, my friend, to meet one of Carolina's loyal citizens. I bring news of a most unfortunate disastrous thing. The Fort has fallen and many soldiers, women, and children have been slaughtered. I am here because my friend, Little Carpenter, claimed me as his captive." He embraced young Henry and began to sob. His tattered buckskins were diminished only by the moccasins that showed portions of his feet.

"How did this all happen? Where is the rest of the company?"

"After the death of Old Hop, principal chief, the Fort was besieged by the forces of Ocanostota, his successor, for six months. Upon his approach, we slaughtered our herd and processed it into jerky. We then were confined to the Fort, relieved only by some of the soldier's Indian wives who brought in vegetables and corn. By August 6, the men began to desert, taking their chances on escape preferring the risk of torture to that of starvation. Little Carpenter lost control of the Overhills tribes and took his family to the woods after appealing to Ocanostota for peace. On that day Captain Demore sent me to confer with the Cherokee. Here is a copy of the agreement as I wrote it. Please read it while I gain my composure."

Henry opened the leather packet and read the document. It stated that the garrison will be allowed to leave with arms and drums and enough powder and ball necessary for the march and what baggage they could carry; that the garrison go to either Virginia or Fort Prince George and that Indians be appointed to escort and hunt; that the lame and sick be received in a friendly Indian town until such time as they could go to Fort Prince George; that the Indians provide horses for which the colony would pay and that the fort, great guns, powder, balls, and spare arms be received to the Indians without any fraud.

Henry exclaimed, "Whew. The Fort was surrendered. Then what happened?"

"We left the fort and headed to Fort Prince George. As we marched I noticed that some of the chiefs in the escort began to drop back. I approached one of them about this and he said that they were not needed as the braves could take care of it. Toward noon as we were resting, a brave galloped to a stop and motioned for one of the remaining chiefs. They conferred in private. I later learned that he brought news that the terms of surrender had been violated and that the Indians had found the great guns spiked and ammunition buried on the grounds. It is rumored that one of the widows living in the Fort had told Ocanostota of the location in order to gain favor.

"That night we camped in a meadow near the mouth of Cane Creek on the Tellico River. About sun up I noticed that there were no Indians left in camp. At reveille the guards reported that we were surrounded by Indians. Captain Demere gave the order to go to battle quarters. Both sides exchanged fire for twenty minutes. The savages came from the surrounding woods and we were caught on all sides in the open meadow. The party was soon overcome. Captain Demere was wounded, scalped and then burned alive while we were all forced to watch. I was seized by Onto, the brother of Round O, who persuaded the chief Ocanostota to take me to Little Carpenter who resided at Tomotley, where after appealing for peace, Little Carpenter took his family in the wilderness. After twenty-eight of our number were killed, they stopped and gathered the rest as prisoners. The prisoners were marched back to the fort. Twenty-eight, the number killed, is the same number as the hostage chiefs killed at Ft. Prince George.

"Some eighty people were taken prisoner. Chief Ocanostota, with his hands on all the ammunition, began to lay plans to siege Ft. Prince George. The chief called me before him and told me I would be forced to help carry the cannon left at Ft. Loudoun to the siege of Fort Prince George. Further, I was made to compose a letter to the commander of Prince George to wit that if he did not surrender the fort they would burn a prisoner a day in front of the fort. Chief Ocanostota stated cruelly that 'The commander would see if he could hold out watching his friends burn before his eyes.' I was alarmed and determined to escape. I managed to get a message to Little Carpenter who bought me as his prisoner. I was moved to his quarters with his family. He later took his family and me on a 'hunt.' We traveled night and day for a week. We first ran into a party of Virginians under Col. Byrd headed to relieve the Fort. On hearing the news of the fort's capture, Byrd turned back to Virginia and we soon met the King's subject Running Bear who agreed to take me to the Governor. Little Carpenter wished us godspeed and asked me to bring a message of peace to His Excellency, Governor Lyttelton. We are dearly paying for the massacre of those chiefs at Fort Prince George. While I was prisoner in the Fort I observed several French officers trying to persuade the chiefs that the English built the Fort to bring harm to them and their families."

Henry, with tears in his eyes, replied: "It is with God's blessing we see you alive. A most amazing story. Your Grace, while you were at Ft. Loudoun, Governor Lyttelton has been appointed Governor of Jamaica and Lieutenant Governor Bull acts in his stead. My family would be honored if you joined us on our plantation while you recover from your ordeal."

"I would be honored and be in your debt."

Upon returning to the plantation and after formalities were met, Henry's father, Thomas, brought out dispatches from the governor of North Carolina and the acting governor of South Carolina. They stated that a campaign was to begin in the spring and that the Neel Rangers were assigned to service.

Captain Stuart refreshed himself and was given clothes and new moccasins. After a supper he related the story of Ft. Loudoun. He composed an account for the acting Governor Bull and senior Thomas sent a servant with the news to Charles Town. He sent an identical letter to the governor of North Carolina.

Later that week at dinner with the Reids, Henry told Nancy of the impending call of the Rangers. The family was quite excited about his account of the affair with Captain Stuart.

After dinner Henry and Nancy walked to the stable. As Henry saddled his horse, she touched his arm and said, "My Darling, as you go to hunt the Cherokees, I want you to wear this scarf to remind you of me."

He took the scarf and placed it in his tunic next to his heart. On an impulse, as he was about to mount his horse he turned and kissed Nancy. She responded warmly pressing hard against his body. "My heart will always remind me of you. I love you, Nancy Agnes."

"And I you. Be careful and come back to me."

Henry turned and rode toward the muster. As he traveled, he thought, "Will we ever stop this war? I grow so weary of fighting people who used to be friends. I would so like to settle down and improve the farm. In fact, I am obligated by my patent to clear three acres a year and we are behind in this effort."

After a few days, Neel's Rangers formed up and started for Fort Prince George. Stuart joined the group. The Rangers were by now battle-hardened. As they rode along, young Henry and Thomas Jr. confided with Stuart that the men had become almost uncontrollable in battle. They were inclined to murder and pillage when in the midst of battle. This behavior was caused by the poor leadership of Colonel Montgomery, who demanded that all males of the enemy be wiped out. Some of the troopers were little better than savages to begin with and now it was difficult to control their lust for vengeance—particularly those who lost families.

Four days later the Rangers arrived at Fort King George. So many troops were there that their tents were spread over the grounds in front of the Fort. Major Anderson met them and assigned their areas.

The next evening the company cheered as the first sound of drums and bagpipes broke the morning air. With regimental colors flowing, the kilted Highland light infantry advanced in perfect formation. Colonel James Grant dismounted from his horse, approached Colonel Montgomery, saluted and gave his orders. The provincial and royal troops now approached 2,600.

On the 7th of June, with flourishes and the beating of drums, the diverse army of provincials, highlanders, and Creek and Chickasaw Indians moved toward the site of the lower towns. Henry and Major Anderson were in charge of the scouts who moved ahead of the troops. Henry turned to the Major.

"The racket that the drums and pipes make are certain to give us a welcome from our Cherokee friends."

"I am a great one for tradition but perhaps a little silence would be golden. I will discuss this with Colonel Grant tonight."

The troop approached the ford where the Indians had attacked Montgomery the year before. Anderson sent the Chickasaw scouts ahead. One of the Chickasaw scouts pointed to a point on the bluff where there crouched a band of Cherokees about one hundred yards behind them. Anderson sounded the alarm just as the reports came from at least five dozen muskets.

The troops ran for cover among the cane breaks along the river. Anderson, Henry, and Thomas Jr. crouched low and found the sergeants. Tom informed them, "Don't fire if you can't see anything. Form in ranks of two. When you see a flash, aim on either side of it. The savages will fire and then run. If you fire on either side of the flash, you have a chance of getting one. Keep your guns loaded." Col. Montgomery came forward and ordered the men into a squad formation.

Major Anderson immediately rebuked him. "Sir, these men are Indian fighters. If you use the Braddock tactic, you will have Braddock success. Do as these provincials say."

"This way of fighting is so uncivilized," grumbled the Colonel.

The firing grew more and more intense. The Scots of the Royal infantry advanced toward the Cherokees many times, only to be rebuffed. The hideous war whoops of the savages chilled the men. Suddenly, the direction of the fire changed. A contingent of Cherokees was trying to get the provisions of flour and cattle in the rear. At about 11 o'clock the Cherokees retreated. A squad under Major Anderson pursued them. Henry and Thomas remained behind to assist with the killed. Several sacks of flour were thrown in the river so that some of the horses and mules would be available for the wounded. The dead soldiers' bodies were weighted, wrapped, and thrown in the river to thwart an Indian attempt to scalp them. Thus ended the Second Battle of Etchota Pass.

The main body of troops proceeded toward the Indian town of Etchoe. At about midnight the army attacked. The Cherokee warriors had abandoned the village to fight the English, so only old men and boys were left to defend the women and children. The Chickasaw rushed in to prey upon their old enemy. Chaos prevailed; the old men as well as women and children were scalped. Soon some of the militia, aware of a bounty on Cherokee scalps, joined in. In vain did Henry and Thomas try to restrain the militia. The King's troops looked on in horror.

Soon Col. Montgomery ordered the village to be burned. All night long the lodges burned, some of them much more commodious than the hovels of some of the backcountry militia. Animals were shot and the crops set on fire. Thomas and Henry began to weep in frustration.

Lit by the light of the burning village, his faced bathed in sweat, and his countenance in grim frustration, Henry spoke to his brother. "Some day we will need to make peace with these people. Such destruction will long be remembered. They face a harsh winter without their warriors, their crops, and means to hunt."

"Yes, it is fearsome to think that we have a just God. Have you heard that the British intend to distribute blankets from their soldiers who died of small pox?"

"I heard that they tried to do that with their enemies up north. I hope it is just talk."

Major Anderson rode up and interrupted, "Captain Neel, form up your rangers. Let them have about two hours sleep and then prepare to march."

"Aye, Sir." Then Henry and Thomas gave the orders to their companies.

For the next ten days, the companies ranged through the lower and middle Cherokee towns burning crops and destroying homes and granaries. Women and children were left destitute as their men stayed away and continued to fight. As the group moved west some rangers grew more savage. Occasionally, even women and children would be shot, scalped or burned in their villages. At one point Henry hit one of his men with a rifle when he was about to tomahawk a young boy. His continued admonition made the massacres clandestine. Henry and Thomas then forbade the trading of scalps for the colonial bounty. This caused much grumbling among the Rangers.

Outside of a Cherokee village near Fort Loudoun the Rangers charged in the mid-morning. The village was deserted except for some women and children. Thomas burst into one of the lodges and found a number of women and children huddled in a corner. The lodge was dark, lit only be a small fire. The women were dressed in tattered European dresses. Their faces were gaunt, their countenances terrified. Children were crying. Suddenly one woman stood up and said, "Spare us, Sir, for we are captives." In response, Thomas called to Henry. They lit a pitch torch and looked around the room.

"By God," exclaimed Henry, "they are all white captives."

One woman stood up, "Aren't you Squire Neel's son?" she asked.

"Why yes. Who may I ask, Madam, are you?"

"I am Marie Hawthorne and this child here is the only one of my family left," she sobbed. Then she came forward and threw her arms around his waist as she slid to her knees burying her head in his stomach.

"There there, Madam, we will take care of you now. All of you. We are Neel's Rangers of the Catawba. You have nothing to fear. Take your belongings and come outside. We are so happy to have found you."

The dozen women and children came out of the structure. Mrs. Hawthorne turned to Henry and said, "Captain Henry, Sir. We have been moved here but a fortnight. The people of this village have treated us with love and kindness. Please don't be harsh with them."

"This pleases me," he answered.

"Drummer, roll a beat." An assembly roll was effected.

"Rangers, we have found this village to be of good report. They have treated the captives well and have tried to live in peace. It will be spared. Anyone who harms them will be faced with a drum head court martial."

Colonel Montgomery continued to advance and burn Cherokee villages until every significant settlement of the lower and middle Cherokees was destroyed. Reflecting on the fatigue of his men, he ordered them back to Fort Prince George. The condition of his men was such that they could march no farther because their strength and spirits were exhausted. Here they awaited news of an anticipated Cherokee surrender. Soon Little Carpenter appeared with several chieftains.

Little Carpenter was greeted outside the fort by Col. Montgomery and James Stuart. Little Carpenter dismounted and approached. He had no war paint. "We come in peace. Our villages are burned, our crops are gone, and we have not enough powder to hunt. Our women and children starve. The pox rages among our people. We would like to become brothers again as we were during the days of Col. Cummings when I traveled to see our Great White Father in England."

"We welcome you. How beautiful are the moccasins of those who bring peace. Come let us eat, smoke the pipe of peace, and then we will discuss the terms."

James Stuart wrote out the terms of the peace settlement. Little Carpenter withdrew in horror at the terms. Four braves were to be brought forward and put to death before the camp or four green scalps be brought to Col. Montgomery within twelve days.

Little Carpenter threw down the peace pipe and stomped around. He broke an arrow. He could not accept the terms and demanded to see Lt. Governor Bull. The request was granted and the Neel Rangers were chosen as escort.

Accordingly, Attakullakulla and the chieftains, being furnished with safeguard, set out for Charles Town to hold conference with Lieutenant Governor Bull, who, on their arrival, called a council to meet at Ashley Ferry, and then spoke to the following effect: "Attakullakulla, I am glad to see you, as I have always heard of your good behavior, and that you have been a good friend of the English. I take you by the hand, not only you but all those with you, as pledge for their security whilst under my protection. Colonel Grant acquaints me that you have applied for peace. I have therefore met with my beloved men to hear what you have to say, my areas are open for that purpose." A fire was kindled, the pipe of peace was lighted, and all smoked together for some time in great silence and solemnity.

Attakullakulla then arose and addressed Lieutenant Governor Bull to the following effect: "It is a great while since I last saw Your Honor. I am glad to see all the beloved men present. I am come to you as a messenger from the whole nation. I have now seen you, smoked with you, and hope we shall live together as brothers. When I came to Keowee, Colonel Grant sent me to you. You live at the waterside and are in the light, we are in darkness, but hope all will yet be clear. I have been constantly going about doing good, and though I am tired, yet I come to see what can be done for my people who are in great distress." Here he produced the strings of wampum he had received from the different towns, denoting their earnest desire for peace, and added, "As to what has happened, I believe it has been ordered by our father above. We are a different color from the white people. They are superior to us. But one God is the father of us all, and we hope what is past will be forgotten. God Almighty made all people. There is today a day but some are coming into and going out of the world. The great King told me the path should never be crooked, but open for everyone to pass and repass. As we all live in one land, I hope we shall all love as one people." After which peace was formally ratified and confirmed. The former friendship of parties being renewed, both expressed their hope that it would last as long as the sun shines and the rivers run.

The conference was held outside of Charles Town because of a smallpox outbreak. The treaty stipulated that all white prisoners would be returned and that the Cherokees would not travel beyond Twenty-Mile Creek. This was later changed by the Indian superintendent, James Stuart, to Forty-Six Mile Creek under the urging of Little Carpenter. The Cherokees wished to keep hunting rights.

After the conference and after bidding a somewhat tearful farewell to Little Carpenter, young Thomas and Henry prepared to leave for their homes in the Wauxhaus. The Neels and Tom Polk first called upon the Clerk of the county and drew patents to the area on the south bank of the Catawba. They received a thousand acres each for their service. Henry dismissed the Neel's Rangers. As they were about to leave, one of the Governor's aides came forward and asked, "Why is it that the Neel Rangers have not come forward with as many scalp bounties as the other Rangers?"

"Sir," replied Lieutenant Thomas, "We forbade them because they had become so blood thirsty, even scalping young children for the bounty."

The clerk continued, "Something is strange about this. You see those two mounting their horses? They just turned in over thirty-six scalps. It is difficult to believe that anyone could have killed that many."

Just then Sergeant Butler rode up and saluted. "My compliments, Sir."

"Yes, sergeant," replied Henry.

"Sir, I observed those two traders buying scalps from our men. When I queried my men they denied anything. Claimed they were buying tobacco."

"Thank you," said Henry, "You are dismissed. May I take this opportunity to thank you for the service you have rendered both colonies and His Majesty."

"Thank you, Sir. It has been a pleasure to serve you." With that Sergeant Butler rode off.

The Neel men approached the riders.

Thomas said, "A word with you, Sir."

"What is it you want Lieutenant? We must be on our way."

"I noticed you had an unusual amount of scalps. May I ask what unit you were with?"

"We served as irregulars with a Waxhaux militia."

"I don't believe there was any other militia than the Neel Rangers."

The stranger looked up in surprise and horror. Then he and his partner turned and rode off.

"Who were those renegades?" asked Thomas.

"I don't know, but I for one am anxious to get home."

# CHAPTER 14

# Departure of a Giant

It was almost dark when the young rangers rode into the compound. Two dogs barked, charged toward them, and then realized the familiar faces. From the porch ran their mother, father and Uncle Henry, who were visiting. Arthur ran out and took their horses. They first embraced their parents and their young brothers and sisters. After a few minutes of greeting, Henry rode off to see Nancy Agnes and the new baby.

Henry approached their home. As it was late, he placed his horse in the barn and proceeded to the front porch. Two hounds came toward him and started barking. Nancy Agnes came to the door saw him and ran toward him. "What a dirty handsome man. I was looking for a husband, but you will do."

"Madam," he said formally, "May I return your scarf which protected me through the war. My Dear, you look lovely." He lifted her up, whirled her around, and kissed her.

"Yes, but we better go inside before we start a scandal."

He was introduced to his new son. Nancy Agnes did not seem to object to the sweat, beard growth, and trail-drenched clothes.

The next evening they joined the rest of the family at Squire Thomas' house. As the atmosphere was oppressively hot, they decided to supper outside. Lieutenant Tom and Henry related their adventures with the militia. Elder Henry recounted how there were orphans, widows, and wounded that needed to be cared for. Tom then told of the widow Hawthorne who died shortly after she reached the plantation. He related that he, Thomas, was caring for her child James. James was raised by the Indians about five years and had picked up all the skills of the savage.

Young Captain Henry described the horror of the atrocities committed by both the whites and the Indians. He then related how he forbade his men to collect scalps. He mentioned how two traders may have bought the scalps the Neel Rangers had taken in a clandestine manner.

Sheriff Uncle Henry stood up and asked, "What did these vile fellows look like?"

The younger men described them.

"You just met our old friends Squawman Johnson and Artimas McGhee. They claimed to be from the Wauxhaus and you never saw them at a muster?"

"Our Rangers are not that numerous. We know all our men. They were never among them."

"Well, they received a pardon from the South Carolina Assembly. That does not mean that if we catch them on the North Carolina side we can't arrest them. I will have to think up a charge. Maybe trading in unauthorized contraband."

"I remember your account of the raid on their compound and how Uncle Henry took back the Hawthornes' horses."

"Yes and that spineless South Carolina Assembly let him go after Little Carpenter brought them in. It is no wonder the Cherokees don't trust us. Those Governors Giles and Lyttleton were the real cause of the war. It seems that the new Lieutenant Governor Bull will govern with more intelligence and peace."

The following Sunday, the Neels traveled to the Reverend Dalton's Waxhaw church. There was much celebration over the news that the new monarch, George III, had succeeded to the throne. According to the Charles Town paper, even though a Hanover, he spoke English and had been raised in England rather than Germany, so everyone was pleased at the prospect of a true English monarch. There was much discussion as to whether the new prime minister would wield as much power as Lord Walpole and William Pitt. Who was this Lord Townsend who seemed to be ready to assume the reigns of power?

Henry was in a daze to be united his wife and family. Nancy Agnes wore a white bonnet tied beneath her chin and a white gown that blazed in the morning sun.

Before he began his sermon, Reverend Dalton asked the Rangers to stand. Tom Polk, Thomas, Henry, and a dozen other rangers were present. The preacher then thanked the Lord for their bravery and safe return. He also prayed for peace in the land.

Thomas senior found that the only ship stores that seemed to bring in money was hemp. He could not find ways to economically market the ship masts. Dragging them to Camden and floating them down the river proved too expensive. The family increased their activities in cows, hogs, hemp, wheat, and blacksmithing. As the plantation lay on the trading path, the family engaged in some intercourse with the traders, including shoeing their horses, repairing tack, and manufacturing knives and hatchets.

In early 1762, Zeke came into the compound on his way to Charles Town. He related that all the tribes seemed to be at peace. He said that the warring tribes were all moving west along the Hiawasee and Tennessee Rivers. The peaceful ones were taking up agriculture and staying in the lower villages. He was somewhat worried about the rumor that a coming King's proclamation on staying behind the

Appalachian watershed would be broken. He related that he was tired of the trail and wanted to buy a piece of land and settle down.

"What of your Shawnee child?" young Henry asked.

"One Who Scampers is grown now and has been chosen by the daughter of a Shawnee Chief."

"What are Alexander's plans?" asked the Senior Thomas.

"I can speak for myself, Sir. I too would like to buy some land. Also, I would like to buy your servant Rachel for my wife," answered Alexander.

"I am afraid that is impossible," replied Squire Thomas with amusement.

"Why? Aren't I good enough for her?"

"No, she is a free woman. You will have to ask her father, Uncle Arthur." He smiled as he continued. "I always wondered why you were around her and her sisters so much. I would be happy to have you as a neighbor and can give you some land."

"I don't wish to be beholden to you, Sir. I want to buy it."

"I will make a deal with you. If Rachel marries you, I shall give her one hundred uncleared acres as a wedding present. I am too tired to clear anymore land anyway."

"You have a deal." Alexander then almost ran to the servants' area.

Zeke turned to the Squire. "Your friends and mine, Squawman Johnson and Artimas McGhee, are trading without a license. I was in the village of the upper Cherokees and talked with Little Carpenter. He said that the two came into one of the villages near Ft. Prince George, got the leaders drunk, and sold them some shoddy goods in exchange for skins. They also raped two young Cherokee girls and took them captive. Some of his braves were trying to track him. I traveled with these braves to Ninety-Six and then left them."

"Do you think that they are going to Charles Town?'

"You know as well as me that they will try to sell the skins either at Ninety-Six or Charles Town."

"I think I shall call Sheriff Henry and go after them."

The next morning Squire Thomas completed the necessary papers assigning one hundred acres each to Zeke and Alexander. Alexander later consented to a Christian marriage to Rachel. Rachel had had a child out of wedlock some ten years before. It was now discovered that the couple vowed a "broom" ceremony in the servants' quarters ten years ago before consummating the marriage bed. Thomas had always suspected as much.

With Zeke, Henry, and his sons, Thomas embarked on the trail of Squawman Johnson and McGhee. He planned to use Zeke's testimony to bring the two to justice. After three days they arrived at Ninety-Six. The trading post had grown in spite of the fact that the good hunting grounds had retreated to the west. Still, many of the Indians brought in skins and produce to be traded. Upon arriving Squire Thomas went to the new justice of the peace and presented some papers with complaints against his favorite antagonists.

The message he received was that the two had been in a brawl and had been thrown out by the tavern owner. They left two days before. After spending the night in the open, the group started for Charles Town. On the second day they came upon a trade train going west. Zeke recognized the trader and conferred with him. He learned that Johnson and two others were passed on the trail the day before. They quickened their pace. That night they camped along a stream.

Around an hour after sunset they heard a call, "Permission to come to your fire."

The Neel party was in the midst of a dinner of beans and fresh rabbit when the call came. "Permission granted," shouted Thomas.

As the party of four approached, a man came into the light. He recognized Thomas and immediately turned and ran. "It's Squaw Man!" shouted Zeke. The Neel party ran for their horses. Just as they got there, they saw a figure jump on his horse and ride away. Two of the Neels' horses had their hobbles undone. Champion was snorting and shaking his mane, obviously very agitated.

Saddling up, they began in hot pursuit. Zeke yelled, "Wait! This might be an ambush!" No sooner had the words left his mouth than a series of shots rang out in the darkness of the forest. Squire Thomas slumped in his saddle. Young Henry rushed to his aid and held him there. Young Thomas and Champion came on the other side. They guided the Squire's mount back to the campfire.

Sheriff Henry yelled, "Zeke, Alexander, and James stand watch. I want each of you to take a different direction. They may come back to ambush us again."

Henry and Thomas took Squire Thomas down from his horse. There was a huge hole in his chest. Air hissed from the lung as he breathed. Blood flowed freely from his mouth. Using the light of the fire the elder Henry placed a neckerchief in the hole to stem the blood.

Squire Thomas looked into their eyes as he coughed up blood. "I don't think I shall make it, men. I hope you will take care of your mother. There is a will in the desk. Henry please take care of it and make a written report to the South Carolina Governor about this."

"Oh Papa," lamented young Henry. There was a gurgle, a gasp, and he was gone.

Sheriff Henry stood and announced, "Although it is dark, we know from whence we came. The moon will help us. Let us start for home. We will go after these miscreants later."

The body was wrapped in a blanket and with tears in their eyes and with much disdain they placed the body on a sling between Tom's horse and his father's. They began their melancholy trip home. In a record three days, they crossed the Catawba and entered the compound. Uncle Arthur grabbed Squire Thomas's mounts. The boys removed the body. Henry rushed forward to inform his mother. Mary was sitting by the fire.

She looked up to see the frightening countenance of Henry. "Henry, what has happened? Where is your Father?"

She stood up and moved toward him. "Mother, he has been called to the Lord. He was shot by Squawman Johnson."

She embraced Henry. "Where is he?" Just then the boys came through the door with the body.

She used the services of Uncle Arthur in embalming Thomas. She placed the body on the dining room table, which they moved to the front room. Candles were placed around the body. "Leave us alone," said Mother.

She then proceeded with Rachel's help to wash and dress him. That afternoon they placed him in a coffin that Uncle Arthur made and loaded a wagon for the trip to the churchyard. Their neighbors gathered and Reverend Dalton delivered the eulogy. The elder Thomas was laid to rest in the churchyard. There was the traditional feast at the Neel plantation but it was not as raucous as the traditional Irish wake. There was too much sadness over the loss of the great patriarch, Thomas Neel. The entire congregation mourned the loss of Squire Thomas, elder, justice, and soldier.

After the funeral the family made its way back to the home of the deceased Squire Thomas Neel. As the new thane, Uncle Sheriff Henry addressed the group.

"What say you? Shall we pursue the miscreants or shall we allow the King's law?"

Uncle James spoke, "I say we do both. However, I don't know which way they fled."

Zeke spoke, "Well, I really ain't ready to clear land. Why don't I scout the Cherokee and Choctaw villages? Perhaps someone can go to Charles Town and determine what they know."

"Yes," spoke James, "Why don't I go and speak to the South Carolina Governor. He must stop this rat's nest in Ninety-Six and the lawlessness that exists."

"A fine idea," agreed the new thane, Uncle Henry. "With all those new people down from Pennsylvania and Virginia fleeing the war up north, there is a great deal of growth around Hillsboro and Salisbury. Perhaps I should make a call there. You two young husbands can take care of things here. I swear on the altar of God that these two miscreants shall hang."

# CHAPTER 15

# Law and Order Comes to the Waxhaw and the Catawba; the Torch is Passed to the Next Generation

Thomas Christopher Neel (1730) developed the thousand acres across the Catawba as a reward for his service in the French and Indian war. Most of the land that had been ceded by the Catawbas and Cherokees was assigned to him by Lt. Governor Bull of South Carolina in 1762. The exact border between the two colonies had not been settled. The land straddled both colonies. He and his bride, Jean Spratt, built a home there. Their house was a copy of the old homes in the Waxhaw. Mother Mary stayed in the big house with the children. Henry and Nancy Agnes developed a new place on Steele Creek. Henry, too, had a thousand acres near the junction of North and South Carolina called the "Corner," not far from the Polk plantation and Widow Jackson's farm.

Thomas quickly rose as an important part of the community. Thomas received a joint appointment by the governors of North and South Carolina to serve on the boundary committee determining the boundary between North and South Carolina. In 1752 Jean had given birth to twins, Thomas Jr. and Andrew. Later John, Sarah, Mary, Jean, and Elizabeth were added to the family of the Catawba. A problem arose because the land assigned to Thomas lay in the disputed area later to be called the "New Acquisition." Thomas had a confusing life. He received his land grant as a reward for assisting the South Carolina militia. Then he was appointed, later, as a member of the North Carolina Assembly. Thomas served on several committees in the Assembly, also, as petitioner on roads and ferries, and certifier of accounts petitioner on land grants. As if he weren't busy enough, Thomas in 1754 served as a member of the committee, along with Thomas Polk, to determine the site of the Bethel Presbyterian Church. He later became an elder in that church. He and Jean were actually citizens of both Carolinas.

\*\*\*

A weekly mail courier brought a copy of the *Charles Town Gazette*. As the courier rode up, Henry, seeing the rider from his front window, advanced to the door. "Greetings, friend, what news do you bring."

"Great news, the *Gazette* here has the terms of the Treaty of Paris signed last February. The bad news is that the council for the Southern Colonies has decreed that all settlement is closed beyond the mountains and that those in Indian lands must be removed."

"Well, that is most distressing. Would you have some refreshment?"

"No, your Grace, I shall fill my canteen at your well and be gone."

"May the Lord bless you."

Henry rang the bell and called the plantation company and spread the word. He sent Uncle Arthur to tell his brother of the news.

Meanwhile, Squawman Johnson and Artimas McGhee had gone first to Charles Town, then slipped by the Neel compound to the wilds near Hillsboro where they blended in with the hundreds of new settlers in the area. The winding down of the war led many Scotch Irish, Quakers, and Moravian Germans to settle the western areas.

Uncle James came back from Charles Town with the news that Squawman Johnson and his gang had traded scalps for bounty. "I cannot understand why His Majesty's agent did not question thirty five scalps among four people. Especially, when we consider that young Henry here could not identify them as part of the militia.

"I also stopped by the Governor's Palace in Charles Town and told him of the murder of our brother. He expressed his regrets and gave a warrant for the arrest of Squawman Johnson and Artimas McGhee and four unnamed persons. As His Majesty's mail packet was in port, he forwarded a letter to the North Carolina governor apprising him of the murder."

By this time Zeke had something to say. "I counseled in the Chickasaw Villages and found that four men had come there trading without a license. The Chickasaws had never seen these traders before but were able to trade some skins for muskets, knives, and pots. The muskets were of the poorest quality. When one of the muskets fouled killing a brave, the villagers became quite concerned. I don't think our friends will be back there."

Young Thomas turned to his Uncle Henry, the Sheriff. "Uncle Henry, what authority do we have now that we have no magistrate to try anyone?"

"I believe we may have taken care of that. I stopped by and talked with the Justice of the Salisbury District. He related that there was much concern for the lawlessness of the frontier here as well as over in South Carolina around Ninety-Six. There are several problems. Many people fled their homes during the Cherokee war. After they returned, they found their homes burned or ransacked, their cattle gone, and an atmosphere of lawlessness. Some turned to the charms of debauchery, both as highwayman and housebreaker. Reverend Woodsman of the Ninety-Six area, in a letter to the Governor of South Carolina, told of the difficulties of the law. The two hundred mile trip to Charles Town in the pursuit of justice was too expensive. A trial with Charles Town jurors instead of local mediation made justice a sham. Because of these difficulties, committees of citizens organized to bring about justice. Rather than submitting to questionable and what they felt were often unreasonable trials in Charles Town, the frontiersmen were punishing and banishing suspects with only the merest judicial restraint. These committeemen are called *Regulators*.

The magistrate claimed he was worried that because of the tremendous influx of new people from Pennsylvania in the area around Hillsboro, there soon might be problems of lawlessness in North Carolina. He informed me that the new North Carolina Governor Tyron had defined five judicial districts. Our area in Anson County is in the Salisbury District. He related that the Governor had seen the petition in which your father first requested a new county to be formed from Anson County. Based upon my testimony, he issued a North Carolina warrant for the arrest of Squawman Johnson and Artimas McGhee and four unnamed accomplices. After expressing regret at the loss of your father, he appointed you, young Henry, as Justice of the Peace and Thomas as a captain in the militia."

Uncle James broke in, "I propose a toast to the new justice." All toasted and then retired to a dinner prepared by Uncle Henry's wife.

In December 1763, the post from the Governor arrived and confirmed Young Henry (1736) as Justice of the Peace and recognized Thomas Christopher (1730) as a Captain in the militia. Henry's brevet rank was changed to a permanent rank of ensign. Other items included:

1) A request for the help of all personnel in the Salisbury district to discourage and remove all persons who settle west of the Appalachian Mountains;

2) A warrant for the arrest of Squawman Johnson's renegades;

3) A memorial to Colonel Thomas Neel in service for the Florida campaign and service as justice in the Providence area;

4) An acknowledgement that the request for a new county had been received and had been approved by an act of the legislature and council to take effect immediately;

5) A proclamation from Lord Egermont, Secretary of State for the Southern Department, requiring royal approval for all negotiations and sales of Indian Land.;

6) A proclamation that American colonial judgeships, as distinguished from justices of the peace, now required the approval of the Crown.

Uncle Henry read the dispatches and then commented. "I believe we will have a good governor, at least he will be better than those South Carolina dandies that led us into a war with the Cherokee. It appears that the Council, the Assembly, and the Governor have been busy. However, this is mostly good news. We have also received a notice from the Secretary of State for North Carolina that the new lands in Providence and the Catawba have been posted. So, my young nephews, you now have a confirmed title to land gained by your participation in the late war with the French and Indians. The bad news is those silk stocking dandies of Edmonton and Wilmington will not likely give legislative rights to the poor upland people. I doubt if we shall get a county without some problems. The Highland Scots displaced by the Battle of Culloden are arriving daily in the Cape Fear and Cross Creek areas. They have fallen in with the rich coastal folks up there. Wilmington and New Bern are jealous of their control. Besides, the Governor desires to build a grand palace at New Bern and find a permanent place for the legislature to meet. I would prefer Hillsboro because it is more nearly the center of the colony. You will notice that we have only two representatives while the older counties have four."

Young Henry piped in. "You mean that after we fought all those Indian and French Battles for the dandies in Charles Town and Wilmington, they will not give us proper representation?"

"That ain't all, my young friend," added James. "Those new settlers in the back-country and near the Virginia Border are completely without any justice system. People are beginning to stir up there. They don't care what jurisdiction they are in nor do they like law much. They just squat wherever they are. Most of them fled from the wars in Pennsylvania and are not too anxious to get involved again.

"I also know that west beyond the Tellico River, John Sevier has already started trading for a good deal of Cherokee land. There are people already moving in there. It will be interesting to see what happens, now that the lordships have forbid the sale of Indian lands to individuals."

"Speaking of Indians," interjected Thomas. "Jean and I would like to adopt young James Hawthorne since he has been living with us since his re-capture."

The newly appointed magistrate Henry replied. "It will be an honor to make this my first official act." He then sat down and made an article of adoption to be read at the Steele Creek Church during the next session.

All segments of the Neel clan, Uncle James, Uncle Henry, Thomas, and Henry continued developing their lands. With the completion of the Royal Highway from Salisbury through Providence to Charles Town, the families began more and more to move from a cash to a credit basis in their trade with the English agents who received products and credited the colonists for manufactured goods. This meant, however, that the families became debtors to their English agents.

` Thomas and Jean Spratt had a steady issue: twins Andrew and Thomas (1752), Sarah, Mary, Jean, John, and Elizabeth.

Henry and Nancy Agnes's family, while starting later expanded rapidly: William, 1762; Mary, 1763; John, 1767; James, 1769; Nancy Agnes, 1771; Samuel, 1773; James, 1775; Henry, 1779; Mary Williams, 1781; and later Jenny

The news was read in the church one Sunday to the effect that the Governor's Council with the consent of the Assembly had formed a new county out of the northern portion of Anson County and a few of the surrounding counties. The new county was named for Ann of Mecklenburg, the queen and wife of George III. The village of Charlotte Town was the site of the new courthouse. The new Squire Henry was asked to form a committee to choose a courthouse.

After church some of the Neels gathered outside the meeting house. Uncle Henry, the Sheriff, spoke, "Now that we are a county, I suggest that we issue additional warrants against the nefarious outlaws that killed my brother. I have taken an oath to bring them in, dead or alive. I have asked Zeke and Running Path to help me track them. I believe they have run north close by the village of Hillsboro. Squire Henry, if you will draw up the necessary warrants we shall be on our way tomorrow."

Henry replied, "Thomas and I shall go with you."

"I believe your place is here. There is a justice court to organize, as well as some concern for the Shawnees who have been threatening hunters. Also, you will need to assist the King's forces in moving settlers squatting on Indian lands. Thomas, I deputize you as the deputy sheriff for the area."

Thomas replied, "Now that the war with the Indians and the French is over, Colonel Lord Stuart will soon be making treaties with the Cherokees, Shawnees, and their allies. I hope the Indians will not decide to launch some kind of attack now that the King's forces have gone. It looks like we are on our own."

Uncle James chimed in, "Yes, I think we should be sure there is family fortification throughout the county in case of Indian restlessness."

Thomas added, "With the defeat of the Highland Scots in the Battle of Culloden, there seems to be a great deal of settling along the coast as well as rather unorganized migrations into the western frontier. Hillsboro has become a hotbed of violence as the forces of justice seem to be overwhelmed. This will put a great deal of pressure on the Indian lands. It will be difficult to move them when they occupy Indian lands illegally."

The next morning Zeke and Uncle Henry, the old sheriff, departed with a pack mule each in search of Squawman Johnson and Artimas McGhee. Henry and Tom gathered and wished them godspeed. Running Path of the Catawbas joined the searchers as they traveled.

Henry (1736) spent the day with his wife Nancy Agnes as she approached the birth of their second child. Nancy, the ideal frontier wife, adapted as the family enterprise rose from mere subsistence to what the amused neighbors of Virginia called North Carolina gentry – a gentry not based on lineage but accomplishment. With not a great deal of labor Mary Neel was brought into the world in 1763 to accompany her brother William born one year earlier. Henry beamed with pride as he held his new daughter. Rachel maintained a family tradition by acting as midwife for yet another Neel generation.

# CHAPTER 16

# Intolerable Acts of the Crown

There were four families at the worship society Lord's day. Squire Captain Thomas Neel (1730) stood and addressed the group as they sat in the great room of his home. "Brethren, I call your attention to the great numbers who are moving into our Catawba as well as the areas south of here. Already a Reverend Woodmason of the Anglican faith is petitioning the South Carolina Assembly for more funds to defeat the 'New Lights' as we are called. We are chastised for our demand of a physical manifestation of the Holy Ghost or evidence of progress toward that happy state when the Holy Ghost dwells within a man's heart. Many of the new settlers are little better than the heathen Indians they replaced on the lands.

The word of Christ's gospel in purity and simplicity is not reaching these new citizens. Further, our weekly trip to Steel Creek or Waxhaw Kirks is difficult, particularly in the winter. Therefore, I propose the building of a new Kirk better able to serve our area. I also wish to petition the Governor to allow the Presbyterians to perform marriages. It goes without saying that the continued denial of this sacrament held exclusively by the Anglican Church is without merit in the sight of God and man. Paying taxes to that invisible clergy is one thing, having no service from it is another. What think you?"

After a brief discussion, the communicants agreed.

Thomas prepared a memorial to the Philadelphia Presbytery, noting the society's intention to found a church on Neel's property west of the Catawba. As the family sat around the room and the children romped outside, Jean spoke. "I received a copy of the *Charles Town Gazette* which contained an editorial. It seems one James Otis, lately the King's Advocate, in 1761 was ordered to obtain writs of assistance to search the home of any person suspected of smuggling. Rather than do this, he became a counsel to those who believed the King's servants should have properly served warrants from a magistrate to search homes for smuggled goods or any other reason. It appears he has thrown the Admiralty Courts in an uproar by his action. In his argument before the Massachusetts Supreme Court he is alleged to have sworn his fidelity to King George, but felt that Parliament, by the Navigation Acts, had deprived them of the rights of Englishmen. What are we to do? Go to war against the Mother country? She has not been too good to us Irish."

Thomas replied, "Now, now my Dear. According to the way I read the article

His Majesty King George III, through his Prime Minister Lord Townsend, wished the colony to help pay for the Seven Years War just concluded. I believe that since the newly minted King is the first monarch raised in England and can at least speak English we can expect a more sympathetic King. Those dandies in Parliament don't seem to realize that we gave up much over here. Our legislatures gave up a good deal of their treasure, many homes and crops were burned, many of our brave militia and citizens died in the cause of England. What have we received in return? Restrictions on settling conquered lands and the withdrawal of His Majesty's troops in North America, leaving us naked before the uncivilized among the savages and the aspirations of Spain and, yes, even France. The good governor of our colony had to build his own navy to flush out the pirates who preyed on our shores. I believe people like Otis should keep up their fight, but for us on the Carolina frontier, I believe we will be well treated by His Majesty because he needs our ship stores of hardwood, ship masts, tar, and hemp. We will always be held in his regard as there is not enough timber left in England for his large fleet."

Henry added, "Well spoken, Brother. Otis's problem was a problem of the Northern colonies. This far from the shore, we are not bothered much by smuggling. That is the problem of our sea-going friends. I think things have improved with the repeal of the Molasses act. Even though we grow our own, there is a principle involved here."

Reverend Dalton asked, "What is that? Fie, does not the learned Prime Minister Townsend know that we have a sweet tooth, too?"

Nancy Agnes spoke, "Perhaps he wants you drunken sots to give up your rum."

They all laughed. Thomas chimed in, "No, just the rum punch which I noticed is not something that you ladies avoid."

"Ah the trials of a frontier woman," she replied cheerily. "You must work from day to day and then put up with such insults by these brutes." She winked at Jean. As it was getting late the families went home.

It was a warm November 1763 day. Sheriff Uncle Henry had received a Writ of Election from North Carolina Governor Dobbs the year before, but the task of founding a new county caused a delay in the election of delegates. The notice of the election had been posted in every tavern as well as the churches. Freemen and landowners assembled as required by the broadside at the tavern in the Charlotte Village. There the landowner rolls were verified. Sheriff Henry Neel spoke. "You all know why you are here. You are to elect two representatives to the Assembly of North Carolina to represent our new Mecklenburg County. Only those who own land and have paid a poll tax may vote, except for tradesmen who have been previously verified by the Crown. First, we will have speeches by anyone interested in this service to the Crown and his loyal subjects. After that we will vote for two individuals. Who will be the first to speak?"

"I wish to announce my readiness to serve," yelled Thomas (1730}.

"I, too," yelled Tom Polk.

An extremely well-dressed gentleman came forward. "I am Christian Huck, lately settled from His Majesty's lands in the Highlands. I am a loyal subject of the King and His church and wish to bring the blessings of our beloved Monarch to this wretched region."

Uncle Henry asked, "I am not acquainted with you, Sir. Where do you own land?"

"I have before me a deed and registered said deed for land I purchased from one Ezekial Johnson at the conclusion of the late war against the Cherokees."

Henry's countenance darkened and he asked, "When was the last time you saw Master Johnson?"

"It has been over a year. It took some time to get the deed back from New Bern."

"Very well, Sir. I have no record of your poll tax so if you will pay it at this time, we will declare your candidacy valid. Gentlemen, if there are no other candidates please get numbers from the lovely lady over there (pointing to Nancy) and see your order.

Tom Polk drew the first straw and began. "As you know the Polks have been in the Waxhaus a long time. We have served well and won most of the time, having lost to one of my worthy opponents only once when he stole the heart of one Jean Spratt."

Someone shouted, "Is that why you are running, for revenge?"

"No, I cannot help it if fair Jean has such poor taste," he replied. Nancy Agnes, who stood nearby with Henry, blushed as the crowd roared.

"But, seriously, I have been a loyal subject of the King, a soldier in his militia, and a member of the Christian faith serving as an elder along with my worthy opponent, Thomas Neel. If elected, I shall serve faithfully and work to bring a better life to the County."

Sheriff Henry: "Thank you, Tom. Now Master Huck, do you wish to address the crowd?"

Christian climbed on to the back of the wagon which served as a stage. He was dressed in a silk vest with ruffles at the edges, a straight back wool coat with tails and ornate cuffs, tan breeches with codpiece, white hose, and wigged hair. He had a tall handsome frame that commanded the attention of both sexes. His piercing black eyes and firm jaw drew admiration of all the ladies. "My fellow countrymen,

I have been in this area but a short time. However, I migrated to this territory after my family was ruined by the Jacobite rebellion in which we tried to shake off the rule of the English. We settled in Charles Town as merchants and have lately purchased this land in your area. We now have a glorious new King who is wholly English and able to respond to our most generous needs. I offer you the blessings of His Majesty's true church as well as connections in Charles Town and England to furnish the necessary specie to help our land prosper. My experiences will help you prosper beyond your wildest dreams."

A heckler shouted. "What will you do about the King's Proclamation that we can't settle over the mountains? Many of our people died for this land and are now going to be forced to leave."

"His Majesty means no harm. We shall be able to settle this amicably. Let us all gather under the protection of His Majesty who has given us generously of his protection and this land. Thank you. And now my good man," he said while sniffing from his snuff box, "I yield the floor."

"Thank you, Sir. Now we will hear from Captain Thomas Neel."

Thomas was dressed in a more formal dress with a cotton embroidered vest, a deer skin great coat, linen trousers, hose and polished shoes with buckles. He wore his tri-cornered hat with a ribbon of the militia.

A bearded face in buckskin with some teeth missing shouted, "You look like a dandy, Captain Neel. You never fought the Frenchie Indians looking like that!"

"Jacob," he replied, "If I were as handsome as you I would not have to dress up like a dandy. And for your comments you are sentenced to be the first one in line at my rum barrel."

The crowd roared. "You always took care of Neel's Militia."

"Thank you, Jacob. First, let me compliment my opponents on their qualifications and suggestions. I want to clear up one thing. The Neel Regiment is just as much a Polk regiment. The Polks and the Neels have served side by side. However, Tom Polk, I remember that you did not suffer too long after the loss of Jean, but married her sister. Now I am stuck with you as a brother-in-law."

Tom interrupted, "We both suffer."

"Tom, it is an honor to have you as a, I hope, friend. No finer miliaman lives. But to the point and to the rum, if I receive your vote I will address the needs of our area which I see are these:

1. The Cape Fear dynasty has too much power. New counties are entitled to the same level of representation as the old.

2. I will increase the specie so that commerce can be carried on in the back-

country, and we will not be at the mercy of English merchants and Charles Town factors.

3. I will strive to develop western North Carolina and get out from under the yoke of the Rice Kings who control both colonies.

4. I will continue to pledge my life, fortune and service to the rights we have as Englishmen.

Thank you. Now may I direct your attention to the rum barrel on my wagon. If you want ale see Polk. If you want tea and cakes see Master Huck."

Sheriff Henry spoke, "Thank you gentlemen. I suppose I could have you line up according to your preference in refreshment. But as I call your name from the poll list please line up in back of one of these three gentlemen."

The crowd engaged in the refreshments. A buffalo had been butchered and roasted the night before. Now men took their knives and carved pieces into their hands or truncheons. Some served their families. At what Henry thought was about the third hour past noon, he ordered the polled to stand behind their candidate as their names were called.

Thomas was within a few feet of Christian while waiting for the polling to begin. "I say, Neel," Christian began, "What mean you by the Rights of Englishmen and the rule of the Rice Kings? You sound like that tyrant and traitor Otis in the northern colonies. I seemed to have heard an insult not only against South Carolina but also against the Crown."

"I did not know that the Rice Kings were the only people in South Carolina. I live in a disputed area which could be either colony. I have served with the South Carolina militia and alongside the King's dragoons. I guess you hear what you want to hear."

"Is that not an insult?"

"What you heard was a good old frontier debate. We like our whiskey straight, our rum, beer, and women warm. We like our religion straight out of God's word. Our recreation is horse racing, wrestling, drinking, praying, and politicking. And oh, yes—tall tales and a little lying. I hope you enjoy them all."

Christian drew back looking bewildered. He turned to see but a few in his line.

Henry counted the lineup. "I now certify that Thomas Neel and Tom Polk are elected as the Mecklenburg representatives to the North Carolina Assembly. Congratulations, gentlemen, and may God Bless your efforts."

After the spirited election, Thomas, the Squire of the Catawbas, proceeded to New Bern for the annual meeting of the North Carolina Assembly. Polk with business in Charles Town came to the Assembly by ship. He agreed to take some of Thomas's baggage.

Spring 1764 began. The crops of corn and a little wheat were in on the lands of Thomas Neel. The cattle were ready to be gathered and driven to the Charles Town market. Things looked well enough for Thomas to begin his journey to the North Carolina Assembly. This was to be a most important meeting for there was a great concern among the coastal Rice Kings of South Carolina for the "New Colonial Policy." As the Neel properties of both brothers were on the border between the two colonies and as the border had not been precisely determined, they were constantly besieged by concerns of both colonies. The previous session of Assembly had been alive with concern. After bidding good-bye to his family and spending the first night at the home of Brother Henry, Thomas and his man servant Samuel began their journey overland to New Bern. He could have taken a boat from Charles Town, but he wanted to gather feelings of citizens about the frontier as he went. He thought perhaps he could pick up some information concerning the murderers of his father. He carried copies of the warrants for Squawman and Artimas but supposed they had fled to the west by now, possibly across the Mississippi. His baggage included a cavalry sword, rifle, and a brace of pistols. Samuel, a trusted servant and son of Uncle Arthur, was furnished with most of the supplies as well as a knife and pistol.

As they headed for Colson's Ferry, Thomas turned to Samuel. "Samuel, how old are you now?"

The lad of six feet dressed in buckskins and a tattered hat answered, "I have seen sixteen summers, Sir."

"What say you for your future?"

"I will follow the trade of my father as a dresser of horses and keeper of the stable."

"Do you ever want to be free?"

"I don't know, Sir. I have never seen any place but my home. I have been treated well, and I love my father, mother, and sister Rachel. I like to listen to Mr. Alexander, for he tells me of lands far away."

Their mounts now were in single file for a narrow portion of the trail. "I was ruminating about my need for an enlarged blacksmith shop. You could be an apprentice and after you learned the trade and some letters you could be free."

"I have watched the blacksmiths and think that would be a good thing to know. However, I would hate to leave my home."

"You would not necessarily have to. I believe that the day is coming when we will have no kind of indenture and all men can work at whatever gifts they have."

"What mean this 'indenture?'"

"That means that one man owns someone like a cow or horse."

"I never thought of it that way. You mean you owns me?"

"In a legal sense yes, but we consider our servants more like a family. We provide you with food, clothes, shelter, and in return you work for us. When people are free they must provide for those things themselves by working for someone else."

"I don't rightly see the difference."

"The difference is that you will probably work harder for yourself than as a servant and will gain some money we call capital to start at a trade of your own. Any money you have is your own. It belongs to you and no one else."

"What if I get married? To who does dat woman belong?"

"Well, I guess she would not belong to anyone. You would be partners."

"This all makes me ponder. Look yonder, I see some smoke."

They entered the village of Colson Mill Ferry. Thomas and Samuel dismounted at a tavern. Above the door faded red letters *Red Boar* hinted of refreshment. After dismounting, they both entered and sat down at a table near the wall. In a strange place, Thomas wanted no one behind him. It was a dark room with a fireplace for cooking at one end and a small candle at each table. The dirt floor was policed by two dogs that ate food dropped or thrown from the tables. There were no women customers. Ale and rum were flowing freely. Half the tables were occupied by country men dressed usually in buckskin. Food was served by two young women who were apparently the daughters of the tavern keeper. Soon the proprietor came forward. He was dressed in a leather apron, wool shirt, and wool pants. "What brings you here, my good fellow and your man?"

"I am Captain Thomas Neel and a delegate to the Assembly to which I travel. What news do you have?

"First, is this Captain Neel lately of the Cherokee Wars?"

"I had a small part."

"Small part! Weren't you with the Neel Rangers? Did you serve under Montgomery and Moore?"

"That was our regiment. Where did you get such nonsense?"

"I am Jediah Smith and served as a rifleman with the Grant Rangers from Camden. The rum is on me, Sir. Sally, see what these men want. What news do you bring?"

"First, this is my manservant, Samuel." The tavern man nodded and looked at Samuel with askance.

"The news from the north is that there is a great deal of concern about the Acts of Lord Townsend. The repeal of the Molasses Act is a stroke of good fortune."

"Do you think that the proclamation forbidding settlement beyond the Appalachians will be enforced?"

"I am not sure. To remove people who fought for the land and had families die during the Indian Wars will bring serious consequences. Especially when we consider that before the Proclamation was made, many soldiers were promised land. I shall take this with me to the Assembly."

Jediah continued, "Well that is a problem. There is a great deal of concern about the law here. Some of the travelers from Anson, Orange, and Grandville Counties tell of the lack of justice. They are beyond the law. If someone is caught stealing a horse, he must be taken to New Bern for justice. This may take weeks. Jurors are drawn from Wilmington and New Bern. They are not 'peers' as I hear it. They are resorting to 'Corn Law.' Many lawless people are blending in with the good people of the population. The dense pine forest separates the western counties from the lower piedmont and the seacoast. There are no navigable streams and only trails linking them to the coast and Governor Dobbs' justice.

"Many people feel the royal justices, sheriffs and justices of the peace are controlled by the Governor's council. They require tax payment in specie. Up there people only trade by barter. There is no money. Some unjust sheriffs seize lands for taxes while the owner is out trying to borrow money."

Thomas replied, "Sir, this is quite frightening. To think that His Majesty's servants would be so distressed. I would like to speak to the justice here."

"That would be Israel Colson over there. He also owns the mill and ferry."

"Thank you, Sir. It is always good to meet a man who served His Majesty's militia so well."

"Thank you. I am honored."

Thomas moved to another table with Samuel and Jediah. "Your Honor," began Jediah Smith, "May I introduce to you Captain Neel, lately of Neel's Rangers."

"Sit you down, Sir and your man as well. What news do you bring?" He put down a turkey leg which was in one hand and the tankard of ale in the other. He was a corpulent man with a jolly countenance. His bushy unkempt beard showed greasy remains of the wild turkey.

"I am on the way to the Assembly as a representative of the Providence area."

"How goes things there?"

Thomas related the concerns about the Townsend Acts and heard in return the same account of the western counties.

Colson continued, "We must find a way to control the western counties. There are committees of vigilantes. They are calling themselves the Regulators and are attempting to protect their communities first from French and Indian raids and now from people who are pouring in from Pennsylvania and Virginia. Also runaway slaves, indentured, abused women, and fugitives from justice are heading to the upcountry. There is a complete lack of Christian education. Now that the threat of Indians is diminished there is nothing that ties the communities together."

"That brings me to my reason for addressing you. I have a warrant for the arrest of one Ezekial Squawman Johnson and an Artimas McGhee for the murder of my father Thomas Neel and for stealing the King's property."

"Your countenance indicated a rather intimate involvement. Please accept my condolences. How did this murder happen?" asked Colson.

Thomas described the murder and gave a description of the two nefarious outlaws.

Jediah commented. "Your Honor, that description would apply to many people. I think we may have seen someone like that a few months ago. I remember someone bragging about how many scalps he had obtained. He remarked about how he served with the Neel Rangers and killed many Indians."

"It is extremely difficult to hide my anger. If it is our wanted men they have not served in the militia since the Georgia campaign. What you have said sounds like Squawman Johnson. Were there any families with them? Such as children and half-breeds?"

"They did not bring them into the tavern."

Colson added, "When they crossed on the ferry the next morning there were families with them. In fact the entire party numbered about a half dozen, all mounted with some children sharing saddles."

A customer chimed in, "Yes, I lost four fine horses but found some broken down animals in the barn. When they recovered I had a boon. The animals the scoundrels left were just about as good as the ones I lost. I think these mounts were ridden pretty hard."

Thomas sat at a table and wrote a note to Uncle Henry asking that a message be forwarded to Zeke at Ninety-Six. He then stood and spoke, "Is anyone going to Charlotte village?"

"Sir, I am." A young traveler in trail clothes came forward.

"My good man, take this to Sheriff Henry Neel in the area of Providence. I will give you a half crown now and the Sheriff will give you another crown on its successful delivery within two days. The terms are so stated in the letter."

"Sir, I am your servant."

"Samuel," said Thomas, "Please take care of the animals and stay in the barn. I want to visit with these gentlemen. Mr. Colson, may I have food and shelter for my servant and animals?"

"It will be our honor and you must stay at my home tonight."

The next morning after a sumptuous breakfast of hoe cakes, venison, and cyder for both Thomas and Samuel, they mounted and turned east. They rode in silence as they descended farther into the coastal plain. Swamps were now prevalent. The late summer had failed to cool the land. Mosquitoes, gnats, and horseflies abounded. Travel became less and less comfortable.

As they rode Thomas continued studying his problems. He thought, "The counties of the west apparently do not have justice and something must be done about the lawlessness. Speaking of lawlessness, we must bring Squawman and Artimas to justice. Where do my duties lie? To the family, to the colony, to the militia, to the King? And what about this Otis and all the things going on up north in Massachusetts? Does the King, who seems so devoted to England, really know what is happening? What are we to think of Lord Townsend, Lord North and this new commoner, William Pitt? How are we to defend ourselves now that His Majesty's troops have left?"

He swatted at a large horsefly shortly after it bit him. The sound awakened Samuel who was dozing in his saddle as they went along. This caused his horse to jump and suddenly run. Samuel brought it under control.

Thomas laughed, "What say you, Samuel? Have you started after your freedom already?"

"Oh no, Sir, I was just dozing and trying to remember some scriptures."

"Scriptures, where did you hear them?"

"Well, Sir, I know we blacks ain't supposed to read, but my daddy Arthur, he know how to read well and read us the Bible ebry night."

"I understand he also preaches"

"Dat he do. I hope I ain't got him in no trouble."

"Not to concern yourself. If you become an apprentice you can learn to read, too."

"I think I am ready to do dat."

They approached the twin communities of Cross Creek and Campbellton. The creek, for which the town was named, began in the gentle hills and descended precipitously to a gentle meander before joining the river where mills had been built. There was a grist mill, saw mill, smith shop, and tavern. Many people engaged in mechanical trades such as wheelwrights, carpenters, coopers, and tanners.

The pair dismounted at a tavern. The noise of the crowd hinted of a Scottish brogue. Celtic speech was also present. Inquiring about lodging, Thomas found a bed which, of course, he shared with a stranger. Samuel drew much better quarters in the stable. The town, incorporated in 1762, flourished under the leadership of the commercial interests who provided services and an outlet for backcountry goods. The Cape Fear River was navigable by small boats the year round. Thomas called upon the justice of the peace and left warrants for the arrest of Johnson and McGhee.

The next evening found them camped along the Cape Fear River, two days from New Bern. After building a fire and a supper of rabbit killed upon the trail, Thomas read a passage from the Bible followed by a prayer. Sam listened intently. After putting down bedrolls, the night sounds surrounded them with katydids, wolf music, owls, the chirp of bats, and the blackness of the skies filled with infinite twinkling lights. This was what Thomas missed the most about the campaigns, not being able to be at one with God's creations.

After a breakfast of pemmican and coffee, the pair headed along the Cape Fear River on the south side until they appeared south of Wilmington. There they took a ferry to the north side and that night camped about a day's travel from New Bern. Late the next day, Thomas found lodging in a New Bern boarding house which catered to the Assembly and Council. Samuel was allowed to room with Thomas as his man servant.

The pair climbed the stairs to find their assigned room. It consisted of two tick rope beds, a desk between the beds facing the window, and two chairs. A stand with pitcher and wash basin as well as two chamber pots completed the accommodations. "Well, Sam, what do you think?"

"The bed looks good to me, Sir."

A knock came to the open door and in walked Tom Polk. "My you look trail worn!" he exclaimed. "I will have my man bring up your baggage. After that, you owe me a drink."

"How was the voyage? I imagine you were sea sick. You look terrible."

"That will cost you a double shot, or I won't let you have your dandy clothes for the Governor's ball."

After instructing Samuel on the placement of clothes, Thomas and Polk went to the public bath where both enjoyed a steaming tub bath. The pair emerged from the experience with fresh clothes. Dressed in conservative colored coat, shirt, and waistcoat, they could have passed for aristocracy if they had powder hair or wigs. After a shave by a barber, they tied their hair in back and proceeded down to the local eatery.

The tavern was noisy. Assemblymen from over the province were there. There was much joviality and back slapping as reacquaintances were made. Polk and Thomas, being freshmen, stood in awe at the activity. They took a table and ordered a meal brought out on a trenchant with a knife and a tankard of ale. They both had brought those new French implements called forks.

"I say there, Polk, may I join you?" asked an elegantly wigged man as he approached them.

They both stood, "We always stand for one of the King's gallant warriors. How are you, Hugh?" responded Polk. "Thomas Neel, you remember Hugh Green of the Wilmington Regiment."

"Of course, Sir. It is a pleasure to meet you. How goes it with you?"

It was then they noticed a pinned sleeve and remembered that he had lost his arm in the raid on the Cherokee Villages.

"We seemed to prosper but the whole area is concerned about three things: the raids of that renegade Indian Pontiac up north, the coming passage of the Sugar Act, and the rumor of even worse acts to come. I suppose you heard of that James Otis in Massachusetts railing against the writs of assistance and the rumored admiralty courts."

Polk replied, "I heard some of it. Why don't you enlighten us?"

"As you remember, the Molasses Act was enacted to help His Majesty's government pay for the late war. Well, it seems it did not bring enough revenue for those dandies in London who suck the life out of us with the high mark-ups on our goods. It seems that a new act called the Sugar Act has been passed. We now have to pay duties on foreign molasses, sugar, wine, and other commodities. One would think this is no problem for us because we can smuggle them in; however, revenue officers now have writs of assistance which do not require the intervention of a judicial officer. We have little recourse. We are concerned here that offenders will be taken to England for trial."

Thomas commented. "That will not particularly concern us in the back country. We still get a bounty for our ship stores and our relations with the Indians seem quite benign. Besides we render our own molasses and there are rumors that we make our own wine, rum, and whiskey." He smiled and gave a wink.

"You don't understand what this has done to the coastal areas. We fear that even greater restrictions are coming."

Tom Polk countered. "Why should we be concerned with the coastal problems? There are not enough honest justices and King's officers in the backcountry to keep order, and, other than you, we found little help from the coast during the Indian Wars. We need the same representations in the back country that you have in the Cape Fear and coastal areas. We have two representatives to some of the old counties' four."

Hugh replied, "There you have it, gentlemen, if we include the danger of that renegade Pontiac, we have the agenda for this session. Let us toast the new session."

"Here, Here," the backcountry gentlemen replied.

At 9:00, the jovial patrons of the tavern drifted to the hired meeting hall down the street. The congregation of assemblymen advanced or staggered in a mixed phalanx. Tar torches lit the way. They approached the door of the hall where they formed a line. Good natured jostling ensued among the crowd of backcountry, Piedmont and coastal gentlemen. Those with ladies preceded them. On each side of the door was a soldier of the Governor's guard standing at rigid attention in red tunics, white bandoliers, and white pants that glistened in the torch light. The strains of a string quartet came from the inside. A massive number of candles attempted to light the room. The smell of candle wax was almost overwhelming. Couples were dancing to the minuet. Frontiersmen were waiting for the country or line dancing to begin.

Thomas was struck by the beauty of the ladies of the Cape Fear region. They seemed to have adopted many of the French fashions. The skirts were hooped with low bodices which gave hints of ample bosoms. Since many of the men had traveled from the far southern reaches of the colony, they were without wives. They looked jealously at their colleagues who were accompanied by such beauty. Some of the backcountry men looked in awe, for they had never seen any creatures so inspiring. Their own women back home usually dressed in drab linsey woolsey and were frequently barefoot in summer.

Both Tom and Sam were drawn to an attractive woman with a stunning green gown, complementing her eyes, an eye-catching diamond necklace, and French earrings – all of which accented her fabulous form. A well coiffured powdered wig and a beauty spot in the manner of the French completed her aura.

"Who is that woman?" exclaimed an excited and fascinated Thomas.

Polk answered, "That, my friend, is the famous Flora McDonald. She fought diligently against the King's forces during the Battle of Culloden in 1746. She masterminded the hiding and escape of Bonnie Prince Charlie when he tried to usurp the throne. She became a heroine for Highland Scots, was declared an outlaw, and was later arrested and imprisoned in the Tower of London. Scots lavished gifts on her. She took the oath of loyalty and was released. Later she married Alan MacDonald and came to America. Here she affirms her loyalty to the Crown and the Church of Scotland and still is revered by her people."

"What an unusual lady."

"Would you like to meet her?"

"Delighted."

They walked over and Polk introduced Lady MacDonald. Tom marveled at the beauty of a woman who was perhaps ten years his senior.

After introductions, Flora remarked, "It is a pleasure to meet you, Captain Neel. I am told of your contributions to the Crown during the battles with the Indians. I have forgiven the horrid English and accepted their horrible oath. However, I now feel like a new person in the colonies."

"I hope you will enjoy it here." replied Thomas.

"I am sure I shall. I would like to journey to the southwest sometime."

"It would be our pleasure to offer our hospitality," mumbled the awestruck Thomas.

"We would both be competing for the opportunity to entertain," suggested Polk.

"Please excuse me, the Governor is beckoning me." With that Flora fluttered her fan and flowed across the room in such a manner as to gather everyone's smile and gaze. After her trials, several children, and approaching fifty years of living, she could still charm a crowd.

A reception line formed. As Thomas and Polk approached the line they were announced as the new assemblymen of Mecklenburg County. The Secretary of State, Treasurer, Speaker of the Assembly, and the Council greeted them with their ladies. The line ended with Lieutenant Governor Tryon, Governor Arthur Dobbs, their wives and, of course, Flora and her Captain Alan MacDonald. The Governor greeted Thomas and Polk and turned to the new Lieutenant Governor.

"I say, Tryon, it gives me great pleasure to present to you Captains Thomas Neel and Thomas Polk of the Neel's Regiment who were responsible for clearing out the Cherokee menace during the late encounter with the French."

"Welcome, my Lord," answered Thomas Neel. "His Lordship is most generous in his praise. I felt we were merely defending our homes."

Polk interjected, "Yes, with both our lives and treasure. Your Grace, it is a privilege to have served for the King and North Carolina."

Tryon responded, "It is a genuine pleasure to meet you. One of His Majesty's superior court magistrates told me of the generous hospitality of the Waxhaus. During my recent survey of the state, I missed your estate but was able to spend one night with your Brother Henry on my way to Salisbury. He has done the King an honor the way he has developed the area."

"It would be an honor to have you sample our humble fare on the other side of the Catawbas, Sire."

The Governor added, "I have asked Lieutenant Governor Tryon to look into some of the disturbances on the frontier from a group called the Regulators."

Thomas replied, "It is wise that his Lordship look into this. Our neighbors to the south have had even more trouble. I understand an Anglican clergyman has complained about the lack of King's Law in South Carolina. A Regulators group has formed there to protect themselves against thievery and to provide civil defense."

Tryon replied, "You are referring to the appeal of Reverend Charles Woodmason. I have seen his report. We may use his findings to help our people."

"I am afraid the good Reverend did not take too kindly to us Presbyterians," retorted Polk.

Tryon responded, "If the Crown wanted all of you to be Anglicans, they would have sent more clergy. We admire what the Presbyterian villages have done in the defense of His Majesty's frontier. The King has spent much treasure in defending your borders."

Tom Polk replied sternly, "When your Lordship has been here longer you may find that we also lost a lot of treasure in burned homes, crops, and scalped families. If the Crown had placed a better governor in South Carolina, there would have been no Cherokee War."

Tryon retorted, "I will ignore your impudence, Sir, because of your service to the King. However, I must caution you to use restraint."

"Your Grace is most generous." They left the line after receiving the hand and smile of Lady MacDonald. Thomas and Polk returned to the punch bowl.

"Well," remarked Thomas, "You certainly did make an impression on the new Lieutenant Governor. I hope he doesn't hang you for treason."

"He might as well know how we feel." Polk added, "A measure of caution is in order."

The North Carolina Assembly convened the next morning. After all the delegates had been certified, the lawmakers debated the lack of representation in the new counties. The old Cape Fear, Wilmington, and Edmonton crowd prevailed because they had the ear of the Governor and Council. The Assembly asked the Governor to look into the dangers to the colony from the attacks of the renegade Indians under Chief Pontiac and to determine if the borders were secure. The final act was to send a memorial to the Council asking for a letter of concern from the Council and Governor over the taxes being imposed by Parliament to pay for the late war.

After a budget was approved and a yearly memorial voted for the Governor, a message was received calling for the Assembly to send delegates to Philadelphia to discuss the threatened acts of Parliament. Just as the Assembly was about to act, Governor Dobbs prorogued the Assembly. Some assemblymen were angered, some were confused, and some were relieved. The latter group was glad to avoid a conflict.

With no further business, Thomas sold his horses and he, Samuel, and Polk took passage to Charles Town and then home. While in Charles Town, Thomas discussed some purchases with his factor, checked his accounts, and then joined Tom Polk and his wagon for home.

Thomas was happy to be home. His acreage had increased to 3,000 as a result of his service in the war with the Cherokees and French. Most of this was from the land ceded by the Cherokees. His cash crops consisted of cattle driven to market in Charles Town, tar for ship stores, an occasional ship mast on order, some corn, and molasses. A small acreage of tobacco was also attempted. His sawmill supplied his needs and those of neighbors. The family grew and now consisted of the twins Andrew and Thomas, John, Sarah, Jean, Elizabeth, and Mary. The orphan, James Hawthorne, continued to grow as part of the family.

Alexander and Rachel, too old for any other children, became the alternative parents of the orphan James Hawthorne. He spent much time there as well as with the children of Running Path of the Catawbas. His hatred of the Cherokees continued to grow. Thomas constantly admonished him to forgive the Cherokees because there were good men such as Little Carpenter who were anxious for peace.

Thomas had been home about a month when Zeke rode in. He had received Tom's letter sent from Colson's Ferry and had turned north to search for Squawman Johnson. The old trader learned that Johnson and McGhee had fled to Kentucky or perhaps Virginia. As the trail grew cold and there was a need to begin clearing the land, Zeke had returned home.

Thomas received acceptance from the Philadelphia Presbytery of the Bethel Church in 1764 and was ordained as an elder. He also became active—as did his brother Henry—in the affairs of both colonies. He hunted, discussed the affairs of state at Charlotte Town, continued to clear his land, and generally kept the prosperity of that end of the colony going.

When Zeke returned from Ninety-Six to the south he brought news of a great disturbance among the South Carolinians. He related more information on the South Carolina Regulators. Some of the backcountry settlers, led by Reverend Woodmason, had petitioned Governor Montague for the protection of laws against the horse thieves who roamed the area. The Governor commissioned a man named Scouil to investigate the matter. In a short time Scouill became so dictatorial that a group withdrew to govern themselves. They called themselves Regulators. They regulated the area by summary judgments upon those accused of crimes. Scouill arrested two regulators who had been engaged in whipping two horse thieves and had them sent to Charles Town for trial.

Those who favored the King's justice rallied behind Scouill. Those who supported 'regulation' rallied, also. Soon there were two confrontations. At length the two factions were ready to fire on one another. The odium of a civil war became an anathema to both sides. Flags were exchanged and fighting, for a time, avoided. A petition was sent to the Governor and circuit courts established, augmenting justices of the peace. Formerly the superior court judges resided in Charles Town, making a two hundred mile trip for trial. Courts were established in Cambridge, Orangeburgh, and Camden, which brought thirty-two horse thieves to trial in two years.

The 1765 session of the North Carolina Assembly began in May after the crops were planted. Thomas and Polk sailed from Charles Town to New Bern rather than taking the overland trip. The premier issue at the Assembly would be the Stamp Act.

On the first day of the Assembly, Speaker John Henry addressed the gathering. On this day, the then new Governor Elect Tryon was presiding as honorary chairman.

Thomas arose. "Your Excellency. I rise to a point of privilege."

"The chair recognizes the Assemblyman from Mecklenburg."

"I propose a moment of silence and memorial to the memory of our gallant, but departed, Governor Sir Arthur Dobbs and then a pledge of fidelity to you, Sire, and a wish for your continued gaining of health."

"Thank you, Master Thomas. Is there a second?" Polk seconded the motion and then it passed.

"Thank goodness," responded the Governor laughing, "I would have been concerned had you voted against my health."

Thomas spoke in low tones to Polk. "I like his sense of humor. He will be a good Governor."

The new Acting Governor William Tryon was born in 1729 at Nubury Park, Surrey. He later served with the First Regiment of Foot guards, his father having bought a commission. He arrived in North Carolina in 1764 as a lieutenant governor. With the passing of Governor Dobbs he became governor in April 1765, his oath being administered before the Council.

After the preliminary business was conducted, time came for the Governor's address. He stood on a small dais. In front of him was the Council or upper House, which served at the will of the Governor and Crown. Seated at desks in the Assembly chamber were the county elected freeholders. The Governor arose.

"By the authority of His Gracious Majesty and the Almighty God, Amen. I want to thank you worthy gentlemen of the Assembly for the kindness shown me during my recent acclimation to the climate of the colony and my ascension to this noble seat. I am looking forward to a period of happiness and prosperity for the King's colony. First, I lay before you the need for more justices. There is apparently extreme unrest among our countrymen on the borders of our state. They must travel too far for justice. I propose more circuit justices and a commission to look into their grievances. We also must have better surveys of the lands ceded by the Indian tribes. This means we must have a better collection of His Majesty's taxes. We need to look at the formation of new counties so that justice will be swift and fair to all who are grieved in the farther areas. We also need a permanent residence for the Governor as well as a fitting place for the Council and Assembly. We need to continue to train the militia in case the conspiracy of the heathen Chief Pontiac would spread to our borders. Finally, there needs to be a final definition of the border between North Carolina and its sister. I implore you to assist the Council in improving the felicity and safety of our province."

The group arose respectfully as the Council and Governor left the Assembly, John Henry having been elected speaker.

Daniel Murdock of Wilmington stood. "Mr. Speaker, I call your attention to a concern just recognized this morning with the arrival of a packet from England. It seems that Parliament has passed and King George approved an act called the Stamp Act which will require every document, almanac, periodical, pamphlet, and even playing cards to be stamped. The Tax Act specifies that we must pay in silver. The transfer of such specie to England will seriously hamper the business of the colony. We have not been consulted on this tax which is allegedly to help pay for the defense of our borders from the French and perhaps an Indian uprising. What need do we have for English troops? They have already withdrawn most of their forces and will use the troops to keep some of our newer settlers out of lands we fought hard to save from the French. Besides, every time the militia fought using English officers, we lost. I would like to go on record as resisting this tax and call on the Governor to forward a letter to the King to the effect that this is an imposition of a tax which is inimical to the rights of Englishmen. The use of Admiralty courts to enforce the Act without trial by jury interferes with our rights as Englishmen."

"Here, here," responded the Assembly enthusiastically.

"Mr. Speaker," responded Tom Polk, standing. He was recognized.

"We of the interior have not the rancor for such a program as you do. We live happily with the Indians now and are quite content with the trade in ship stores, a little tobacco, and cattle. We seldom would need the stamps. However, I would like to express support for Mr. Murdock's concerns."

Daniel Murdock converted his comments to a motion. A memorial was sent to the Governor and Council imploring them to write a letter of protest against the Stamp Act expressing the Assembly's concern over its anticipated hardships.

"Mr. Speaker," Dan Murdock continued.

"The chair recognizes Mr. Murdock."

"I understand that the Secretary of State has received a circular letter from the colony of Massachusetts requesting an inter-colonial congress to coordinate colonial opposition to the Stamp Act. I therefore move that this Assembly respond to the proposal."

Murmurs of shock swept the house. The Chairman gaveled to order. He asked for a second to Murdock's motion. Just as the vote was about to be taken, the Sergeant of Arms appeared and read a notice from the Governor announcing that the Assembly was now prorogated and dismissed. An uproar erupted. Assemblymen rose from their chairs and jeered the Sergeant of Arms. Speaker John Henry gaveled loudly.

Daniel Murdock rose to his feet, "Mr. Speaker, Mr. Speaker!"

The chair recognizes the representative from Wilmington.

"Mr. Speaker, we have been deprived the rights of Englishmen to express ourselves. I for one can no longer be a part of this farce. I am walking out. We cannot allow ourselves to be the only colony not to participate in the conference concerning the Stamp Act."

Murdock was among the first ten to leave the room followed by others.

Tom Polk turned to Thomas Neel and remarked, "I don't think we have a dog in this fight."

John Henry banged is gavel and announced, "This Assembly is adjourned until such time as the Governor calls us. I urge all members to use restraint in this time of crisis."

Thus, North Carolina became one of the four colonies which did not take part in the Stamp Act Congress. The colony of North Carolina experienced its first major internal split. The Crown faction supported the Stamp Act, the merchants and lawyers who would pay the stamps opposed the act, and the areas such as the western counties did not care. The three factions engaged in small conclaves of debate before departing for home.

Before the Stamp debate the Assembly had been able to pass the Establishment and Vestry Acts, making Anglicanism the official religion of the colonies. The Act also set the Governor's salary and gave the Governor power over the appointment of clergy. The bill passed, however, by only a bare majority. Members of the upcountry districts rebelled in horror at the thought of the possibility of having Crown control over their Presbyterianism.

On the ship home, Thomas, Polk, and Polk's manservant had four days at sea to discuss the events. The first day they were invited to the Captain's mess. The party consisted of Polk, Thomas, the Captain, Henry Laurens, and Josiah Brewton. The latter two were assemblymen of South Carolina.

It was a superb dinner of pot roast, turnips, carrots, and plum pudding with a claret wine. Josiah Brewton remarked, "I was much impressed with the new Governor; however, I believe those older counties are going to have to give up broader suffrage to the newer provinces."

Thomas replied, "Yes, and we must give more attention to the governmental needs of the frontier. With all those people coming down the Wagon Road and settling the back country, we can't seem to keep up with their needs."

Josiah continued, "Yes, and let's not forget all these Highland Scots coming in after the defeat at Culloden. They are settling near us in what little land is left around Charles Town, as well around the Cross Creek area."

"I have talked to some of them as well as some of the Moravians and Swedes. None of them seemed to be concerned about what is happening with the restrictions the Crown places on us," said Thomas.

"Quite," added Polk. "They tell me that they just want to be left alone. They have never had land before and are allowed to worship as they please through benign neglect of the Crown. What think you about a boycott to bring the Parliament to reason?"

Josiah responded, "Most of our markets are the Barbados for our rice and England for our indigo. A boycott would ruin us because we could not sell our produce. How goes it with you people west?"

Polk continued, "Most of our farms are self-sufficient and we can live with or without a boycott. However, our means of advancement and cash are tied up with ship stores and cattle. The British could not support their navy without our ship stores and you need our cattle."

Thomas added, "Let us hope this can be settled by reason with good feeling for all. I propose a toast to the King."

Over a dinner of stew and beer the next day, Thomas initiated a discussion. "Those people who live on the coast, but specifically those who live in Wilmington, are agitated about the Revenue Acts which do not specifically affect us. But the passing of that Vestry Bill does cause me concern. My family has consistently fled the horrors of bishopric rule and here we have Anglicanism thrust upon us. I did not hear our South Carolina neighbors mention the religion question."

Polk responded, "It is a clear case of the coastal kings having control. They will not allow us full representation from our counties and they will vote the way they please. Here we stand on the frontier protecting their arsses from the heathen while they sit fat and happy making profits cheating our Indians and us with high prices. With all the new people coming in from the Wagon Road, we soon will have a majority anyway. How much blood did those silk stocking dandies spill in the Indian Wars?"

"You make a good point, my friend. They are railing against taxation without representation and at the same time passing taxes on us without our full representation. Which is worse, tyrants who are in the colony or tyrants across the sea?" asked Henry Laurens.

"On that issue, you notice that many of us in the west did not consider tweaking the mother country's nose a good idea. I for one would hate to lose my ship stores business if we were to irritate the King," concluded Thomas Neel.

They arrived at the docks on the Ashley River. Polk, having written a letter some weeks before predicting the date of their arrival, was met with a carriage and wagon from his plantation brought by a servant and one of his sons. Both called upon their factors and loaded the wagon with supplies previously ordered from England and Boston.

The travelers then proceeded up the Royal road past the rice and indigo plantations of the coastal plain. Polk spoke, "These coastal people certainly live differently than we do. Their houses are finer, usually of brick, and they look down on we backcountry folk as bumpkins while their women dress like French whores and never do a day's work. I even heard that they hire servants to wet nurse their babies. Also, wives refuse favors to their husbands and the amorous men then spill their seed with the servants. That is why there are so many mulattos here. Then the light chocolate wenches of such union breed again and again with white masters until in three generations they pass for white."

Thomas asked, "Does passing for white mean that much? If they contribute to the common cause and obey the laws why should we care? With the shortage of clergy and magistrates in the backcountry, bastardry is a way of life. Most of the marriages are common law."

"Aye, you have a point. I can see the day when neither race, status, nor property will be used to determine who will participate in government."

## Chapter 17

# Unrest Continues

The joyous return home was met with many chores. The Neel plantations prospered with the ship shores of tar, pitch, and hemp. With the accumulation of land, the common husbandry was first to clear the land of forests through girding, burning, and chopping down. The first crop was Indian corn. During the first years, the corn yield approached one hundred bushels per acre. When the yields declined, peas and beans were planted for one year and yielded thirty to forty bushels per acre. Afterward wheat was grown until the land would no longer support it. For the final or "old field" stage of husbandry, fields were turned over to livestock. The final fate of the land was a recovery to forest products. Since field crop literally destroyed the land after a few years, the Neel family did not assign many fields to crop during this period of land recovery. This cycle of planting and abandoning was called slash and burn agriculture. Lands were cleared by burning and girdling since a man could barely clear one acre a year by axe.

It was at this time that Jean's home was completed, a close copy of her sister-in-law's home in the Waxhaw. It was a two-story home in what later would be known as the Federal style, consisting of a center hall with two primary rooms on each floor. Two smaller rooms were off the hallway in the lean-to section attached across the rear of the house.

Using imported materials and furnishings from England as well as home-dressed woods, the rooms were furnished with a combination of molded and reeded wood work. A striking fireplace with a sophisticated mantle dominated the dining room. The recessed panels were partially covered in wainscot. The ceiling and floor were finished in hand planed tongue and grooved boards. Large flat stone slabs adorned the front of all fireplaces. These were believed to trap and hold heat. The formal parlor gradually accumulated imported chairs, lounges, and tables from England.

Thomas and Polk reported the events of the Assembly to Waxhaus and Bethel Churches. At the conclusion of the Bethel service, Thomas was discussing matters with his brother Henry when he was approached by a rather demanding Christian Huck.

"I say there, C-A-P-T-A-I-N Neel." He drew out the word "captain" in a rather guileful manner. "What has your Assembly done to thwart the design of those artless northern rebels?"

"It is good to see you are in good health and voice, Master Huck. I am not sure of your meaning."

"I refer to the trouble I read about in the *Charles Town Gazette*, specifically, those scalawags, James Otis and the infidel Rousseau are fomenting republican ideas. Their drivel represents attacks on the King."

"Well, as you probably heard, the lieutenant governor will soon receive his commission to assume the office of the departed Governor Dobbs. William Tryon seems very reasonable. Our Assembly chose not to send a delegate to the Congress in New York called by Massachusetts and Virginia to protest the Stamp Act. As you may have heard, Otis railed against the acts of Parliament."

"That is interesting. I heard that the Governor prorogated the Assembly before you could decide. I believe His Majesty has a right to tax us for defense of the frontier. The Stamp Act is very efficient. Had I been elected, we would not have had any of this nonsense."

"Had you been elected, I would hope you could have persuaded those coastal dandies to allow us to have the same representation as they have. On another matter, my friend, I want to thank you for girdling the trees on the property next to mine."

"I have not engaged your property, Sir."

"My twin sons Andrew and Thomas, while surveying our land, found your servants girdling the trees. They inquired of the workmen, who said they were under your employ. By the way, my brother, Sheriff Henry Neel, had to call out a portion of our militia when some people on Sugar Creek occupied some of the land without plating the same. Some of them were on your land. When Sheriff Henry Neel tried to remove people from both properties, they rebuked him sorely. It was necessary to call a small portion of our militia to quell them. We have made an agreement with them to pay our quitrents. We made no such agreement with the occupiers of the land you claim."

"That is preposterous. How dare they occupy my land."

"May I suggest that we set up a joint meeting and survey the land together? I have plenty of land but do wish to set the boundaries. By the way, the squatters are not paying His Majesty's tax either."

"Very well, I shall send my man next week to work with you."

"I am obliged, Sir."

Thomas (1730), brother Henry (1736), and a newly appointed Christian Huck as justices continued to adjudicate disputes over land. Huck had been added among the new justices approved by the governor and assembly. Many people coming down the "Wagon Road" squatted on lands without regard to the ownership.

There seemed to be a general peace among the Indians because of the land that had been ceded after the late war. Governor Tryon organized the colony into five judicial districts; Mecklenburg became part of the Salisbury district. Master Huck as well as Thomas were both judges in the district and served together on occasion. Each district reported to one of the justices of the State Supreme Court. Anson and Rowan were also the original counties of the Salisbury district. One of the Supreme justices appeared two times a year in each province to hear appeals and transact business for the Crown. Below the Pee Dee River, many of the Highland Scots, survivors of the 1746 uprising, took advantage of the King's peace, swore an oath of allegiance, and received free land of the Crown.

In the winter of 1765, the Thomas Neel compound was greeted by a small guard and Justice James Matthews of the Supreme Court of North Carolina. His lordship rode a fine large stallion. He was dressed in the uniform of a Colonel in the North Carolina Militia.

Thomas, dressed in his best, and Jean in her new gown recently sent from Charles Town, greeted the entourage. The excited family, twins Andrew and Thomas, John, Sarah, Mary, Elizabeth, Jean, and orphan James Hawthorne, stood in awe.

Justice Matthews was shown to one of the bedrooms upstairs and his escort bivouacked in the field and barn. Jean and her staff prepared a fine dinner which included a claret wine, wild boar, wild turkey, venison, and turnips. Coffee, cider, and apple pie finished the meal. Henry from Providence and Sheriff Uncle Henry and their families joined the feast. The children, fed first, were put to bed, except for the twins who were now fifteen. A stew and beer had been prepared for the escort.

After dinner with the soft glow of candles and the sparkling warmth of the fireplace, the women were excused. The men drew their pipes, poured another wine, and Thomas spoke, "Sir James, what news do you bring?"

"First, let me thank you for your hospitality. The pleasures of this meal are enough of a reward for the trip. However, I bring some distressing news. About a month ago a body of men marched down the avenue at Wilmington and halted about three hundred yards from the Governor's mansion. A representative of the Assembly who was the head of the delegation sent a message that they wished to speak with Mr. Pennington, the King's appointed solicitor for the Stamp Act. Governor Tryon replied that Mr. Pennington was a crown officer and that he would receive all protection needed him. Mr. Harnett replied that he should be released or they would enter by force. The issue was resolved when Mr. Pennington resigned his commission by writ and in front of Mr. Harnett. The writ contained an oath that he would never issue stamped paper in the province. Needless to say the writ did not contain the accursed stamp. This same oath has been required by His Lordship the Governor, and of all county clerks and other public offices. I have brought you your documents."

Thomas asked, "This is a different approach than those of the brethren of the north. I hope this will bring peace to the colony. We here would not have been affected much by the stamps because most of our transfers are accounting transfers."

Brother Henry interrupted, "Yes, and those dandies in the Council and the Assembly do not allow us to have the appropriate amount of representation. We are not getting money for fords and bridges, while a portion of our quitrents go to coastal dandies."

The jurist replied, "That brings up another concern. We are not getting the King's taxes from some of the over the mountain and backcountry areas. How goes it in this county?"

Uncle Henry, the Sheriff replied, "Most of our people do not have any wealth to tax. The yeomen live on subsistence farms and have no produce to sell. What commerce they do have is by barter, exchange of services, or theft. There is no specie and now that the Crown has not allowed the colony to print its own money, things are even worse. There is also a great deal of concern for the Governor's plan for a palace at New Bern. The people think that is too far away from the over the hill Country and our area. What would seem to be a better place would be Charlotte Town or Hillsboro—some place not so far away."

Matthews replied, "I suppose His Lordship is concerned where most of the population dwells and the need to promote commerce. Most capitols, if not all, are by the sea. Besides, for a good deal of the population the river systems are the most convenient means of travel and communication. However, there is a great deal of concern about these groups called the Regulators. It seems a group headed by a man named Husband claims that the justices and sheriff up in the western counties are corrupt and that it has been necessary for the community to take matters of law in their own hands. This is particularly true because of the large numbers of people pouring down from Pennsylvania and Virginia over the old Trading Path. It is now so well traveled that wagons can use it. The mule trains of Master Zeke will soon be rare. They are now living under so called 'Corn Law.' By this means local committees control the commerce and taxes of the contested area. For enforcement there have been beatings and featherings without the benefit of trial.

On another matter, have you heard that this Seiver and Boone are making sorties into the Tennessee and Kentucky areas? This would be a violation of the 1763 edict on settlement beyond the Appalachians."

Jean entered the room. The gentlemen rose. All eyes were fixed on her French styled green gown. She interrupted, "You gentlemen have talked too long. It is time you retired for the night. Brother Henry and Uncle Henry, you may have Andrew's room. Your Lordship, we will show you the guest room. Breakfast will be at first light because of your need to go to Charlotte Town for the court day."

Judge Matthews spoke, "Ah! What a great feast it was, Madam. It is unfortunate that I was deprived of your company and charm. Instead I was ground down by the growlings of these wretched male creatures."

"Thank you, Sir. You are most kind. We women have been put on earth to tame you animals." She winked at the magistrate winsomely.

Henry remarked, "Jean, you have a great deal of work left to do with my brother Thomas." Laughter broke out at the comment.

Next morning the men all headed to Charlotte for the court date. The journey took half a day. During this time Thomas, Henry, and Lord Matthews discussed the events of the day in a rather light and non-confrontational manner. Thomas and Henry recalled the Cherokee campaign and the ineptness of the South Carolina government in the conduct of the Cherokee wars.

They arrived at the village and there met the other three justices of the district including Christian Huck, newly appointed as justice of the peace for the district around Charlotte. That afternoon the five judges heard pleas concerning the need for roads and ferries, the protesting of taxes, and the lack of specie. Finally, the justices discussed the needs for the next quarter session. The sheriffs were instructed to carry out the collection of Crown taxes in kind as well as specie. Christian objected to this flagrant denial of the King's ordinances, demanding taxes in specie, but no one responded. The court and county business concluded, the men retired to the town tavern. Henry, Thomas, Uncle Henry, and Justice Matthews were seated and sharing a spot of rum punch. Christian Huck came in and was asked to join.

"I say there, Your Lordship," queried Huck, "how goes things in New Bern? Has this Massachusetts rebel Otis had any effect on the common people?"

"Our good acting governor, Tryon, met with some of the leading merchants and tried to overcome the resistance to the Stamp Act. He offered to pay from his treasury the duty on tavern licenses and many of the legal documents required by the Act. The burghers refused his offer. Shortly after, three or four hundred 'Sons of Liberty' forced the Stamp Master, William Houston, to the courthouse in Wilmington and compelled him to sign his own resignation. But I bring you good news. There is a great deal of sympathy in Parliament for the abolition of the Stamp Act. It has not been successful and has driven a wedge between the mother country and the middle North American colonies. William Pitt, the Whig leader in Parliament, has pointed out that both the new provinces taken from the French, such as Canada and the Spice Islands, all receive better treatment than we do. This motto, 'taxation without representation' has grown to a serious concern among the people of our English colonies."

Huck responded, "I don't know why His Majesty does not send some troops down here to discipline this rebel lot. If they are not under control soon they will turn this continent into a democracy with all its rabble running around without proper gentlemen to guide them in their best interests. If people think there are tyrants overseas, wait until they see the tyrants we have in a democracy."

"Ah," commented Thomas, "We have a disciple of Plato here. If we have an aristocracy to guard us, who will guard the guardians? Some day the people will be heard. The frontier here in Carolina may well be the model of what the continent will become—yeoman governing themselves."

A grimacing Huck replied, "Then who will protect my family from this mob?"

"Our militia, composed mostly of yeomen, did a remarkable job against the Indians and French in the last unpleasantness. Perhaps they can be of service to you. By the way, as a justice I understand you are required to organize the militia in your area. If you need any assistance, you may call on us."

"I am quite well equipped for the task. I have some very capable lieutenants who manage quite well. Besides, my presence at the Battle of Culloden is well documented."

Henry asked with a smile, "Did not your Highland Scots lose and were forced to take an oath to the King?"

"Sir, I resent the tone of your remark. We surrendered in order to save our families, not only from the English but in order to overcome the possibility of the lowland tribes raiding our villages. In addition, we took an oath to serve the King should he be threatened. The King gave us land here around New Bern, but I preferred the Providence area for its beauty and neighbors."

Henry, sensing he went too far replied, "I meant no offense, Sir, I apologize." To himself he thought, "I shall see how good he is the next time his militia is called. If he outranks the Neel Rangers we are in for a might bit of trouble."

CHAPTER 18

# Troubles of Tryon

On June 25, 1765, Governor Tryon received his royal commission a few months after the death of the ailing Governor Dobbs. As his first act he issued a proclamation in response to a notice from London declaring the Stamp Act repealed. The good Governor decided that now, during this era of good feeling, was the time to stop moving the capitol at each call of the Assembly. He felt that the northwest Edmonton location where the Granville party wanted it might be too close to Virginia. The powerful Granville area, mostly English, felt the capitol of the old Albemarle grant should be chosen. Tryon felt that a central location such as Camden or Hillsboro would have some value. The majority of the population lived in the Cape Fear region, and he did not want his government too far from a port and the sea. James Davis, the public printer and editor of the colony's first newspaper, the *North Carolina Gazette*, wrote:

> Can you see the PUBLIC RECORDS carted from Place to Place, and your
> Properties and Estates trusted to the mercy of a Shower of Rain., and at the
> Discretion of a Cart Driver? Forbid it Heaven!

Thus began the fight for the first permanent government site. The Assembly appropriated 5,000 pounds for the construction to be followed by more funds later. By 1767 the central portion of the "palace" had been completed. The cost grew to 25,000 pounds. The frontier people thought the location too far from the populous counties of Orange, Rowan, Mecklenburg, and Anson. The palace was completed in 1770 as one of the handsomest government facilities in America.

1767. Both the Neel scions, Thomas and Henry, were visiting after Sunday service at Bethel. It was a nice spring day and their families spread a picnic lunch under one of the hickory trees that was just beginning to bud. The younger generation, Andrew and James, were visiting with the young ladies of the congregation. Jean turned to her husband, "It seems our children are getting along rather well with some of the ladies."

"Yes, Andy my brother seems to be interested in your distant cousin Laureena-Smith and James has been trying to attract one of the Polk girls. I hope the boys don't have to race like I had to do to win the most beautiful woman of the Waxhaw."

"Well, I don't know where the girls could get an adequate horse. The blood lines of Champion and Victory have brought forth a strain of horses for which some young maiden could not compete."

Nancy Agnes, Henry's spouse, remarked, "That Laureena is a charming young lady. She has a healthy countenance and a fine form. I hear she comes from near that crude Ninety-Six and yet she has the grace and manners of a lady. I heard she was educated in Charles Town. Notice how smitten Andrew is."

At length Andrew, the younger brother of squires Henry and Thomas, did marry his distant cousin Laureena Smith. The Smith plantation adjoined Andy's property.

Zeke searched the northern counties for Squawman Johnson and Artimas McGhee. He returned in 1767 with the news that the counties of Orange, Granville, Halifax and Anson were upset over the banditry and lack of honest government. The constant theft of horses seemed to fit the pattern of the murderers of father Squire Thomas Neel. Zeke brought with him a tract which had been printed by a Herman Husband in Nutbush, Granville County, June 6, 1765. Henry read while Uncle Henry and the family of Providence listened.

> We the subscribers do voluntarily agree to form ourselves in an Association, to assemble ourselves for Conference for Regulating publick Grievance and abuses of Power in the following Particular, with others of the like Nature that may occur.
>
> 1$^{st}$, That we will pay no more Taxes until we are satisfied they are agreeable to Law and applied to the Purposes therein mentioned; unless we cannot help it, or are forced.
>
> 2nd, That we will pay no Officer any more Fees than the Law allows, unless we are obliged to it, and to shew our Dislike and bear an open Testimony against it.
>
> 3rd, That we will attend our Meeting of Conference as often as we conveniently can, and is necessary in order to consult our Representative on the Amendment of such Laws as may be found grievous or unnecessary; and to choose more suitable Men than we have done heretofore for Burgesses and Vestry-men; and to petition the Houses of the Assembly, Governor, Council, King, Parliament &c. for Redress in such Grievance as in the Course of the Undertaking may occur; and to inform one another, learn, know and enjoy all the privileges and Liberties that are allowed and were settled on us by our worthy Ancestors, the Founders of our present Constitution, in Order to preserve it on its ancient Foundation, that we may stand firm and unshaken.
>
> 4th. That we will Contribute to Collection for defraying necessary Expenses attending the work according to our Abilities.

5th. That in the case of Difference in Judgment, we will Submit to the Judgment of the majority of our body. 1

Uncle Henry, the Sheriff, observed, "That sounds like a 'Corn Law' to me. You know that Granville District has always been a problem. When the Royal Colony was formed in 1729, Lord Granville did not sell his property to the Crown. Those colonies formed from the district have been ruled by some of the so-called aristocracy which has not concerned themselves with the yeomen. I have heard that the sheriffs have set up places for the collection of taxes and required people to appear there. If they do not, property is confiscated. They require specie but most people are engaged in trade. The officers are charging more than the Crown's prescribed fees for service. Horses and other property are stolen but when a complaint is brought before the court there is little action. When there, the accused is found not guilty. However, if some individual is not able to pay his taxes, he is placed in the county work crew until his taxes are made. In the meantime, he cannot attend his farm and finally may have to sell it, usually to one of the sheriff's friends at great loss."

"Yes," continued young Henry, "Governor Dobbs thought he had ameliorated the problems of the area when he established taxes and fees for court cases and had the Crown appoint the sheriffs and clerks; however, since that time these officers have instituted cruel abuses for their own gain."

***

In 1767, other events occurred for the Neels of the Waxhaw. A new Cherokee reservation line was run. The tribe agreed to cede more land in exchange for some trade goods because the lands were pretty much "hunted out." Not all of the Cherokees were happy with the ceding of these southern portions of their lands. A small band of young warriors from the northern towns of the Hilawsee descended upon two settlers' cabins, burning them out and capturing their cattle. The families fled to Charlotte. Captain Thomas Neel, joined by Lieutenant Huck and five rangers, proceeded through the Catawba reservation to the newly ceded Cherokee lands. There they found the burned cabins of the displaced settlers.

Huck commented, "I say, these savages were thorough. Look at the destruction."

Polk remarked, "Not too thorough. They took no scalps this time. I don't understand what they were doing here."

They camped that night near a stream. Rabbits made the meal. Guards were posted. In the morning, as they were completing their breakfast, the Rangers were alerted at the cry of a jay three times.

"That is Little Carpenter," suggested Thomas. Soon five warriors came into the camp. The aged brave and two companions led five fine unmounted Cherokee horses.

"Is this the son of my brother, Henry Neel?"

"Well, almost Uncle, Sheriff Henry is my uncle."

"I come with a wampum belt of peace. Some of the young braves of the Keowe raided some settlers in your newly bought land. They have been punished by the tribe. The Council has decided to give these five fine horses as a token of our regret for this."

"Thank you, Uncle. Your bravery and concern for peace is well known. Your gift is most generous as the Cherokee horses are renowned for their strength, speed, and beauty, and I will recommend to His Honor Governor Tryon that they be accepted as payment. Youths sometimes have hot blood. I hope none of our young people have disturbed your lodges."

"We met an occasional long hunter, but if they are not interfering too much we make no complaint. We allowed settlers living in our boundary to harvest their crops before moving into the new areas for settlement."

"Come, Uncle, let us smoke a pipe of peace." After a common meal, the giving of the wampum belt of peace, smoking a pipe, and the telling of lore, the Indians departed and the Rangers headed for home.

Huck commented, "I say Neel, that old chief seemed quite friendly. What is his story?" Thomas then related the story of Little Carpenter and the Cherokee War.

Huck replied, "Why didn't you just kill all the savages when you were on the campaign?"

"My dear Master Huck, the blood of innocent women, children, and old men should not stain the standard of the Neel Rangers and the King's name. We had a difficult time keeping some of the militia from taking vengeance for the atrocities committed on their families. After all, the South Carolina Governor's blunders are what started that war. We must learn to live at peace with these people. They were here first and do not realize the benefits of our so-called 'civilization.'"

"I suppose you are right. The Cherokees were able to keep the French from overwhelming us for a while and are a good guard against the Spanish in Florida. I do not understand why we have to give that area back to them."

Upon arriving at the village of Charlotte, the horses were turned over to Justice

Huck for his sale to reimburse the settlers whose land was decimated. The rest of the Rangers, including Thomas, headed for the Waxhaw.

In 1767 the families of the area were treated to a visit from the Governor. A ball was held in his honor in Charlotte. Uncle Henry, Henry, Thomas Christopher and their wives attended the ball. The bachelor twins of Thomas, Thomas and Andrew, also attended. On the way home in the new family carriage, Sarah remarked to Thomas Christopher, "I am much impressed with the new Governor. I don't recall that Governor Dobbs ever visited us."

"Well, he actually did. You see he helped develop the land on the other side of the Catawba where our fathers first settled. Did you know the new Governor has been quite ill adjusting to our climate and one of his young children died of the fever?"

"I heard something about those misfortunes. Anyway, that is quite a trip for a social call."

"Actually he came to survey the new line for the Cherokee territories. Little Carpenter was quite taken with him. I thought his retinue of one hundred was terribly costly. I believe the Rangers could have accomplished the task at a fraction of the cost."

When the party reached home, Thomas found a dispatch calling for a muster of the Rangers. The Governor's purpose was to prevent a rebellion in His Majesty's Provinces of Orange, Anson, Granville, and Halifax Counties.

In the summer of 1768, Henry, Thomas, Polk, and Christian Huck responded, as well as a half dozen other area militia companies. They reported to Orange County. Thomas Christopher was placed in charge of the small company, which consisted of mainly officers and officials of government. Picking up Christian Huck at Charlotte Village, the Rangers followed the road to Salisbury.

Camping one night just below Salisbury, they were greeted by two trail-worn ruffians. A sentry brought two people to Thomas's tent.

"My stars, young Thomas. Can't an old friend get a meal without being treated like some Frenchie Indian?" It was Alexander and one of his companions.

"I will take care of these men, Corporal. They look mean but are quite harmless."

"Harmless! Why I could take on the whole pack while looking backward."

"Now, now Uncle Alexander. Get some food and try to explain to me what an old trail rat is doing here."

Taking a trencher of stew, a spoon, biscuit, and coffee, he began. "This here is Jose. He really don't know what he is. He claims he is part Spanish, Negro, and Choctaw. Anyway he looked lonesome so I thought I would adopt him."

Alexander spit into the fire, broke some wind, and belched.

Thomas retorted, "I hope you haven't taught him any of your high society manners."

"I taught you, didn't I? Anyway, I was coming back to tell you that Zeke thinks he has spotted Artimas and Squawman."

"Where?"

"Up in Hillsboro, Orange County. It seems that some of these settlers are agitating against the sheriffs and justices about the way they collect their taxes and things. A group of people armed to the teeth came up to the sheriff with a piece of paper, something about Nutbush Address. Since I can't read I jus' listened. It seems this dandy named Edmond Fanning holds nearly every office there, including head of the militia and justice."

"I read about this Notbush Address. It protests the abuse of fees for government service, the unfairness of the courts, and unfair sheriffs. But go on."

"Well, a group of these Regulator fellers led by a man named Husband went to His Honor Fanning and asked for a meeting. This here Fanning yells at them and tells them that they are in something called an insurrection and that they did not dare question his authority. About that time, the sheriff seized a Regulator's horse, bridle, and saddle for taxes. The Regulators then rode into Hillsboro, rescued the horse and fired shots into Fanning's house. Man, were they agitated.

"His Honor was not there when the horse was seized but when he returned he called out the damn Orange County militia and ordered the arrest of William Butler, Peter Craven, and Ninian Bell Hamilton, the leaders of the mob. The officers of the militia grew scared and suggested a truce but wrote Fanning that they was bidin' for time. Husband was voted to discuss a truce with the militia. While under a flag of truce, he was arrested and put in jail with William Butler. Husband was scheduled to go to New Bern for safekeeping."

"How did you know all this?"

"Zeke and I talked it over. He knows that we black folks have a good memory, especially when we see the white folks' stupidity."

"Thank you, Uncle, I am always pleased to be in the presence of such greatness."

"You whelp. I could still lick you. Cain I go on?"

Thomas and Henry nodded.

"I was standing by the tavern the next morning and up rode about seven hundred Regulators yelling, cussing, and brandishing pitchforks, muskets, and claymores. They was 'agiiiitaaated.' The county officials counted the weapons and released the prisoners. Just then Fanning rode up and told the leaders that the Governor would receive their petition. Husband gave him the petition."

Henry broke in. "Yes, I understand the Governor said that Fanning exceeded his authority and that is why he has called up the militia. Fanning has been placed under arrest for extortion. Governor Tryon could not trust the Orange militia to raise enough men. That is why he called out the Rangers."

"Well, anyway," continued Alexander, "I noticed that in the back of the mob were our friends Johnson and McGhee. I walked slowly over to find Zeke. But for some reason I kind of stood out in the crowd. The two spurred their horses and ran away. Zeke and I tried to follow them but the trail grew cold."

Alexander and Jose departed the next morning. After two days, the Rangers reached the village of High Point where the militia was bivouacked. Neatly arranged tents defined a rectangle with a broad thoroughfare leading up to a tent with the Union Jack and the Governor's colors flying from two staffs.

Captain Thomas Christopher Neel first reported to the adjutant's tent. He was greeted, duly registered, and asked to report to the Governor's tent. He walked to Governor Tryon's headquarters. The Rangers were dressed in the green uniform of a Dragoon regiment. He was greeted by the Corporal of the Guard and escorted in. Thomas saluted. Governor Tryon, dressed in the uniform of a colonel of the Lancers, rose from his chair behind a small desk. "Ah, Captain Neel, how good to see you again. I understand you have a problem determining whether you are in North Carolina or South Carolina."

"It is a pleasure to serve the King from either colony."

"Thank you. Let's get at our situation here. My predecessor, your friend Governor Dobbs, was drawn to the problems of the western areas of the province. It seems that we have appointed some rather opportunist officers as justices, sheriffs, and clerks. You may have heard, I am sure. It seems these lawless Regulators have gathered a force to help us with our prosecution of some of our accused officers. It will be the duty of the militia to help subdue this mob. We will demonstrate before them tomorrow. Please take your men, find them food and sustenance. We march tomorrow."

At the second hour after daylight to the beat of drums the various militias fell into formation, each carrying its colors. The Neel Rangers, followed by Huck Dragoons, advanced smartly behind the Governor's guard. They proceeded to the top of a hill where they looked down on the camp of about 3,500 farmers summoned by the Regulators.

Seeing the forces, the Regulators agreed to let the trials proceed and went home. At length Husband was acquitted, but Butler and two others were fined and imprisoned. The Governor's friend Fanning was fined one penny and forced to resign his position as registrar.

Thomas and Henry were packing their horses and tightening the girths when Zeke and Alexander approached. "Well, look here, we have the young Neel whelps. I hope you have not allowed yourselves to be beat by them Regulators."

"If we had, it was because we had such poor training from trail rats I have known."

"Listen to that," snapped Alexander. "You'd think they would respect their elders. Anyway, while you was playing soldier we trailed the murderers, Johnson and McGhee, to Boyd's Crossing on the Virginia Border and then lost them. I think they'se now in Virginia. We alerted every sheriff along the way but most of them think we are Regulators and aren't real interested in helping. When we approach a Regulator, they think we is the Governor's spies. Anyway, it was good to meet with our old families in the Shawnee village. They will hold the outlaws if they come their way."

Thomas added, "I really appreciate what you are doing. Why don't you come on home for a while? We probably will be back later. The Regulators are not through."

***

Thomas and Polk rode to the October 1769 session of the Assembly. As they called on taverns along the way, they heard of startling activities of the Regulators. A band of thirty from Edgecombe County attempted to rescue one of theirs from the Halifax jail. Their compatriot had been jailed because he could not raise the specie for his taxes. A group of Anson county patriots succeeded in breaking up the court as the sheriff tried to collect taxes. A group in Rowan County brought charges of extortion and corruption to the grand jury, but the office refused to bring true bills of indictment.

In the summer the Regulators turned to the Assembly in an attempt to obtain justice. Governor Tryon dissolved the Assembly and ordered new elections.

Thomas and Polk arrived at New Bern and took lodging at an inn. After refreshing themselves in the pubic bath they joined the other assemblymen in the Tavern. To no surprise they found Squire Huck holding forth on the need to crush the rebels.

As Tom and Polk entered the dark tavern, one of the Regulators stood up and addressed Polk, "Sir, what would you have us to do? No one listens to our pleas. When we bring forth charges to a grand jury we must travel two hundred miles for a testimony. When we have a jury trial we must do the same. We cannot pay our taxes with the dammed specie and our products cannot be substituted."

"There is nothing but rebellion in your counties. We should call out the militia to crush you."

"Sir, I will not tolerate such insult. I demand satisfaction."

Tom and Polk stormed in and stood between the two forming factions.

"Master Huck, may I present Abner Conner of the King's militia who fought in the Cherokee wars with distinction. I believe if you had known his record of loyalty, your countenance might have been different. Especially since he left his good arm at the battle of Keowee and might be at a small disadvantage in an affair of honor."

"Thank you Captain Neel. I was not aware of the gentleman's service to the King since I am newly arrived in this colony. I sincerely apologize and pray your forgiveness. Please, Sir, may I purchase drinks for the house in your honor?"

"I would be most honored, Sir," replied Abner, extending his left hand.

The next morning, October 23rd, the Assembly met. A petition was put forth by the Regulators outlining their concerns about the behavior of the King's officers and the lack of concern for the conditions of the western counties. Before the issue could be brought forward, several resolutions were drawn up by the rich "Rice Kings" questioning issues between the American Colonies and the British government. The issues were similar in outline to concerns of other colonies which had been fomented by the Committees of Correspondence. The Governor's response was to dissolve the Assembly and call for a new election.

The Assembly quickly convened across the street upon hearing the news that the Regulators had assembled in Cumberland County for the purpose of marching on the Assembly. The Assembly's response was to pass the "Johnson Act." This strengthened the power of the attorney general and declared persons outlaws should they refuse to appear in sixty days after a court notice. Further, those persons so declared could be killed without imputation. The Governor was further authorized to call the militia.

The assemblymen were shocked by the outrage of the Regulators. Superior court judges were too frightened to hold court and told the Governor so. The essence of the condition was that local justice in the affected counties shut down. This was caused by a general call of the Regulators to the counties of Bute, Edgecombe, and Northampton encouraging patriots to join them. The leaders further agreed not to allow the collection of any fees or to allow courts to be held.

All through the spring the tension between the Governor and the Regulators continued to grow. The Governor called for volunteers from the militia, but enlistments were slow until a bounty was offered. Guns, ammunition, swivel cannon, and other equipment were sent from Fort Johnson at Cape Fear for use by the militia.

Even with the new election, the impatient Regulators were not satisfied with the slowness of the deliberative body. They broke into courts of justice, drove justices from the bench, and contemptuously set up mock Corn Law trials. Attorneys who charged more than the prices fixed by the Assembly were dragged through the streets and citizens who did not have the same beliefs as the Regulators were assaulted.

The issue was brought to a head in September, 1770. While Judge Richard Henderson was presiding over a superior court in Hillsboro, a Regulator mob led by Husband, Hunter, Howell, and Butler stormed the court and attempted to assault the judge. William Hooper, an assistant attorney general, was dragged and paraded through the streets. The mob broke into the recently finished Fanning house, burned his papers, destroyed his furniture, and demolished the building.

Because of the Regulators' threats, the Assembly passed a series of laws relating to appointment of sheriffs and their duties, fixing attorney and officer fees, providing for the speedy collection of small debts and creating the counties of Wake, Guilford, Chatham, and Surrey in the region where the Regulators were most numerous.

# CHAPTER 19

# Battle of Alamance

Governor Tryon reviewed his troops at Fort Johnson consisting of 1,068 men and 151 officers. General Waddell approached from Salisbury with 236 troops and forty-eight officers from Anson, Rowan, and Mecklenburg counties, including troops from the newly formed Tryon County.

Captain Thomas Christopher Neel was placed in command of the Mecklenburg and Tryon Militia, composed mostly of the Neel Rangers augmented by forces from Charlotte under Lieutenant Huck. They served under General Waddell. A detachment of eight rangers scouted ahead of the Waddell troops. They moved in the dusk picking their way along the road to the Yadkin River.

Thomas spotted some campfires on the other side of the river. Dismounting he crept to the edge of the bank and heard the raucous laughter of the Regulators. Making a quick estimate he started back to alert the camp of General Waddell. At about dawn, his tired squad was quickened by the sound of shouting around the bend in the road. The Neel Rangers dismounted at his signal. He motioned for the squad to stand ready as he scouted ahead. Checking their pistols, Thomas Christopher and Master Huck crept through the forest. Moving cautiously through the piney and cane groves, they soon spotted men holding four wagons at bay. "Get down off your wagons and you won't get hurt."

A lieutenant had jumped down from the lead wagon and accosted the leader of the group. "I am a lieutenant in His Majesty's militia and consider you under arrest for interfering with the King's business."

A tobacco stained bearded man rode his horse up to the lieutenant and spat on the ground near him.

"I reckon we are in the same business neighbor. I am working for the King's justice which has been a might scarce in these parts. Just tell your men to stand by and we will go about our work. Since you are outgunned and outdrawn, I suggest you move peacefully and you won't get hurt."

The lieutenant turned to his men. "You men get down from the wagons and stand over on the other side of the road. We don't see any need for anyone to get hurt."

Master Huck whispered to Thomas, "That man is Ezekiel Johnson. He is the one who sold me my land."

The renegades pulled the trees on all the wagons save one, slapped the rumps of the horses and watched them run away.

Thomas's face reddened as he bit his lip. "This is one of the men that ambushed us and killed my father," he whispered.

Thomas then considered his situation. His group was a couple of hundred yards back. He was outgunned. They might surprise SquawmanJohnson and his squad, but they would have only two shots. Already the King's troops had put away their weapons. Finally, Neel made his decision. He motioned Huck and retreated back to the rest of the squad.

"Mount up Rangers and check your weapons. This King's militia has been ambushed by a band of outlaws. On my command we are to charge the group with sabers and pistols."

As Thomas spoke, a tremendous explosion rent the air. Flames shot up from around the bend. As the squad galloped toward the spot, they were scattered off the road by three panicked wildly charging teams coming at them. Through the dust Tom shouted, "Reform and proceed." The Rangers cantered at a precision gallup only to be met by a squad of the King's militia running after the teams. Tom signaled the troop to halt. The lieutenant came forward.

"I am Lieutenant Atwater of the New Bern militia, Sir. Can you help us."

"I am Captain Thomas Neel and this is Lieutenant Huck. What has happened and how can we be of service?"

"We were under convoy to deliver supplies of food and gunpowder to General Waddell. We were entangled in an ambuscade and two of our four wagons were destroyed and the remainder stolen."

"Are your men militiamen?"

"No, they are mainly draymen who volunteered themselves, wagons, and horses for the King's service."

"I think our best course would be to pursue the renegades. If you catch one of the horses, have one of your men or yourself report the incident to General Waddell. Good day, Lieutenant."

"Good day to you, Sir."

"Men, we will proceed single file with two men on the point." Turning to his young sons, "Andrew, you and Thomas scout ahead. See if you can find one of those wagons. Forward ho!"

In a few hundred yards they rounded the bend and found the parts of two wagons and two large black holes where wagons had once been. The pace quickened as they followed the tracks of the wagons in the road toward the Waddell camp. Shortly the tracks diverged from the main road toward a barely developed trail in the woods. In about an hour, the twins Thomas and Andrew drew up. "Father, I mean Captain, we found the wagons abandoned about one hundred yards ahead with some of the food stuffs still in it. The other wagon was filled with gun powder. I think the teamsters were aware of our presence and escaped on one of the horses."

Captain Thomas scribbled a message. "Thomas, take this report to General Waddell and inform him of what you have seen. Ask him to bring some men back to pick up these supplies. We are going after Squawman."

Huck protested, "I say, Captain Neel, won't we be outnumbered? Is it not better to have General Waddell send out a party?"

"Lieutenant Huck, you make me realize that this is more of a personal matter with me because of the murder of my father. Andrew and I are going ahead to find this group. Please take charge of the squad and take them back to camp. Mount up, Andrew."

"I wish you godspeed, Sir," replied Huck saluting.

Unknown to Tom and young Andrew, as they chased after Squawman Johnson, General Waddell had broken camp and was headed for the Yadkin. Just as Waddell's command crossed the ford of the Yadkin, they were met by the Regulators. Fire was exchanged, and seeing he was outnumbered, Waddell withdrew and fortified his position on the north bank of the river. The date was May 9.

As Tom and his son Andrew trailed Ezekial Squawman Johnson and his gang, they came upon a clearing where they found two militiamen bound and tied to a tree. As Andrew loosened their bonds the two related that they had been captured and beaten by the leader of the group called the "Black Boys of the Carrubus." Only the appeal of the group kept the leader from killing them.

"What was this leader like?" asked Thomas.

"He was a large man with a large unkempt beard stained with tobacco. He frequently spat near us as he kicked and cursed us."

"What was your mission here?" asked Thomas.

"We are part of the Anson militia, and we know you to be Neel's Rangers. We were attacked as we marched across the Yadkin. The force was superior to ours and General Waddell withdrew. I think mainly because our militia is so poorly trained, he did not feel we would fight. We have dispatches for Lord Tryon in Hillsboro telling him of our predicament."

"Well, hop on behind us and we will see that your mission is completed."

Tom and Andrew, with the Anson troopers riding double, proceeded to Hillsboro. Tom contained his rage that the pursuit of Squawman Johnson had once again been thwarted by duty.

That evening as the two horses and their burdens came into Hillsboro, they were directed to the Governor's camp. There they were challenged by a sentry in the uniform of the Fusiliers. Fusiliers were trained in rapid musket fire and took pride in their skill.

"I am Captain Neel of the Neel Rangers, and I have dispatches for His Lordship the Governor."

Andrew, Thomas and the two Anson militiamen dismounted and proceeded to the tent which flew the Union Jack and the standard of the state militia. On either side of the tent stood a corporal of the guard. Seated at the table was the regimental command. Thomas approached and saluted. "I am Thomas Neel of the Mecklenburg Tryon Neel Rangers with urgent business with the Governor."

"Well, I see the eyes of the old warrior have grown rather weak. Does he not recognize an old companion of the Cherokee campaign?"

"Major, or excuse me, Colonel Anderson. What a pleasant surprise! What brings you into the militia service? I thought you would be the lord of some English estate by now since you were going to marry the Governor's niece."

"You should feel fortunate she chose me over your brother, Henry. I fled England to get away from her and her family. Ah! That is another story. By the way how is he?

"Henry married the lovely Nancy Agnes Reid and lives like a drunken lord on Steele Creek near Charlotte."

"I am pleased he is doing well. What news do you bring?"

"I have urgent communication concerning the condition of General Waddell's forces. Lieutenant Thompson here has more details. But please allow me to introduce my son, Andrew."

"It is a privilege to meet you, Andrew. I have a son about your age in England. We are indebted to the service of your father. But let us get to the problem at hand. Please wait." In a moment, Lord Tryon, dressed in the uniform of a Colonel of the Lancers, appeared. They all saluted.

"Captain Neel, how delightful to see you again. What mischief have you been into now?"

"Sire, General Waddell has been attacked by a force of the Regulators and these men have dispatches for you."

Lieutenant Thompson then related the tales of his capture, punishment, and the news of the attack on General Waddell. After hearing the reports, Tryon turned to Anderson, "I want a council of war within the hour. We will assemble in that church over there," he instructed, pointing to a Presbyterian church in the Hillsboro square.

Thomas and young Andrew refreshed themselves, enjoyed a sumptuous meal and were given a tent for the night's rest.

On May 11 1771, Tryon, with a force of over 1,000 drawn from the Carteret, Orange, Beaufort, New Hanover, and Dobbs Counties, fell in behind the drummers and the small pieces of artillery. Their purpose was to go to General Waddell's aid and finally to crush the rebellion. The Governor had on May 3 conducted a full dress review of his troops while he waited for General Waddell. The Governor's troops camped on the banks of the Great Alamance Creek on March 14. The fires of the Regulators could be seen at night.

That night Thomas attended Tryon's council of war. He wondered how his troops were faring under Lieutenant Huck. As the Governor, seated in front of the Presbyterian meeting house, outlined his next course, a sentry interrupted.

"Your Lordship, a Reverend David Caldwell wishes to speak with you. He claims to be a representative of the Regulators."

"Show him in."

A rather short, clean shaven man with his hair drawn in a pigtail under a tricornered hat and wearing leather britches, vest, and coat entered the church. He approached the Governor after passing down the aisle to the amusement and wonder of the officers present. He bowed before the Governor.

"State your business," growled the Governor.

"Sire, I am David Caldwell in the Lord God Almighty's service and wish to bring peace to the region and avoid bloodshed. We know you are a fair man, and I come as your servant for bringing peace to the two parties. As a token of the sincerity of our group, the Regulators, I have brought Colonel John Ashe and Colonel John Walker who were captured by the Regulators outside of our camp. What I have been asked to do is seek terms for the resolution of these matters."

Sitting royally in his campaign chair as if on a throne, the Governor scowled at the Reverend. "My good man, I am indebted for the return of our officers and appreciate your attempts to resolve our present condition. My officers will give you your reply in the morning. Please help yourself to refreshments and return tomorrow. You are released on your parole with the understanding that you will not divulge any information concerning the strength of our forces."

Caldwell bowed and left the building. Ashe and Walker were then admitted.

"Gentlemen, I desire to hear of your adventures."

Ashe spoke. "Sire, we were scouting the Regulators and had found some cover some one hundred yards from their camp and were attempting to determine their numbers. A half dozen armed men came from behind and surprised us. Being in uniform, we requested quarter. We were immediately bound. As we stood, a big man with a tobacco stained beard spat on the ground, kicked the feet out from each of us, and began to kick us while we were on the ground. The good reverend fired his pistol in the air and told the miscreant to stop, which he did. We were then taken to the camp and presented to a Mr. Husband who seemed to be in charge."

"Yes, we know this Harmon Husband was jailed for failure to pay taxes among other things. After acquittal, he led a rebel group of legislators. But, go on. What can you tell us of their forces?"

"They appeared to be a loosely governed mob. Some are not even armed except for scythes. I would estimate their number at around 2,000. There appeared to be little drilling. The camps were not set up in a military manner."

"Thank you, Colonel. You two officers have been through a great deal. Please check with my surgeon and then refresh yourselves."

The Governor conferred with his officers and prepared the order of battle in case it was needed. He ordered Thomas to scout again.

The next morning at sunup, Reverend Caldwell appeared. He was escorted to the quarters of the Governor.

The Governor stood fully uniformed. The reverend bowed. "Sire, our group presents to you a resolution amended from the address first presented to Governor Dobbs in 1765 at Nutbush Granville County."

"Yes, I have read this document and have generously adopted many of the requests, including the trial and sentencing of some of the offending officials."

"Sire, fining the Registrar, Edmund Fanning, who is standing over there, a penny for his extortion while imprisoning our accused has not been well received. Our people feel this is hardly equal treatment."

"Such insolence. I will not hear of such outrageous accusations against my adjutant. Was not your leader Hermon Husband acquitted of even more serious charges? I will not negotiate with the Regulators while they remain in a state of war and rebellion. They must disarm immediately and return to their homes or face the consequences. Sir, you are dismissed to carry this message back."

Reverend Caldwell bowed his head and in obvious disillusionment, passed through the camp and into the camp of the Regulators.

Meanwhile Thomas slipped across the lines and observed the camp. He watched as Reverend Caldwell approached Husband's tent. Thomas could hear the conversation.

"Where is Master Husband?" asked the Reverend.

"He has just fled. He said he would have no part of a rebellion," replied one of the supposed officers.

Just as he spoke two riders came very close to where Thomas was hiding. They were Husband and Squawman Johnson. Thomas was again torn between duty and revenge. He looked longingly at one of the horses tied about fifty yards from him. If only he could go after Johnson. He also thought of his duty to report on the conditions. Impulsively, he pulled his pistol, took aim at Squawman, and fired. The bullet missed, but caused the two riders to spur their mounts away. He waited for the inevitable discovery. He was surprised to hear a great deal of gunfire to his left. Some squad was engaged in target practice. His shot had blended in with the gunfire, and he was safe.

He observed a small group gathered around the reverend and a man later identified as James Pugh. He heard a chant "Fire and be dammed. Fire and be dammed." Thomas decided it was time to return to the Governor.

Slipping back across the lines, Thomas reported to the Governor that the Regulators were rejecting his conditions, but that they did not seem to be well prepared. He was not aware of who their new leader was since Husband had simply ridden away, and there seemed to be no discernable chain of command. He was delighted to find that the Neel Rangers had been detached from General Waddell, still west of Hillsboro, and were in camp.

That night in a glorious and emotional reunion, the elder Thomas Neel told his twin sons, Thomas and Andrew, of his adventures and how he had fired on Squawman Johnson.

The dawn of May 16, Reverend Caldwell appeared with the "Fire and be dammed" reply of the Regulators. The Governor gave the rebels one hour to surrender. The hour passed and the Governor's response was announced by fire from the cannons. The cannon fired for fifteen minutes. One of the batteries was overcome, first by snipers in the woods and finally with a rush upon their position. The rebels now had one cannon against the batteries of the militia. The militias were ordered forward. Many refused to fire on their neighbors. Governor Tryon rose in his saddle and shouted, "Fire on me or them!" The battle began.

The battle raged for two hours. During the time many of the Regulators deserted and the heroic capture of the cannon soon came to naught as the rest of the mob refused to follow up. The militia advanced in ordered drill, which caused the Regulators to scatter.

The rebels soon took shelter behind rocks and trees in order to fire on the militia. The Neel contingent was ordered to attempt a flanking maneuver on the right side of the arena. This time mounted Thomas and his company traveled to the extreme right of the battle zone. There they charged the Regulators while the main body charged from the front. Soon Regulators were throwing down their arms (some of which were only knives and farm implements). The militia moved toward the surrendered Regulators. Unfortunately, the Governor sent Edmond Fanning, his nefarious adjutant, to speak to the surrendered rebels.

Fanning, in the dress of a major, advanced toward the dissolute wretches. Some stood erect in defiance while others appeared dejected.

"To His Majesty's loyal subjects. All who wish to take an oath of allegiance and are not seen as promoters of this conspiracy will be pardoned and allowed to go home. Those who do not or are among those we will identify will be held under arms. Those who wish to swear allegiance will form over with Colonel Anderson and sign a parole. Those who do not will remain with me. I shall now read the list of people who will face charges of leading an insurrection."

When Fanning finished reading the fifteen names, all except James Pugh were placed in a wagon. Fanning turned to the prisoner.

"James Pugh, your being one of the most notorious of the people of this rebellion, including threatening and harming King's officers in Hillsboro and other environs, are by the authority of Governor Tryon and the King sentenced to death. Colonel Anderson, form a squad for execution. Reverend Caldwell, you may attend to the condemned."

Colonel Anderson then called upon a sergeant to form a Sergeant's Guard. The distraught rebels stood at one side while the regiments of the militia stood by units on the other. Reverend Caldwell knelt to the figure tied to the tree and prayed with him. Then Anderson asked, "Prisoner Pugh, do you have any last words."

"I regret that I have not been able to provide for my family. My lands have been taken from me by corrupt officers such as Edmond Fanning. I die proudly standing for my rights not only as an Englishman but also as a Carolinian. I do not wish to be blindfolded. May God have mercy on my family. Our blood will be a good seed in the ground that will soon produce one hundred fold."

Fanning yelled, "Colonel Anderson what is the delay?"

"See you in hell, Fanning," yelled Pugh.

The Sergeant of the Guard then formed a squad of twelve men. They stood some twenty paces from Pugh. His voice rang out. "Check weapons, stand attention, ready weapons, aim, fire." Smoke and fire rang out as the figure slumped to the ground. A group of rebels were allowed to remove his body to a waiting wagon. The silence among the Regulators was deafening. The paroled were allowed to pick up their weapons and carry away their casualties which numbered two hundred dead and wounded. Governor Tryon assigned his surgeons to treat both parties. The militia dead, nine in number, were given a military funeral and buried on the spot. Eighty militia had been wounded.

On May 21, the Governor and his troops marched to Sandy Creek where they collected supplies and took more citizens under oath. On the 29th they moved westward and joined General Waddell and his troops on June 4. Then they marched to Hillsboro where the prisoners were tried before a court marshal chaired by Edmond Fanning. Six were condemned to death and the remaining nine were pardoned.

Governor Tryon received a notice that he had been appointed Governor of New York. Before departing with Edmond Fanning, the militia held a formal review in his honor. The Governor spoke, thanking the troops for their valiant service to the King. The troops gave a rousing cheer as his entourage left for Wilmington and New York. Thomas noticed that the cheers for Edmond Fanning were rather weak. Tom thought perhaps Tryon took Fanning with him in order to save him from the simmering hatred of the Regulators.

Colonel Ashe was left in charge of the King's forces. Josiah Martin, assuming the governorship, arrived and continued taking oaths. By July 4 some 6,000 Regulators had taken the oath. However, many fled westward to Virginia, Tennessee, or Kentucky. By 1772 some 1,500 had left, with others staying behind only to sell their land. This massive move broke the 1763 settlement agreement with the Indians regarding settlement beyond the Appalachians.

CHAPTER 20

# *An Uneasy Peace*

By July 10, the dismissed Mecklenburg Tryon County Militia turned back toward their homes. The second night on the trail from Hillsboro they arrived at Salisbury. Colonel Anderson traveled with the party, which included Captain Huck, Captain Thomas Neel, and Lieutenants Andrew and Thomas. The troops were given a day off to refresh themselves. The five officers took a table in the tavern.

Young Thomas, one of the twins, spoke after receiving a tankard of ale. "If I may, Sirs, I am disturbed about what I have heard. Here this Edmond Fanning gets excused with a few pennies fine for extorting the people which prompted the revolt. At the same time, one of the Regulators was shot and six hung for defending their lands. There may be something to these reports I read in the *Gazette* concerning the unrest in Massachusetts."

"Do I hear the beginning of a rebellion amongst the younger Neel clan?" queried Huck.

Young Andrew replied, "I don't think it is just to leave those families without relief and support when their husbands were killed fighting for their land. Did not your people do the same thing at Culloden Moor in 1746?"

With flushed face Huck retorted, "We were not fighting for such a wretched land as this. I was forced to leave under the Culloden Oath. Let them move to a different colony if they do not like our government."

Young Thomas answered, "To them it is not wretched. They had defended the land against the onslaught of Shawnee and Cherokee and defended the King's borders against the French without a great deal of help from Lord Townsend across the sea. By the way, tell us about this Culloden Oath."

"The Oath, my young friend, was taken by the survivors of the slaughter of Culloden by Lord Cumberland. Those families, such as mine, who came to the aid of Bonnie Prince Charlie were forced to give up their weapons and forbade the wearing of their clan plaids. I memorized the oath as required by my father. It went like this:

> I do swear, as I shall answer to God on the great day of Judgment, I shall not,
> nor shall I have, in my possession a gun, sword pistol, or arm whatsoever, and
> never use tartan, plaid or any part of the Highland garb; and if I do may I be
> so cursed in my undertakings, family and property -may I never see my wife

and children, father, mother or relations—may I be killed in battle as a coward, and lie buried without burial in a strange land, far from the graves of my forefathers and kindred; may all this come across me if I break my oath.2

So you see, good young friend, I admire your courage, but I must warn you that your talk borders on treason and I have sworn to uphold the Crown."

"My honored friend, it seems to me you would want to question oppression given the history and courage of the Scots. What is treasonous about questioning actions against people asserting their rights of Englishmen as your people once did?" asked young Thomas.

"Do good Englishmen thwart the statutes of His Majesty, such as openly ignoring the law against settling beyond the 1763 treaty with the Indians? And what is this I hear about this Seiver buying land from the western Indians in defiance of His Majesty's declaration?"

Captain Thomas, the elder, decided it was time to intervene. "I know this Seiver. He has led a great many restless people. I, too, share your concern for his behavior. But come, let me buy another round and we will drink to the King's health." With this young Thomas and Huck shook hands as they were served.

The trip home began next morning with a parade and salute by the officers of the Neel Rangers. The militia then traveled south with men veering off as they passed near their abodes. At Charlotte Village the Neel boys bid good-bye to Master Huck and headed to their home in the Catawbas.

Thomas arrived at the plantation in time for the wheat harvest festival. The Neel plantation was third on the list of communal harvest. One half dozen families, including the Spratts, came while the fields of the two families were harvested. After three days a festival was held. Horse racing seemed to be the biggest event since Thomas had one of the best one-mile tracks around. The progenitors of Champion and Victory upheld the houses of Spratt and Neel by winning three of the races.

Jean appeared with an imported parasol and a Queen Anne dress of lavender, with a white linen bodice. Seated watching from a grass-covered knoll facing the river, she commented, "Thomas, I still think Victor added more to the quality of our line than did Champion. Look at Victoria's grace and beauty as she runs. Much like her mother."

Country gentleman Thomas, clad in a linen coat, embroidered vest, large hat, leggings and boots, commented, "Look at the skill and grace of the rider, Mary, much like her mother, but not as beautiful."

"How dare you talk of my daughter that way, Sir."

"Ah! How fortunate I am to have such a fine farm and fine family." The conversation was interrupted by a courier. He delivered a message from the new Governor Josiah Martin. Thomas broke the seal.

"What does it say?" asked Sarah.

"It is posted from New York and states that the new governor will be arriving in August and has asked for a meeting of the Assembly. He relates that he has called for a meeting of the Assembly for August 12, 1771. We also have a notice that our brother Andrew is now a Captain and is a member of the commission to finally fix a boundary between North and South Carolina. I am also to assist William Moore, Robert Adams, Ephraim McClure, and John Bond to build a new court house. It will be interesting to find out where a justice will finally have a permanent home instead of meeting all over the county."

He called his son Andrew from his frolicking and dancing and told him the news.

The next Sunday the Neel clan met at the Waxhaw Presbyterian church, even though Thomas was an elder of the Bethany Church in New Acquisition. Baptisms were performed and a lesson presented by Reverend Dalton. At the conclusion of the service, the families gathered in the grove by the church. There was much discussion of the events of the day, including the no importation agreement which was passed by a rump session of the Assembly and was to take effect soon. Most agreed not to use English manufactured goods even though the Neel plantation trade would be hurt because of their intercourse in ship stores and crops. At length the discussion turned to other things.

Fifty-something, Sheriff Uncle Henry spoke. "The time has come for me to pass the torch. I have asked the Governor to appoint someone else sheriff. I just can't in good conscience continue."

Henry (1736) asked, "Uncle, what causes you such concern?"

"My main concerns are the quit rents. As they get more prosperous, landowners pay rent in order to avoid militia service. Soon they refuse to pay. Some both refuse to pay and to serve. Besides, I want to devote my time to the pursuit of Artimas McGhee and Squawman Johnson. I have heard they have gone to the Wautanga across the mountains."

"Yes," replied Captain Thomas, "I fired on Johnson as he ran away from Alamance accompanied by Husband, the leader of the Regulators."

Zeke, who had made one of his rare church appearances, announced, "Even though I am old, like Sheriff Henry, I long for the trail. I will go with him on his mission to hunt down the scoundrel. He has been at large long enough. Besides, he killed my good friend, Squire Thomas."

"I would be honored. We should leave in three days for the Wautanga. Since my wife has passed on, I would like to register my will which gives my earthly goods to my children."

Mother Mary, murdered Thomas's widow, stood up, "I would like to propose a toast to my brother-in-law and long time friend, Henry."

And the church said, "Amen." Mother Mary walked over to her brother-in-law, Henry, gave him a kiss on the cheek, and embraced him. "Take care of yourself, Henry. I will miss you."

The men gathered in a cluster and lit their pipes. They were dressed in their Sunday best. Squire Henry (1736) (brother of Captain Thomas) drew on his pipe, looked skyward for a minute and commented, "I heard that there are many people from overseas who own land here and do not pay taxes. Can't we do something to make these people help us? They were not here for the fight with the Indians and the French. Cannot they do their fair portion?"

Assemblyman Captain Thomas replied, "Yes, we should do something about that. The merchants and the large rice plantation owners seem to be in league with these other dandies. They can attach our property if we do not pay for our debts to them, but we can do nothing for gaining redress for unfair quit rents. This is one more point that reinforces what that firebrand Otis up in Massachusetts has to say. Also, these acts by His Lordship Townsend, the Crown's Prime Minister, show that he doesn't seem to realize that we did most of the fighting with the Indians and the French. So, why should we pay a tax to support a war which was for the benefit of the empire?"

Reverend Dalton added, "Yes, and at the risk of treason, I must state that we of the Presbyterian faith should have the right to perform marriages and baptisms more clearly defined by the colony. How can we have only a bishops' church recognized as the performer of these rights when their clerics appear only seldom? I cannot accept that all the marriages I have performed are illegal and that all of the children born of these marriages are bastards."

"I agree, and I will fight anyone who says my children are 'bastards.'" replied Thomas.

` Henry commented, "It is difficult to be a justice for His Majesty's colony when there are so many things with which I cannot agree."

Thomas, with a disquieting counsel, answered, "This gives us a great deal to discuss when the Assembly meets. It will be interesting to see just how the new man operates."

\*\*\*\*\*\*\*\*\*\*\*\*\*\*\*\*\*\*\*\*\*\*\*\*\*\*\*\*

August 12, 1771, Master Huck, Tom Polk, and Thomas Neel were standing in line at the Governor's ball in the newly completed palace. The Assembly had been called by the Council to swear in Governor elect Josiah Martin. As usual most men were without their wives and looked longingly at the ladies as they were escorted through the line and through the minuet. As the trio looked on, Polk commented, "I am glad I don't have to learn those dandy games like the minuet."

Huck replied, "I personally find the minuet quite invigorating; however, not as invigorating as the Highland Scots fling."

Polk interjected wryly, "You must demonstrate how the Highlanders do it some time."

Thomas with a wink retorted, "I guess Robert the Bruce must still be with us. Next thing will be a huzzah for Bonnie Prince Charlie. Say, look the reception line forms."

As they moved through the line, the greeters of the new Governor were dressed as if in a uniform order of the day -ruffled shirts, waistcoats, coats, knee breeches, worsted or silk stockings with buckled shoes and some with pumps. As they moved through the reception line, Thomas stopped in front of the speaker of the Assembly, Richard Caswell.

"Did you get my letter of concerns about the rents and church petition?" queried Thomas.

"Indeed I did. We can expect an interesting time when you consider who His Lordship has chosen for his Council."

Later the line moved. When the trio came to the Governor and his lady, Colonel Anderson, his newly appointed aide, winked at them and said, "Your Excellency, may I present Captain Thomas Neel, Lieutenants Polk and Christian Huck of the Waxhaw and the Catawbas. They are the famous Neel Rangers of the late war and the uprising of the Regulators."

"Gentlemen," said the Governor with a warm smile, "It is a genuine pleasure to meet you. Your prowess has been attested by Governor Tryon when I met with him a little more than a fortnight ago. Tell me what counsel you can you give me?"

Thomas replied, "Sire, I would recommend that you go to the country of the Regulators and assure them that their voices will be heard. They are a proud and free people who are ready to love their sovereign if only they are cared for and heard."

Huck interjected, "Not to worry, Sire, we crushed them. They will never bother us again."

Polk interjected, "Particularly when you consider that they are voting with their feet and heading west."

"Is that not against the King's Proclamation of 1763?" asked the Governor.

"When they see an empty land, most of those displaced Irish want to occupy it," commented Polk.

"Good day, Gentlemen, thank you for your comments."

The trio bowed and made their exit.

As they gathered near the punch bowl, Christian commented, "I say old man, you seem to almost encourage those renegades to break the King's law regarding settlement."

"I just state the facts. I heard that nearly every pardoned Regulator is attempting to move to Kentuck or Western North Carolina. I hear Seiver has quite a settlement on the River of the Tennessee in the region of the Watonga," said Polk.

"I hope the natives don't mind," sneered Huck.

The next week the Assembly took up raising the sinking fund tax to pay for, among other things, the Governor's palace. Even though the obligations had already been committed, the Assembly revoked the tax of one shilling per poll levied in 1748. The Governor vetoed the bill as a "fraud and a violation of public faith." In retaliation, the Assembly drew up a resolution indemnifying or compensating the sheriffs for not collecting the tax. The Governor, in retaliation, dissolved the Assembly.

Speaker of the House Richard Caswell ordered the treasurer to indemnify the sheriffs of each county (the sheriff collected the taxes). The Governor then issued a proclamation demanding that the sheriffs collect the taxes. Most of the sheriffs ignored the Governor's order. The sheriffs reasoned, why not stay home and avoid the inconvenience of collecting the taxes? The popularity of the Assembly grew because there was no need for the citizens to pay their taxes. The seeds of revolution had been sown.

On the boat back to Charles Town, Polk and Thomas listened to Huck's harangue about the threats of insurrection. He was particularly disturbed that as a merchant in Charles Town his warehouse had suffered financial loss because of the non-importation agreement on English goods. Polk and Tom wondered if he might have made up the losses through smuggling. At Charles Town, Huck excused himself to attend to his business there. Polk and Tom caught the new weekly stage service to Charlotte.

During the year 1772 Andrew, brother of Thomas (1730) and Henry (1736), was appointed to the court of the inferior bond, as witnessed by his brother. The inferior courts had not been affected by the Assembly's action concerning courts. Young Thomas II (one of the twins) was appointed Registrar of Tryon County. The state boundary had now been approved and the estate of Thomas and Jean lay on both sides of the boundary. That year the petition arrived from the minister for

Colonial America granting the authority of the Presbyterian Church to solemnize marriages. Polk was chosen Clerk of the County of Tryon.

With the drawing of the boundary, Captain Thomas Christopher's land was still a part of the new Tryon County, North Carolina, as well as half in the "New Acquisition" in South Carolina. Thomas continued as an Assemblyman in North Carolina for a time while serving in the militia of both Carolinas.

Both of the elder Neel brothers followed the events carefully. The relationship with the Crown's officers and the Carolina colonies continued to fester. The Neels reached the height of their loyalty to the Crown when they assisted in the War of Regulation. Now came the time of reflection. First, the Stamp Act really didn't bother them very much. Governor Tryon had been able to keep the good will of the Northern colony even though other colonies were more aggressive. However, when neighbor William Hill's forge was hampered by the Iron Act, which controlled the production of certain iron goods, the brothers became alarmed. The farmers depended on Hill for such items as hinges, plows, and occasional fire arms.

In March 1773, after the Assembly had exercised the right to attach the property of foreigners in debt to North Carolina, the Crown instructed royal governors to not assent to any bills that attached property of people who never lived in the colonies even though they were not paying taxes.

December 4, 1773. In retaliation the Assembly refused to appropriate funds for the Governor's courts and denied the right to create such courts without the "aid of the Legislature." The Governor appointed Maurice Moore, Richard Caswell, along with Chief Justice Martin Howard as judges of the new courts of oyour and terminer. Oyour and terminer come from the Latin, meaning roughly "hear and determine." These courts were held under the control of the Governor.

March 2, 1774. The new courts had no funds. In essence there was no effective court system. Governor Martin called the Assembly again and tried to get through a new court bill without the "foreign attachment clause." A compromise was reached for inferior courts and the oyour and teminer courts, but the former judicial system was compromised. This established the power of the Assembly as an independent body, an important concept in the cause of revolution.

June 10, 1774. Lord North's ministry came to the aid of the East India Company by passing the Tea Act. All other taxes had been revoked, but the tax on tea was maintained to help the East India Company and also to establish Parliament's right to tax. This action coalesced the colonies and led the North Carolinians to join the Committees of Correspondence, which were sharing information in the other colonies.

CHAPTER 21

# *Trouble with the Crown*

The recent tax on tea became the dominant conversation at taverns, church gatherings, and court houses. Both Captain Thomas Christopher and his brother Henry from Providence and Waxhaw were amused to hear that their wives were holding "non-tea" parties using sassafras root and the new import, coffee. People were pledging not to use tea until the coercive acts were repealed.

The patriarch Henry and Zeke sent a message from Kentuck.

> To: Captain Thomas Neel Esq. and Andrew Neel, Catawba River
>
> From: Henry Neel about July 1774
>
> Dear nephews:
>
> Zeke and I are still on the hunt for Artimas McGhee and Squawman Johnson here in Kentuck. Yesterday we shared cups with His Majesty's Agent Lord John Stuart. We enjoyed a few stories about his captivity and rescue. He then complained about the perennial problem of unlicensed traders. We then related to him our mission to catch McGhee and Johnson. His Honor grew strangely silent and gave his salutations and good-byes. We now believe that our nemeses are in the upper Cherokees, perhaps the Tennaco. We ran into a hunting party of Dragging Canoe, one of the principal chiefs of the Cherokee. They demanded tribute and were not too friendly until we inquired into the health of his father, Little Carpenter. Dragging Canoe then related as to how much his father admired his so called white brothers. There is a strange feeling of unrest among the Indians. Dragging Canoe related that the tribe was disturbed by anyone crossing the Appalachians. They seem to tolerate hunters but told us settlers would be removed. Love to the families.

At the Tryon County Muster, Henry's company from Mecklenburg assembled for training. Captain Huck's western militia trained separately.

In the evening after the shooting competition, Thomas and Henry sat by the fire, and as they were smoking Thomas read the letter from Uncle Henry.

"I certainly appreciate what Uncle Henry and Zeke are going through although I think part of the reward is the long hunt. I wonder about our friend Stuart. With our current troubles with the Crown's Townsend, I am not sure where the

173

Cherokees stand. With the defeat at Alamance, many of our fellow Carolinians have drifted over the mountains. Who will Stuart help if trouble comes?"

Thomas answered, "That is a good question. As I toured with the men, there was a lot of discussion. It seems that some of the troops are beginning to call the extreme loyalists 'Tories.'"

Henry remarked, "They must be damn few. Most of our muster wouldn't want to be associated with those sons of cavaliers and Highland Scots. I suppose our people are Whigamores then. By the way, do you know where the name came from?"

"Oh, I suppose from the Whig opposition in Parliament. It originally applied to Presbyterians. I am not sure the term would apply to those of us who are loyal to the Crown but do want the Crown to redress some of our grievances. I wonder how all those new Highland Scots see the King."

"That is right but it means to 'whig' or urge a 'mere' or horse."

Thomas asked, "Let's hope their urging of the horse doesn't get carried away. On another matter, where is our illustrious friend Huck?"

"I hear that he is taking the western militia company on a little hike. I believe most of his company is sympathetic to the Crown. He is a curious fellow. He has a trading business in Charles Town but spends most of his time here in the back country and continues to hold office here."

Thomas responded, "That reminds me, brother Sheriff, you need to call an election in both Mecklenburg and Tryon counties to pick candidates for the Provincial Congress called by the Speaker of Assembly, Colonel John Harvey. It seems that our good friend Master Harvey wants to send delegates to a Congress in Philadelphia, as he puts it, 'to discuss certain coercive acts against the welfare of the English colonies.'"

Henry responded, "I know, I already had an election in the Mecklenburg area and Huck won. He gave a great speech condemning Harvey and threatened us all with treason. He also treated everyone to roast pig and some ale. That crazy Scot has learned that ale can get more votes than rhetoric. I suppose Tryon County will have an election soon."

The rest of the evening was spent with the men discussing the relative strategies of muskets versus long rifles. The consensus was that the militia did not favor the faster-firing, but inaccurate musket, and favored instead the more accurate rifle. Young Andrew summed up the argument.

"If you are going to hunt bear you better shoot to kill on the first shot. You cannot rely on the quantity of the lead thrown by a musket if it is not accurate. Better one shot to the head than five at random." They lifted their coffee cups in agreement.

\*\*\*

Captain Thomas visited Charlotte Town to drop off some skins and purchase a few supplies. His customary source was, of course, Charles Town, but he thought a little scouting in the west could pay dividends.

He had just loaded his supplies in the wagon when he was greeted by Christian Huck. "I say there Neel, so good to see you. You must join me in a repast at the Mighty Boar."

"I would be delighted, Master Huck."

They found a relatively quiet corner in the dark tavern. Only one door and a window provided light except for a few smoky candles. A serving girl came up and took their order for two of the local ales.

Huck began, "I usually don't imbibe in ale but the Mighty Boar has an unusual body to their beverage, don't you agree?"

"Very refreshing. How goes it with you and your family?"

"The mercantile business is suffering from the cursed non-import agreements. The London merchants are retaliating by not importing our goods. My factors in London sent a missive continually wanting to foreclose. These damnable Committees of Correspondence are usurping the authority of the Crown."

Thomas nodded compassionately, "'Tis a pity. We can't foreclose on property here owned by citizens in Great Britain, yet they try to foreclose on us."

"I suppose our attempt to foreclose on them is what caused our problems in the first place. The Assembly should have never initiated that fight with the Governor on the issue of property foreclosures from those across the sea."

Thomas winced, steeling himself again for the inevitable question. "This issue of taxation without representation is taking on a life of its own. I hear you were elected to represent your district in the congress called by Colonel Harvey, the speaker of the Assembly."

Huck answered, "Damnable business that. When the Governor refused to call the Assembly, this nefarious Assembly Speaker, John Harvey, called an illegal meeting anyway. I do not appreciate the sending of flour and other goods to the closed port of Boston on his order. We are getting too involved with the rebellious people of Massachusetts. Harvey will keep up this nonsense until there will be troops down on us. Only the Governor can call such a meeting. These so called 'Sons of Liberty' and Committees of Correspondence are going to drive this colony into rebellion. Mark my word."

"I have an open opinion on the subject. I can see no harm in meeting to see what the colonies of Massachusetts and Virginia have to say. Closing the port of Boston over the Tea question does not bode well. You remember we confiscated some of the stamps back in '65. Besides, I hear our brethren up in Edenburg had a Tea party of their own and disposed of some of His Lordship Townsend's tea. Perhaps we can moderate any hot heads up north. We owe Massachusetts and Virginia more than Great Britain for the help we received in our fight with the French."

"I say it is treason and Harvey and his henchmen should be hung."

"I surmise, my friend, that you will not be attending."

Huck replied. "I shall go and espouse my fervent support for the Governor and the Crown."

Tom continued, "The Governor means well, and we all support the Crown. However, the rights of Englishmen should not be subverted by Lord Townsend and his lackies."

"As a friend, Thomas, I shall forget your treasonous remarks."

Tom stood up in anger, pounded his fist on the table and upset his tankard, "Is it treason to expect our concerns to be heard by the Crown? Is it treason to be taxed for an army that never helped us in the first place? How long has it been since you have seen a member of His Majesty's military here to help us? We differ my friend; I covet your friendship and respect your opinions. You must excuse me. I must reach my brother's place by nightfall."

Christian Huck stood up in amazement, stepped through the door to see Thomas depart. Wearily, he trudged to his plantation which was west of the village of Charlotte. A servant greeted him and grabbed the horse. His wife Martha and his two children welcomed him. After they embraced, Martha said, "Come, friend husband. We were just sitting down to supper."

The couple moved to the dining room of the newly constructed Georgetown-style mansion. After greeting the children, Huck sat down on his elegant imported chair and pulled it up to a contemporary table. He gave a short prayer and began his repast of stew, bread, and rum.

"You seem quite troubled, friend husband."

"I am very perplexed and filled with melancholy about the state of our affairs. We have suffered some loss of capital with our mercantile business because of the wretched non-importation. I am obligated to the Crown, first of all for the parole given my family after the Battle of Culloden, and second, because of the land they have given us in the Carolina Colony. I hope we are not seen as in league with this rabble because I would hate to see our lands back home in Scotland confiscated because the Crown perceives us as disloyal. The Irish here seem to feel they fought the French themselves in the recent war. They do not cherish the love and protection of the Crown that we do. I tremble what will happen if these Irish Presbyterians continue their press towards anarchy. I have friends in the Irish. We serve together in the militia. I just wonder what will become of the militia."

"Yes, at the regimental militia musters I have visited with Jean Neel as well as her husband's brother Andrew's wife, Laureena. They are such strong women, though their radical Presbyterianism worries me a bit."

Christian continued, "I have decided to answer Harvey's call for a Congress even though it is illegal. Only a governor can call a meeting of an Assembly."

She replied, "You and the Assembly will be in our prayers. We are in a perplexing state. If we were to anger the Crown we could lose my inherited lands in Scotland and maybe our lands here in the Piedmont. The boycotts could ruin our mercantile business."

The family retired for the night, but Martha continued to fret over the conditions of the colony. Her family had emigrated with the Hucks after the defeat of the Scots at the Battle of Culloden. Her older brothers and two uncles had been savaged after they surrendered to Lord Cumberland, the leader of the English army. Her father had taken the pledge of Culloden and was granted clemency.

She enjoyed the festive season of Charles Town but preferred the coolness of their Piedmont plantation. With all of the agitation, which was the conversation of her social world of quilting bees, harvest seasons, and church meetings, she was now in a constant state of worry about their future. Their life had contrasted sharply with the former hard times in Scotland when the British forces had been so cruel. However, she was disturbed by the crudeness of the Irish Presbyterians and their lack of social graces common to a Highland Scot. The Irish Presbyterian worship was so lacking in splendor compared to the elegance of the Church of Scotland services. The Irish Presbyterian semi-legal courts under the presbyters seemed to be the only justice and most of their justice was beginning to disfavor the Crown. She despaired at the lack of the quieting influence of Episcopal clergy in the backcountry and wondered why the Crown could not send better judges and clergy. She wondered why the justices of the peace were Presbyterian elders. Sleep wearily came late that night.

CHAPTER 22

# *Troubles for Governor Josiah Martin*

The Tryon and Mecklenburg Counties elections for the New Bern Congress called by Speaker Harvey were an uproarious affair with speeches overwhelmingly against the Tea Act. Unquestioned support for the Crown was significant by its absence. The people pledging unquestioned support were first called loyalists and then "Tories." Those favoring an address for grievances were now called rebels and then "Whigs." The original name for the Tories was an appellation for supporters of papists and later royal English rule. The term "Whig" was originally an appellation for extreme Coventry Scots of the 16th century who opposed the royal party and frequently marched against the English. The Tryon County election sent Thomas and Polk to New Bern. Mecklenburg sent Christian Huck, a Tory, and William Hill, a Whig.

By August 13, 1774, seventy-one delegates, representing thirty of the thirty-six counties and four of the six borough towns, met in New Bern in the court house not far from the Governor's new palace. Governor Josiah Martin, who succeeded Governor Tryon, declared the meeting an illegal assembly.

It did not take long to understand that this was clearly a revolutionary body. The Tories, after making a few speeches, left. Huck was among them. The discussions by those remaining took place at the court house. At first their conversations and rage centered on the courts controversy, the failure to tax delinquent properties whose owners were across the seas, and the disturbing trend of taxation without representation. For the first time such phrases as "social contract," "taxation without representation," "rights of the governed," and other radical French republican ideas were heard in the hall. The Assembly took a vigorous stand against parliamentary taxation, which it considered illegal and oppressive, endorsed the general congress in Philadelphia, and declared an economic boycott of trade with Britain. After pledging support for Boston, the Assembly appointed William Hooper, Joseph Hewes, and Richard Caswell as delegates to the First Continental Congress. The Assembly was now the First North Carolina Provincial Congress.

In the absence of the Governor, who cowered behind the "Tryon Palace" walls with his family, the delegates voted to establish Committees of Safety for each county and a five member committee for the province as a whole. Thomas was appointed as militia commander for Tryon County and Henry for Mecklenburg.

The third brother, Andrew, had patented land in South Carolina near Ninety-Six and would be serving as a company commander there while still holding property in Mecklenburg.

Upon returning home, Thomas and Polk called on Sheriff Henry and reported the news to the families of the Catawba. Henry (1736) took his commission in the new Continental Army with pride. He would not be a member of the militia again until 1779.

The ladies of Tryon County, where Col. Thomas Christopher lived, and those of Mecklenburg, pursued their "non tea parties" with more vigor. Attendance at them became a test for the budding Whig and Tory factions. Thomas reviewed the actions of the first North Carolina Congress with the congregation at the weekly Bethel Kirk meeting. After services, Thomas reviewed with the minister a copy of the Rowan County memorial to Congress on the Tea Act of 1774. "Reverend McPherson, have you seen the resolves from Rowan County?"

"I read something about it in a tattered old copy of the *Charles Town Gazette*. I am troubled in the extreme. We seem to be headed in a terrible direction. These resolves seem to define some of the issues which irritate many of the people."

"Such as?"

"They claim that the essence of the British Constitution is that no subject may be taxed but by his own consent, freely given by himself in person or by his legal representative. They further state that a Non Importation agreement of British Goods would begin in October 1775."

"Yes, and I hear they mentioned the Boston trouble, also."

Thomas continued, "We here in the west have not been particularly inconvenienced by the acts and have faithfully served the King when called to do so. We may now be asked to form committees of safety and raise a militia which in our case is to convert one from existing militiamen. This militia business could bring trouble. Where will the loyalties of militia lay – with the Crown or, if we separate, with the local populous? I pray we will not have to make a choice."

The next Tuesday a courier rode up with a dispatch. Young Andrew, Thomas, John (children of Captain Thomas and Jean), and Jean gathered as Thomas read.

"Very amusing. One dispatch dated March 6, 1775 is from His Excellency Josiah Martin condemning the action of the First North Carolina Congress. The second dispatch is from Speaker John Harvey calling for a meeting of the new Provincial Congress on April 3, 1775. I guess I should make ready to go. Our sons, Thomas and Andrew, can you help here with the estate? James Hawthorne should be given more responsibility and could be a great help."

Jean commented, "Are you a soldier or a farmer? Why is it always the Neels doing the fighting? I noticed that many of our neighbors aren't as passionate."

Thomas replied, "I believe we must act. It won't be long until James Stuart, who at one time sat at my table, will be exciting the Cherokees, Creeks, and Shawnees into rebellion. Mark my word."

Jean and Thomas embraced and then he was gone.

# CHAPTER 23

# *Resolves*

Henry arrived at his Steele Creek home, and discussed the happenings with the Waxhaw church. He was joined by his wife Nancy and neighbor Billy Hill. Nancy looked up from her faux tea. "At the last militia muster, I was sitting with some of the wives discussing the Tea act, the closing of Boston, and the adventures of you men folk at the North Carolina Assembly."

"You mean the North Carolina Congress."

"Whatever." She continued, "Anyway, I was sitting with Mildred Huck and some of her friends. They do not know what is to become of them. They fear the radicals such as your brother Thomas and your brother Andrew of Ninety-Six are going too far. Now with these Committees of Correspondence and the Councils of Safety, they worry about certain lawlessness. They are afraid of the Indian menace as well as the breakdown of the courts which have left only the justices and sheriffs without authority. This Continental Congress has been blasphemous to the ministry and soon will turn on King George himself, she fears."

"I suppose she has heard of the formation of our two regiments for the new Continental Army."

"That she has. She is puzzled. She asked whether the militia would protect us now that we have no courts or if the Presbyterian elders had taken over the governing of this colony?"

The next morning brother Thomas Christopher Neel from the new York County, South Carolina, carved from Tryon, North Carolina, arrived at Henry Neel's compound. He was accompanied by his son Andrew. The new county birth was a result of a realignment of the borders between the two Carolinas. The South Carolinians called the area *New Acquisition*.

Henry and his eldest son William had just returned from assigning the work of the day to the field hands.

"Welcome Thomas. To what do we owe this great honor? You must come in and break bread with us."

"I would ride clear to Boston to sample some of Nancy's delicious entrees. What are we having?"

"Oh, only coffee, candied ham, ground corn pudding, and biscuits. I suppose you would not be interested."

"Only when ducks cease to swim and eagles no longer fly."

Nancy Agnes called out to the kitchen building for the servant to bring in some more plates and soon the guests gathered around the dining room table. The children were excited to see their uncle and grown up cousin. After hearing the family news, Henry spoke.

"I know this is more than a social call. What brings you to the heart of the Waxhaw?"

"You may have heard about the problems up near Boston of a massacre by the King's troops and now a clash in Lexington, Massachusetts. It seems that the Whigs there were gathering gunpowder, weapons, and ammunition in order to be ready in case the forces of the King attacked. At a place called Concord Bridge the patriots and the forces of the King clashed. As the patriots fought Indian style, the redcoats were severely hurt and the Continental Congress is set on taking some kind of action. Meanwhile, the Mecklenburg Committee of Safety has summoned us to Charlotte to take part in drafting a resolve. Accordingly, we will probably disband the militia and set up a new one composed of patriots for the cause of North Carolina and not the lackies of the King."

"Well, I guess I will join you within the hour. We should make Charlotte by nightfall."

Henry turned to his eldest son, "William, saddle Josephus. Nancy, please fix lunches for us. I shall pack and be with you shortly."

That night the elders Thomas, Henry, and Andrew arrived at the Boar Tavern in Charlotte. All available beds were taken; however, they found lodging in the home of a member of the militia, Abner Holiday.

The next morning Ezekizl Polk, Tom's father, appeared before them. He reviewed with the at first raucous and now somber crowd the events of the past year, including the Boston troubles, clashes with the governor over attachment of foreign lands, and the rumored excitement of the Indians. The final complaint was the aggressive nature of the King's troops, although very few were stationed in North Carolina.

Committees were assigned, and on May 31 the Mecklenburg Resolves were finished. Among things stated were the following:

1. The power of Parliament over the colonies was denied.

2. The laws and commissions of the Parliament and King were temporarily suspended.

3. Since laws were suspended, it was necessary to establish a government for Mecklenburg County until the Provisional Congress could establish new ones.

4. All inhabitants were to participate in forming nine military companies and select officers.

5. Each company contained two "selectmen" to settle minor conflicts concerning debts of the company.

6. Selectmen were also commissioned to hear cases concerning larceny and a select board of eighteen was to meet quarterly to hear disputes over forty schillings. Convicted persons could be confined until the Provincial Congress could establish a mode of procedure.

7. Quit rents and taxes were to be turned over to the Committee of Safety for disposal as public exigencies might require.

8. Anyone who received or attempted to exercise a commission of the Crown would be deemed an "enemy of the people."

9. Anyone who refused to obey the Resolves would be considered a criminal.

10. The resolves were to remain in effect until the North Carolina Provisional Congress acted or until the King and Parliament gave up "arbitrary pretensions with respect to America."

Cheers resounded as the Resolves were read. The proprietor of the Boar Tavern toasted the Resolves and treated a round to the house.

Henry turned to Thomas, "I hope they will be this happy when Sir Henry Clinton and his minions from Boston descend upon us."

Thomas replied, "Yea, we were able to hold the French without a great deal of help but the Crown was more enthused about West Indies sugar than our continent. This time it will be different. If you don't mind, I think I shall call on friend Huck. He should see a copy of these before he gets himself in trouble. I understand the *North Carolina Gazette* will publish the Resolves soon. Andrew, why don't you go back with Henry? I should be home in a couple of days."

The next morning Thomas headed northwest toward the Huck plantation while Henry and his brother Andrew turned south. Andrew had affixed his signature to the Resolves.

At about noon Thomas approached the elegant plantation house of Master Huck. His horse moved slowly but majestically up the tree-embraced drive to the house. A Georgian house with colonnades on the front supporting a porch and a balcony loomed from between a row of well groomed trees. As he approached, he saw Master Huck just bidding good-bye to the post rider.

"Colonel Tom, what an unexpected pleasure. I am glad to see you are taking refuge from that rabble at Charlotte this week."

"Friend Huck, I appreciate your warmth, and I hope your trust. I come as a friend concerned about your welfare."

"And I yours on this hot day. Won't you come in? Samuel, take the Colonel's horse, rub it and give it some provender. Mildred, look who is here. Hanibal, fetch us some cups of sack. Sit down, sit down."

Thomas and Christian moved to the portico. After an exchange of pleasantries about the families and some concern over the affairs up north, Thomas made his move. "My friend, we are headed for trying times. The Mecklenburg Committee of Safety has rejected all commissions of the Governor and King. This means you and I have no offices. Hopefully, this condition will end when the King and Parliament come to some sort of agreement with the Provincial Legislature."

"My word, that is preposterous. It is anarchy and calls for the Johnson Riot Act, passed during the Regulator crisis, to be put in force."

"My friend, that is impossible. Soon the Congress will go into session, and that will end the tenure of the Governor. However, let me get to my point. I have admired your citizenship, your prowess in the field, and your support of the militia in whatever we did. I know of the difficulties you will have because of the Culloden Oath. The crisis is that the Mecklenburg Resolves declare that anyone who does not submit to the Committee of Safety and Selectmen's authority will be considered a criminal. I myself have some choices because half my lands lie in South Carolina, a colony which so far has passed no such resolves. I hope you will be able to take an oath in support of the Resolves. I know your choice will not be easy. You hold your lands at the pleasure of the King and could forfeit your warehouse as well as overseas lands."

Huck's countenance grew to a scowl, "I cannot believe this. You, a loyal officer of the Crown giving in to this rabble?"

"Please take this advice in the manner intended. You may have neighbors who will turn against you. Your family may be in danger. My only admonition is that as a long time friend, be careful."

Huck grew red faced and clenched his fists. "Can this misery never end? We Highland Scots came here for relief from terror, and now it has followed us here. Samuel, get the Captain's horse. I believe he is leaving. Good day, Sir, we shall meet again perhaps as enemies."

"We have been friends. Let's not forget that. May God protect us both."

Thomas turned, waited for his horse, and rode silently away. His shoulders slumped, and he suddenly felt very weary. He doubted if he would ever see this part of the country again.

When passing through Steele Creek he called upon his brother Henry, the justice of the peace. As they sat under the tree in front of the manse, Thomas wearily related the meeting with Huck.

Henry reacted, "All this euphoria sounds like independence. It stirs the blood, especially from your boys Andrew and Thomas. When I saw them last week they were highly agitated and were stating things which at one time would be considered treason. By the way, please look after my family. I have volunteered for the First North Carolina Regiment of the Continental Army."

"Congratulations. I will be in constant check with them. I wonder just how many people are going to support the proposed North Carolina Provincial Congress and the new Continental Congress. I will probably turn my allegiance to South Carolina since my lands now lie in the new York County of the New Acquisition."

Henry asked, "Now that you are a half citizen of South Carolina, what have you heard about our neighbors to the south?"

"I haven't heard much. Just like Master Huck, many of them have mercantile operations with the mother country and are not sure where they stand. Since Charles Town is a better port than Wilmington, I suspect the Crown will try to occupy it some day like they did the Port of Boston."

Henry continued, "My family is worried about the Cherokees. Will Lord Stuart, His Majesty's southern Indian agent, stir them up or will he try to keep them neutral? I admire him, and I think he respects us.

"I am glad you agreed to look after my family as I go with the Army. Young William is but thirteen years old, and we have only servants to defend the place. I hope that Little Carpenter can contain the Cherokees; however, since they have ceded most of their land this side of the mountains, I don't believe he has much influence. I have heard some bad things about his son, Dragging Canoe."

"How did his son get that name?"

"When he was about ten years old, the Cherokees planned a raid. Dragging Canoe is alleged to have begged his father to go. Anyway, the warriors left without him. Apparently the party traveled by water and then had to portage around one of the falls on the Catawba. As the braves were carrying the canoes around the falls, they were surprised to see Little Carpenter's son dragging his canoe by himself. He had followed the party. He has been a war chief for some time. Apparently, Little Carpenter is the peace chief. Little Carpenter, though, is getting old and has lost much of his influence."

The air was suddenly rent by young William's lusty clanging of the dinner bell. Nancy yelled, "Are you two old warriors going to talk forever, or are you coming to supper?"

Thomas replied, "Only if you will give me one of your famous pies and allow me to spend the night."

"I shall suffer," she replied with a coquettish wink and a toss of her hair.

The supper and vespers were followed by news of the Catawba Neels. Thomas related that their younger brother Andrew, his wife Laureena Smith, and their children had relocated and patented some land in South Carolina near Ninety-Six in the new lands recently ceded by the Cherokees. He heard the farm had little commercial potential yet. Thomas added that there was still a great deal of support for the King in the backcountry areas.

The next morning Thomas hit the trail to his plantation on the Catawba.

# CHAPTER 24

# *Hillsboro Congress*

The post brought news to the Thomas Neel compound that the New Bern Committee of Safety had drawn up an "Association" similar to the Mecklenburg Resolves. The *North Carolina Gazette*, in a manner not complimentary to the Crown, related that Governor Josiah Martin had fled New Bern and established himself at Fort Johnson after first spiking the cannon at the New Bern palace and transferring ammunition to the *HMS Cruzier*. Later he fled to the *Cruzier* after realizing Fort Johnson could not be held with so few of His Majesty's troops. According to the article, the patriots burned the fort as the good Governor watched from the decks of the ship with his family. He later fled to Charles Town and offered his services as an officer of the Crown. These services were not accepted.

Unbeknown to the Neels at the time, from the safety of the *Cruzier* with his family, Josiah Martin wrote Lord Clinton and the Minister for Colonial service, Lord Germain, of his plan to liberate the Carolinas. He felt that the Highland Scots, former Regulators, and other loyalists would rise to the occasion and rout the rebels should the Crown land troops for support. The now displaced Governor proposed that an army be sent to New Bern or Charles Town and that if this plan were effected, the loyalists of the interior, particularly the newly arrived Highland Scots, would rise up and defeat the rebels. This was particularly so since the Governor had lifted the restrictions on the Culloden Oath related to Tartan dress, swords, and pistols. Suddenly, these contraband items had been appearing from nowhere.

Thomas resigned from the Assembly and the proposed new Congress because most his interest now lay with Charles Town, South Carolina. In fact, with the formation of York County, South Carolina, he became their representative to the South Carolina Congress as well as Chairman for the Council of Safety. He received the Rank of Colonel of the Neels Rangers Militia of the New Acquisition, or York County.

Brother Andrew continued developing land near Ninety-Six, even though the affairs as clerk of North Carolina's Tryon County were taking more and more of his time. At a communion meeting at the Bethel Church one Sunday in April, Thomas, Andrew, Henry, and Thomas's twins, young Andrew and Thomas, were relaxing after a dinner on the grounds. The Waxhaw Church members and the

Mecklenburg Neels had journeyed from their homes to attend services and catch up on the news. Thomas reported on a rumored slave revolt. According to the rumor he heard, the slaves were being agitated by the deposed North Carolina Governor Martin to rise up against their masters. Supposedly, they had been promised land over the mountains and freedom in exchange for their help against rebels.

Jean interjected, "I really doubt that our slaves would do that. We have never sold any family and will never break one up. They have been with us, some including my inheritance, for decades."

Mary added, "Yes, I feel that way about ours too. And we, like you, have been freeing those who have mastered a trade. Although slavery is unjust, cruel, and a curse, I cannot think of what those poor souls would do if they were released without the skills to succeed. Besides, haven't old Uncle Arthur and his daughter Rachel been granted their freedom? Yet they have not sought to leave."

Henry answered. "I think if some revolt were planned our servants would tell us about it. However, I read in the *Gazette* that slave patrols are forming around New Bern and any Negro without a pass from his master is queried and beaten severely. You know there was an uprising during the war with France but that was on Stono Island, South Carolina, and near Florida. Those rice and indigo cavaliers down near Charles Town treat their servants terribly. Their slave holdings are so large they cannot get to know individual slaves very well. And they cannot get an indentured person to work for them. So the slaves run off."

As they were speaking, a post rider sped into the yard with a lathered and panting horse. Thomas spoke, "Whoa there, Jonathon. What news causes you to be in such a hurry?"

"Master Tom, I bring you some disturbing news. His Majesty's troops in Boston marched out of the city on April 16, intent on capturing some arms and ammunition the militia had stored in Concord. Minutemen were alerted by citizens Daws and Revere, who warned the countryside and caused an uprising. At Concord Bridge there was a clash and about a dozen patriots were killed. However, on the way back to Boston many of the Red coats were killed or wounded. Congress has activated the Continental army and placed that chap Washington as the head."

"Yes, I have heard of this event. Oh, I remember this Washington. He was with Braddock. As a colonel in the Virginia militia he served on the frontier with some distinction. He seemed to lose a lot of battles though," observed Thomas.

"This is indeed bad news. What is to become of us?" queried Mary.

"Well, the militia got along just fine in our past skirmishes; I don't know why we can't live through this," responded Thomas.

\*\*\*

August 20, 1775, the Third Provincial Congress met at Hillsboro, located at almost the center of the province of North Carolina. It was now chaired by Samuel Johnston who had been elevated to the position of Speaker after the death of Harvey. An early attempt by the Congress was to induce the Moravians, former Regulators, and Highland Scots "by Argument and Persuasion to heartily unite with us for the protection of the Constitutional rights and privileges of America." This Congress, which did not contain many ardent loyalists, including Christian Huck, all signed a "Test Oath," affirming loyalty to the King but supporting the rights of Englishmen. They pledged a regiment to the Continental line in answer to an appeal by William Hooper, Joseph Hewes, and Richard Caswell, delegates to the Continental Congress in Philadelphia.

The North Carolina Congress passed *An Address to the Inhabitants of the British Empire,* which outlined the colony's participation in the revolutionary movement, the moderate character of the Congress, the desire to support the Crown, and a denial of the goal of independence. An additional address was aimed at Moravians, former Regulators, and Scots Highlanders, imploring them to support the protection of the constitutional rights and privileges of citizens and the defense of American liberty.

September moved the Congress, reacting to continuing news up north, to pass legislation for raising 1,000 Continental soldiers which included two regiments of five hundred men each. Four hundred troops were to be stationed in the Wilmington district and two hundred each at Edenton, New Bern, and Salisbury districts. Shortly after, the Congress passed a resolution to raise 3,000 minutemen (militia) to be split among battalions in six military districts. The Continentals were to be maintained as separate units from the militia. The field officers for the First Regiment were Col. James Moore, Lieutenant Col. Francis Nash, and Major Thomas Clark. Henry volunteered as an ensign in this regiment. The Second Regiment was commanded by Col. Robert Howe, Lieutenant Col. Alexander Martin, and John Patten as major. Each regiment of 728 consisted of eight companies with a captain, two lieutenants, one ensign, four sergeants, four corporals, two drummers or fifers and seventy-six privates when at full strength. Each soldier was given one pound of beef, three quarter pound of pork or salt fish per day, one pound of bread or flour, three pints of peas or other vegetables, half pint of rice or corn meal, and a quart of spruce beer. Each company received three pounds of candles, nine gallons of molasses, twenty-four pounds of soft soap, and eight pounds of hard soap.

The crowning achievement was the creation of a provisional civil government of forty-six of the leading men of the province to draft a plan of government by September 9. A plan was completed which set up the structure of the government. The Congress authorized trade for arms and ammunition.

On November 1, 1775, Henry attended the muster of the Mecklenburg Militia and the First Continental Regiment. Colonel James Moore, after the roll call, addressed the troops.

"Company stand at ease. As you are no doubt aware, Captain Huck has formed a militia in support of the Crown, and, as can be seen by our ranks, many of our militia have separated to his cause and have laid claim to some of our arms and ammunition. As of September 1st, the North Carolina Provincial Congress, in answer to a plea from the Continental Congress in Philadelphia, has authorized a continental army. I have been offered the command of the First Continental Regiment which will be recruited out of Tryon and Mecklenburg Counties. I now offer positions in this regiment for which reimbursement will be made for the service. There will be billets available for three months, three years, and the duration of the war. The Mecklenburg militia, or what is left of it, will be in command of Captain Polk. While the Continental regiment is away, the militia will be defending our homes. Those who wish to join the regiment may sign with Lt. Col Nash and Ensign Henry Neel at the table."

The militia then separated among those wishing to remain with the North Carolina Congress and those who wished to join Huck. All the remaining took the Oath as either a part of the Mecklenburg Militia or the First North Continental Regiment.

> I do swear, that I will be faithful and true to the United Colonies; that I will serve the same, to the utmost of my power, in defence of the rights of America, against all enemies whatsoever; that I will to the utmost of my abilities, obey the lawful commands of my superior officers, agreeable to the Ordinances of Congress and the Articles of War to which I have subscribed and lay down my arms peaceably, when required so to do by the Continental Congress. So help me God.

Nancy Agnes had become agitated earlier when Henry volunteered for service. However, she took the new developments in stride as a frontier wife.

It was November. Henry had risen through the ranks from brevet ensign to ensign of the Continental First Regiment. His company was drilling with their newly furnished muskets and recently acquired blue and buff uniforms of the

Continental Army. As an officer, Henry wore a blue uniform with a red lining and lapels trimmed in red. The cuffs were buff with white pants. A dispatch rider dressed in a Continental uniform rode up, dismounted, and saluted Henry. "Ensign Henry Neel."

"At your service, Sergeant."

"I bring you orders from Col. Moore who will serve under command of Col. Richardson. We are assembling at Salisbury in three days to march to the relief of our neighboring patriots at Norfolk."

Henry read the dispatches and then turned to his company. "Patriots, our brethren in Virginia have appealed for our aid. The Royal Governor, Lord Dunsmore, with British Regulars, has initiated a campaign of burning homes, plundering plantations, and seizing slaves and other properties. Return to your homes and be prepared to muster when the sun is at ten o'clock tomorrow. You will need a full pack, all ammunition you have, and your horse. We will be mounted infantry. Commissary Sergeant, come home with me. We will collect some livestock to take with us. We must have provisions for about a month."

Henry returned home and broke the news to Nancy Agnes about his departure. "I am proud of you, my husband, and we will find ways of keeping the farm going while you serve the province. We have trusty slaves and neighbors who will provide security."

Henry arose early the next morning to an early breakfast, kissed his children and Nancy goodbye. He then spoke to his eldest slave, Uncle John, who had been allowed to arm himself along with a half dozen others.

"I think the Cherokee are mainly at peace with us. If you run into any threats try to make it to Charlotte with the family. If not, have Mistress Nancy call on the Polks or Jacksons for help. See to it that our fort is well supplied in case there is not enough time to get to Charlotte. Thank you for all you do, my friend."

"Master Henry, you can depend on me. This is my family and land too."

"Thank you, I knew you would defend my family as well as your own."

"Yes, I heared about them King's people in Virginny that come in and carry off Negroes from their homes"

"How do you know such things?"

"I ain't supposed to tell but they'se are many Negroes hiding in the cane breaks and some of us servants gives them food."

"Well, be careful that they don't come in and skin us alive."

"They'se good people. They'se really my uncles and cousins who was sold up to the north by Master Huck."

"He did? I cannot believe it. I shall depend on you my friend, and as soon as your son masters tanning and blacksmithing, I shall give him his freedom. The offer of your freedom still stands."

"I'se too old, but thank you, Master Henry."

Henry called to his company sergeant who had rounded up cattle and hogs for provisions. The troop assembled with two commissary wagons and began their trip to Salisbury, arriving there at night fall. For the next week the regiment under Col. Richardson made its way to Virginia. The regiment at first used the Wagon Road for part of the way. This brought memories to Henry of his trip over the same country with Zeke Proctor as a young lad. The regiment soon departed from the Great Road and headed east to Hillsboro. There they were greeted by members of Congress. They continued to New Bern, then across the dismal swamp to an area northwest of Portsmouth where they were greeted and joined by the Virginia troops of the Continental line. The troops had remained in remarkable spirits even though some had not received their promised clothing and shoes. Animals driven on hoof furnished food for the troops as they moved toward Virginia.

On December 11, 1775, the troops approached the community of Great Bridge over the Nanosecond River in Norfolk. The restless Continentals stood on the docks making obscene gestures at the ships in the harbor. Sometimes in reply the ships would lob occasional shells at the town. Most of the Tory civilians had to be evacuated to the ships in the harbor. Some Continental skirmishers engaged foraging parties who came ashore on occasion. For a while things were at a standstill. Col. Howe, commander of the Continental forces, called a council of war and afterward Col. Moore ordered the Neel Company to dismount and advance toward the fortifications in front of the bridge.

Henry ordered his squad to dismount, form into a column four abreast, and be ready to fire by twos. Two artillery pieces christened "Old Mother Covington and Her Daughter" blasted at the fortifications. The British had no artillery since they were relying on the ships of His Majesty for support. In the process of unloading and placing ordnance, the enemy panicked when they spotted Henry's group on the road. Soon the entire regiment engaged in close battle. Henry's squad, now drawn in a skirmish line, advanced toward the bridge. Henry separated his rifle men and addressed them. "Gentlemen, it seems almost like murder but you long hunters, I want you to go to that copse of trees and see if you can pick off the officers. Good hunting."

Henry turned to the rest of the troops, "When I give the order we will charge the bridge."

The cannonade stopped. Colonel Howe fired a flare. Henry and the other troops charged. From the west, the troops of the Virginia line charged. The loyalists consisting of Lord Dunsmore's militia and some regular troops fled in rout. They dropped muskets, equipment, and packs as they fled in terror. Henry held his troops in check, but the Virginians were so incensed by the action of the loyalists that they charged the town of Portsmouth, looting and burning the homes and establishments of known Tories. Finally, a cease fire was announced and the British troops were allowed to board ships for New York with their wounded. As the loyalist troops passed Henry's company, a voice called out, "Ensign Neel!"

Henry turned to see a colonel of the British grenadiers on a stretcher being cared for by both British and American surgeons.

Henry drew near, recognized the face, and knelt down. "Major, I mean Colonel Anderson!" he exclaimed. "How wonderful to see you. Are you badly hurt?"

"I have a wound in the shoulder. I think one of your Continental riflemen was aiming for my head."

"Thank God you are safe. May I do anything for you?"

"I believe everything has been done for my comfort. I am quite perplexed and afraid for the outcome of these misunderstandings. I love my King and I love the friends I have made in this country. I have admired the way the colonials defended their country against the French and Indians. I only wish we could have peace."

"And so do I. Will you be going back to England?"

"I don't have much desire for England. My family lost most of its fortune and the estate is in dire circumstances. My wife turned out to be a shrew. She has had affairs with some of the noblemen in the area. We have lost our children. We will probably try for an annulment or something."

The two of them were now left alone.

"I guess it is a good thing I did not learn the minuet. Perhaps I would have been stuck in England," commented Henry.

"I fear I have nothing to return to. I have only my commission, and now with the condition of our estate and going on half-pay while inactive, things are not well."

Two privates and a British sergeant came up. "It is time to move you aboard, Sir."

Henry saluted, "Seriously, Colonel, if I can ever be of service call on me in the Waxhaw. Please write me and tell me how things turn out for you."

"You are most kind, Sir. Give my regards to your brother." With that he was lifted up and carried away.

Henry thought to himself, "I only wish he were on our side."

The Congress of the Virginia and the Continental Congress now celebrated their first victory. That night with much gaiety the Continentals from both colonies rejoiced. Wrestling, dancing, and lying about accomplishments prevailed. Col. Howe, against his better judgment, ordered a double ration of rum. It was during the festivities that Col. Moore called Henry aside.

"Captain Neel," he called.

Henry saluted, "Thank you, Sir, but in the dim light you must have misread my rank."

Moore continued, "I have not misread your actions. I am recommending you to the rank of captain. You may obtain this as a brevet until such time as the Congress or the Legislature approve. You will take over the company. Captain Smith has been incapacitated."

Two days later, the now Brevet Captain Henry Neel ordered his bleary eyed, hung-over company to mount up for the trip home. He questioned his own wisdom at having his company loose in the gin mills of Norfolk. Some had brawled with His Majesty's sailors. As he inspected his company, he noticed that there were no fatalities and but a few injuries. Only four were left behind for treatment.

He called newly-minted Ensign Lewis. "Jake, why, if we are leaving four wounded men behind, do we not have four empty saddles? And why are some men riding double and with Royal Navy uniforms?"

"Well, Sir, it is like this. These men are deserters from the English navy and wish to join the Continental line."

"Why was I not informed?"

"We did not know until last night when we drug our riff raff out of the taverns and these bleary-eyed wretches just came along. They are impressed seamen and are only too anxious to escape the boatswain's whip. They seem such nice fellows. Besides, that gives His Majesty some problems finding enough men to man his ships."

"Well, I guess we will take them. I can't believe the Congress would object. I hope His Majesty's problems don't become our problems. Hmmp."

"I don't think so, Sir. If they cause any trouble we can always turn them over to a press gang for a 'British re-enlistment.'" Lewis chuckled at his own joke.

The Continentals were called to a muster where warm congratulations and gestures of appreciation were read from the Virginia Committee of Safety, thanking the troops of North Carolina for their service. The order was given to proceed. Col. Moore dropped off "Mother Covington and Her Daughter" with the New Bern Committee of Safety with his compliments as they passed through the settlement. The voices of these two brass patriots would be heard again soon. When the Regiment reached Hillsboro, they were saluted by the Provincial Congress. In a week the Neel Company was home and furloughed.

Henry received a warm greeting upon returning home. During the interim, there had been some villages raided by the Cherokees around Rousmor's mill. There were no casualties. Brother militia Col. Thomas Christopher Neel authorized one of his companies to investigate. Their show of force resulted in a conference with the Cherokees. It seemed that the news of the land being ceded had not reached the ears of that particular raiding band.

# Part Two

In this part of our story we find ourselves in three locations. The youngest of patriarch Thomas's children, Andrew, signed the North Carolina Mecklenburg Resolves and was to be a part of the North Carolina militia serving in the southern portion of South Carolina in the area of Ninety-Six.

Henry, still living in the Waxhaw/Steele Creek area, would continue to serve in the North Carolina first Continental Regiment. Thomas Christopher, who helped set the new boundary between North and South Carolina, would resign as part of the North Carolina Assembly and become a member of the South Carolina Congress. In this "New Acquisition Area," he was appointed to the York County Committee of Safety, and served as the Colonel and commander of the Neel Regiment operating first around Ninety-Six. He joined the Florida/Georgia campaign and participated in defense of Charles Town. His regiment consisted of men from both North and South Carolina.

We should perhaps discuss the family of Andrew Neel, third oldest son of Thomas and Elizabeth Neel. Thomas (1710), as recorded earlier, was the son of Henry (DOB 1683). Thomas moved from the upper Cape Fear to the Providence area in 1735. He had four sons, Thomas, John Henry (also known as Henry), Andrew, Samuel and James, as well as daughters. His youngest son Andrew settled in Tryon, now Lincoln County, but spent much of his time developing some South Carolina land near Ninety-Six. He married Laureena Smith and from this marriage produced at least three children: Aaron, Sarah, and Thomas. His wife was the daughter of Aaron Smith whose land abutted Andrew's. Andrew became an important factor in the affairs of both Mecklenburg and Tryon County. He also served in the militia and fought at Moore's Creek Bridge, the Snow and Indian campaigns. He was originally an adjutant in the militia under Col. William Graham. This chapter makes him the protagonist for a short time. The monument mentioned in Chapter One lists "Andrew" as Clerk of the Court and in another place as the signer of the Mecklenburg Resolves. There is an Andrew who signed them. The monument mentioned Andrew as having been killed at Rocky Mount in 1780. We believe that Andrew is the nephew of the Andrew of the 1730's, but more about this later.

Because many of their activities occur in the same time frame, we will sometimes treat the characters' stories as separate narratives.

CHAPTER 25

# Fight Begins and Andrew Marches to Fort Ninety-Six

March 1775 the South Carolina Provincial Congress organized the military forces into three regiments, two on the coast and one ranger regiment in the interior. The Royal colonial regiments in the interior were dissolved since the Whigs, or rebels, did not fully control them. The Council of Safety thus hoped to eliminate all forces who would not take the oath supporting the Provincial Congress.

The Tryon North Carolina Safety Committee on August 14 formed their association. The committee subscribed to a document uniting themselves "under the most sacred rites of Religion, Honor, Love of our country to resist by force in defense of our Natural Freedoms." They further required all of the inhabitants, but especially the militiamen, to take an oath of support "for the Association and the preservation of rights and liberties."

The leadership of South Carolina Congress was divided. Conservatives Rowlin Loundes, Michael Brewton, Thomas Bee, and Thomas Hayward Jr. wanted to proceed slowly. William Henry Drayton, Arthur Middleton, Christopher Gadsden, and Charles Pinckney were more vigorous in pressing the Whig demands. News of disturbances led the Council of Safety to issue a Declaration of Alarm which at first called all militia to active duty and would have placed the colony under military law. The militia protested that they did not wish to give up their civil law. The mobilization order was rescinded. The German communities were not interested in the Whig cause because they seldom drank tea (the cause celebre of the boycott) and could not see the difference between being taxed by the Crown or being taxed by the legislature. In northwest South Carolina, a number of influential backcountry leaders took actions to thwart the Whig cause. Among them were Robert Cunningham, Thomas Browne (who had been tortured by the Whigs), and Thomas Fletchall. Fletchall, a justice of the peace and a colonel of the militia, had received a letter from the Committee of Safety requiring his regiment to take the oath of allegiance to the Provincial Congress. He reported back that the letter was read to his regiment but all refused to sign and had taken another oath supporting the cause but declaring their loyalty to the Crown. This prompted the Congress to send a mission to the backcountry to assure their loyalty.

In the spring of 1775 Captain Andrew, native of North Carolina, Tryon County, was completing some outbuildings of his new second farmstead near the Entree River ford. It was a hot day and he and some slaves were engaged in placing some trusses on the new cabins when his nephew Thomas (one of the twins) rode up.

"Welcome, young Thomas, what brings you here to South Carolina?"

"A rumor of great repast and comfort from Aunt Laureena Neel."

Putting on his blouse, Andrew turned to his servant. "We can fix that, come to the house. Jacob finish up. Be careful of the sun."

Young Thomas was mobbed by Andrews's three young children. They soon completed their usual ritual of robbing the pockets of his coat which contained hard candy.

Laureena came running from the house and embraced her nephew. "How is my Thomas? Have you found a woman to put some weight on you yet? You are so skinny. We will have to fix that. Sadie, bring us some punch from the spring house."

All three sat down on a circular bench around a large sycamore tree.

"What news do you bring?"

"I spent the night at Ninety-Six and heard some distressing news. There I learned of some horrible misfortunes of one Thomas Browne, a Scot gentleman of some importance from Georgia. It seems he made some disparaging remarks against the Committee of Safety in Georgia. He was submitted to torture by tarring and feathering his legs. He refused to recant even as his feet were blistered. He was run out of his settlement. However, some of his loyalist friends took him in and nursed him. Now recovered, he is one of the most militant loyalists in the area. There is also a rumor that Colonel Tom Fletchell lacks a loyalty to the Provincial Congress. He called his regiment together. Wait, weren't you there?"

"No, my Company is not under his regiment anymore. We are under Major Robinson. But, go on," answered his Uncle Andrew.

Thomas continued, "Anyway the Provincial Congress sent a letter to Col. Fletchell asking for a test oath of loyalty to the State as opposed to the His Majesty's Townsend Government. He replied that he read the Provincial Congress's letter to the troops but no one in the militia wished to sign. Instead, they drew up their own association and all signed it. He further stated that he utterly refused to take up arms against the King until it became his duty to do so. I really don't know what will come of this."

Andrew replied, "I have heard of this Fletchall; he rules the Fair Forest area like a king. Oh, I remember him. A giant of a man, but a most charming and charismatic fellow. I am sure he exercised a great deal of influence on his troops."

"Yes, and there is a rumor that Uncle Henry's friend, the Indian agent Lord Stuart, is stirring up the Indians. He will probably ask them to remain neutral if there is a fight; however, King George looks pretty good to the Indians with his 1763 proclamation against settling on the Indian lands by white intruders."

"I would hate to see another Indian War. We fought so hard to bring peace. Since Siever and his bunch made a treaty getting the middle Cherokees to cede lands without the authority of the Crown or the Congress, I think we are headed for trouble. That Over the Mountain area was more or less saved for Indian settlement, especially because of the proclamation of 1763. Your father and I have always admired Stuart as a just man as well as Chief Little Carpenter. I have heard that his son, Dragging Canoe, is quite vicious and not at all like his father."

The evening was spent reminiscing about the Catawba and the early days. The next morning Thomas left to return to the old Tryon plantation of his father, Thomas Sr., in a part of York County, South Carolina. It was a little before noon of a hot August day. Captain Andrew was again at work with his men on the new cabins. As he turned back to the mansion for dinner, he was greeted by three men on horseback. As they drew closer, they dismounted.

The larger of the men spoke. "I am William Drayton and these gentlemen are Reverend Oliver Hart of the Baptist faith, Reverend William Tennant, also a servant of the gospel and a patron of St. Andrew. Do I have the pleasure of addressing Captain Andrew Neel?"

"You do indeed, Sir. It is an extreme honor to be visited by the distinguished clergyman and the Speaker of the Provincial Congress. Your patriotism precedes you. How may I be of service? But before you answer, you must partake of a dinner. Laureena," he called, "we have company!"

"We bring you greetings from your brother congressman, Colonel Thomas Neel. We welcome the invitation and the companionship of your family."

Dinner was served outside under the trees. William Drayton began. "I am here to re-assure the population of the support of the Congress and to solicit help in suppressing those who would be disloyal to the Congress."

Andrew interrupted. "You mean, Sir, to shore up support of the Congress and try to suppress those loyal to the King?"

"Precisely and candidly put, but I prefer to think we persuade rather than suppress. What is the disposition of your company?"

"To a man, my company has sworn the test oath to the Congress. I understand that all of Colonel Robinson's as well as my brother Thomas's rangers have sworn an oath of allegiance. You are aware, of course, that the Neel Rangers are based mostly in North Carolina."

"But what have you heard of Thomas Fletchall's Regiment?"

Andrew then related what young Thomas had told him earlier.

"We wonder about Fletchall. We are not sure where his loyalties will eventually lie. Some zealots tortured his friend Thomas Browne, which could have angered him severely. On August 15th last I addressed a group at King's Creek on the Enoree. While there it was announced that Robert Cunningham, Master Brown's friend, was at hand. Someone suggested that we have a public disputation on the present crisis. After the debate, of which I believe I held my own, we invited Cunningham to dine with Rev. Tennant and myself, where we tried to convince him of our cause. After our refreshment, Thomas Browne limped in with Dlyrymple's *Address from the People of England to the People of America* from which he discoursed quite forcefully. I continued my exhortation but did not succeed in getting any signatures of loyalty. Two days later Tennant and I called on Col. Thomas Fletchall's residence in Fair Forest. Soon the party was joined by Cunningham, Brown, and of all things Col. Robinson. Brown had been busy distributing the pamphlet prepared by General Gage concerning *Dlyrymple's Address* with much acceptance. At breakfast the next day, we used all our charm and persuasion to convince Cunningham and Robinson, and all we got from Cunningham was the statement that he could never take up arms against the King and the proceedings of the Congress in Philadelphia were 'impolite, disrespectful, and irritating to the King.' Brown became so enraged that we were almost provoked to violence."

Andrew replied, "It is a great thing you did going among those people. I hope someday they will change their minds."

William Drayton continued, "I believe that Fletchall controls that area's people like those of a feudal lord. I have heard that Governor Lord Campbell secretly went there to shore up support for the King. By the way, Major Kirkland is rumored to have joined Fletchall with his company. I hear he was disappointed over being passed over a command by Mason.

"On another matter, you should be called to muster in a few days because of some unrest among the Indians."

Andrew answered, "You are probably referring to Lord Stuart the agent and the rumor that he has been enthusing the Creeks and Cherokees. I have heard that he has stressed neutrality. Where else have you gentlemen gone?"

Tennant answered. "We have met with Moravians and other Germans, as well as Quakers and Highland Scots. Tis a shame that Scots of our precious Presbyterian faith are so in bed with the Crown's Anglicans. In a word, our only success has been with you Irish Scots who came mainly from Ulster, Pennsylvania, and some English dissidents. In order to win the Cherokees and Chickasaws to our cause, we are going to rescue arms and ammunition from Fort Charlotte and give them to the tribes as a message of good will. We are not going to repeat the mistakes made in the late war where goods were taken from the Indians and massacres resulted. We are not sure what the strength of the backcountry is but this should help. May God have mercy on us."

At length Tennant, Hart and Drayton departed toward the west and the Tenneco River. They then moved to Ninety-Six from whence Tennant traveled to Georgia and returned to Charles Town by the Savannah River. Henry Drayton stayed on at Ninety-Six where he ordered Major Andrew Williamson of the Ninety-Six militia regiment to stand by. He also alerted Colonel Richard Richardson and Colonel William "Danger" Thompson to be ready with their men to act quickly if necessary.

It wasn't long before William Henry Drayton, as he tarried in the back country, began to realize that the inhabitants were not of a mind to separate from the Crown. Further, the Provincial Congress was split on its vision. One group wished for a reconciliation with a protection of the rights of Englishmen. The other, under Drayton and Arthur Middleton, wished for separation. In his trip through the backcountry, Drayton found that the long neglect and ridicule he and other of the southern Rice Kings had forced on the backcountry made his task exceedingly difficult. However, in the "New Acquisition," or the area ceded by North Carolina, he found support. This was the seat of the Neel empire. The estate consisted of some 3,000 acres of Colonel Thomas Neel, farms of his twin sons Andrew and Thomas, and across the line in North Carolina, the estates of his brothers Andrew and Henry.

Interpreting the mandate given to him by the Provincial Congress in Charles Town, William Henry Drayton exercised that power liberally. His task was to separate the leaders of the backcountry Tories from their militia. His targets were Moses Kirkland (who recently changed sides when denied a promotion with the Whig militia), Robert Cunningham, and his brothers, Thomas Brown and Thomas Fletchall. His first move was to muster the militia under Col. Richard Richardson to Ninety-Six. He then issued a Declaration warning people against Moses Kirkland. Kirkland responded by fleeing to Charlotte and the Governor's protection.

Drayton raised 1,000 militia at Ninety-Six to confront the Tories. Thomas Fletchall responded with 1,200 Tory militia. Not wanting a confrontation at this time, Drayton invited Col. Fletchall to Ninety-Six for a conference. Brown and Cunningham refused to attend.

What emerged on 16 September 1775 was the Treaty of Ninety-Six in which the Tories promised not to assist British troops in any way, and the Rebels agreed to punish any of their people who molested or harmed a Tory. The Treaty ended with an ominous sentence: "All persons who shall not consider themselves bound by the treaty must abide by its consequences."

When the corpulent three-hundred pound Fletchall returned to report the treaty to his compatriot, "burnt foot" Thomas Brown wrote the Royal Governor of Georgia complaining that Fletchall was drunk when he signed the treaty and that he was not bound by the treaty. William Henry Drayton wrote Cunningham asking him if he were bound by the treaty. His answer was that he was not so bound. As he was eligible for arrest under the Whig interpretation of the treaty, Robert Cunningham became a fugitive hidden by his many friends. Thomas Brown went to Charles Town to see the Governor, was captured by the Committee of Safety and ordered to leave South Carolina. He moved to Augustine, Florida where he formed the King's Loyal Rangers. Thus two of the antagonists of the Tory cause were neutralized, at least temporarily.

Thomas was conversing with Alexander and his son Thomas Jr. when Henry Drayton and a guard of four militia rode up. He arose and approached the patrician who was on his splendid mount.

"Master Drayton, what an honor, what brings you to York County?"

"Col. Neel, a rumor of fine repast here as well as to solicit your help with the Cherokees. There is a rumor that John Stuart is arming the Cherokees against us."

The group enjoyed a splendid meal in which the events of the day were discussed. Jean was a little perplexed at the thought of another fight for the militia. She could not reconcile the thought of Thomas's absence and the need for more supervision at the farm.

The next morning Thomas, accompanied by James Hawthorne and the twins, Thomas and Andrew, joined Drayton. They met at the Congarees with Good Warrior and other Southern Cherokees. Drayton gave the usual "Friends and Brother Warriors" speech, discussed the Whig point of view and promised guns and ammunition if the Cherokees would support their cause. Thomas inquired concerning his friend Little Carpenter and was told that he was with the Over the Hill Cherokees as the peace chief. However, his son Dragging Canoe was now a war chief. The Drayton party departed after the signing of the treaty.

In order to appease the Indians, the South Carolina Committee of Safety in July 1775 ordered a portion of the militia under Major Mason to occupy Ft. Charlotte on the Savannah River. His mission was to seize and hold the fort and move a wagon load of ammunition and guns to the Cherokees as a message of good will. Col. Robinson also appointed Captain Perris to meet with the leaders of the Cherokees to explain the gift. Both sides accused the other of enlisting the

Cherokees. Be they Tory, Whig, or neutral, this stirred up memories of the Indian wars of ten years before.

On October 1, 1775 the Provincial Congress elected William Henry Drayton as president. On the same day Robert Cunningham was captured by the Neel Rangers near Ninety-Six and within the week was brought before Congress. There imprisoned, he was without any recourse to contact from the outside.

The news infuriated the Tory faction in the backcountry. On November 3, Robert's brother, Patrick Cunningham, and sixty men captured the wagon carrying the 1,000 pounds of powder and 2,000 pounds of lead liberated from Ft. Charlotte on the Savannah River by Whig forces under Major Mason. This was the load promised the Indians by Henry Drayton. Major Mason and Captain Caldwell found themselves captives of the Tories.

Meanwhile, Whig General Moultrie had organized the defenses of Charles Town and had driven the British Navy from the harbor. The Governor on board one of the ships was to spend some time on the high seas having evacuated Charles Town. He was soon joined at sea by Governor Martin fleeing North Carolina.

In November, 1775, Andrew was assigned as commander of a company of the militia between the Tyree and Enoree Rivers in South Carolina. Andrew's North Carolina Company moved to South Carolina and the village of Ninety-Six. There was growing concern about the loyalty of some of the citizens of the area around Ninety-Six near the two mentioned rivers. Captain Andrew was especially concerned because he had some property in that area of South Carolina.

Newly appointed Governor William Drayton reported the news to the Provincial Congress. Col. Thomas Neel, as the head of the York Committee of Safety and a county representative, rose and proposed an expedition to recover the goods taken by Cunningham. The debate was spirited and went through over one hundred resolutions. Arthur Middleton, friend of Drayton, lead the faction for vigorous prosecution while Rawlin Laurens lead the more conciliatory group. The latter still hoped for a resolution of differences with the Crown. Finally on November 8, 1775, by a vote of fifty-one to forty-nine, the Congress passed a resolution calling for a "draught" of militia.

> To Col. Richard Richardson
> Sir,
> There being a necessity of assembling six Companies of the regiment of Rangers, Capt. Polk's Company of Volunteers, and draughts of militia to act in the interior parts of this colony; and ye being the eldest field officer now ordered upon this service, of course the command of the detachments upon

this service vests in ye. And hereby ye are ordered, to draught form your regiment of militia , including militia Volunteers, and to demand of Col. William Thomson, Col. John Savage, **Col. Thomas Neel,** and Col. John Thomas, or the commanding officer of each of these regiments (including militia volunteers) present, respectively, and they, and each of them, are herby ordered to supply ye with such numbers of men with their officers to be draughted from those of any of those regiments, in order to act under ye command as ye shall judge necessary.

On the 3rd day of this instant November, Patrick Cunningham, Henry O'Neal, Hugh Brown, David Reese, Nathanial Howard, Henry Green, and sundry other armed persons unknown, did, in Ninety-Six district, cause and raise a dangerous insurrection and commotion, and did, near Mine-creek, in the said district, feloniously take a quantity of ammunition, the property of the public, and in contempt of the public authority: Therefore , ye are here by instructed and ordered, with the troops aforesaid, or and party of them, to march, and to act in such manner as ye shall deem expedient, to seize and to apprehend ; and with those troops or any part of them, ye are herby ordered to seize and to apprehend, the bodies of Patrick Cunningham, Henry O's Neal, Hugh etc. (Bold on Neel's name added from McCready text)4

Thus began William Henry Drayton's first session with the South Carolina Provincial Congress. The act further ordered:

1. Col. Thomas Fletchall to surrender Patrick Cunningham and his associates.
2. Transmit to Major Andrew Williamson the thanks of the Congress for apprehending Robert Cunningham.
3. Committees of the several districts to prevent the removal of the effects of any debtors out of the colony (probably to discourage Tories who were trying to flee).
4. A list of draughts including one hundred from Col. Fletchall and one hundred from Col. Neel.
5. Mentions the rations and pay for service.
6. Militia Volunteers forbidden to take the field on horseback (probably to prevent an easy retreat).

President William Drayton, accompanied by Col. Richardson, marched toward Ninety-Six where Major Williamson bivouacked with regiment. Andrew was now temporary Captain and commander of his brother's Neel Rangers. Thomas, who had previously stayed behind with the Congress, arrived at the Whig bivouac with his company. He dismounted, ordered his company to camp, and proceeded to the tent of Col. Robinson. He was greeted by Major Williamson.

"Captain Neel," he exclaimed "Good to see you again. How is that wonderful family of yours?"

"'Tis fine, Sir. And how is your health?"

"It is an exciting time. A time when our blood flows strongly for freedom. But enough of this. Captain Johnson will give you your assignments."

"My compliments Captain Neel, what is your strength?"

"We have a mounted company of seventy militia trained by monthly muster, but mostly riflemen. We have a wagon train of three for our baggage and provisions for about a month."

"Excellent, excellent. Let me describe our mission. A few weeks ago, the Provincial Congress of South Carolina gained knowledge that His Lordship James Stuart had been meeting with some of the tribes but primarily the Cherokees. The Congress then asked a company of Kirkland's troop under Major Mason to go to Ft. Charlotte on the Savannah and relieve them of some ammunition and other trinkets for appeasing the Cherokees. They did and Captain Caldwell was left to garrison. Upon returning to Ninety-Six, the goods were stolen by Major Cunningham of Fletchall's militia. Unfortunately, the remainder of your Major Robinson's squadron have now gone over to Col. Fletchell."

"What have we heard from Col. Fletchall?" asked Andrew.

"I suppose you heard about how the good Colonel Fletchall refused to take the oath of the association and instead took one of his own. He called a muster of the general regiment at the Enowee ford. At that time Major Kirkland attended the muster. Kirkland was disappointed that the South Carolina Congress did not approve him as a regimental commander instead of me. Six men of his company came back and told us that Kirkland had joined the Loyalist's forces under Fletchall and that most of the whole upper country has joined him.

"These men reported that your Major Robinson, a portion of the Neel Regiment, including Captain Polk's Company, and the companies of Robert and Patrick Cunningham have joined those forces. In essence, your old commander has now become a loyalist as have at least 1,500 others. The entire people from the Broad to Savannah Rivers have come out against the Congress and for the King. With the addition of your Rangers we now have six hundred fit for duty. I suggest that you double your pickets and commission a twenty-four hour alert."

"I cannot believe that Polk would engage in such duplicity."

"These are trying times for us all. These are weighty questions for us to decide.

We are outnumbered and can expect an attack soon. Anyway we were called here by the South Carolina Council of Safety to defend this village."

Andrew met with his company and gave them Major Williamson's orders. He looked at the fort. It was really a village with a jail, twelve dwellings, a court house, store, tavern and corrals. Barricades and ditches were prepared to meet the forces of Col. Robinson. The complement near the fort now consisted of Major Williamson's two companies and Andrew's company. They awaited President Drayton and the forces of Col. Richard Richardson. A well was dug and a barricade constructed. Whig forces cowered behind the rapidly erected defenses. Before their eyes on November 22, with drums beating, fifes playing and banners flying, Patrick Cunningham and his insurgents marched in and took possession of the court house, jail and invested the stockade. Drayton had 560 men fit for service. Cunningham's Tories had 2,000.

The Whig forces began to re-fortify their portion of Ninety-Six by digging trenches and throwing up abutments of wagons. Andrew was standing near Major Williamson. They mounted and approached Major Robinson. Williamson turned to Andrew and said, "It looks like the good leopard has changed his spots from green to red."

Robinson drew up and while still on his horse saluted and spoke, "Well look here, Neel. I wondered what happened to Neel's Company. You missed the muster at the Congarees."

Andrew replied, "I did not receive my orders in time to meet you, but proceeded to our ultimate objective which was Ninety-Six."

"Then you are unaware that enlightened companies of the Neel Rangers have now taken an oath of loyalty to the King."

"I can't believe my brother would allow such a thing."

"Your brother Col. Thomas has placed me in command. The Polk and Cunningham's regiments have joined with Col. Fletchall's Regiment and hope to bring peace to the area by enforcing the King's law. Captain Patrick Cunningham has captured the ammunition bound for this fort with which the so-called South Carolina Congress had hoped to arm the Cherokee. Thank God we saved the country from this nefarious deed. You might as well yield. But enough of this. Major Williamson, we command you to hand over the remaining ammunition and supplies your forces confiscated from Ft. Charlotte, and further we call upon all of you to take an oath of allegiance to the King."

Drawing up smartly in his saddle, Williamson looked Robinson straight in the eye and replied, "I respectfully refuse as I have taken an oath in support of the Provincial Congress and therefore cannot take up an oath to support a King who will allow a tyrants such as Lords Townsend and Germain to take away our freedoms. However, I would like to have something like the honors of war and we will give you the village."

Robinson then turned to Williamson and Andrew. "That comment amounts to treason, and Captain Andrew Neel as your commander I must warn you that if you and your company fail to come with me I shall be forced to charge you with insubordination and deal accordingly."

Andrew replied, "Major, as you will recall, when I was in North Carolina I signed the Mecklenburg Resolves in which I swore an oath in support of the patriot cause and the Provisional government. I cannot and will not invalidate my oath. My brother, Col. Thomas Neel, is the commander of this regiment and until such time as he orders me I shall remain loyal to my last command from him."

"Major Williamson, you have one hour to surrender the post and all of your arms and ammunition. Should you refuse, you will be declared an enemy of the Crown and dealt with accordingly."

"Robinson," he replied, "our families have served together a long time. If we surrender, we will be acting against our lawful legislature as well as endangering the lives of our families by causing the Cherokees to anger. We chose to defend our righteous cause."

"Very well then," Robinson replied. "May God have mercy on our souls."

Andrew Neel and Williamson returned to the fortifications. Andrew spoke. "Major Robinson has been a long time friend of our family. He fought well in the Indian wars. I cannot understand his sudden lack of resolve."

"Well, my friend, these are trying times. Families will be torn asunder as the Continental Congress debates what they are to do. I am just afraid that if the Indians get started, both loyalists and patriots will pay. Upon hearing of the growing militancy, I was commanded to set a force to occupy this outpost and arrest the justice of peace, your brother's old nemesis, James Matthews. You know, one of the reasons those backcountry people are worried is that the Tories have spread a rumor that the ammunition we were to give the Indians would be used to raid the settlers."

As they were returning to the lines, Williamson and Neel were greeted by Lieutenant Lewis. Major Williamson shouted. "Hold your fire men. Fill your canteens and get your rations. Be prepared for a siege. Look lively. Each man in a company will fire only once until the entire company has fired once. Change positions after each shot. Let's not try to kill them yet just scare the hell out of them!"

All day the shallow gunfire continued. No one seemed too anxious to cause any damage. There were even some good natured exchanges as the opposing forces looked across at each other.

"William," one soldier yelled to another, "with that aim of yours I don't see how you ever killed any squirrels."

"Are you fighting for the King or sore that I stole your girl? And keep your damn head down so I won't shoot you."

"If I were as mean as you, I would hunt bears with a switch. I cannot understand why Sue would marry someone as ugly as you."

For three days the sporadic desultory fire continued with no let up. The forces within Ninety-Six were more comfortably seated than those of Williamson. On the first day Robinson ran up a black flag of "no quarter." By the third day a white flag was waved for parley.

Williamson, accompanied by Andrew and Robinson rode between the lines. Andrew was surprised to see Speaker of the Congress William Henry Drayton accompanying Major Robinson.

"Your Excellency," remarked a startled Williamson, "What a surprise! What brings you here?"

"I arrived last night and have parleyed a truce with Major Robinson. Major Robinson, please proceed."

"Major Williamson, I propose a truce. You must leave the fort and free Justice Mathews and any prisoners you have. You will be allowed to return to your homes unmolested with arms and any ammunition you can carry on your person plus all the wagons and livestock you have brought—except for your field pieces which will be turned over to me. I do this as a humanitarian effort. You will also be happy to know that Captain Polk's company will be joining you as well as others of that rebel kind. Let us hope that our differences can be resolved by some peaceful means and we can return to our salubrious relationship we so earnestly solicit. We must both accept an agreement that this will end our animosity and that both our forces will remain neutral in this present unpleasantness."

"I accept your generous terms with the hope that you will pursue our mutual interest to ameliorate the concerns of the Cherokee tribe. We fought together to bring peace to the area. Let us try to keep the tribe at peace with us. In addition, I propose that we negotiate later for the ammunition taken from us which was meant to pacify the Cherokees."

Papers were then exchanged and signed. The paper swore a truce and a promise to live in peace. While the ceremony was going on, William Drayton approached Williamson and told him that the cannon would be secretly returned at a later date.

"God bless you, Tom, and may God have mercy on our souls," was Robinson's reply.

Captain Polk's company fell in with the regiment and they returned to the Catawba. Major Kirkland's company was not among them.

The companies returned back to the Catawba area. Upon their arrival and hearing of the desertions, Col. Thomas Neel called for a muster. He then conducted a court marshal concerning the desertion of two of the companies to the cause of Fletchall and his band of loyalists.

Col. Thomas Neel (1730) sat in his tent at a camp table. Two candles barely illuminated his frontier militia uniform. Just returned from a session of the South Carolina Congress, he frowned as he read the peace agreement. Thomas winced to find that two Tory leaders, Brown and Cunningham, had not signed the treaty agreement. Major Williamson attended him. Thomas turned to his companion.

"While you were gone I received a letter from President Drayton congratulating you on your mission. A second letter arrived from the Committee of Safety condemning us and Drayton for the Ninety-Six Campaign."

"Must be quite perplexing. These are trying times," replied Major Williamson.

Captain Polk appeared. He ducked into the entrance, came into the tent, saluted, and stood at attention. He was dressed in deer skins, the uniform of the backcountry.

"Tom, er Captain Polk, at ease," Thomas began, "You are called before this court of inquiry to explain the desertion of your company. Please enlighten us as to why you joined the forces of Fletchall."

"Well, Tom, er Colonel," he began, "my company was under Major Kirkland and was obligated to obey his command. We at first did not realize we had been drawn into Col. Robinson's change of sides. It was only after we had surrounded the fort that we realized there were two forces. I approached Major Kirkland and asked why we were serving under a Union Jack. He replied that his companies were now in the service of Col. Fletchall, who wished for peace, and was against the Townsend Acts but was not going to fight against the King. I was extremely perplexed about where my duty lay. I tried to contact Andrew and his company, but they had already crossed over. I gave the men a chance to vote. They chose to go with the Congress. Hearing this, Col. Robinson ordered us to the rear where we stayed until the truce was called and then joined Major Williamson's command. I apologize for any inconvenience caused the Neel's Rangers and offer both my loyalty and resignation."

"What say you, Major Williamson?" Col. Tom winked and turned to his Major Williamson.

"Why should we lose one of the best company commanders because of a lack of communication seeing his men have already taken an oath of loyalty."

"Captain Polk, I refuse to accept your resignation. Return to your company with my compliments. I now declare Captain Kirkland and his company in mutiny and will bring charges of desertion and mutiny at such times as he is caught. Major Williamson, dismiss the regimental muster. I am going home."

# CHAPTER 26

# Colonel Thomas and the Snow Campaign

After the siege and peace of Fort Ninety-Six, Col. Thomas Neel received a report from his brother Andrew and Tom Polk regarding the peace arrangements and everyone relaxed. Thomas heard that the provincial President, John Drayton, had met with the Cherokees, together with the new South Carolina Indian agent, to explain the loss of the promised ammunition which Cunningham had stolen from the Whig forces enroute from Ft. Charlotte on the Savannah to Ninety-Six.

On November 15, 1775, Thomas Neel (1730) relaxed with Jean and their children as they awaited supper. The crops had been harvested. It was a good year, in spite of all the political excitement. Fruits had been dried, fodder for some of the animals had been stored, and many cattle and hogs added. Thomas was at home after the long debate concerning the theft of ammunition meant for the Cherokees. Thomas Jr. and James Hawthorne joined the family in the great room. A servant came in, "Master Tom, there appears to be a troop coming." Thomas arose from his chair and headed for the porch. An officer in the troop dismounted and saluted.

"Col. Neel, I am Lieutenant Thomas Ingless of Col. Richardson's muster. I have dispatches for you from the South Carolina Committee of Safety."

"Thank you, Lieutenant. I knew this was coming. I helped debate it. Please take some repast. Will you stay the night?"

"I am sorry, Sir, we must be contacting other militia." With that the squad rode off.

The men walked into the room. Jean arose from her sewing anger gleaming in her eye, "I don't know what it is, but you are not going off playing soldier again. Your family obligations take precedence."

"Let us first see what it says."

Thomas tore the string from the packet and broke the seal. He read silently and began.

"It seems that our Major Kirkland has never surrendered after stealing the ammunition headed for the Cherokees. Col. Richardson has been ordered by the Congress to assemble troops to search for him. Further, the Neel regiment is to assemble at the Fork of the Saluda."

Jean spoke. "Did not the peace agreement at Ninety-Six forbid hostilities? Why is Richardson calling a muster?"

"I am not sure that Col. Richardson is bound by the agreement. There is some communication that the forces of Robinson have broken the agreement and raided some of the property of those who support the Congress near McClarin's store. Anyway, I heard his forces were moving toward Col. Fletchall's fiefdom on the Broad River."

"Thomas, ride over to Polk's and Uncle Henry's and tell them of the muster. I am not sure if Henry is still there. I think the Continental Regiment has been called away. Tell them to assemble on November 20 at our place on the Catawba."

"Young Andrew, you ride to Uncle Andrew and notify all the militia on the way. Tell them to start the notification tree."

"Uncle Arthur, prepare a wagon with corn, flour, and the usual vittles. We will also need about ten cattle for use on the way. James, act as quartermaster and keep track of our expenses. Now let us pray."

In three days two hundred men of Neel's regiment had assembled at the Catawba River. They began their march to the militia under Col. Richardson. Coming with Polk's company were young Thomas, Andrew, and James Hawthorne. Thomas and Andrew had given up their King's uniforms for the fringed deer hunting blouse, deerskin leggings, and trail boots.

As the Neel Rangers approached the Congarees, they were met by the final company of the ranger regiment commanded by Thomas's brother Andrew. A cheer went up as the two groups met at the crossroads.

Andrew drew ahead of the troops and approached Thomas. Andrew was also dressed as a frontiersman and mounted on a large black stallion. Both men had the black cockade of the Revolution on their hats. Each carried two pistols in their belts with a rifle mounted on their saddles. As Andrew rode forward, he greeted Thomas who was well mounted on the son of Champion, a large dapple stallion. The breath of the horses was visible in the cold November morning.

Mockingly, Andrew moved away from his troops and saluted. "Good morning Colonel. I see you have given up your fine King's uniform. How goes it?"

"Listen, Captain, as a member of the South Carolina Provincial Congress and as chairman of the York County Committee of Safety, I shall not brook such insults."

"I had not realized I was in such august company!"

Next morning Andrew continued with his brother Col. Thomas. "I do not feel comfortable with this little excursion. I was a party to the treaty agreement with Col. Robinson at Ninety-Six in which I agreed not to take up arms against Fletchall."

"That is a question that will have to be answered."

On the first of December, the Neel Regiment reached Dutch Fork and camped near McLaurin's store fifteen miles from the Saluda River. Thomas reported to Col. Richardson's force of 2,500 men. Newly minted Col. Polk with six hundred men was on a march from North Carolina with a regiment. The Neel Regiment joined with two hundred men and Col. Lyles with one hundred and fifty, along with other regiments of rangers as well. They hoped for the arrival of the First North Carolina Continental Regiment which would complete the complement. One of the companies of the Continentals was commanded by newly promoted Lieutenant Henry Neel.

As the Neels rode along, Andrew turned to Thomas. "I really admire Henry's joining the Continentals, but I favor the militias."

Thomas interrupted. "There are very few militias as well trained as the Neel Rangers; however, we have a devil of time getting the troops to leave their homes. I know General Washington is in favor of a standing army which can be moved anywhere on the continent."

Andrew continued, "That is all well and good, but a militiaman will fight harder for his home than a continental."

Thomas replied, "Wait until they see a bayonet or a broad sword charge. Excuse me, I must get back to my men before the muster."

As the Neels approached the night's bivouac the tall gray haired Col. Richardson was addressing six of Tory Fletchall's captures.

"I am charging you men with trying to foment rebellion against the Congress of South Carolina. I am going to release three of you. You are to return to your homes with this proclamation: 'to wit. You must deliver the bodies of Patrick Cunningham and Henry O'Neal and any other who led the siege at Ninety-Six and deliver the ammunition taken by Cunningham, the arms of all the aiders and abettors of these robbers, murderers, and disturbers of the peace. And further, you must submit to the oath of allegiance in support of the Philadelphia Congress and the Congress of South Carolina.'"

"Sir," pleaded one Captain Johnson of Fletchall's militia, "I was at Ninety-Six and under the terms of the agreement we were to disband, which we did, and were not to be molested as we are now."

"You ingrate, you would have me believe that you had not robbed and harassed your neighbors who have taken the oath of freedom?"

"But, we did take an oath under Fletchall. I protest our treatment, Sir."

"Put this man in irons. That oath was in support of Fletchall's militia, not the Congress. The rest of you Fletchall men can return to your homes. But remember we must have Cunningham and O'Neal as well as our ammunition."

"Greetings Col. Neel, what an honor to have a representative of the Congress with us. By the way, your son just arrived."

"Sergeant Adams, take Col. Neel and Captain Neel over to the tent of Ensign Neel. My, this is confusing. Does anybody else in the Waxhaw but the Neels fight for the Congress?" Robinson asked.

"Thank you, Sir," replied Col. Thomas, "but there is one more. My brother Lieutenant Henry is with the Continental First Regiment of North Carolina. We are quite prolific."

Richardson smiled, "Just leave a little of the war for the rest of us."

As they approached the tent, young Andrew and Thomas ran and embraced their two namesakes. Out limped James Hawthorne who also embraced them.

"What do you trail bums have to say for yourselves?"

"Thank you Sergeant, what happened to you?"

James answered, "We got into a little skirmish coming here and I got winged. Should be healed soon."

Col. Thomas said, "Enough of this. Praise God you are all safe. By the way Jimmy, I suppose you will be asking me if you can court Mary Ann soon. Of course, it all depends on how many bad habits you have picked up from Uncle Alexander," he said with a chuckle. "I shall expect a call when I get home."

"I would be obliged, Sir. But now I wish to engage some Cherokees to avenge my family."

***

That afternoon Col. Richard Richardson conducted a court martial. After hearing the evidence, the court decided that the five men who deserted James and the brothers would be placed as advanced scouts and would "volunteer" for the next "forlorn hope."

Richardson called a council of war at the McClarin Store. "Men, I would like to explain why we are fighting. Col. Fletchall, although he outwardly has submitted to the term of the Ninety-Six agreement, has enthused the population for Lord William Campbell who rules bravely as governor from a ship outside the harbor under the protection of the Royal Navy. And I guess he communicates with his subjects by carrier pigeons." The officers laughed.

"Now we shall pursue these people until we find those who stole the ammunition. Be ready to march in an hour. See that your men have at least three days rations. Do what you can for their comfort as it is beginning to snow and will be some tough going. Try to avoid any looting other than minimal forage. However, if you need blankets, take them. Remember we are trying to get these people to join our cause so treat them gently, unless of course, you run into Master O'Neal or one of the Cunningham boys. The Committee of Safety also has warrants out for Hugh Brown, David Reese, Nathaniel Howard, Henry Green, and Jacob Bochman. You are dismissed."

The force under Col. Richardson advanced steadily into the Tory country. As they rode, Andrew turned to his brother Thomas and said, "Col. Richard Richards, being a member of the Committee of Safety, had some trouble getting them to vote on this expedition. I heard it took one hundred votes again before the Committee could barely agree to call up the militia. Since I was a party to the agreement at Ninety-Six, I am somewhat disturbed by this. However, if the Fletchall bunch really did raid some of our Whigs, I could get over the discomfort."

"Well, as you know, dear brother, even before we had Regulators in North Carolina, there were some in South Carolina. The then Governor Bull sent a force under Scoville to root out the people who were harassing the officers of the Crown. Scoville became a dictator and crushed the resistance. Thomas Fletchall took over as his successor and has ruled in the interest of the crown ever since. Some Whig farms have mysteriously been raided by Indians while Tory farms are left without any harassment. That is one of the reasons we don't feel too bound by the Ninety-Six agreement."

"I feel better already."

"By the way watch out for the youngsters, Andrew, Thomas, and James Hawthorne. I don't want those young hot bloods getting into trouble again."

"I wouldn't worry. They probably take after us both."

"That is why I worry. By the way did you hear that Tom Sumter has been given a command? It seems he was given command of Kirkland's regiment when it was about to be disbanded. Some feel that the regiment is really a bunch of Tories. They seem to be quite loyal to me."

"Yes, they do," remarked Andrew, "but I know Tom, he has a lot of families on both sides."

"Speaking of changing sides, Col. Richardson told me that Richard Pearis, to whom the Committee gave a commission as Indian agent, has now joined the Tories. He had accompanied President Henry Drayton when he met with the Cherokees concerning the powder and ammunition, but when he did not receive a command was induced to change sides. Now he will probably work on the Cherokees to turn out against us."

"My, you are full of good news." Just then a courier rode up.

"I am looking for Neel's Rangers."

"That is what my flag says son, what can I do for you?"

"Dispatches from Col. Richardson." He then handed the packet to Thomas who opened them and exclaimed, "There is some intelligence that the King's men are forming near the Cane Break on the Saluda. Our regiment is to march there with the forces of Col. Danger Thompson."

Thomas ordered a forced march through a falling snow and on December 21 arrived within a view of the Tory campfires. On the morning of the 22nd, the Neel Regiment as well as the forces of Thompson surrounded the Tories. Just as they were about to attack, they were discovered. The Tories were unable to form a skirmish line. Their leader, Patrick Cunningham, escaped on a bareback horse. Six of the Tories were killed before Thomas and Thompson could restore order. No Whigs were killed. In the meantime, Col. Richard Richardson sent his son to Charles Town with Col. Thomas Fletchall, Captain Richard Pearis, Captain Shuberg, and others under guard. Fletchall had been hiding in the trunk of a hollow tree. The Congress confined Col. Fletchall in Charles Town. When the city fell to the British in 1780, he was restored his commission with the Royal forces.

The expedition returned to Dutch Fork where the troops were dismissed to their homes. The three brothers went their separate ways. This was to be known as the Snow Campaign, fought in one of the worst snow storms in the history of South Carolina. Col. Thomas was quite disturbed to hear that Samuel Johnston and his company had deserted and probably joined the Tories. All of the Neel brothers headed for their homes in hopes of making that goal by the new year.

CHAPTER 27

# *Captain Henry and the fight at Widow Moore's Creek*

We now turn to a more detailed discussion of Henry Neel born 1736 and his family. Far less colorful than his brothers Thomas and Andrew, Henry prospered in the Providence area northeast of Charlotte near the Waxhaw. The term "Waxhaw" refers to the area occupied by a former Indian tribe with that name. He became the sheriff and justice of the peace in the area as well as a captain (in our story) in the militia serving as a company commander under Huck's regiment. Huck is, of course, a fictitious character. Henry and Nancy Agnes Reid continued to develop their estate on Steele Creek, about ten miles north and across the Catawbas from brother Thomas. Henry participated in some of the Indian wars (1755 to 1763); however, unlike the estates of brother Thomas which lay along the Catawba River and shared the borders between the colonies of North and South Carolina, Henry's land lay adjacent to the Cherokee lands and was on the trade route to Salisbury. His primary concern was usually defending himself and his family against the Cherokees and Shawnees.

Henry had, as a tradition, named his first son after his father. Thomas will be the adopted son of Andrew later in the story. Andrew in this story is Henry's (1736) brother.

Henry, an officer in the North Carolina militia, resigned to become an ensign in the North Carolina Line First Regiment. The Provincial Congress had authorized the regiment at the request of the Congress in Philadelphia. Henry took his commission in the new Continental Army with pride. His wife Nancy later sewed the buff uniform of a brevet captain, a commission he received after the Battle of the Great Bridge in Virginia. With his new dragoon boots purchased in Charles Town, she felt he was one of the handsomest men in the colony.

Andrew and his brother Henry both received a post from the New Bern Committee of Correspondence stating that a Donald MacDonald and Donald McLeod had both been brought before the North Carolina Committee on Safety since they were rumored to be recruiting among the Highland Scot settlements near Cross Creek. They had resided at the home of Alan MacDonald (Donald MacDonald's cousin) and his wife Flora MacDonald, whom Polk and Thomas had met at the Governor's ball. Proponents for the Committees heard through one of the patriots in the area that Alan MacDonald and McLeod were speaking in Gaelic to the inhabitants. They were hauled before the Committee of Safety to answer charges of treason against the colony. Their defense was that they were merely visiting their clansmen on their journey north. A later communication from the Continental Army in Massachusetts asked of their whereabouts. It seems that the two visitors were officers of the British regulars at Bunker Hill. The Safety Committee had been chastised by the Selectmen for their carelessness. There was now a great deal of concern about the backcountry and its loyalty.

January 1776 began cold and blustery. January was sometimes fierce in the Piedmont, but the swamp areas to the east were relieved to be beyond the yellow fever and hurricane seasons. This area of the Piedmont was the site of Henry Neel's farm. Henry Neel's family gathered on the manse at Steele Creek enjoying the holiday season. He had just returned from the Battle at the Great Bridge in Norfolk. Henry was one of the more enlightened Presbyterians who now celebrated the pagan Christmas much to the chagrin of some other staunch, old time, Presbyterian elders. Henry and Mary were relaxing when one of the boys came in.

"Father, the post arrives."

Henry opened the large oaken door and stood on the porch. A sergeant's guard in the dress of the North Carolina Continental Army rode up. The sergeant dismounted from among the four man troop and saluted. "Captain Neel, Colonel James Moore has called the First Continental Regiment to assemble at Wilmington on January 15. Your orders are to assemble your company immediately and report for service."

"Thank you sergeant. Have your men take some refreshment and draw such rations as you may need from the kitchen. By the way, I am only an ensign not a Captain. I don't believe I have been raised above a brevet."

"Sir, I only addressed you by what was on the orders. I heard you had been promoted. Thank you for the offer of lodging. You are most kind." He saluted, and the company, after a meal and refreshing their horses, rode to find the rest of the regiment.

Wearily, Henry said good-bye to his family. Before leaving he called his overseer Uncle John. "Uncle John, I must again rely on you to manage the grounds and protect my family. You may issue arms to those seven servants we trust and fortify the family fort against Cherokees. Some of the militia should warn you if there is trouble from the Cherokees or Tories. If things look bad, try to get everyone to the Polk's place. Have someone take this note about my leaving to Col. Thomas

Neel and Captain Polk. What do your friends in the woods have to say about the Cherokees?"

"Well, suh, Alexander came by from the Thomas Neel plantation and tole that he had talked with Chief Little Carpenter, and he say that they'se gwan stay out of this white man's mess. He also ask why I didn't ask for my freedom like he got. I tole him I ain't got nowhere to go. I never learned to manage money like white folks, so I'se kind of feared to try."

"As I said before, if you ever want the little paper for you or any member of your family, let me know."

"Someday I would like freedom fo my son Jacob as soon as he learn the black-smith trade. I'd worry about where he go without being kidnapped and put back with a cruel master. And if'n my daughters want to marry a freeman, I would like their freedom."

"Consider it done old friend. I can't believe I could get along without you. Beware of those fugitives in the swamps. If you get too friendly, they may rob us."

"No fear, Ole Kicker here should keep them under control," he replied, caressing his prized Pennsylvania rifle which Henry had given him some time ago.

"Oh yes, keep those envelopes with my permission to bear arms with you at all times. Some of these outlaws may try to jail you as a fugitive, although I pity anyone who would discomfort Neel property. I just hope those patrols can read. The militia will also be making rounds to see that the Indians stay in their villages."

"God bless you, Sir, and hurry back."

"God bless you, my friend." He spurred his horse and was away west.

On January 17, 1776, Captain Henry Neel assembled his mounted company at Charlotte. They were acting on behalf of the newly formed Continental Army. The company was somewhat experienced, having taken part in the rout of His Majesty's troops at Norfolk, Virginia. An hour before sunset on the second evening, Henry was scouting with Lieutenant Lewis. They were approximately two miles from their camp, having been alerted by one of the scouts. Suddenly, they heard the sound of fifes, drums, and bagpipes on the other side of a hill. Creeping down a creek bank and peering from the bushes, they saw a parade of men. Henry turned to Lewis and whispered, "Look at that, it's Master Huck!"

At the head of the column riding a splendid charger was Master Huck dressed in kilts and the blouse of a British officer. Huck was now a colonel of His Majesty's loyal militia, marching toward Cross Creek with most of his company, augmented by some of the Regulators. Henry had heard that Huck had not taken the Test Oath and was working in service of the King.

From behind the cover of the bushes and scrub pine, Henry marveled at the banners, the fife and drums, the bag pipes, and the kilted Scots. Each wore the head dress of a Scottish clan. Strapped to each Scot's back was a four foot broad sword. Most wore kilt and around each ankle sock was a dirk. Henry was puzzled at the dress because it was outlawed by the Culloden Oath. Some of the men were armed with muskets and pistols. Bringing up the rear, armed with scythes and pitchforks, were irregulars in irregular dress. Henry guessed them to be the Regulators Governor Martin had tried to recruit.

Henry turned to Lewis and in a low voice said, "I hope our friend Huck has not sent out scouts and that our boys don't make too much noise. Let's stay put and see if we can capture someone at the end of Squire Huck's column." He had barely spoken when he saw Huck point to a clearing and choose a spot for his troops to camp for the night.

Stealing quietly back to their horses, they walked them while returning to camp. Henry ordered his company to move quietly away after first apprising them of what had happened. A mere company could not do well against Huck's regiment. They marched in the dark for about an hour and camped near a river and ate a cold supper.

Lieutenant Lewis slipped out with a couple of men and returned at about midnight to Captain Henry's camp with a captive. Miraculously, Lewis had escaped detection as had the noisy baggage wagons of the Neel Company. Lewis brought the captive to the tent of Captain Neel, the only tent erected that night. Henry was seated in the tent on a camp chair behind a camp table. A bearded disheveled man stood before him with the dress of a back woodsmen. Henry caught a look at him through the small light of his candle.

"What be your name, man?" asked Henry.

"I am Wilber Harris, and I donna know what goes on here."

"What do you mean?"

"Well, sir, first our militia gets called out by the Committee of Safety and then we hears this Captain read a message from Governor Martin. We cain't understand how the Committee of Safety would be with Governor Martin. This here Captain says that if we help run out the rebels we would get two hundred acres of free land and parole for any crimes against the Crown. We also would pay no taxes for five years. Now I don't have no crimes against the Crown except when I stood around at the Battle of Alamance, but it sounded good to me. Anyways this fellow Col. Huck comes by our muster with those noisy Highland Scots and told us we have to join him at a muster at Cross Creek where we will join up with a larger group. I ain't one to cause trouble. I don' want any count with this trouble with British. I jes don understand those Highlanders; they don speak the King's English. They keep singing those worrisome dirges, something about 'Where shall I gae to seek my bread. Where shall I gae wonder?' Ifn they don know where they are going, why should I go with them? I jus want to earn a living and raise my young'uns."

Henry chuckled and asked Harris to sit down. He wrote a message for Col. Moore at Wilmington. "Lieutenant Lewis, pick two good men and have them take this intelligence to Col. Moore. I want you to stay with me and see that the prisoner is kept under guard." Lewis saluted and was dismissed.

Turning to Harris, Henry continued, "My good fellow. You have been through a great deal. I, of course, cannot release you now as you can understand. You will be fed, bound and placed under guard. When we reach Wilmington, you will be released. If you take our Test Oath, the Provincial Congress has promised land to all who serve in the Continental Regiments."

"I am grateful, Sir. If I may, did not you serve with the Crown at Alamance?"

"That was my brother. By the way have you heard of men named McGhee or Johnson that served with you?"

"I believe they fled to Kentuck, but last night I thought I saw them talking to Col. Huck."

"Thank you. Help yourself to some cold vittles. We will return your firearm later."

"I am obliged."

Shortly before daybreak the company broke camp and headed north toward Wilmington and on January 11 joined Col. Moore's regiment. There he met his brother Captain Andrew Neel's militia company which had marched from southern Tryon County.

As Henry was reviewing some reports, he was disturbed by a jovial voice.

"Well, I see that this is where my brother has been hiding while I have been fighting the Scouvites in South Carolina," challenged brother Andrew.

"Has the provincial militia any respect for the real fighters, the Continentals?" Henry continued. "What news do you bring?"

As the day progressed, both Captain Neels left their lieutenants and ensigns in charge and visited, catching up on family news. Henry was particularly impressed with the news of Ninety-Six.

During the journey scouts were placed many rods in front and back of the company to keep some distance from Col. Huck, but Henry was not too worried about their location because the Huck Regiment was the noisiest company that had marched since the days of Caesar.

On February 16, Moore's regiment marched out of Wilmington and camped seven miles from the Highlander-Regulator camp. The Continentals were joined there by one hundred and fifty minutemen under Colonel Alexander Lillington, two hundred men under Col. Kennon, and one hundred partisan rangers under Col. John Ashe, including Andrew Neel's company. This was the same Ashe who was captured by the Regulators at Alamance. Earlier, Governor Martin had ordered his refuge warship, *Cruizer*, up the Cape Fear River as a threat to the Whig forces at Wilmington. The sharp shooters of the Whigs soon drove some disembarking Royal Marines back to their warship which then retreated back to sea. The frustrated Governor sailed his refuge ship to Charles Town to keep company with the deposed Governor of South Carolina.

While camped on the banks of Rock Fish Creek, the Whigs received a copy of Governor Martin's proclamation from Tory General Donald MacDonald firmly urging Moore to rally under the royal standard. Moore, under a flag of truce, sent General MacDonald a copy of the "Test Oath" that the local Committee of Safety had drawn up and suggested that he and all his men subscribe to this and avoid bloodshed by joining the Patriot army.

Henry's company somehow lost contact with Huck's Tory company and finally reported to Col. Caswell about twenty miles out of Wilmington. The Whig force under Caswell, a former Speaker of the Assembly, withdrew his forces defending Corbett's Ferry on the Black River and proceeded to take possession of the bridge on Widow Moore's Creek twenty miles above Wilmington.

Col. Lillington's one hundred and fifty man Whig militia arrived at the bridge on the twenty fifth ahead of Caswell and the Tory forces. Moore's Creek, some thirty-five feet wide, wound around swampy terrain which could be traversed only by way of the bridge. Lillington and Caswell with eight hundred and fifty men arrived on the 26th and bivouacked on the west side of the bridge.

Earlier MacDonald was moving his loyalists to Brunswick across the River from Wilmington. Caswell, lately returned as a delegate from the Continental Congress, approaching with eight hundred partisans, spotted the Scots crossing the Black River. The Whig Col. Moore sent Lillington and Ashe to join Caswell. Moore proceeded in a round about way which would place him on the Highlanders' rear, also blocking the route to Cape Fear.

Henry's company along with the forces of brother Andrew, Ashe, and Lillington arrived at Moore's bridge on the night of February 25th. They immediately erected bulwarks and trenches on the east side of the bridge. The trenches were anchored on one side by the deep creek and on the other by a swamp. Across the creek they placed our old friends the cannon, *Mother Covington and Her Daughter*. Caswell joined the regiment on the west side of the bridge and was given command. He destroyed the works on the west side, removed stringers from the bridge, greased the spars with tallow, and waited for MacDonald.

This was the same Donald MacDonald, along with his colleague, Donald McLeod, who was with the British forces at Bunker Hill. Returning to Boston after having been questioned by the New Bern Committee of Safety, they landed again at Wilmington and contacted Highland Scots, including Donald Mac Donald's cousin, Alan and his wife, the famous Flora. Flora and Alan lived in the Cape Fear area and their estate was used as a base. The survivors of Bunker Hill reminded the repatriated Scots of their pledge of support for the Crown.

Flora and Alan had come to the Scottish settlement after the Battle of Culloden in 1746. Flora is alleged to have had a romantic interlude with Bonnie Prince Charlie and helped the Jacobin pretender to the Scottish and English thrones escape back to France. She was captured, imprisoned in the Tower of London, and later released after taking the pledge of loyalty to the King.

The Boston visitors, as mentioned earlier, were discovered and hauled before the New Bern Committee of Safety. The pair claimed that they were merely visiting friends and were released. They were now the Governor's representative in rallying the Loyalist forces. In early February McLeod had married General Donald MacDonald's daughter, Laureena.

On the eve of battle the elder Tory leader, General Mac Donald, became ill and could not leave his tent. His new son-in-law, McLeod, was given command. The Tory forces of approximately 1,600 camped some six miles from the bridge. They were composed of Scots, about one hundred and fifty former Regulators, and irregular militia. The promised Royal troops that Governor Martin had asked for and depended upon for control of North Carolina were still at sea. Unknown to Martin, their course had been disrupted and the fleet scattered by severe storms.

The Tories held a council of war. There was much discussion as to whether they should charge the earthworks or withdraw and find another path through the swamps. Eager young Scots were itching for a fight and overruled the caution. At about 1 a.m. on the 27th the troops under McLeod began to advance. The going was slow through the thickets and swampy ground. Men grumbled and cursed. Only half of them were equipped with firearms. The Scots proudly luxuriated in their restored firearms, kilts, and broadswords. As the Scots marched with fife, drum and bagpipe, some, especially Regulators, began to drift away. An hour before dawn the Loyalists came upon what they thought would be the Whig forces of Lillington on the east side of the creek. They met only smoldering fires there. The newly dug trenches were empty. McLeod rallied his men in a small dry clearing nearby. He gave the rallying cry, "King George and the broadswords!" With drums and bagpipes skirling, Captain John Campbell and seventy-five picked broadswords proceeded across one bridge stringer and Captain McLeod across the other. The Tories frequently slipped on the tallow and some of them fell into the creek. They advanced toward the earthwork on the west side.

Campbell drew his four foot broadsword from behind his back, raised it above his head with both hands, and gave the cry again, "For King George and the broadswords!" Just as they charged the earthworks *Mother Covington and her Daughter* began to speak with grapeshot. Eight hundred muskets discharged at once. Campbell fell, advanced, took more shots and fell again, slain. Campbell thus led the last broadsword charge in history. The battle ended in less than ten minutes. Thirty of the seventy five under Campbell died. The Whigs lost one man. The Tory forces fell back in disarray, some splashing into the swamps for cover. The Regulators who had accompanied the Highland Scots simply melted away. Captain Henry's company waited for the slats to be replaced in the bridge. Infantry troops charged across before the bridge was entirely restored. As soon as all the slats were replaced, Henry's company began their pursuit. They soon came upon small groups yelling, "Quarter, Quarter!" Col. Lillington gathered up these defeated groups, confiscated their firearms, and allowed them to return to their homes with broadswords. They were released upon their pledging to not take arms against the Provincial Congress. Thus ended the first clash of Whigs and Tories in North Carolina.

Henry made inquiry among the captured concerning McGhee and Squawman Johnson but received the same reply—"Fled to Kentuck."

That night around the campfire, the troops were startled to learn that the Whigs lost only one man. The next morning the Whig troops were saddened to see families descend upon the battle ground and claim the bodies of their loved ones. The moan of the mournful bagpipes and dirges filled the air. The Whigs tried to comfort the Tories and offered their physicians as well as the services of a Presbyterian preacher who followed them.

Master Christian Huck who did not participate in McLeod and Campbell's charge, climbed on a horse and fled back to the Tory camp in the rear. He appeared before General MacDonald who was ill in his tent some seven miles from the battle. Flora MacDonald attended the aged leader. She recognized Huck from the Governor's Ball. Huck appeared before his ill commander. "Sir, I bring you distressing news. Our forces have been soundly defeated and your son-in-law Captain McLeod died in battle."

The old man grew sullen and gray.

"Col. Huck," sobbed Flora, "It is grave news you bring. Have you heard of my husband, Alan MacDonald?"

"He charged the Moore's Creek Bridge, and I believe he was captured. You must flee because the rebels will soon be upon us. There appears to be no one able to resist them. Most of my company has broadswords. The Neel Rangers took most of the militia arms when they severed themselves from our militia."

"I cannot leave my husband's cousin. I shall throw myself on the mercy of the rebels."

"I see that it will be difficult to move General MacDonald. I know the commanders of two Whig companies. I shall compose a plea to them on your behalf." Col. Huck then took a candle and sat on a camp stool in the tent. He was barely aware of the confusion as horses and men came screaming past the camp fearing their fate if the Whigs should descend upon them.

> To Captain Henry Neel and Capt. Andrew Neel
> My dear friends:
> It is quite distressing to see us come to arms against each other after our close association in so many campaigns. However, I must impose on our long friendship and ask you to grant a favor. Madam Flora MacDonald is a gallant woman who once befriended Prince Charles. She nurses her husband's cousin General Donald MacDonald. Please grant her the courtesies due a great lady and assist her in any way you can.
> It greatly distresses me to see such dear friends in conflict.
> I am in your debt.
> Col. Christopher Huck, His Majesty's Colonial Militia, Charlotte.

He then brought the news to General MacDonald that his new son-in-law, McLeod, was killed and that they were about to be overrun. The old man gasped and expired in Huck's arms. Just then there were shouts coming from the swamp. Huck and a small group of his company climbed on their horses and sped away.

Henry came into the camp within minutes of Huck's withdrawal and drew his horse to halt by the commander's tent. Two kilted Tory sentries stood at attention. He turned to one.

"Sergeant, for you the war is over. Your troops are surrendering. Take your arms over to Lieutenant Lewis and assist him in treating your wounded."

Henry ducked into the tent to find the expired General Donald MacDonald with Flora weeping over him. Henry drew up to his height. "Whom do I have the pleasure of addressing?"

She looked up at the somewhat dirty blue and buff uniform of a Captain in the Continental army. Weeping, Flora stood up, and faced the American officer. She was a woman of some fifty years, well endowed and preserved. She projected an aura of gracious animal charm. She smiled through her tears, "I am Flora MacDonald and in there is my husband's cousin General Donald MacDonald who has just expired."

"My regrets, Madam. We must find some quarters for your comfort and an escort to your home."

"Are you Col. Neel of Neel's Rangers?"

"No, that is my brother. I am Captain Neel of the First Continental Regiment. Why do you ask?"

"I met your brother at the Governor's reception of Governor Moore. You are equally handsome. I have a message from Col. Huck for you." She handed Henry the note from Huck.

Henry read the note. "Madam, I have news of your husband, Alan MacDonald. He has been captured and will be sent to Wilmington. If you wish I will talk to Col. Lillingham concerning your accompanying him."

"Oh, good. Where is he now? And what of my son?"

"I believe they are back at the bridge and should be brought up in a little while. Do you wish General MacDonald to be buried here or taken to his home?"

"I would like to talk to his widow. What have your heard of my husband's cousin Donald McLeod? He recently married General MacDonald's daughter."

"I have no information. I shall prepare a wagon for you and an escort. I shall send an orderly to take care of your comfort. If you will excuse me." Henry then returned to the chaos of the camp.

In about an hour Henry returned with two tired men, one about fifty-five and the other about twenty. Their tartans were dirty and there was strain on their faces. Upon seeing Flora their countenances brightened.

Flora raced to her husband and son and embraced them, sobbing. She explained that MacDonald had died and that Captain Neel had befriended her. Just then the striking figure dressed in the buff and blue of the Continental Army came and saluted.

"I am Col. Lillington of the First Regiment of the Continental Army. I wish to express my condolences over the death of your leader."

The two Scots stood at attention. "Thank you, Sir."

"First I must ask you. Do you swear to the loyalty of support to the North Carolina Congress?"

Alan replied, "Sir, my family has sworn the Culloden Oath and cannot under penalty of death to ourselves and family support an oath against the Crown." Flora began to sob.

"Then you are our prisoners. However, I shall grant you a parole to your Wilmington estate for thirty days in order that you may prepare your affairs and assume the burial of your leader, General MacDonald. Further, any of your men who wish may take the pledge of the Congress and be paroled to their homes. Anyone refusing to take said oath will be prisoners of the Congress of the colonies. What say you?

"I shall not stand in the way of anyone taking the pledge, but I cannot."

"Very well, on signing your parole, you will be given thirty days to complete your arrangements and then you must report to the provost at Wilmington for assignment. My surgeons and ministers are available for the comfort of your men. Good day, Sir." A provost sergeant then appeared with the necessary parole documents.

In the morning Flora MacDonald, her husband Alan, and Alan junior departed by wagon under escort. She sat beside her husband in a second seat in the wagon. Beneath her bonnet her brown eyes teared as she smiled at Henry as he stood near with his company. Henry touched his hat in response. Alan and their son were imprisoned to the end of the war. Flora and her children were given safe conduct to Nova Scotia. Three of her children were buried near Wilmington. At the end of the war they settled in the Skye Island area of Scotland where she finally became a heroine of both the English and the Scots.

No Whigs were killed in the battle but one, Private John Grady, critically injured. He died that week. The patriots recovered 1,500 muskets or rifles, three hundred and fifty shot-bags, one hundred and fifty swords, and 1,500 pounds sterling. Some of the captured Scots were allowed to go to Nova Scotia, some banished, but most of the non Scots were paroled to their homes. The battle ended February 25, 1776, lasting only about ten minutes. It is sometimes referred to as "the other Concord Battle." Both this battle and the actual Battle of Concord occurred before the signing of the Declaration of Independence.

Henry's Continental company received another battle ribbon on their banner and returned home. They did not choose to search for Huck. The Battle of Moore's Creek is remembered as the first decisive battle in North Carolina and the last battle of a charge led by broadswords.

CHAPTER 28

# New Country and the Defense of Charles Town

The Continental Congress appointed General Charles Lee to command the southern troops. Lee was a former British general who had cast his lot with the patriot's cause. Lee was a polite, well-bred, and sensible man with few oddities. And yet, he was almost a comic figure with his scarecrow body and long nose.

Lee's egotistical nature prompted him to rail at Congress for his being slighted for the command of the Continental Army in favor of a colonial upstart named George Washington. He felt his long service as a British officer should have trumped Washington's continual defeats in the French and Indian War.

Lee waited in Halifax, Virginia, for a rendezvous with his Virginia riflemen. The lack of discipline by the Virginia troops troubled him. He was pleased with the addition of the First North Carolina, as the veterans of Moore's Creek and Norfolk Great Bridge were battle hardened and showed potential for steadiness in conflict.

Lee began his march south from Halifax by way of Tarboro and New Bern. Henry's company and the rest of First North Carolina Continental regiment were chosen as a part of the escort. Henry was delighted at the prospect of returning home. After journeying past those two towns they marched through Hillsboro. There the First Regiment was feted to honors as they paraded through the streets to the cheers of the populous. On June 1, Lee's forces arrived in Wilmington just as the King's troops weighed anchor and headed south. Lee, as commander of the Southern department, had trouble believing that the British would strike Charles Town even though he had been informed that the fleet has left Wilmington. By the time General Lee reached Charles Town and observed fifty-one British ships in the harbor, he was overwhelmingly convinced otherwise.

The North Carolina First Regiment and others, raised in haste to stop an invasion from the sea, were sent to defend its sister colony to the south. The seven hundred and fifty First Regiment Continentals under command of Lieutenant Colonel Thomas Clark marched through Charles Town to the music of drums and fifes. Captain Henry Neel felt thrilled as his Continental company was saluted. People cheered at the arrival of the Continentals while militia jeered at their slightly better equipped comrades.

Many of the back country Continentals had never seen the South Carolina capital city. Houses, sometimes three stories high, were festooned by exterior columns and beautiful balconies. The houses were set with the end to the street to catch the evening breezes on the piazzas for each floor. Gardens abounded with Carolina jasmine. Ferns grew in the shade and oleanders bloomed in the sunny spots. Portraits by the leading artists of the day were displayed in elegant drawing rooms. People were awed by the Charles Town rich. At the same time, the city had a large and growing population of artisans, craftsmen, shopkeepers, and others engaged in one business or another, and, of course, slaved and indentured servants.

Clark's Continental troops were bivouacked in an old field of Haddrell's meadow by the inlet to Sullivan's Island. It was swampy land and caused sickness among the troops. They suffered in the heat. By this time the regiment was in dire straits for food and clothing. The lack of pay for six months finally led to rioting. The South Carolina militia was called in to quell the disturbance. Thomas and Henry managed to get a paymaster who arranged for payment. Cloth and skins were obtained for clothing and moccasins.

British General Clinton landed troops on Long Island. General Lee rushed Lt. Colonel Thompson's Third Regiment of South Carolina Rangers, reinforced by two hundred of Clark's First Continental Regiment, to oppose them. Both troops were ferried across the inlet and landed on Sullivan Island in back and north of Ft. Moultrie and facing the British across the inlet to Long Island. Henry's Company, now under the direction of Col. Clark, was camped on the sea side and busily built entrenchments. That night as he retired to his tent, Henry heard a familiar voice.

"Sergeant, I seek the whereabouts of my kinsmen, Captain Henry Neel."

Henry, recognizing his brother, yelled out. "We do not allow any dandies of the Neel's Rangers in here, especially when they leave our province and become representatives to the South Carolina Congress." He emerged from his tent.

Laughing, he ran to embrace his older brother. "What a pleasure to see you."

"And you."

Henry continued, "I know you have distressing news. So why don't you begin."

Thomas recounted the Scoville campaign and the circumstances related to their brother Andrew and his family as well as the demise of Johnson and Artimas.

Henry's countenance grew sad. "You know I stopped over at my place on the way down and heard about Andrew. We plan to adopt young Thomas and Sarah into our family."

"Sounds like a good plan. Your place should be relatively safe being close to our friends in the Catawba and sympathetic Whigs." Thomas added somewhat prophetically, "Perhaps, since your place is in a relatively peaceful area, you should resign and provide a safe haven for Andy's family."

"Well my enlistment is up in '77, and we shall see then."

The two elder Neels, joined by Henry's nephews Thomas and Andrew, enjoyed the evening around their campfire. They enjoyed a vesper service as well as a roast lamb and rice dinner followed by pipes and reminiscences. Thomas told of the actions of the South Carolina Congress and Henry described in detail Moore's Creek and the Great Bridge. Late in the evening Thomas and his sons retired to the Neel's South Carolina regiment.

The next morning, June 26, 1776, the North Carolina troops were awakened by drums beating to quarters. At the same time they heard the guns behind them as Ft. Moultrie opened up on the British fleet as it felt its way through the channel between Stono and Sullivan Islands. At the same time on the north end of the fort, the troops were assembling as the British began to wade across the seventy-five yard inlet between the two islands called the "breach."

The veteran riflemen of the militias and the North Carolina Continentals began popping at heads in the water until they noticed they were drowning. They then started firing long range at those on the beach of Long Island. Soon Col. Clark ordered his commanders to assemble.

"Gentlemen, I don't believe those poor wretches over there will be able to swim across. I want you to instruct your men to fire only when they have a clear target. The British are terrified at the thought of the frontier rifle. If they see you are missing targets they will soon get over that premonition. By the way, congratulations and stay alert."

By nightfall the firing ceased. Clark brought back the news that the British had lost two ships sunk and four damaged. Many were stuck on the sand bars. He related that the palmetto log and sand earthworks were so effective that the British shells were wasted. However, the nearly 3,000 balls were harvested from their burial in the sand by the defenders and many returned to their owners from fortification's guns. By July 14, Long Island was evacuated by the British and the fleet sailed from the Charles Town harbor. Parades, speeches, and fireworks were in abundance celebrating the departure of the forces.

Representative Thomas Neel of the Neel Rangers, present in the South Carolina Congress after the Battle of Sullivan Island, listened to the debates concerning separation from England caused by the Continental Congress's Declaration of Independence. He had spent some time wrestling with the concept of independence but finally surrendered to it, particularly since his brother, Andrew, in North Carolina had signed a similar *Mecklenburg Declaration* earlier. His participation with Governor Tryon against the Regulators and his frequent service to the Crown colony made for constant mental turmoil. He thought that the Townsend Acts did not work any particular hardship on him. For example, he did not care for tea. To the contrary, the potential loss of a ship stores and livestock market was bound to cause him loss of treasure. His long friendship with Huck and Lord Stuart, the Indian agent, weighed heavily on his mind. However, the losses to Andrew's family of the Indian raids were the determining factor in finally approving of a separation from England. Thomas Neel's reverie did not last long. The Neel Regiment was sent to the Ninety-Six district because Indian raids outraged the frontier.

In December, 1776, the new General Assembly met. President John Rutledge began a tradition of addressing the body. He praised the wider diffusement of representation. The more remote districts were now represented. This was only partially true because there was no uniform method of choosing; sometimes it was by mere caucus. William Hill told of a problem of the New Acquisition (where he and the Thomas Neels lived between the Broad and Catawba Rivers). It seems the five chosen representatives of the area were challenged. In answer, a more organized election was held and five more representatives were elected, giving the area five more votes in the Assembly. After years of derision and neglect, the seaboard planters became most accommodating to the back country settlers because they were the first line of defense against the Creeks and Cherokees.

There arose in the Assembly a lively debate by the Reverend Tennant, who had previously toured the interior with President Rutledge to generate support for the Congress. Tennant objected to the taking of tax money to support a church that he did not attend. He railed against the issue of other churches, such as the Presbyterian and Baptists being unrecognized for marriage, education, and burial. He posited that there could be no republic if there were state supported churches. "The rights of conscience," he maintained, "were inalienable, and all laws binding upon it *ipso facto* null and void. The law acknowledges only one society as a Christian church; it does not know the other at all."

The new Assembly in the next year passed ordinances supporting the freedom of religion. They adopted the Declaration of Independence and passed an ordinance establishing an oath of "adjuration of the King and allegiance to the State." They enjoined the president to administer the oath to all the late officers of the King of Great Britain. A seal, which included the palmetto palm, was adopted by the Assembly, and is the same used by South Carolina to this day. The adoption of a Declaration of Independence was the last straw for John Rutledge who still hoped for conciliation with Great Britain. After some discussion as to the flexibility available in the constitution, the Assembly installed Rawlins Lowndes, a former conservative, as president of the South Carolina Congress. The date was March 6, 1776.

The debate over independence came to an abrupt end when on August 12, 1776 the news and a copy of the Declaration of Independence reached Charles Town. Guns went off and parades were initiated down the streets. There were bonfires, fireworks and speeches. Andrew Neel, as the Clerk of Mecklenburg, had sent a note to the Congress in Philadelphia signed by some of the selectmen, declaring that the colony would not be a part of the union unless the taxation for churches was dropped and freedom of religion guaranteed.

Very little doubt lingered that the colonies were now headed in an irrevocable direction toward independence. War news from the north raised the hopes of all. In December 1776, Washington, in a surprise move, routed the Hessians at Trenton, New Jersey. He followed this by another victory at Princeton. By January Washington was in winter quarters at Valley Forge. The Continental Congress had fled Philadelphia as the British, after evacuating New York, had marched and occupied the capitol city in September 1777. The Congress fled to Lancaster, Pennsylvania. In October came the gleeful news that a British Army coming down from Canada led by General Gentleman Johnny Burgoyne was defeated with 7,000 captured by Generals Benedict Arnold and Horatio Gates. This was the first Continental forces victory using European battle tactics. In November of that year, the National Congress adopted the Articles of Confederation. North and South Carolina soon ratified the document.

The Thomas Neel plantation continued to be developed with the addition of the lands of Andrew and the leasing of the lands of Master Huck near Charlotte. A feeling of peace descended on southeastern North Carolina and all of South Carolina. Thomas was able to attend the sessions of the South Carolina Congress as well as spend time back at the plantation. He rented a small cottage in Charles Town and on occasion was joined by Jean and other members of his family.

The third or fourth Sarah in our story was the daughter of Col. Thomas and Jean Spratt Neel. It was during this period that Sarah was married to James Johnson. They developed a small farm within the Thomas Neel Catawba property.

# CHAPTER 29

# The Cherokee Uprising

June 1776. The news from the Congress in Philadelphia regarding debate on a motion for independence fell excitedly on the ears of the South Carolina Provincial Congress. The Royal Governor attempted to rule from a man-of-war in the outer reaches of the harbor and was soon joined by the Royal Governor of North Carolina, Josiah Martin, recently arrived from New Bern in another man-of-war.

Col. Thomas Neel served on the Committee of Safety for York County and was a representative to the South Carolina Provincial Congress when he was not employed as commander of the Neel's Ranger Regiment. In June 1776 he was in Charles Town with the Provincial Congress. Henry served with the First Regiment of the North Carolina Continental Army stationed at Sullivan Island. Andrew, the youngest of the three brothers, joined with the North Carolina militia attached to Major Andrew Williamson's Regiment in South Carolina near the Congarees River. He had been there since the conclusion of the Moore's Creek campaign.

A rumor made the rounds of the North Carolina Congress that His Majesty's Indian agent, John Stuart, was stirring up the Indians again. The Neels' former friend (they had once rescued him from Cherokee Indian imprisonment) had left his Charles Town mansion under threat from the Select Committee and now ran the Indian affairs from his enclave in Florida. He appointed Alexander Cameron to go among the Cherokees and enthuse them toward an attack on the settlers coinciding with the proposed British attack on Sullivan Island. The attack failed because the news of the assault and the subsequent withdrawal of the British was late in getting to the Cherokees. The Cherokee uprising arose without the support of the southern British invasion.

The Provincial Congress had assembled in the hall of the former Provincial Assembly when news came of the efforts of Indian Agent Cameron. Because the British had labored so hard to keep the settlers out of the backcountry, the Congress was concerned that the Indians would be in sympathy with the British and perhaps would rise up against the settlers in the back country. The body debated as they faced westward to the backcountry while worried about the British fleet at their back. While the debate was going on, the executive body, known as the Council of Safety, sent Captain William Freeman to meet some of the chiefs and headmen of the Cherokees at Seneca near the Georgia border. The purpose was to assure the

Cherokees of the friendly disposition of the white people toward all Indian tribes. Captain Freeman returned with the news that the tribes could not be relied on while under the influence of Cameron.

The Council of Safety then entrusted Captain James McCall of Major Williamson's Regiment to meet with the Indians and attempt to capture Alexander Cameron and bring him before the Congress. McCall was accompanied by Captain James Baskin, Ensign Patrick Calhoun, twenty-two Carolina volunteers, and eleven from Georgia. Among those were young Ensign Thomas Jr. and young James Hawthorne. The Council ordered McCall to also try to reclaim property plundered by the loyalists and Indians.

Young Ensign Andrew (son of Col. Thomas Neel 1730) and Sergeant James Hawthorne had just returned to the Williamson Militia at the Congarees. Upon arriving, they called on Major Williamson who ordered the two to join McCall at the Cherokee Ford on the Savannah River. The boys were dressed in their fringed frontier shirts, ranger hats, leggings and moccasins with buffalo coats for the cold weather and sleeping. They rode some sturdy horses with packets for food and extra blankets.

It was an unusually crisp June morning when they boys left the Catawba and headed south of the Cherokee and Catawba Indian borders to the muster at the Congarees. The Piedmont had started to bring forth its summer glory. Rhododendrons and fruit trees were well into their summer magnificence. Birds of all types were back and added to the bucolic rustic nature of the backcountry wilderness. They were above the line where yellow fever and malaria usually struck and were following an Indian path. Occasionally, they would pass a settler's home and if they suspected them to be loyal to the Congress would stop; if not sure, they would ignore it.

On June 20th James and Andrew reached the rendezvous at Cherokee Ford. They reported to the command tent of Captain McCall.

"Ah, the illustrious Neel Rangers. What a pleasure to see you." A tall, gray haired, distinguished soldier rose from his camp chair and extended a hand which they took eagerly. Captain McCall was a veteran of the Ninety-Six campaign as well as the Snow Campaign under Col. Richard Richardson.

"I trust you had a good journey."

Ensign Andrew spoke. "It is indeed a pleasure to serve with you. May I present my friend, Sergeant James Hawthorne?"

"Yes, I have heard of the pending blessed event of uniting the Neel clan with one of our finest frontier families. I was shocked many years ago to hear of the massacre of your family. However, I see you have done well."

"Thank you, Sir," replied James, "I only long for the opportunity to repay the debt I owe those savages. You may be a trifle premature about that uniting. The young lady has not given her consent yet."

Captain McCall continued, "I hope you won't have a chance to avenge on this assignment. Our duty is quite clear. We are to take our party of some thirty-three rangers from the Carolinas and Georgia into the lower Indian villages and try to impress on them our friendship and hospitality as well as, to quote, 'Gently persuade them to give up some of the goods and livestock' they have plundered. I assume you are well mounted and need no supplies. If you do there is a provision wagon available. You should draw your powder and ammunition, some trail food for about a week, and prepare for a muster in the morning."

"Aye, Sir." They both saluted and left. They were soon exchanging greeting with some of their former comrades. After a supper of venison stew and cornbread they slept out that night, taking guard duty on two shifts.

At sunrise Andrew and James were awakened and summoned to a small carefully concealed fire where coffees and jerky awaited them. The detachment mounted up and left Seneca and the Savannah River. The rain that day dampened their spirits but seemed to drive away the mosquitoes. For the rest of the week they called on Cherokee towns and were greeted with friendship and hospitality. James Hawthorne grew strangely quiet whenever they entered a village.

He confided in Andrew, "Whenever, I get near one of these villages, I cringe. I need to take revenge on the way they treated my family. If we get to Keowee I don't know how I will control myself."

"You went through a great deal losing your family and having to live with the tribe for so many years. I guess that is why you are such a good tracker and hunter."

On the morning of the 26th Captain McCall approached James. "Sergeant Hawthorne, I want you to go with me to the next village as a translator; the village is the principal village of Keowee." They then turned. "The rest of the company will stay here. Be sure to post skirmishers and guards. Good day, gentlemen, and may God be with you."

Captain McCall, James, and a Catawba guide mounted up. In half an hour they approached the village and were met by the chief man of the village, Running Deer. The Cherokee village was a settlement of perhaps one hundred families. McCall rode to the principal hut and dismounted.

"Hail mighty Running Deer, I come in peace and friendship from the Council in Charles Town."

"What kind of warrior are you? What news do you bring?" asked the chief through James as an interpreter.

"We come as brothers to show our friendship and assure you of our love and affection for your tribe and to try to overcome the evil words of certain people from across the seas."

"That is good. Wait, is not the one who speaks for you the adopted son of Atta ku-lotta chief of the Tennaco Band."

James replied without a smile but with clinched fist and crossed arms. "Yes, Uncle I was adopted by the band after my family was slaughtered. Later I returned to the white people."

"Enough of this. Your reputation for lack of respect for your elders precedes you. You are an outcast of the tribe."

James asked, "Can not the great chief honor the tribe hospitably?"

"I'll show you hospitality." Suddenly from inside the council house, a group of braves rushed them. James jumped on his horse and was away but managed to tomahawk two would-be attackers. He received a tomahawk wound in his thigh. McCall was caught and tied to a pole.

James rode hard to the camp and alerted them. Only minutes after, the camp was charged by a company of Cherokees. Ensign Calhoun ordered a circle with firing by twos. After a horrific fight the detachment was able to fight its way out. Their remaining horses escaped. Calhoun and three others were killed.

Andrew and James were found with a group of a dozen survivors headed to Ninety-Six. In command was Ensign Polk. All horses had been lost and the group proceeded on foot. James struggled with a crutch and continued to bleed. After a half day crashing through the brush Thomas and James fell further behind. Ensign Polk approached them. "We need to separate. Our trail signs are wide open. I am assigning Peter Neilson, Jason Abraham, and Albert Chesney to help. The rest of us will go ahead to Ninety-Six to give a report and will send someone back after you with horses. May God bless you."

With that they were away. Andrew and his small detachment began to work their way down the trail until they came to a small stream. Under the direction of Andrew they plunged down the stream for a mile and came back up into a thicket. They carefully erased their footprints on the sand and disappeared into the woods where they waited. They heard the voices of Indians at the ford and soon heard the splashing of water which meant that their trail was found. Andrew's party checked their loads and waited. Soon a warrior appeared in the stream about twenty feet from James. James threw his tomahawk and struck the would-be assailant in the head, killing him instantly. Andrew ran out and tried to grab the horse. He also dragged the lifeless body into the brush and hid it.

"Men, let's move out. Perhaps our pursuers will not know which way this scout has gone."

"This man is Fine Bear the son of Atta ku-lotta, the chief. We will now be a part of a blood feud."

Andrew added, "This will not speak well of McCall if he is still with them and alive."

James replied, "I can't imagine the lack of hospitality. Visitors are not to be treated as we were even if they are enemies."

They limped along through the thickets occasionally crossing the trail but hiding their footsteps as best they could. Twice James fainted. The group took turns carrying him on their rifles. At dusk Albert Chesney approached. "Andrew, I have heard some calls in the woods that undoubtedly are Indian scouts. James will soon die. Let's give him a gun, conceal him here, and move on. Perhaps we can get a squad to come back and get him."

"No, I will not leave him. You go on." With that James and Andrew were left alone. Andrew propped up James against a large oak tree, gave him a sip of water and a piece of jerky. He tore part of his linen undershirt and re-wrapped the wound. James seemed to revive. They stayed there through the night.

At first light as the two sat upright against a tree they heard the rustle of bushes and saw coming toward them five Indians with tomahawks raised. Both of them fired their rifles and hit their marks. They then grabbed their pistols and fired again killing another two. The fifth ran in terror.

The men reloaded. Andrew stripped his assailants of knives and tomahawks and then read the trail of the departed brave. At about a quarter mile he found four Cherokee horses tied to trees.

He took two of them and returned to James whom he helped onto one of the horses. James appeared to be more alert. They proceeded up the trail at a rapid rate. The second morning they arrived at Ninety-Six and reported to Col. Williamson. He was seated in his tent having coffee with his fellow officers. Two arose and took James from his horse.

"What goes with you, young Neel?"

"Sir, the detachment was attacked by Indians at Keowee and Sergeant Hawthorne is wounded."

"Sergeant Smith, get two men and take this man to the surgeon. Go on man. What happened?"

Andrew then related the events which led up to the capture of Captain McCall. He related the death of Ensign Calhoun and their two fights with the Indians.

He ended with the statement, "I now have a blood feud with Peter Nelson, Jason Abraham, and Albert Chesney for abandoning us."

They both looked up at a commotion and there stood Captain McCall. His deer skin trail clothes were torn; his bearded face was drawn and appeared extremely tired.

"McCall," asked Williamson, "Tell us man, what happened to you. First sit down and have a spot of rum for strength. Orderly, bring this man some breakfast. You must eat first and then tell us what happened."

McCall staggered to the camp chair, ate hungrily for a few bites and then began his story.

"We came upon the village of Keowee on the 27th and up to that time had been greeted well by all the chiefs we met. I left the detachment behind and took young Hawthorne with me as an interpreter. Oh, hello there young Neel. I see you made it out. What happened to the rest?"

"We are not sure, Sir, but we are glad you made it."\

Williamson interrupted, "Go on, go on."

"As Hawthorne and I were talking with the principal chief, Running Deer, he recognized and seemed to be quite agitated with Sergeant Hawthorne. Suddenly, as we were talking we were rushed by a band of Indians. Hawthorne killed two and escaped while I was pinned before I could make a move."

Williamsons interrupted, "Hawthorne is alive and being treated for wounds he received."

"That is most welcome news. After my capture I was forced to witness the torture of one boy of a captured family. A twelve year old boy was suspended by his arms and wood splinters eighteen inches long, lighted at one end and sharpened at the other so that the torch would not be extinguished were thrown at his form. There was much shouting as the warriors scored by puncturing the boy's body. He was a brave lad and did not cry out which seemed to enrage them. After about two hours of this the boy, whose body was full of these fiery darts, expired. His body was then thrown to the dogs.

I then threatened my captors with annihilation should they harm an emissary of the Congress who was on a peaceful mission. Should I be harmed, much Indian blood would be shed. Shortly after that I was confined to a dark hut with a mat filled with all sorts of vermin. Running Deer approached me and in perfect King's English related that Agent Cameron wanted to visit with me. I refused. Then one night a young maiden came into the hut and loosened my ropes. She related that she had been captured by the Indians at age eight and did not want to return to the ways of the white man but did not want to see the tribe punished. I crept into the night, found a horse and escaped. It has taken me ten days to get here."

Just as he was finishing, the nefarious trio, Neilson, Abraham, and Chesney staggered in. They were unaware that Andrew had returned. At this time he had gone to see how Hawthorne was faring.

"Captain McCall, Sir. It is so good to see you again," stated a startled Neilson.

"Thank you, Sergeant."

Col. Williamson, with a firm grimace on his face asked, "I understand that you were with Neel and Hawthorne on the trail. Have you heard from them?"

"They both perished, Sir."

"You are a scoundrel and a coward, Sergeant. They were abandoned by you and are within the camp. Sergeant, place these men in chains. We will have our court martial later."

There was a court martial that afternoon and the three men were to be confined to foot on all skirmishes, reduced in rank, and would be the point. Should they desert, all their lands would be forfeited to the militia.

In a week James had recovered enough to take to the trail. Andrew and six of the other Neel detachment rode back to the Neel place on the Catawba.

It was a hot July day when Andrew and James came into the compound. Col. Thomas was home from the Congress and was poring over the plans for the militia with Polk. Jean greeted them along with James's adopted mother, Rachel. James Hawthorne was placed in a bedroom in the house where he was well taken care of by Jane, Mary, and his foster mother, Rachel. He continued under their care with Mary spending more and more time with him, sometimes under the trees in the yard and sometimes with long walks. As they were returning from one of their walks they came upon Jean and Thomas having refreshment under the large oak tree.

"Col. Thomas, Sir." James began

"Yes, James."

"I would like to have the hand of this lovely daughter Mary in marriage."

"Really. Mother, do you want such a scoundrel as this in our family?"

"Ah well, since I have observed him for a number of years and find that he has a great appetite, is a fine hunter and Christian, I guess we could do worse. I am so glad." She arose, broke into tears, and embraced them both.

"I guess that settles it," said Thomas, "I have observed these two mooning around for a number of years." She nodded tearfully.

A week later Mary and James Hawthorne were united in matrimony by Reverend William Richardson at the Bethel Church. In the same ceremony, Mary's sister Sarah was married to Samuel Johnston. Both couples took land near Squire Thomas Neel's plantation.

# CHAPTER 30

## A Time of Sadness and Revenge

On July 20, 1776, as part of North Carolina Royal Governor Josiah Martin's plan, the Cherokees attacked on a front from Virginia to Georgia beginning at Eaton's Station. This was to be a concerted attack with the British occupying Charles Town. Happily, the British fleet was repulsed by the work of General Moultrie, but this fact was not immediately known in the back country. The Cherokees numbered some 12,000 fighting men with 3,000 musket warriors.

The first awareness of the raid came when Francis Salvadore, a prominent Jew and member of the Provincial Congress from the area northwest of Ninety-Six, was startled by the screams of Aaron Smith, a young neighbor riding up to his home. He met him at the front door. Aaron then related that the Indians had attacked his father's farm and all his family had been murdered including his sister, Andrew Neel's wife Laureena, who was visiting. Salvadore immediately swung onto his horse and reported to Major Williamson's residence some twenty-eight miles away. There he found one of Captain Smith's sons who also escaped. The rest of the week reports came in to Williamson of other atrocities. Among those killed was the progenitor of the yet to be born General Wade Hampton. The people of the region were destitute of arms because the best of their rifles were sold to the rifle regiments and the rangers. Men had to place of their families in places of safety before they could take up arms with the militia.

The news soon was to reach Captain Andrew Neel (1742) by courier on his other farm between Ninety-Six and Tryon County. There came a knock at the door. Andrew swung open the door to see three militiamen.

"Captain Andrew Neel?"

"At your service."

"The militia has been summoned to appear at Col. Williamson's plantation. There Cherokees raided on the Saluda and several families have been killed."

"Killed? What about the family of Aaron Smith?"

"I understand they have all been killed."

"Oh, merciful God. My wife was there assisting her sister who was about to give birth." Turning to his children he said, "Thomas, you, Aaron, and Sarah go to Uncle Thomas immediately." Turning to his servant, "Moses, saddle up my horse and a mule. Please load about two weeks trail supplies. You are to be in charge of the farm. I leave within the hour." He called to his oldest, Thomas, age fifteen, and placed him in charge of the family.

"What has happened to Mother?" protested daughter Sarah.

"I am not sure, Dear, but I will find out. You must be brave and go to your Uncle Thomas and Aunt Jean. Daddy will be back in a few days." Andrew then embraced them, mounted his horse and headed to the Smith place near Ninety-Six. His other property adjoined the Smith's.

The next day he arrived at the smoldering Smith Plantation with tired animals, having pushed them to the limits through the night. Major Williamson and the militia were already there. There was only a chimney left as a monument to where a fine house had been. Fresh graves of his father-in-law Aaron, his mother-in-law, three children, and his wife Laureena were arranged in rows under a large oak tree.

Major Williamson, who was supervising the cleanup, turned to see Andrew ride up with his animals lathered from the hard ride. Andrew jumped to the ground and stood in front of the Major. Andrew looked around at the house foundation, the naked chimney, and the ruins of out buildings. "Were there any survivors?" he pleaded.

"Only two of the boys, one who brought the alarm to Mr. Salvadore. I am so sorry, my friend. Your wife is buried over there."

Andrew stumbled to the grave and fell prostrate upon the fresh earth. "Oh, my poor Laureena. Why did you have to come here?" he sobbed.

Williamson knelt down, placed his arm over him and tried to console his sobbing friend. Andrew stood up, his deep-set eyes piercing at Williamson with a determined countenance.

"As God is my witness, these heathen will suffer."

Williamson continued. "When we arrived there was still some smoking ruins. We sent out scouts but they have not returned. The family was all scalped. Here are the arrows we pulled from your wife's body. I am terribly sorry Andrew. Here are some of the belongings."

He handed a necklace, ring, a pair of baby shoes and blanket. In the blanket were two arrows.

"I must go now. I see some more militia approach."

With bowed head in sorrow, Andrew continued to turn the arrow shafts in his hands. He was startled from his melancholy by the sound of four horsemen. He saw them dismount and speak to Major Williamson.

Soon a well-proportioned sandy haired frontiersman, James Hawthorne, approached. "Uncle Andrew, you are here. I just heard the news. I am so sorry."

"Thank you, Jimmy. This is truly a sad occasion following so soon on your wedding. How is your wound?"

"I heal slower than my vengeance. What are you doing with those arrows?"

"They were taken from the body of my beloved Laureena."

"May I see them?"

"Of course."

"The shaft is from a willow and has the mark of a canoe. The feathers are from an owl. A carefully crafted point made of onyx portends of a ceremonial arrow. The canoe means only one thing—Dragging Canoe. He wanted us to know who killed. He crafted his arrow from a precious stone. Amazing. This is far away from his village in the Over Mountain."

"Didn't you live among his clan?"

"Yes, we were raised together in the house of his father, the one people called Little Carpenter. They tried to make us brothers." His countenance grew grim.

"We were taught many things as warriors together. But I can never forgive his uncle, Soaring Eagle, for what he did to my family back in the French War."

James walked over to Major Williamson and gave his report. Williamson was startled at what he heard about the arrows. Meanwhile Andrew tried to control his rage. He had lost his wife and his father-in-law's family, save Aaron Smith. He kicked at the ground, then smoothed the dirt of Laureena's grave, and placed a twig which still contained some oak leaves on it. He marked the grave with a cross made of a board from the ruin and began to chisel out Laureena's name.

James came over. "Uncle Andrew, we have been asked to scout ahead while the rest of the militia gathers. Are you willing?"

"Yes, but let's send a message back to your father-in-law, Col. Thomas."

Andrew then wrote a message describing what happened and telling that he and James were on the way to scout for the raiders. Assembling his mule with supplies, Andrew mounted his stallion and accompanied by James, started on the trail after the Indians. As they were approaching Rayborn Creek, they were met by Major Downes and one hundred and fifty militia under his command on the way to join Major Williamson. That night they bivouacked at the old Lyndley's fort near the ford at the fork of the Saluda River. Many of the settlers had fled to the fort for protection. The next morning, the 15th of July, the fort was attacked by eighty-eight Indians and one hundred white men, most of them dressed as Indians. The Cherokees and their loyalist friends were not aware of the arrival of Downes. They had not realized the fortuitous circumstance of the fort being reinforced. After gaining entrance to the defense perimeter momentarily, the attackers ran and were pursued by the militia and men from the fort. Several attackers were left dead on the field, including two chiefs.

Andrew and James, accompanied by a mounted company, rode after the fleeing assailants. They soon heard the sound, "Quarter, quarter." Andrew was startled to see that a few Indians were not Indians but Tories dressed in Cherokee paint.

As he looked them over he noticed two rather older men who began to drift out of the clearing where they had been captured. James barked, "You two there, stop or you will have your skulls split by a tomahawk."

They turned and were ordered to sit down. Major Downes turned to the captured Tories.

"Men, you are charged with an assault on a people's fort. You will be sent first to Charles Town to be dealt with at the pleasure of the South Carolina Provincial Congress. If you cooperate, you shall better insure more favorable circumstances." Turning to one of his lieutenants, he ordered him to take their names and locations of their property.

Suddenly James rushed two of the captives and drove his tomahawk into the head of one of the captives which glanced off, cutting off only his ear. Artimas McGhee writhed in agony on the ground. James was shortly constrained by the militia.

Major Downes reported. "What goes there, Sergeant? What caused you to attack these men?"

"This is the man who attacked our house and was with the Cherokees when they murdered my family in the War with France."

Then Andrew knocked the other man down and began to choke him. He too was restrained.

"Now what brought this on?" inquired Downes.

"This man murdered my father. Let me save the Congress the trouble of trial."

"Calm down, Captain. We will take all of these men to Ninety-Six. I am sure your brother in the South Carolina Congress will take of the matter with alacrity and care."

"Johnson, you are an ingrate, heathen, and I hope you rot in hell. I don't want to kill you outright; I would like for you to suffer first," retorted Andrew.

Both McGhee and Johnson raised their bound hands toward their heads and looked away, expecting another blow. Blood streamed from the place where McGhee's ear formerly sat.

Downes then detailed a squad of twenty to take the captives to Charles Town. Their hands were bound behind their backs and tied together on captured Indian horses. Downes then turned his troops toward the muster at the Williamson plantation. The Downes force accompanied by James and Andrew returned to Ninety-Six where the forces were gathering. Andrew was granted leave to move his family.

Andrew's trip to his settlement was sad as his heart was filled with memories and rage at the loss of his wife. As he approached the wood lot near his home he found his servant and was greeted by a sobbing figure.

"Jacob," he asked, "What troubles you?"

"Oh Master Andrew, them Indians attacked us and killed Miss Sarah and Master Aaron. My wife and I managed to save Master Thomas. He is here in the woods with us and some of the other survivors. Oh, woe is me."

Andrew's eyes narrowed as he looked at the countenance of his weeping friend.

"Oh Lord, will this ever, ever end? You tell the others to stay hidden. Bring Thomas here. Did you save any of the horses?"

"Yes, Sir. And some livestock."

"Get a horse for yourself and Thomas and come with me."

Jacob and Thomas emerged from the forest. Upon their approach young Thomas, dressed in frontier deerskins, alighted from his horse as did Andrew. They embraced.

"Father, it was terrible. Shortly after you left a party of Indians came asking for food. As Aunt Priscilla turned from answering the door, they rushed through and grabbed Sarah and Aaron. I ran to the shed and got the spare rifle, came back and fired. Then I threw a tomahawk. They ran off. I then found Sarah and Aaron dead. It was awful. I must have the scalps of those Indians."

"Where are Sarah and Aaron?"

"Uncle Jacob took all of us into the woods. He was afraid of another attack."

Andrew continued to embrace Thomas after he told his story. Tears came across his trail-hardened face. His red whiskers helped hide a dreadful grimace. Composing himself he went on. "You did well, Son. Now let's go home. Let's all check our pieces to see if they are ready." Andrew, Thomas, Jacob, and two other servants mounted their horses and soon came to the compound. Andrew surveyed the area. Apparently there was nothing burned. He rode to the house and tied his horse in front. The door was ajar. Walking into the room he found furniture tipped over and on the floor in a gingham shift lay the body of his daughter, ten year old Sarah. Her blond hair shone in the shaft of sunlight through the door. An ugly gash was against her temple with a pool of blood on the floor. Near her was her brother Aaron who had been named for his grandfather Aaron Smith. As Andrew examined Aaron's eight year old body, he found bruises about his head. Young

Aaron held a tomahawk in his hand tinged with blood. There was an arrow in his chest. "Oh, my poor children. What is to become of all this?" He held Aaron once again.

"When I came in with the rifle an Indian with blood streaming down his face was hitting Aaron," continued Thomas. "I leveled the rifle at him and he let Aaron go. He then threw a hatchet at me but I ducked and shot him. An Indian near the door then shot an arrow into Aaron and another one at me. I took the pistol and fired. They ran away. Uncle Jacob came in with a rifle and took us away." He began sobbing again; Andrew held him.

"You were a brave lad." He looked at the forms of his children on the floor. He was hugging Aaron when he heard a whimper. He then heard a small cry, "Daddy, Daddy."

"Oh Sarah! You are alive." He stumbled to her. "Jacob, bring me a pan of water and get Priscilla." He held Sarah and began cleansing the hatchet wound with a cloth. He embraced and held her as Priscilla gently cleansed the wound. Sarah looked into her father's eyes as he wiped away her tears. She could not speak because of the horrors she'd endured. After burying his young son, Aaron, Andrew gathered up his family and filled the wagon with belongings. They left most of the furnishings. Sarah was placed in the back of the wagon amid bags of grain and bedding. Thomas and Uncle Jacob drove the remaining five cattle and four unmounted horses. Andrew drove the wagon. They headed south. That night they arrived at the home of Andrew's older brother, Col. Neel.

The wagon and entourage entered the grounds, accompanied by the howling of Col. Thomas's hounds. Alexander, who had returned from a fruitless search for Johnson and McGhee greeted them and ordered some of the servants to take care of the horses.

Aunt Jean came out accompanied by her daughter Mary, new bride of James Hawthorne. Jean, with anguish in her eyes asked, "Andrew, what happened?"

A solemn Andrew had alighted from the wagon and lifted young Sarah from the back. Priscilla, the black servant, had been tending to her. As he turned with young Sarah in his arms he replied, "Both the Aaron Smith place and my place have been attacked by Indians. Laureena and her family are dead, young Aaron is dead. I have only Thomas and young Sarah left." His lower lip quivered as he tried to gain his composure. Aunt Jean replied, "Oh you poor man. Take young Sarah into the house. Mary, see if you can get some repast for them. Young Thomas, come here and give Aunt Jean a hug."

Gangly, slim Thomas ran to Aunt Jean, hugged, and wept. "Now, now it will be all right again. Come in and take some rest." They walked toward the house.

As Col. Thomas was still making his way home from his meeting with the South Carolina Provincial Congress, the women of his family and the servants were managing the plantation. The elder Thomas had received the call for the Williamson muster. His sons Andrew and Thomas were waiting his return before departing with the Neel Rangers. Andrew (their uncle) recounted the events and then told of his plans to leave Sarah with Aunt Jean there, but on the morrow to take Thomas to his other brother Henry across the Catawba on Steele Creek.

After leaving Sarah with her Aunt Jean along with his wagon, his servants, Priscilla and Jacob, and livestock, Andrew and his young son Thomas left in the morning for the compound of Henry Neel. They arrived at noon and were greeted by Aunt Nancy. As an officer in the Continental Army, Henry was not at home since he was serving with Col. Francis Nash in Virginia. Aunt Nancy looked up from the window where she was sitting nursing young Samuel. She saw Andrew and Thomas ride up. She cried to her eldest son William, age thirteen. "William, I think your Uncle Andrew and cousin Thomas just rode up. Please go out and invite them in."

William and the other children, Mary and John, rushed out of the house just as the two buckskin riders' horses were taken by Zeke Proctor, who happened to be visiting.

"What are you two scoundrels doing here? I thought you were at Ninety-Six?" Andrew dismounted and embraced the old family friend. "I have lost my family save Thomas and young Sarah." He wept uncontrollably. Zeke continued to embrace and comfort him.

"Come inside to your Aunt Nancy and tell us about it. You children take care of Thomas and put away the animals."

By the time Zeke and Andrew had entered the house, Nancy had placed the baby in the crib. She turned and embraced her grieving brother-in-law. Andrew then repeated the story of the two massacres and the capture of McGhee and Johnson.

Zeke arose from his stool near the fire. With contorted and flushed face he commented, "Oh, I must have a blood revenge against those two miscreants. Where are they?"

"I suppose on the road to Ninety-Six or Charles Town. Anyway when my brother Thomas (1730) hears about it, he will see that they get a fair trial and then hang 'em."

"Jimmy Hawthorne already gave it a good start by cutting off McGhee's ear."

Andrew spent the night at Henry's farm comforted by his sister-in-law Nancy as well as Henry's children. The next morning, having placed his son with the family of Henry Neel, Andrew retraced his steps back to his brother Col. Thomas Neel. He found Thomas home. Thomas brought news of the Declaration of Independence from the Congress at Philadelphia.

As the two brothers sat under a tree that late afternoon, Thomas began, "It distresses me greatly over the losses you have suffered. I don't believe you should go on this muster. You have given enough."

"I will not go home until my family's life has been avenged. My beloved Laureena's soul will not rest until I have found her murderers."

Andrew then related the incident with the arrow shaft and queried, "What will be done with McGhee and Johnson?"

Thomas replied, "They are still being held at Ninety-Six. I understand from what I heard at Charles Town that they will be tried there."

"I hope they won't have the same magistrate justice as the time you were there back in the sixties."

"I understand our friend the Justice James Francis has fled the province. You remember him. We rescued Artimas and Squawman from the Creeks and gave them to Little Carpenter, Peace Chief of the lower Cherokee, to return them to Justice Francis at Ninety-Six. Justice Francis refused to try the two miscreants for stealing and released them. As I recall, the Colonial Assembly refused to prosecute even though the Governor wanted it. This made the Cherokees angry because Squawman and Artimas had killed two of their braves. I don't know where Francis will find friends. Perhaps he has made it to Florida with the unfortunate Robert "Burn Foot" Browne. You remember him. He is the fellow who was tortured by some misguided Whigs and debated President Rutledge at McClearin's store. Rumor has it that he has formed a legion in Florida and is raiding into Georgia."

"That is good. One less for my blood feud. What will be the effect of this Declaration of Independence?"

"This is a glorious time. It is an exciting time—to think a people have thrown off the rule of a monarch and established a republic. Republics have always failed in the past because they cater to the lowest level of people's desires and by the second or third generation, the people give up their freedom. The English did not fare too well under Cromwell's republic in the last century. It will take a lot of courage to no longer 'be in subjection to your rulers' as is commanded in the scriptures. We have neighbors who are still loyal to the Crown and have not taken an oath in support of the Congress. We now have the Indians in rebellion. It is a time for glory and tragedy. We must determine if we will live like free men or retreat from the onslaught of the savages and cower under the heel of the far away monarch for protection. Also, as we choose to live in freedom, can we govern ourselves? I heard one Tory say 'It is better to have one tyrant in England rather than ten thousand at home.'"

Andrew answered, "I have given so much. I am now ready to give more."

"May God bless you." responded Thomas, "Tomorrow we join our muster. The Neel's Regiment will be here in the morning."

The next morning the Neel Rangers assembled at the Neel plantation. The complement contained Captain Andrew, Ensigns Thomas and Andrew, newly minted ensign Hawthorne, and Major Tom Polk's company. The entire Regiment just topped two hundred men all mounted. The rangers were dressed in fringed buckskin blouses and leggings, moccasins or trail boots, and a beaver hat with a red and white ribbon in the brim.

Each man carried a hatchet in his belt, a knife in a sheath on his belt, canteen, shot pouch with paper cartridges, powder horn and either a musket or rifle. The horses of the officers represented the best of the provinces. The Neel regiment had managed to equip its troops with some fine horses. Most were a cross between the warm blooded and trail horses, relatively swift yet large and able to go long distances. The riflemen were mostly in the company of Polk and were known for their sharp shooting ability. The regiment was a remarkable blending of the role of light and heavy cavalry.

Col. Thomas turned to Major Polk. "Major Polk, is all of the regiment accounted for?"

"Col. Tom, we have one hundred and ninety common present for duty. Some have been given leave due to family problems and disease. We invite your inspection."

The men all stood by their horses as Thomas rode down the ranks. Each man stood more or less at attention with his piece on the right side held by his hand. The left hand was raised across the chest of each man in salute as Thomas passed. Thomas completed the inspection and brought his splendid charger, Champion II, to a halt facing the ranks.

"I am impressed by your attempt to look like Continentals as you stand at attention. You kind of scare me. I am glad you sergeants have been drilling so well. Our success on the expedition against the Scouville Tories has followed you. We have been asked by the Congress to help Major Williamson in his fight against the savages who have ravaged the frontier near the Saluda and Congarees. Some of you have suffered some tragedies including my brother here who has lost his wife, in-laws, and a child.

"Most of you know by now that the Continental Congress debates independence from England. We are now given the responsibility of governing and defending ourselves. We don't know what the British Indian agents have done, perhaps stirred up the Cherokees. As we answer our muster, let's remember to be soldiers. If any of you have not yet taken the oath in support of the Congresses of South or North Carolina and the Congress of America, you may do so after we are dismissed. If you do not wish to take said oath, please leave us now. We are disciplined soldiers. We are not to loot or molest the enemy, especially Tory neighbors. Remember, we must live with them after this war is over. Now please pray with me.

Our heavenly Father, who has been with us through many trials, be with us as we become swords of your justice. Protect our families and may thy richest blessings rest upon us. You are great and we are small. Bless the Confederation of States in America and continue to guide us in what we do. In the name of Christ our Redeemer, Amen. Three cheers for the Congress of the Confederation of States in America!"

There followed three enthusiastic "Huzzas."

"We will depart by companies. Each night you will draw rations from the wagons. Drill and target practice will be required tonight. Let's move out."

An arrangement of drums was set upon one of the horses. To the beat of the drums, the Rangers moved out of the compound. A merry air was piped by two fifests. The children, mothers, and servants waved as the mounted Rangers moved in double file down the dusty road to the south.

The Rangers arrived at the Williamson Plantation July 22, 1776. As was his custom, Col. Thomas Neel, after reporting to Major Williamson, bivouacked his troops separate from the main force. The sergeants immediately saw that the horses were cared for. Neel's Rangers were the pride of the militia and had allegiances to both of the Carolinas.

So that there would be no discussions of command, Col. Thomas Neel brought a commission from the South Carolina Provincial Congress elevating Major Williamson to Colonel and giving him command of the forces. His command was soon re-enforced by the Col. Jack's regiment from Georgia.

Around the campfire that night, Andrew and Thomas were joined by James Hawthorne who related the events since Andrew had left. He said that troops continued to arrive and that a supply train under Captain Warley and his regiment had arrived that morning.

The next week was taken with drills and instructions to the troops. On July 30th the troops moved out toward a suspected Tory and Indian camp on the Oconore Creek about thirty miles distant. As the troop pulled out, Williamson called Nelson, Abraham, and Chesney forward.

"I promised you men that you would be placed on the point at every skirmish because of your cowardice in the matter of James Hawthorne. I want you to know if you fail to do your duty or desert, all your lands will be forfeited, you will be hanged, and your family will be placed in servitude for a length of time. However, should you serve well and at the pleasure of Ensign Neel and Ensign James Hawthorne, you will have your misdeed erased from the record. Do you have any questions?"

Nelson spoke, "No sir, we appreciate the opportunity to redeem our names in the service of the Province. Thomas and Jim, we want to make amends for what we done." James and young Thomas nodded and looked away.

"Good, you three take the point with Ensign Neel and the two prisoners who better guide us well or they will be strung up like a butchered deer."

"Drummer, sound the march."

A force of three hundred and thirty consisting of the Neel's and Jack's rangers then proceeded. After about a mile the drums were ordered silent. At the head of the column were Congressmen Salvadore, who first brought the alarm, Colonels Williamson, Neel, and Jack. Williamson related that Alexander Cameron's deputy to Stuart, His Majesty's Indian agent, was camped on the Oconore Creek with some Cherokee braves from the village of Essenecca.

The only ford was on the Keowee River which separated the two forces at the Essenecca camp. After trooping all night, Williamson was greeted by James Hawthorne who reported that the parolees, Nelson, Abraham, and Chesney were missing. He thought that the troop was headed for an ambush. It was about two o'clock in the morning. Suddenly, on both sides of the column fire broke out. Salvadore fell from his horse and was down on the ground. Andrew saw him fall and saw his servant administering to Salvadore. The forces of Williamson fled in confusion. Lieutenant Col. Hammond, coming up with twenty men, rallied the men and charged the Indians. The Cherokees from Essenecca retreated. Upon securing the battle field, they found Salvadore dying after being scalped. Williamson knelt beside the small Jewish congressman. Blood flowed from his bare scalp. With a husky voice he asked, "Did we triumph?"

"We certainly did." He breathed a sigh, closed his eyes, smiled, and died. Thus ended the life of the first Jew to die in the American Revolution. The supposed servant administering to him in the dim moonlight was really a scalping Indian.

Williamson lost three men and fourteen were badly injured. Williamson burned the Essenoca on the eastern side of the river and sent Col. Hammond across to burn the western side which included six thousand bushels of Indian corn, peas, and other articles. Williamson then retreated to Twenty-Three Mile creek.

On the eighth of August, Neel's regiment was ordered to attack the Indian camp at Oconore. The Rangers were joined with the Ninety-Six militia regiment.

The complement reached six hundred and forty mounted dragoons. The camp was found deserted. They moved on and destroyed the towns of Ostoy and Tugaloo. On the twelfth of August, Neel's Regiment was camped in a clearing. The topography now consisted of almost pathless mountains, dark thickets where visibility was about ten feet, rugged paths, narrow defiles, and towering cliffs above winding water ways. Col. Thomas was camped with his officers, except for brother Captain Andrew who was checking on the rations of the troops.

As they gathered around a campfire with a deer carcass roasting over the fire, Thomas spoke to his company commanders and their sergeants.

"I have checked with Captain Andrew and he related that we have posted skirmishers out about a mile and have found no enemy. In view of their defeats there are probably none in this area. However, after tonight we shall not have such a large fire—at least not after dark. I want you to all be in control of your passion. That Smith boy, Aaron, is extremely agitated about the death of Salvadore, my brother Andrew seems to be ready to initiate a blood feud, and James Hawthorne claims his gun does the killing of Cherokees, and he has no control over it. We must control our passions. These Cherokees are human beings and have been deluded by the forces of the King. They have refused the council of the peace chief Little Carpenter and have instead taken up the cause of his son, war chief Dragging Canoe. However, we must wipe out all their ability to raid our people and perhaps move every Cherokee from the lower and middle regions, perhaps sending all of them over the mountain."

Tom Polk added, "Yes, there is a big division among the Cherokees. It seems that Seiver and perhaps Boone went among them in the area of the Tennaco and made a treaty without the authority of the British or our Congress. Little Carpenter ceded some land to them. When Dragging Canoe found out, he rejected the treaty and proposed to drive out any settlers, although he did not want to discontinue trading. It is the war chief Dragging Canoe who is causing all the murders in spite of the counsel of his father Little Carpenter."

Thomas continued, "Yes, this makes my heart very troubled. We at one time considered Lord Stuart, the Indian agent, our friend as well as Little Carpenter. Now they have turned against us. At any rate let us check our troops and turn in. We will break camp with four days rations in the morning after breakfast."

The next morning the regiment, followed by others, crept single file along the narrow trail. Hawthorne and young Thomas were on the point helped by Thomas's old friend Running Bear of the Catawba tribe. They continued a cautious advance until on the morning of the 12th of August. Hawthorne came back with the news that there was a body of braves hidden outside a clearing up ahead. Col. Williamson called a council of war and after much discussion decided to force a stand. Just as he was about to give the order he heard shots and screaming. Williamson ordered the Neel regiment to advance dismounted. Col. Thomas then ordered his men down the narrow path through the dense forest. Soon they came upon James Hawthorne and Uncle Andrew in a hand-to-hand fight with a half dozen Cherokees. Three Cherokees were already on the ground. Upon the approach of Polk's company, the Cherokees ran. Immediately, both men knelt to the nearest brave and started scalping. Taking their knives they first made a circle around the skull. Then sitting on the ground they placed their feet on the shoulders and then pulled the scalp off by the hair. They were in the midst of the second scalping each when the troop approached.

Just then Col. Thomas rode up. "James and Andrew, I order you to stop." They did not. He turned to a sergeant, "Restrain these men." Two squads of four soldiers each grabbed the two enraged soldiers who held onto the scalps of two of the braves. Blood was splattered about their blouses. They were panting and crying. Andrew yelled, "Let me go. These are the savages that murdered my family. I must have revenge."

James screamed, "Why don't you let us kill them all? They murdered my family. What kind of leader are you?"

Thomas ordered, "Have these men bound and sent to the rear. They must be restrained until they can contain themselves."

Holding up a bloody scalp, Andrew replied, "I will kill the first man who takes away this scalp."

Thomas replied, "Let him keep the scalp. Brother Andrew, I order you to calm down."

Suddenly shots rang out from the woods. Polk yelled. "We are surrounded."

Williamson ordered. "The Polk Company will advance to the clearing. The rest of you will fire by two's into the woods for cover and then move by company to the clearing."

Immediately Polk Company moved forward while the remainder of the two regiments fired blindly into the woods or at muzzle flashes using the old axiom of firing to the left or right of the flash. This assumed the assailant would move after the volley. Occasionally, a yell was heard as a shot went home.

As the group advanced, both Andrew and James broke loose. The Polk Company paused at the entrance to the clearing and was met by a group of Indians ready to fight in the open.

Polk ordered, "Make a skirmish line at the tree line and be prepared to advance firing by two's."

The men paired off so one could fire while the other loaded his musket. They advanced by firing rank.

"You may fire at opportunity!" yelled Polk.

Thomas came up with the remainder of the regiment as Polk's company began firing into the Indian camp in the clearing. Just then Andrew and James broke from the tree line and began running toward the Indian defenses. The remainder of Polk's company broke thinking there had been an order to advance. Those left in the Neel's regiment broke ranks and ran toward the Indians. A bloody fifteen minutes ensued. Thomas came upon Andrew and James busy with their two man war. Three braves lay dead at their feet. Andrew had picked up a Cherokee baby and had drawn his knife. James grabbed the baby. "We do not kill babies."

By this time the Cherokees had left the field with sixteen of their warriors dead. Andrew sat sobbing on a log. His nephew Thomas Jr. at his side, Col. Thomas approached his brother, "Andrew, you must contain yourself. I am sending you and James back to Ninety-Six with the wounded. You are just too unsteady for me to depend on you."

"I am sorry, Tommy, but I just lose my head whenever I am near these savages, particularly when I am confronted by one of the clan of Dragging Canoe."

"I think Dragging Canoe is now over the mountains in Tennaco or Holston. You need to go back to your home and get a hold of yourself."

"You may have heard that I do not have much of a home," Andrew answered.

The regiments then burned the villages and supplies of the towns of Tomassy, Chehohee, and Eustash. The expedition was ordered back to the base camp on August 2nd. Upon returning to camp, Williamson found that a number who had not been chosen for the raids had gone home suffering from fatigue, lack of clothes and other necessities, and concern for their families' welfare. Furloughs were granted. The group was to rejoin at Essenecca the 28th.

James Hawthorne and Uncle Andrew left the camp. James returned to the compound near Col. Thomas. Andrew crossed the Catawba to visit his children. One night James Hawthorne's wife Mary found him gone. Zeke Proctor who had been visiting was also gone.

Andrew and Zeke rode through the night and met James at the barn of Col. Neel just at dawn. They then proceeded quietly toward Ninety-Six taking a circuitous route around the Williamson plantation where the muster assembled.

On the second day they stopped at a clearing outside of Ninety-Six. Andrew spoke. "Men, we all pine to secure vengeance upon McGhee and Johnson. They have been responsible for killing our loved ones and have stirred up the Indians. I have two scalps on my saddle and want two more; however, I am willing to share.

Let us plan how we can release these miscreants from prison and then give them the trial they deserve."

James spoke up. "How are we to share our vengeance? They can only be killed once."

Andrew interrupted, "What is that sound?" Shots rang out near the jail. They looked and found a band of Indians swarming near the door of the Ninety-Six jail. Soon they saw the Indians leading two men out to awaiting horses.

Andrew continued, "I don't know what is going on, but I suspect someone has denied us our justice. Let's go into the fort and see what the problem is."

As they rode toward the tavern, bells were ringing and people were scurrying from their homes in various stages of dress, but equipped as all frontiersmen in emergencies with horn, patch and ammunition box, hatchet and rifle all tied together as was the custom on going to rest.

Old Zeke, yelled. "Dismount, they will think we were the attackers."

They dismounted and walked their mounts with a rifle in hand. A drum was sounding a beat to quarters as Zeke approached Sheriff Simpson who was still lacing his britches. He asked his deputy, "Hezekiah, what goes here?"

"A band of those damned Cherokees broke into the jail and freed some of our prisoners."

Andrew asked, "It wasn't someone named McGhee or Johnson was it?"

"Yes, and some braves. Some of the drunks in the place decided to stay. Apparently they killed two deputies."

Hawthorne approached, rolling the shaft of an arrow. "Our friend wants us to know who is causing this mischief. Here is another of the fine arrows of Dragging Canoe."

Zeke interjected, "My, he gets around. I heard his braves were busy over the mountain."

Andrew surveyed the scene and thought to himself, "We are about to be drawn into the Ninety-Six militia. My desire is to go after these reprobates."

Turning to his two companions, "Men, let's go have some breakfast. Excuse us Sheriff."

Angrily Zeke turned to him, "Are you crazy? We must attend the muster."

"Do you think a muster is ever going to catch a raiding party? We must go on our own," replied Andrew.

"I know we can be found guilty of desertion, mutiny or something like that, but I think we should go ahead," answered Hawthorne.

"Well, let's quietly go to the south of town and then circle around to the north. They must have about an hour head start."

The men then excused themselves pleading hunger for two nights on the trail and started south. After about a mile they circled to the north. They progressed quietly down a narrow forest path circling north. They paused by a stream to let their horses water. As they crossed the stream they heard a voice from the underbrush.

"Halt. You are surrounded."

Zeke yelled. "Alexander, you skunk you don's scare nobody."

"Well, I should. You white scoundrels make enough noise to silence every owl in the forest. I have followed you for two days and you never even knew it. How come you can't invite a black man to your party?"

Zeke replied, "That is because you are too mean and ugly. Not because you are black."

"Someday I am going to get some new friends. Why has God cursed me with someone like you?"

"That is because I am the only one ugly enough to put up with you. Why did you follow us?"

"There may be a couple of imbeciles who don't know what you are about. Besides you need me to take care of you. That is why you have been able to live so long."

Andrew interrupted. "Now, now you two. You have fought each other for thirty years. Let us declare a truce. Uncle Alex, it is good to see you. Are you able to walk with your bad legs?"

"The thought of getting those old enemies makes me young again. I am sorry to hear of your family's loss. James, have you been behaving yourself? What are those things on your saddle?"

"Well, Uncle Alex, these are trophies of two Cherokees who will not kill again."

"That scalping is bad business. I thought I learned you better."

Zeke with a note of sarcasm spoke. "Are we going to hear a sermon or go after our friends? Let's get started. Sir, Alexander and I, with his permission, will take the point. Remember silence can save your life."

Alexander with a smile replied, "At last a son of a great African King gets the respect he needs. It will be an honor to serve with one of peasants of the realm."

Alex again brought smiles to everyone. They moved out with Zeke and Alexander on the point—James and Andrew following. At about noon they found the trail of the Indians. Andrew thought to himself that the following posse would be confused by so many horsed men on the trail. However, they could take advantage of the fact that the Indians would know that a large body would take some time to get underway.

They journeyed until the trail went cold and after Zeke declared it safe made a small fire and roasted a couple of rabbits they killed earlier in the morning. Arising at day break they proceeded up the trail. James Hawthorne was now taking the lead due to his skill in reading a trail. Most of the time he was off his horse. Suddenly he stopped and addressed the group.

"It appears to be about twelve horses. Strangely, six of them are shod. They have the mark of the Neel blacksmith."

Andrew interjected. "Those must be mine. I shod them at brother Thomas's plantation after I bought them from the Cherokees. Can you tell how large they are?"

"They look to be about medium weight much like the Cherokee horses."

Zeke asked, "How old is the trail?"

James answered, "From the looks of the dung, I would say no more than a day."

Toward dusk James who was at the point and about one hundred yards from the others stopped and motioned for the group to stop and disappeared into the woods. Soon a sound like an "ugh" came from the forest and then another.

He soon appeared with two scalps. "I hated to do that; these wretches were probably innocent. Anyway they are silent. These are the sentries. Let's leave our horses and have one person hold them. Uncle Andrew, we need surprise and with your rage at your losses I want you to stay behind."

Andrew answered, "My heart says no. But my head says you are right, I am not in control as barely are you."

Zeke suggested, "Let's all disappear into the woods and separate about twenty feet. We will imitate a deer in the way we progress—slowly and quietly. When we reach the camp, I will fire the first shot; you will then know it is time for you to attack. Let's see if we can grab our two friends and take them back with us. A mere shot would be too good for them."

The three disappeared. Andrew took the steeds off the trail and waited. Soon he heard shots and yelling. He untied the horses and stood with their bridles in hand at the edge of the trail.

His attention was drawn to the sound of horses bounding down the trail. Quickly Andrew took a trail rope and tied it to a tree across the trail and wrapped it around another tree on the side where he had tethered his horses. He had just finished when two riders came upon him. Quickly he cinched the rope and it arose to the height of a horse's head. The rope struck both McGhee and Johnson at the neck and unhorsed them. They lay dazed on the ground. Andrew recognized them immediately, fell upon McGhee and drew his hatchet. He missed his head but laid a great wound on his right shoulder. Andrew then turned, found Johnson dazed with head bowed but standing with a knife drawn. Andrew drew his knife and turned to face him.

"Ah at last. The patience of the Neels has been rewarded. A thousand times I have dreamed of this moment and now it is before me."

Johnson drew his pistol and pulled the trigger. The flint fell on the pan but no powder ignited. Johnson drew his knife and the two men circled as McGhee lay moaning on the ground. From his right hand Johnson's knife arced toward Andrew, but he dodged it. Andrew then feigned to the left, came down with his knife in his right hand and inflicted a wound on Johnson's shoulder cutting the buckskin-covered flesh.

"You bastard," Squawman grunted, "I will kill all your clan."

Johnson changed hands and squatted low looking for an opening.

"There is still room in my saddle for one more scalp," sobbed Andrew.

This time the large burly Johnson rushed Andrew. Andrew stepped aside and tripped Squawman as he went by. Squawman tumbled to the ground. Now Artimas, no longer dazed, staggered up and raised his pistol. Andrew threw his hatchet, which hit Artimas's hand causing the pistol to discharge into the air. Squawman McGhee now staggered erect and Andrew found himself confronted by both of these old trail rats.

"What are you going to do, Neel? You cain't kill us both." taunted McGhee.

"I can sure as hell try. Grab your weapons." Andrew replied as he backed up against a tree.

Just then a voice came from back of Andrew and toward the trail. "Drop your knives or I will blast you."

There stood Zeke, James, and Alexander. With pistols drawn, Andrew turned toward Zeke and Alexander and said mockingly, "You old farts are always spoiling my fun. Where have you been?"

Still holding their pistols, "Well, we didn't do much; everyone ran."

Alexander took the rope from the tree and bound the two miscreants. They were pushed down to the ground near the trees.

Zeke contemplated aloud. "Well, what do we have here? The posse will be here soon and will want these misfits. Did you notice how careless they were letting these foes get away? Do we think they deserve another chance to catch them?

James asked, "Did the Sheriff even know we were here?"

Andrew replied, "He did see us but may have thought we went home."

Zeke interjected, "Andrew, you have pretty much had your revenge. Your brothers Henry and Thomas have not. I suggest we take them back and have them answer the warrant drawn from your Grandpa Hank's warrant of about ten years ago."

"You just spoiled my fun." answered Andrew. "As Justice of the Peace in Meck-lenburg County, I can issue a warrant."

"Well why don't you?" Zeke suggested.

"Here ye, Here ye, be it known that Artimas McGhee and James Johnson are wanted for murder, theft, extortion, and cavorting with the enemy. As a menace to the safety of the province, the state of North Carolina, they shall be brought to the Justice Court of Mecklenburg dead or alive."

James observed, "I guess that takes you out of it, Uncle Andrew. You can't give a fair trial if you are trying to kill them."

"Maybe I could conduct a trial after they have some accident."

Artimas and Squawman were placed upon horses after first doctoring their wounds. Zeke couldn't help sneering, "Johnson, your face looks a lot better with one ear. He, he."

His answer was a scowl and then a buried head. Zeke continued. "I must know, after you cheated those Cherokees for so many years, how did you keep them from scalping you."

Squawman answered, "I married a Cherokee. I was brought before a council fire and there renounced my white race and was adopted by the tribe. I have the scars on my breast to prove it just as Artimas does. As a part of our adoption and to spare our children we took part on those raids. I appeal to you men as Christians, not to spare me but find our families and see that they are taken care of."

Andrew slapped Squawman and was restrained by Alexander. "You want mercy after murdering families. Were you in the raid on my place and on the Smith place?"

"I ain't going to say," he sobbed. "Please don't hurt my family. Can't you raise them to be Christians like you?"

James added, "Now isn't that sweet. There didn't seem to be much mercy when your friends murdered my family and took me captive."

The two prisoners sulked in silence. They were loaded on to the horses tied to the saddle. One of their horses was tied to Zeke and the other to Alexander. Alexander at six foot five looked even bigger when he stood beside the Indian ponies of the captures. After much discussion the body decided to head for Charles Town and turn them over to the Provincial Assembly. Andrew pointed out that although they would be headed to South Carolina, the original summons of some fifteen years ago was in North Carolina. So to North Carolina they went. Besides, he felt his new summons was better.

On the second day Artimas came down with a fever. His shoulder wound had turned putrid. Twice he fell from his saddle. That night somewhat south of the

Williamson plantation they camped. Artimas was placed near the fire and kept covered. Alexander was placed on watch and circled the camp.

Artimas motioned for Zeke to come beside him. In a weak voice he said, "I can't talk very loud, please lie down here so you can hear me."

Zeke drew back the blanket and saw that there were no weapons. He handed his pistol and hatchet to Alexander then flopped to the ground where he prepared to listen on one elbow.

"Zeke, I have not led a good life. I have cheated, I have killed, and I have hurt that Hawthorne family terribly. I want you to know that it was not me that killed old Justice Henry Neel. It was Squawman. I know I deserve to die, but promise me my family will not be hurt. I don't think I shall live long. But I want to tell you of some of the French treasure we hid after the Great War. You know that big oak tree in front of Master Huck's house?"

"Yes."

"If one should walk fifty paces from the tree toward the edge of his large barn, one would find a large rhododendron. Under that bush is a strong box which contains some loot we took from the French. Please use it to help my family and those we have harmed."

"May God bless your soul. We will try."

Squawman screamed, "Shut up you fool. That is part my money."

The dead man did not answer. They buried Artimas and began their journey. As they were riding Zeke rode up next to Squawman. "Johnson, we have been around a long time. I can't say we have ever been friends but have worked at the trading game. How could you continue to be accepted by the Cherokees after you cheated them?"

"Well, you see, they expected me to cheat. But they also believed I cheated the white man more and they were right." Squawman chuckled.

The next night they reached Andrew's old place. Andrew grew pensive and silent. Johnson was taken inside and tied to a chair while the party prepared supper. James and Alexander took care of the horses. A watch was established for the night and supper started. Johnson was left bound to a chair. After allowing him to eat supper Johnson was rebound by Andrew. Johnson noticed the ropes were rather loose. Everyone retired except Andrew who kept the first watch.

Andrew placed saddles on two horses. He placed one horse in front of the house and another by the tree on the side. He waited. Shortly, Johnson stealthily crept out of the house and on the porch. He was barefooted. Seeing the horse, Johnson mounted and galloped away. Andrew jumped on his horse and yelled. "The prisoner has escaped. I am going after him."

The pair rode hard through the night along the widely used trail. At times the heaving horses drew within a length of each other. Suddenly Johnson crashed into the woods. He rode about one hundred feet in the dense forest when he was caught by a limb which broke his neck. He fell to the ground. In the dim half moonlight Andrew dismounted. Johnson's horse was hindered from further running by the dense growth. Andrew knelt down over the badly deformed face of his nemesis.

"Well, Neel, you got me. I can't move my arms or legs. Please shoot me."

"I may, but first you will be scalped."

He laid his pistol on the ground and took up his knife. As Johnson yelled he began to slowly make a circle around his scalp. "That is for Sarah, that is for Mother Smith, that is for Father Smith, that is for her brother Aaron, that is for my son, and that is for all the others."

Blood flowed around the wound. Andrew placed his feet on the shoulders of the prostrate Johnson, grabbed his dirty matted hair, and pulled his scalp loose from his head.

"Please Neel, shoot me, shoot me."

Hearing the howling of a wolf Andrew turned, "I shall leave you to the wolves and bears. May God rest your and my soul."

He mounted, took the reigns of the other horse and headed back to his house. There was a candle burning and all the party was awake.

"What happened?" asked Zeke.

"It seems that our friend got away, and I tried to find him."

Zeke continued, "It seems a little strange that there are two horses with saddles out there. Did he have time to put a saddle on a horse before he got away? How could he get away with such a fine sentry on duty? How come you have an extra horse? Shall we go after him or does that bloody shirt and scalp in your hand mean it will be unnecessary?"

"Draw your own conclusions. Most of my vengeance is satisfied."

Andrew took off his blouse and threw it outside. He went to his cabinet, took a buckskin blouse, went outside and washed, put on his new blouse, sat down, and began to weep. The other men left him alone, turned and went to sleep. Alexander kept watch and comforted Andrew for some time.

The next morning over a breakfast of eggs taken from the now wild chickens, some ham from the store house, and coffee, Zeke began to speak. "I suppose we should be making it to Williamson's muster, but I don't like the idea of that war party of Cherokees who freed our friends still running around. I wonder if they will try to find them. We only killed a couple and I will bet there were at least a dozen curious braves out there. Do you think they will come after their friends or just go away?"

James answered, "If that arrow shaft was Dragging Canoe's I don't think he will stick around. On the other hand he knows that Williamson is patrolling the area."

During this time Andrew dressed the scalp. Suddenly, he looked up. "My friends we have two issues. The first is the alleged treasure of Master Huck and the other is two families, not counting mine, who are in need of help. Of course, we also have the issue of Williamson muster."

Alexander spoke, "Technically, I have never been a part of the muster. Suppose I go find that treasure. Zeke, you are too old to be running around after those people. You should go with me. When we find the treasure, we could turn it over to Tom Neel and then find the families of Artimas and Johnson and give 'em aid."

James answered. "I think the Cherokees will adopt those children, and we will have a terrible time getting them."

Now partially recovered, Andrew finishing his tanning and drawing on his pipe concluded, "I think Alex and Zeke should go ahead and find the money while we report to muster."

Zeke laughed, "I hope they don't shoot you for desertion."

Andrew answered. "I suppose they will think we are still on furlough. Thank you for all your help. Look out for Dragging Canoe."

James responded, "I imagine he is already over the mountain."

Late that morning they parted. James Hawthorne and Andrew Neel headed north and that afternoon they arrived at the Williamson plantation. There they found the Neel Rangers on the way to Esseneca for Col. Williamson's muster.

That night was spent giving Col. Thomas Neel an account of the events concerning Artimas and Squawman. No mention was made of the scalps which hung on Andrew's saddle horn, although Tom did give them a curious glance and then smiled. Turning to Andrew he asked, "I suppose these men were given a Christian burial."

Andrew answered, "They got what they deserved."

The next morning the Neel's Mounted Rangers got underway. This was the only mounted unit as most of the militia was required to leave their horses at the muster area and proceed on foot for fear they might desert. As the Neel Mounted Regiment proceeded, Thomas drew up to his brother Andrew some paces away from the troop.

Thomas spoke, "Brother Andy, you have suffered much and the grief you bear is more than I can imagine. But you cannot forever keep up this blood feud. You will get yourself killed and maybe others. I implore you to me more careful and become a better example to young Hawthorne."

"My lust for revenge will not be satiated until I confront Dragging Canoe and make him pay for what he has done."

"Just be careful and don't get others killed with you. As you may have heard Col. Williamson is in command of the South Carolina troops, General Griffith Rutherford is in command of the North Carolinians but under Williamson and will be acting with us. The Virginians under Col. Christie are moving west and will attack the Overhill Cherokees. Williamson has already cleared many of the lower Cherokee villages. We suspect that many of our militia ranks have been augmented by former Tories who are afraid of the Indian raids."

September 12 the Neel Rangers were bivouacked with Col. Andrew Williamson's forces. Williamson assigned a force of three hundred men to guard the newly completed Ft. Rutledge at Esseneca and advanced with a force of 2,000 militia, which included General Rutherford and the North Carolinians. (Neel's Rangers contained both North and South militia who lived on the southeastern boarder of North Carolina. They were all in North Carolina before the border reassignment in 1771.)

The Neel Rangers took the lead, guided by a Catawba Indian. As they mounted up, Col. Williamson came up to Tom with an Indian. "Col. Neel, this is Running Bear, our guide to the headwaters of the Tennessee."

Both men jumped from their horses and extended both arms in an Indian embrace. Tom spoke, "My brother looks well. How goes your family?"

"The Earth Mother has blessed us well. It has been many moons since we hunted together. I hear you are now a great chief."

"Not so great as you, a great chief of peace of the Catawbas. I feel it is a great privilege to once again join around the camp fire. This is my brother Andrew." Andrew nodded but did not smile.

"I have heard of you, Andrew. You have done great things to assist my people. How goes your brother across the river?"

"Henry serves with the Continental Army up north with our great Chief Washington."

"You mean General Washington. Do you think I did not study the white man's skin that talks without learning a little?"

"Well, pardon me!! My chief is not only brave but smarter than I am," Thomas said laughingly. They rode on. Running Bear and Thomas were soon separated by a few paces from the rest.

"I suppose you heard about Andrew."

"Yes, I heard his family was slaughtered by Dragging Canoe and that he has a blood feud against him. He has changed since I last saw him."

"Yes, and he wears the scalp of a brave and also Squawman McGhee on his saddle. Notice how they are both on the right side. He saves the left for Dragging Canoe."

"The Cherokees are beginning to believe he is a ghost, but a man with such vengeance has false courage."

"Our sacred skin teaches us that the revenge belongs to the Lord. With his angry blood he could be a danger to us all," replied Thomas.

In two days the 2,000 militia paused at the entrance to the Raban Gap. This was as far as the wagons could go. Fortunately, many of the wagons were pulled by mules as well as horses. Back packs were placed on the mules filled with flour, ammunition, powder, and dried meat. There was some concern about the continual hunting because of fear of alerting the Cherokees. However, Running Bear of the Catawbas pointed out that it would be a deaf and blind Cherokee who would not know they were coming.

This was the last night for tents. As Thomas was about to retire in his tent an orderly appeared, "Col. Thomas, a militia captain requests to see you. He said you would remember a veteran of the Regulators."

"Send him in," commanded Thomas.

He lighted a candle. Before him appeared Master Christian Huck dressed in bedraggled trail clothes which were quite out of character for him. His countenance was firm and drawn as he looked at his friend.

"Huck, what on earth are you doing here?"

"I have come for many purposes, among them to say good-bye, but also to warn you."

"Aren't you with the King's forces?"

"I have not taken your blasted oath, but Thomas, I am torn between the obligations to my King as detailed in the 13th chapter of Romans which demands we be in subjection to our rulers and to my love for my friends."

"Yes, I saw the order to confiscate your lands. Where is your family?"

"They have fled to Florida. And we may be fleeing to the Barbados or perhaps to Scotland. What I would like is a safe conduct to Florida so that I may search for and join them."

"That can be arranged. Those King's Florida Rangers of Thomas Browne are doing a great deal of mischief with their raids. I will only ask that you will not raise any hand against the Provincial Congress until you reach Florida."

"Of course. I also have two slaves and a wagon hidden in the next village."

"Well, I will include them, but you must get out of here at daylight. I shall have Jim Hawthorne meet you at the river and give you save passage into Georgia." Taking out his pen and paper from his portable desk he scribbled a letter. "There. My letters will probably be enough. Let's have one last drink."

He took two pewter cups and poured rum in each. "It isn't the claret you are used to but the meaning is the same."

"With such an old friend nothing is finer."

Thomas proposed, "Why don't I bid for your confiscated lands and when this war is over you can buy them back."

Huck smiled. "A capital idea. And if the King's forces win, I shall try to do the same for you."

The cups clicked. He then called James Hawthorne who was both surprised and delighted to see Huck again. Thomas shook hands.

Huck spoke, "By the way, the Cherokees heard of a ghost named Neel who takes vengeance on Dragging Canoe for the massacre of his family. Their shaman has seen Neel in a dream tormenting those who killed his family. Dragging Canoe left yesterday with his loyal band and their families for Overmountain to be with his father Little Carpenter."

"Thank you. Good luck. The newly commissioned Ensign Hawthorne will go with you. James, your duty is to scout and see that Master Huck gets across the Savannah safely. Then you are to return."

"May we meet in happier times, Thomas."

There were tears in their eyes as two old friends embraced. He called his aide. "Lieutenant, take this note to Col. Williamson." The note was a copy of the one given to Huck and asked for safe conduct. He also related news of Dragging Canoe.

The next morning, leaving some of the baggage including tents, Col. Andrew Williamson left three hundred men to guard Fort Rutledge, passed through the Rabun Gap with two thousand troops and guided by Running Bear and his Catawbas reached the headwaters of the Tennessee. This was an area of impassable laurel thickets and narrow trails against steep mountain sides. It was an area impossible for dispersing scouts.

The column passed on to the town of Coweechee where on the 17th of September they hoped to find General Rutherford's forces from the northeast of North Carolina. Finding he was not there, the column pushed on following the Coweechee River. Thomas was reminded of the ambush during the French and Indian wars near Fort Prince George. He sensed the same conditions as they threaded through the tight underbrush. The summit of the mountains rose some two hundred feet above the river, broken in stages where grassy mold accumulated and where sweet brier, laurel, and azaleas were luxuriant. Vines struggled in the mountain crags under an occasional umbrella of ash, pine, and dogwood.

On September 19 with the Neel Rangers in the lead, a sudden war yell rang out followed by shots. In the narrow trail there was little cover. Thomas ordered his troops dismounted and they began firing at the flashes in the cover. The Cherokees had them penned down. After about a half hour of firing, Col. Williamson managed to make his way up to the front. There he found Col. Thomas and Running Bear in conversation.

"Col. Neel, what is the problem? Why can't we move forward?"

Thomas replied, "It looks like one of the ambushes in the French and Indian War. The sides are narrow, there is no way to flank, and we can't see them. I have taken some casualties."

Col. Anderson then ordered. "I want you to charge straight ahead. We will give you some blind cover by firing into the undergrowth."

"Aye, Sir, Rangers dismount and prepare to charge."

Within minutes the regiment charged in disciplined order. They stopped, fired volley by two's, and then loaded and charged forward only to stop and fire again. The undisciplined Cherokees fled. A total of thirteen of the rangers lost their lives in the charge. Thomas conducted a religious service for the men that night, and they were laid to rest in a small meadow.

On the 26th of September the forces of General Rutherford and Col. Williamson met at Hiwasee. There the forces attended a service and listened to the Reverend James Hall, chaplain for Rutherford's forces.

Hall's words reflected the grim, self-righteous, combative Calvinism prevalent in the early southern back country. Indians were referred to as murderous heathen, and the troops accordingly considered themselves engaged in a holy war in which all actions against such an enemy were justified.

` As Thomas listened with Running Bear he remarked, "I hope the good Reverend realizes we will be living with these people some day and that they have souls, too."

"Some white men are very strange," replied Running Bear.

What happened the next weeks was a blood bath in the valleys, literally with fire and sword. Settlements were burned and crops destroyed, forcing the remaining Indians to subsist the winter with roots and small game. Many of the militia was surprised to see the credible development of both the housing and agriculture of the Cherokee villages. It was all Thomas could do to keep down the atrocities visited by some of the renegade militia members. He frequently found James Hawthorne and his brother Andrew missing on "special assignments."

General Rutherford with his North Carolinians had passed through the Suwaan-nanoa Gap, marched down the Broad River crossing War Ford and continuing down Hominy Creek, and on down the Tennessee River.

Meanwhile, Neel Rangers moved in a detached manner and came upon a village on the Tennessee. As they approached, an ambuscade drove them back. Thomas was startled to see Andrew rush forward and engage a brave in hand-to-hand fighting in typical "no holds barred fashion." However, little could be done because the Rangers were trying to break through the attack. Finally, the Indians retreated. There lay Andrew with an arrow in his side. Beside him lay a young brave with an ear gone, a hatchet in his head and one of his eyes out.

"Thomas," moaned Andrew, "I have taken the big one," blood bubbles gurgled from his mouth. "Please take care of my family. You will find a will registered in Tryon County with a copy in Mecklenburg. I have loved you very much." He then gasped and died.

Thomas wept and began to pray. "Oh Lord, your servant has gone to join you. He has served the Lord's cause well. Please speed his soul to your presence. In the name of Christ our Savior, Amen."

As he sobbed, Thomas covered his brother with a blanket after first removing the arrow. He handed the arrow to James who knelt over the brave with the Catawba guide Running Bear.

"Colonel Thomas," cried James, "this arrow has a canoe on it."

"Yes, this young brave is Fierce Bear, son of Dragging Canoe. I guess Dragging Canoe must have tried to stop the fight by killing Andrew. He used a ceremonial arrow instead of a musket. He must have known who his son was fighting. He is not through yet. He will want the body of his son. I don't understand why he left his body. Perhaps the fighting was too fierce."

The five dead Cherokees were buried. Thomas wrapped the body of his brother in a blanket and secured the blankets with rope. He then roped the body to the back of a mule and sent James Hawthorne back to his home with the body. Col. Williamson dismissed the Neel Rangers and Thomas prepared to go home.

Two days after the battle, the forces of Williamson were camped in one of the few meadows. In the morning mist they spotted two Cherokee braves coming toward them in the zigzag of peaceful intent.

Thomas and Running Bear rode out to meet them. Running Bear immediately recognized the older man.

"Hail Uncle," he responded to Little Carpenter. "My heart is in joy to see you."

"Young Running Bear and Chief Thomas, it is with a sad heart that I come to you in peace. We wish to have peace for a few moons to bury our dead and prepare for the winter. But I come for the body of my grandson, Fierce Bear, who was slain here two days ago."

Thomas interrupted, "He was slain while fighting my brother, Andrew, who was shot by Dragging Canoe."

"My heart is troubled by what happened. My son, Dragging Canoe, has taken the role of a war chief. He was in this area trying to excite braves into fighting. You too, have lost your war chief, the one you call Andrew, but the one we call Angry Ghost. I want peace because we have lost most of our stores for the winter on the morning sun side of the great mountains. Dragging Canoe has gone toward the setting sun with a party of braves but asked me to find his son."

"Oh, great Chief," replied Thomas, "we both have suffered greatly. We will lead you to the place where we buried the braves." Thomas then assisted Little Carpenter with exhuming the body.

Little Carpenter turned to Thomas. "My friend, the gods of war have placed us on the sides of evil many times. However, our families have been like brothers."

"Yes, you are a great chief. But tell me one thing. Why did your tribe help those people who cheated you, Artimas McGhee and Squawman Johnson?" asked Thomas.

"Yes, my friend, I remember when we traveled together to the land of the Creeks and brought them back for the governor to try. His council chiefs let them go. Somehow my son and other war chiefs were tricked by them. Besides, the man you call Squawman married my son's sister in law. They had been a part of the war party of the tribe. That party now identifies with the King's forces. My son and I have had many talks around the council fire. Now I just want our people to live in peace."

They then clasped arms. "Live in peace my old friend," wept Thomas.

"I always wished I could have seen the King again," replied Little Carpenter sadly. He climbed on his horse, joined by his two braves and the body of his grandson. He rode away.

The mission with Little Carpenter completed, Neel Rangers were dismissed. Thomas arrived home in four days. As the funeral for Andrew was conducted, the little Bethel chapel was filled with residents from both sides of the Catawba River. However, Henry was now a Captain with the First North Carolina Continental Regiment and was in Virginia unable to attend. Nancy Agnes brought her family including Thomas, Andrew's son, who was now living with the Henry Neels.

Thomas read a eulogy from Governor Rutledge. Reverend Dalton and Reverend Williamson conducted the burial service.

By the first of October, the resistance of the Indians below the Tennessee River effectively ended. Dragging Canoe retreated down the Tennessee River to Chickamauga Creek where he set up a new settlement with remnants of disaffected Creeks, Shawnees, and even a few white loyalists. This band continued forays into the Nolichucky and Watauga settlements for the remainder of the war, continually battling John Seiver and Issac Shelby in the region of what is now Tennessee until the 1780's.

Most of the Cherokees just quit fighting and spent the winter trying to find enough food to survive. The 3,000 troops who had come through their land had foraged the area to almost nothing. The Whigs had driven off their livestock and thinned the forest of game. Buffalo all but disappeared from the area. Small game, fish, and roots were the winter fare. In May, ancient Little Carpenter led the major chiefs to a peace conference where much of the lands in South Carolina and some of North Carolina and Georgia were ceded to the new Continental Congress. Dragging Canoe did not attend. He sulked in the faux State of Franklin west of the Appalachians.

# CHAPTER 31

# *Florida Campaign*

Loyalist Thomas Browne, still smarting from his torture in 1775, organized the King's Rangers in Florida and raided Whigs in Georgia and South Carolina. He occasionally liaisoned with a King's vessel to furnish provisions. Most of the King's forces had left South Carolina by July 26th for Staten Island, New York; however, some vessels continued to patrol the areas of Wilmington, New Bern and Charles Town looking for privateers. Privateers under commission from both North and South Carolina captured British merchant ships and relieved them of their cargoes.

On August 3, 1776, General Lee assumed the victory of Charles Town and claimed solitary honors in spite of the brilliant repulse of the fleet by Col. Moultrie. The news of the Declaration of Independence reached Charles Town. General Lee, during the celebration, addressed the men of the Carolina Continentals who stood in formation by the waterfront commons. Lee hit upon an idea, which he thought might overshadow Washington's efforts in the north and perhaps elevate him to commander of the Continental armies.

"My brave comrades, when the history of this continent is written the finest chapter will be reserved for the defenders of Charles Town. We must not rest for I have planned even greater glory. Did you know that the nefarious rangers of Thomas Browne are raiding our brothers in Georgia from their bases in Florida? Did you know that as I speak the equally nefarious Col. Prevost is marshalling his forces to strike at our homes? As your leader I shall lead you against this band and bring glory and honor to you as we stride through Florida and its riches. You will be awarded slaves and treasure to compensate for the hardships you experience. Are you ready for glory?" His voice rose to a shout on this final message.

Cheers rang out.

"Fine. Unit commanders meet in my quarters at the hotel within the hour."

Two days later amid the drums and fife, the First and Third North Carolina Continentals on foot (just returned from the north), the South Carolina Mounted Neel Rangers, and various militias began their march to Florida 1,500 strong. Little logistics were provided, not even a medicine chest.

By August 3 the main body reached Savannah. Various parts of the units were stationed at small Georgia communities along the way. The late departure of the

Royal Governor, James Wright, had not given the colony much time to prepare a patriot force. The Royal forces in Florida of Thomas Browne, British Col. Prevost and his brother Governor Prevost failed to do battle. The starving Continental and militia troops were forced to forage among the planters as well as pull down houses for firewood. Disease pillaged their encampment, Sunsbury, where fourteen or fifteen perished a day. Provisioners from South Carolina charged exorbitant prices for goods and delivered them sparingly and infrequently.

In the middle of the misery, General Lee turned the command over to General Howe and responded to a call to Congress to join Washington in the north. This tenure ended when the British Colonel Banastre Tarleton at length captured him while he dined in a tavern.

Captain Henry Neel's company had been assigned to a small settlement outside of Sunsbury. There was constant foraging by his troops and engaging the enemy's Royal marines who landed frequently to raid plantations for provisions for their troops. As the company dwindled by desertion and sickness, Henry grew despondent. He had picked a small cottage as his headquarters. Late one evening in September he received his brother, Col. Thomas.

Thomas stopped and tied his horse in front of the house. Henry heard him. "Good to see you, Thomas. But you better guard your horse. We have eaten most of ours."

"I know. I was surprised you weren't part of General Lee's Continental guard when he started north to join Washington."

"My troops are too sick. Besides, he wanted the best supplied of the regiment with him. Look at my men. Your Rice King friends in the South Carolina Congress don't supply us with anything. We fight your battles and get nothing except gouging from your filthy merchants. Where are the clothes, the food, the pay we were promised?"

"That is what I want to discuss with you. As you know your enlistment is up, I believe, in March. I think in view of your younger family, and the need to take care of Andy's children, you can best serve your country by returning to the back country while I do the work of both provinces down here in Charles Town. In fact, as a member of the Committee of Safety I am ordering your company back home."

"Thank you, Thomas. Will you inform Col. Moore?"

"I just came from the headquarters. Col. Moore has died and Col. Clark is now commanding what is left of the regiments that General Lee did not take with him."

"Oh, that is terrible. He was such a good man. What of the funeral?"

"Within two days."

Henry's company gathered at the military funeral for Col. Moore. His body was placed on a wagon for the trip back to the Waxhaw. As the term of enlistment was nearly up for Henry Neel's company, and the South Carolinians did not wish to supply the Continentals with clothes or other provisions unless they re-enlisted as South Carolina Militia, most of them headed west and home.

Henry's company had attended the funeral as a small military remnant of the once proud victors of Moore's Creek, Great Bridge, and Sullivan Island. After the salutes to the fallen leader and a speech by Col Clark, they were dismissed.

With a nod from Henry, Lieutenant Lewis barked, "Company attention." Henry strode to the front of them.

"Men of the Neel Company, words cannot express my admiration of you and what you have done. We are saddened by the loss of our great commander, but now the First Continental has been disbanded with honors. You have taken on the greatest fighters in world, the Highland Scots at Moore's Creek, the best of the British Army at Great Bridge and Sullivan Island. Now it is time to go home to your loved ones—to make peace with your Tory neighbors, to start a new nation. I shall always treasure my time with you and wish you godspeed." He turned away with tears in his eyes.

Suddenly one of the troopers stood and yelled, "Let's give three cheers for Captain Neel!" And they did.

The company, dismissed, began the trek back to North Carolina, many riding in wagons as they were too sick to walk. The forces of Col. Prevost had defeated Lee's vision of glory in Florida and Georgia simply by retreating. The British forces never lost a man. The Whigs on the other hand lost one-third of their 1,500 by disease.

Henry and those of his company of the Waxhaw continued up the road to Charlotte. They stopped each of five nights at plantations along the way. Sometimes they ran into Tory sympathizers who turned them away or tried to sell them provisions. Very few horses were left and Henry gave his to a wounded neighbor. As they left the rice lands they began the climb to the Piedmont. They trudged forward cheered by the sight of sweet brier and laurel. The uncleared swamp lands became less present. The topography gave way to flatwoods with nothing but jack pine and red cedar with tangled pine breaks. Finally they could see the mountains in the fog and the gentle hills of the Catawba valley. The girded trees of newly developed lands were interspersed with the small patches of yeomen farmers. Men began to drop off as they neared their homes. Pines, chestnuts, and hemlocks began to appear along the road in areas and continued with rick rack fences marking lands behind them when a farm was near. They were in the Waxhaw at last.

It was a beautiful February morning. A cool breeze waved the grass that sparkled under the dew. The road had now narrowed to a path barely large enough for one wagon. Henry approached his Waxhaw farm near Steele Creek. He was met by a young fifteen-year-old on a horse. The slender lad had the deerskin dress of a frontiersman with a belt containing a knife. He had been on a hunt. He held a rifle across his saddle. A wide beaver hat almost hid his face.

He stopped and looked at the bedraggled form in front of him. The skeleton bearded face with sunken eyes carried the remains of a combination continental uniform and frontier clothing. He carried a rifle with a tomahawk and pistol in his belt. The butt of the rifle was his cane.

"Halo, stranger. Where go you?"

Henry queried, "Can this be William the son of the haggard soldier from the wars in the east?"

The horse let out a whinny of recognition and moved his head up and down. The hound began to jump on Henry in recognition, yapping in ecstasy. In screams of recognition the lad jumped from his horse and embraced Henry, "Pa, I heard the Regiment was coming home. It is good to see you. Here, hop on old Ted and let's go home."

A tear ran down Henry's face as he struggled to mount the horse behind his son. "It is good to see you, son. Have you taken care of the place?"

"I would like to say I did, but Uncle John and cousin Thomas just told me what to do."

"I know John is a wonderful farmer; I consider him a friend more than a servant."

Shortly, they came into the compound. Both dismounted. William smacked the horse on the rump and it headed to the barn yard. The door burst open and five young Neels tumbled out yelling for their father. Henry embraced them all. On the portico came Nancy Agnes his wife holding young Jenny.

Here was supposed to be a middle aged lady of the soil of some forty years. Yet to Henry she was a vision. Her eyes shown from a snow white face the skin of which had been protected by broad bonnets as she had supervised the fields. She wore a linsey woolsey dress with a high collar and sleeves. Her feet were shod in moccasins. Henry with tears in his eyes approached and wrapped his hands around his young daughter and his wife. Nancy wept and shuddered and in soft and gentle voice commented, "I thought I would never see you again. Oh, I am so glad you are home. So many of the neighboring ladies will never see their husbands again." Suddenly, she pushed him away.

"My, you look like you have starved to death," she scolded, trying to master her composure. "You know we like people to wash here once in a while. Mary, go heat some water for your father. We must get some of this dirt off him."

"While you do that I have some presents." He took from his pack knives for William, James, John, and Samuel. He then gave small dolls to Mary, Nancy Agnes, and little Jenny. His nephew Thomas received a trail knife.

"Thomas, this knife belonged to your father. It has been used to avenge the death of your grandparents, mother, and brother. Treat it reverently."

"Uncle Henry, I shall treasure it forever." He hugged the knife to his chest and ran off to be by himself.

Henry related his travels in South Carolina and recalled the accounts of Moore's Creek and Great Bridge. He told of his brother Thomas's work with the South Carolina Provincial government. Mary and young Nancy Agnes swooned over the accounts of the beauty of Charles Town.

After a sumptuous supper Henry toured the farm with Uncle John.

"John, you have done well. How can I thank you enough?"

John looked at the ground and then replied, "Captain," he did not use *master.* "I have enjoyed my life here. Your family is my family. However, I would like to have a larger plot to raise more produce. Mistress Nancy has been teaching my daughter Rachael how to sew and read and perhaps someday she could have her freedom."

"Freedom for a former woman slave is very hazardous. Any single woman regardless of race can not survive alone. I hope one day she can find a freedman she could marry. Do you know Samuel over at brother Thomas's place?"

"I met him when I drove the wagon to family gatherings. He seems like a fine young man."

"I understand he may have his freedom anytime he wants it. He has mastered the blacksmith trade and should be able to support himself. He seems like a fine prospect. Perhaps Rachael could accompany you on a trip to Col. Neel's someday."

"That would be most pleasurable, Suh. I have noticed Rachel sneaking off to talk to him at some of our gatherings."

Henry wept and embraced his old friend.

When at last Nancy and Henry were alone, seated on a bench at the end of their bed, he turned to his bride and asked, "How did you fare, my love?" Nancy looked up into his eyes and replied, "We managed. Uncle John took good care of us. We even made some money when William at a mere fourteen managed to drive some cattle to Charlotte. Our new tobacco crop is doing well. We combined with the Polks and Widow Jackson and pulled a hogshead of tobacco to Charles Town with John and some of the young Polk and Jackson boys. I am worried about some of the things that young William learns on those trips. He sometimes gets a little impudent."

"That is just part of a man growing up; I wouldn't worry. Were you bothered by any Indians?"

"Not really. Uncle Henry and the men were quite capable of defending us. Running Bear or others of the Catawbas came by about once a week allegedly for water or food or to offer a kill, but actually just to see how we were getting along. He is a great friend."

"You can depend on Running Bear. It is so good to be home. You are a brave woman." He then embraced her.

"Oh, my husband, I have missed you," she responded as she felt the sinewy arms beneath his linen night shirt. It wasn't long until he blew out the candle and embraced Nancy in their bed for the first time in months.

Henry soon adjusted to life as a farmer. With the repulse of the fleet at Charles Town, the Waxhaw were generally at peace. Many of the Tories took the oath to support the Provincial Congress. Henry was reassigned to the Waxhuas militia and attended the monthly drill. He was much in demand as he had received military training with the Continental Army.

CHAPTER 32

# General Prevost Before Charles Town

Col. Thomas Neel spent a great deal of time in Charles Town as the commander of the Neel Rangers and as a member of the Provincial Congress now called the Assembly. He purchased a small house in Charles Town. He longed for his Piedmont home in the New Acquisition and regretted the legislative sessions. After General Moultrie's forces at the fort repulsed the British ships, they left the harbor of Charles Town. The Sheriff's Muster elected Thomas with Polk to represent the New Acquisition area of York County. His twin sons Thomas and Andrew as well James Hawthorne remained at the estate on the Catawba River taking care of the plantation. Jean joined the elder Thomas during the legislative session, leaving Mary as mistress of the house up north. Thomas almost exclusively engaged with the Neel's Rangers and the Assembly, allowing little time to visit his Catawba River home.

South Carolina during 1778 was in the throes of establishing a new government. The newly formed Assembly passed a bill abolishing support of the church. There was an attempt to change the state constitution of 1776, but it was vetoed by Governor Rutlege who then resigned. There followed a series of three governors during the year as no one wanted to take the position. Finally, Christopher Gadsden reluctantly accepted the chair.

The debacle of the first invasion of Florida led to the disbanding of the First Continental regiment and Henry Neel's return home. General Howe, the new Commander of the Southern Continentals and the militia still clung to a fort in Sunsbury, Georgia, below Savannah. The fort's purpose, commanded by Colonel Lachlan McIntosh, was to counter the fort that Tory General Augustine Prevost had built on the St. Mary's River in order to conduct forays into South Carolina for forage and supplies.

It was December 1778. Col. Thomas and Jean had returned to the plantation on the Catawba and were anticipating a feast with the family as well as with Henry Neel's family from Steele Creek. There was much excitement as it was announced that the servant Samuel had been granted his freedom but would remain with Thomas as a master blacksmith. In turn Henry had granted freedom to his young servant Rachel. They had met, romance had bloomed and now they were joined in marriage at the Bethel Church. Thomas officiated at the ceremony.

The 19th of December, Thomas received a notice of the landing of a British force near the Savannah River and a request for the Neel Ranger's to return to Charles Town. There were Jean's usual protestations that the family had done enough.

Thomas assembled the Neel's Rangers again in Charles Town. Here he learned that Col. Lachlan McIntosh, of the Third Continentals had withstood the troops and Rangers of Col. "Burnt Foot" Browne and General Prevost at Sunsbury, challenging Prevost to "come and take me." Prevost declined the invitation and retreated back to Florida. However, he was attacked at the Ogeechee Ferry by Lieutenant Colonel Sam Elbert and two hundred Georgia Continentals. In anger Prevost and his men went on a rampage in Georgia pillaging all the countryside as they went. There was no distinction between Whig and Tory estates in their rampage.

Thomas and Polk arrived at Charles Town shortly after Christmas. As they lingered in the Queen Charlotte Tavern before the Assembly, Tom began, "Now that Washington has sent General Lincoln to lead us, what will be our next move?"

"His first move will be to find an army and the second will be to try to get the militias to be released to him," replied Tom cynically.

"It appears the British have devised a new strategy."

"What, pray tell, is that?"

"The *Gazette* believes they plan to occupy Georgia, the newest colony, and from there pacify the Carolinas. This morning's *Gazette* reports the landing of a Lieutenant Campbell who has been aboard the new *Savannah* and has 3,000 troops including two so-called loyal militia from North and South Carolina."

Thomas responded. "I suppose that the North Carolinians are the remains of Huck's old regiment and some of those people we tried to subdue at Fair Forest."

"Yes, but Huck took an oath didn't he when I paroled him?"

"I suppose he did, but he can't just stay down in Florida doing nothing when he has to listen to our friend Col. Thomas, the hot foot, Browne. Besides, the fleet of Commodore Hyde Parker anchors off the Savannah River with additional troops."

Thomas suddenly turned and exclaimed, "Look at that!" A body of haggard Continentals drug by, heads down. The men had the sunken eyes of fatigue. They limped along with the aid of their rifles.

Behind them was the corporal's guard escorting General Howe. Recognizing Polk and Thomas he returned their salutes, dismounted and came to them. They exchanged salutes again.

"Col. Neel and Col. Polk, how good to see you even under these trying circumstances."

"General Howe, what happened?" queried Thomas.

"The British captured Savannah and defeated our forces. I must report to the Governor and ask him to call the Assembly."

Thomas replied, "My compliments, Sir. Your contributions to our cause have been legend. Our prayers are with you as you go to your new assignments as determined by the Congress. If we can be of service let us know."

"Your prayers would be better spent if you prayed for my successor, General Lincoln, who will soon find he has no army to command when he takes my place."

The next day Howe addressed the Council and the South Carolina Congress. He related how his seven hundred troops were met by a force of 3,000 under Archibald Campbell. They fought from a well fortified position but were surprised by a force from the swamp in their rear. Five hundred Continentals were led to the prison ships and only one hundred and fifty escaped. He reported that the citizens in the lower part of Georgia were coming in droves to take the oath of the King. He thanked the legislature. There followed an introduction and later a reception for General Benjamin Lincoln. Howe left for an assignment in the north.

General Lincoln's presence encouraged the population of Charles Town. A fire in the town destroyed many structures near the waterfront. Here and on the west side of the peninsula fortifications were built consisting of a wall and a moat. The General had to contend with a governor who guarded his militia, three regiments of continentals whose enlistment maturity and desertion shrunk his numbers. In addition, the local population sold provender for the army reluctantly and tried to avoid taking Continental currency. Thomas and Polk continued their dual roles as assemblymen and colonels in their respective regiments.

Lincoln drilled his Continentals and by April he was ready to challenge the British at Augusta. Except for occasional raids by the Loyalist forces of Col. Thomas Browne from Florida, there were few engagements.

Across the river from Savannah was Purrysburg which commanded one of the best crossings between Savannah and Charles Town. Lincoln was at last ready for the relief of Savannah. On April 20, 1779, he moved toward Augusta with 2,000 light troops leaving his baggage and artillery to follow. On April 22 he wrote Col. Moultrie, who was left in command of Charles Town, to send his artillery and all Continental troops, except the second and fifth regiments. Moultrie ordered these two regiments to remain near Purrysburg and guard the crossing as long as possible. Moultrie was ordered to defend all fords passes leading to Charles Town, and if attacked to hold until Lincoln could come back from his sortie into Augusta, Georgia.

Col. Thomas's regiment had about fifty horses of its force of one hundred and fifty. This could accommodate one hundred double mounted as dragoons (mounted infantry) or fifty single mounted as cavalry for scouting. His assignment was to scout the west and south of Charles Town while leaving the remainder of the body on the west wing of the Charles Town defenses near the Ashley River. This was the uncompleted portion of the defense perimeter. Slaves and some of the militia worked feverishly to prepare a bulwark.

` Thomas left the position on the Ashley and proceeded on the north side of the Savannah with augmented companies from Polk's regiment. His purpose was to scout all possible fords. It was a dry spring and the rivers were down. On the 23rd of April, Thomas was scouting with his party near the crossing at Ebenezer. Through the dim fog, he heard the clanging of canteens, the groaning of artillery carriage and other tell-tale sounds of an army on the move. Turning to his scribe, he wrote to the recently promoted Moultrie:

> To: Gen. Moultrie.
> *I strongly suspect a crossing by enemy forces at Ebenezer. I shall fall back to Purrys-burg to assist in its defense. However, we shall continue to reconnoiter the enemy to determine, if possible, his intent.*
> *Your obedient servant. Col. Thomas Neel, Neel's Rangers, South Carolina Militia.*

He then dispatched Thomas Jr. to the General.

General Moultrie sent a message to General Lincoln, who was accompanied by Governor Rutledge, concerning the intelligence of Col. Neel.

In reply, General Lincoln requested that his artillery be sent to the Georgia campaign as well as all Continentals except the second and fifth who were to reinforce Purrysburg and to hold the same as long as possible. General Lincoln asked that General Huger's corps come forward and suggested that the enemy Col. Thomas spotted was merely a feign to distract Lincoln.

Thus, the forces around Charles Town were reduced to about 1,200 troops. The view of Lincoln, that the invasion of General Prevost was merely a distraction, continued to be challenged by Moultrie as he pleaded for more troops to defend Charles Town. On April 29, the King's forces under Prevost attacked Purrysburg. After a spirited defense, the forces under McIntosh and Neel made an orderly retreat northwest toward Dorchester. The Cavalry of the Neel regiment was dispatched west to follow General Prevost.

A rear guard was left at Coosahatchie under Col. Laurens. General Moultrie started forming a defense line at Tullifiny Hill. His orders to Col. Laurens were to hold the enemy in order to gain time for Lincoln to send troops.

Scouting ahead of Laurens, Thomas's cavalry found that the forces of Prevost were crossing at Ashland Ferry. He sent a message to Moultrie and related that he was falling back.

Moultrie commanded Laurens and his force of three hundred to assist Neel with a rear guard. The gaining of some time would give an opportunity for a force from Washington, and perhaps some more troops from Lincoln, to reinforce them.

As Lauren's detachment moved west along the Ashley River, he was intercepted by Col. Thomas. Thomas drew up with two diminished companies of cavalry. He saluted the young Colonel, resplendent in his copy of a continental uniform. Here was the contrast of South Carolina manhood, a backcountry gentleman in the buckskin of the New Acquisition militia saluting a privileged youth of the South Carolina Rice Kings.

"Well my young friend, it is good to see you. How goes your father?" queried Thomas.

"Colonel Tom, it is good to see you. My father serves in Philadelphia if it still holds. How is your family?"

"Young Andy is playing politician up in the New Acquisition. Tom is with one of my regimental companies."

"How does it look ahead?" asked Laurens.

"We spotted some advanced forces crossing at Ashley Crossing and threw them back. However, they will be coming again."

They rode to the top of a hill and observed the enemy.

"I believe that we can attack and rout them," suggested Laurens.

The astonished Thomas turned in his saddle and looked directly in the young man's eyes, "I thought your orders were to delay and not engage."

"Yes, but opportunity is ours. We cannot let this gift be rejected."

"I protest, sir, my orders are to scout and I cannot partake of your adventures. I shall report your disregard of orders to General Moultrie."

"As you wish. We cannot fail." He then turned and rode away. Thomas recalled his small command and continued to scout.

By mid morning the intense clatter of musketry greeted him. He turned with Col. Polk to the top of the hill where he recently viewed the river with Col. Laurens. They saw that the forces of Laurens had driven a small sortie of Prevost's forces across the river, and were engaged on the east or south side of the Ashley.

"That damned fool. That is the whole force of the Prevost army he has engaged – three hundred militia attacking 3,000 of the King's Highlanders and trained militia. Polk, what should we do?"

Col. Polk put down his spy glass and turned. "We will have to throw our country boys into the cauldron and save those lower South Carolina areas."

The distraught commanders returned to their commands. Thomas turned to his troops. "Well, those swamp dandies have done it to us again. We will have to go save them. Mount up. Company commanders of companies A and B will form a dismounted skirmish at the top of the hill. The rest of us will charge the crossing making a hell of a lot of noise."

In short order, the two companies formed a line at the top of the hill over-looking Ashley crossing. The remainder of the company charged down the hill at full gallop yelling and brandishing sabers in the air. They were met by fleeing troops as the forces of Laurens were retreating across the ford with Highlanders in hot pursuit. The river was shoulder high at this point. Most of General Prevost's troops waited for a boat to cross. At the sight of cavalry bearing down on them, the advance forces of Prevost fell back giving a portion of Lauren's troops time to regroup behind the Rangers who had since dismounted. The sight of the frontier shirts and distinct crack of the long rifle caused the British troops to withdraw further. The marksmanship of the Pennsylvania rifle was well known to the British. Officers knew their crimson uniforms were the primary targets.

Both the Rangers and Lauren's troops withdrew in good order to the hill where Thomas's dismounted company poured shots on any enemy troops that got within two hundred yards. At length they all withdrew to Tullifiny Hill where General Moultrie hoped to make a stand.

Thomas and the rescued Laurens appeared before General Moultrie. "Col. Laurens, what do you have to say about all this? Were you not ordered to refrain from a confrontation?"

"Your Excellency, I saw what I believed to be an opportunity to wipe out the troops of Prevost as he crossed the river."

"Let us see if I understand this. With a force of three hundred you were going to rout a force of three to four thousand of the King's finest, including the 71st Scot Highlanders?" Moultrie almost screamed.

"How many men did you lose?"

"One half of my command never made it back across," was Lauren's reply.

Moultrie continued, "Col. Neel, how many did you lose?"

"One man was thrown from his horse by a close artillery and broke his arm, Sir."

"Col. Neel, you are to hold this hill until nightfall so I can withdraw my forces back to Charles Town. I shall send an urgent message to General Lincoln for more aid. I understand that Count Pulaski arrived in Charles Town with a small force and that Governor Rutledge has brought a regiment back with him from the assault on Savannah. General Huger's forces were not returned to us. We have only 1,200 men to defend against the three to four thousand trained troops of Prevost." He then saluted Thomas.

"Thank you, Sir. We will do the best we can. I suggest that Col. Lauren's remnants retire with you." Thomas looked at the dejected and frowning Lauren who will forever be blamed for his unchecked enthusiasm and the loss of his command at Ashley Ferry.

Thomas formed a skirmish line at the base of the hill and placed the remainder of the Neel and Polk regiments at the top of the hill. All afternoon his riflemen from behind shrubbery and rocks at the top of the hill shot at anything that moved in front of them. The musket troops at the bottom of the hill waited in readiness for an attack that never came. Thomas slipped down the base and called his three captains together.

"I want you to number your men off by two's. An hour before sun down, I want your one's to set up three rounds of fire and then go up the hill. The riflemen will commence an intense fire. Then the two's will do the same. I want everyone on the way to Charles Town by nightfall."

At noon the skirmish line of General Prevost advanced to the base of the hill. The rattle of musketry erupted from behind the Whig lines. The British halted and withdrew. Soon the main body came forward with the Highlanders in the van to the beat of drums, fife and bagpipes. The Whig lines spoke again. Clouds of black powder soon obscured the line. Then the "ones" retreated. The Highlander charged only to be hit when the second echelon swung the action. The Highlanders stopped and then retreated. The Whigs retreated and joined their companions at the top of the hill. From there they made an orderly withdrawal to Charles Town.

As they rode toward the port city, Polk turned to Thomas. "I certainly don't understand why General Moultrie did not make a stand at Ashley Ferry or here in the narrow neck between the Ashley and Cooper Rivers. If that British fleet breaks through again we will be in great danger."

"Yes, just between the two of us, Moultrie has not done much for victory since he drove off the fleet back in 1775. I hope General Lincoln will not continue to feel this move by Prevost is feigned."

The next morning the regiments crossed over the fortifications which were completed from the Cooper River except one-quarter mile near the Ashley. Tom and Polk paused only briefly and commanded the sergeants to dress up the ranks. Then the two regiments proudly marched down the streets of Charles Town as the citizens cheered.

Tom turned to Polk and related, "If they only knew how really weak we are they would be praying and not cheering."

"Yes, but isn't it a grand feeling to be appreciated?"

Tom, after inspecting the duty stand and bivouac of his regiment, turned to his Charles Town home. The next night Thomas was awakened from a sound sleep by Sergeant Johnson.

"Sir, there is some action near our lines. Col. Polk wants you immediately."

With that he returned to the bedroom, embraced Jean, put on his clothes, and galloped through the streets to his troops. Thomas arrived to see fire flashing all along the fortification in the direction of the enemy. Soon a dazed group of men came through the lines carrying their wounded and killed amounting to twelve. Among them was General Huger.

Thomas arrived and asked the stretcher bound Huger, "Ben, what happened?"

"We were ordered by the Governor to close the gap left open for a passage through the abatis. When we were returning, friendly fire got us."

The next morning there was a memorial for the slain. General Moultrie asked one of Huger's officers who gave the order to advance that night. The answer came back, "The Governor."

Moultrie contained himself until after the service and then turned and sent a curt message to the Governor.

The next morning the General appeared before the Governor and Council dressed in his finest Continental blue and duff with a sword at his side. Standing at his full six feet, he addressed them.

"Sirs, we are in great peril. I did not authorize the raid of General Huger. If the Governor is to be in charge of militia while I command the meager Continentals, we will advertise our weakness before the enemy and will be defeated."

Governor Rutledge swelled up in pride and looked at General Moultrie, "Sir, the militia belongs to the state not the Continental government. We are not fighting to keep tyrants from overseas merely to replace them with tyrants at home."

"Sirs, I have served the state well these past five years. However, if I cannot be in charge of all the forces in the defense of Charles Town, appoint someone who can. I cannot have people being shot at by their own men!" His fiery eyes glistened.

Thomas, dressed in his frontier buckskin arose, "Your Excellency. I have served with this man off and on for five years. He is our most qualified and is adored by the troops. I suggest we work toward a compromise."

Governor Rutledge replied, "What does the esteemed colonel from the New Acquisition have in mind?"

"As a member of the militia and the Congress I propose that General Moultrie be given command of all military decisions and your Council the decisions related to non-military."

The Governor turned to his Council. "What say you?"

The Council assented to Neel's suggestion.

"What say you, General Moultrie?"

"I agree. All civil matters will rest with the governor. All military commands will be unified through me and both militia and Continentals are to report only to me."

All available labor and troops were engaged in preparing a perimeter abatis. There was still an open wing on the southern side. Thomas's and Tom Polk's regiments were stationed in this gap after the loss of General Huger's command.

As an assembly man of the South Carolina Congress, Tom would frequently go to the Congress Hall to hear the latest gossip, solicit and give opinions. He was particularly interested in the status of the General Prevost expedition toward them. Seeing the Governor, Thomas greeted him. The Governor asked Thomas to attend a joint meeting of the council of the Charles Town and the Council (formerly the Committee of Safety). After all of the participants were seated, Governor Rutledge stated the purpose.

"My fellow citizens we are in peril and face a great danger to our lives and cause. The forces of General Prevost hover at our gates. We have not heard from General Lincoln approaching behind Prevost nor have we heard any skirmish fire which would lead us to believe there is attacking from that direction. General Moultrie, what is the status of our forces?"

"We believe we have a strength of 1,200 troops counting militia and Continentals. However, we have shrunk from some 2,000 as militia leave their companies in order to defend their homes from the forces of Prevost who is ravaging the land as he approaches the city. Two militias were dismissed or deserted as they approached their own homes."

"And General Lincoln?" one of the Council asked.

"He returned one regiment to us but still holds ambition of restoring Augusta to our hands. He has split his command and is sending a regiment toward us. I have, as have you heard, no report for three days."

The Governor continued, "And what is your estimate of the forces of General Prevost?"

General Moultrie answered, "Col. Neel here counted two regiments of Highlanders from their regimental flags. There is a detachment of Royal Marines, a detachment of artillery, some Tory regiments, and several irregular battalions of unknown strength. I estimate between 3,000 and 3,500."

Young Laurens interrupted. "I protest, sir. I believe their strength is at least 5,000."

Moultrie continued, "If I may sir. I believe a spirited defense would delay the enemy long enough for General Lincoln to arrive."

"If it is a delay you need, then I shall give it to you."

"I propose cease fire while we negotiate for terms. If we could delay Prevost for perhaps twenty-four hours, perhaps Lincoln will be in his rear, and he will retreat."

The Council all agreed with his proposal. Col. Moultrie was asked to solicit General Prevost for terms. Moultrie at first refused, relating that he felt the enemy could not force his lines and relating that according to their agreement the previous day the civilians would negotiate any terms and not the commander. However, if so ordered he would pursue terms. The message was sent in Moultrie's own name in the person of his aide Kinloch.

The message read:

*General Moultrie, perceiving from the motions of your army that your intentions to besiege the town, would be glad to know on what terms would be disposed to grant a capitulation should he be inclined to capitulate.*

General Prevost retuned his answer on the 11th. It was signed by Lieutenant Colonel J.M. Prevost, the general's brother commanding the advance.

*Sir, the humane treatment which the inhabitants of Georgia and this province, have hitherto received, will, I flatter myself, induce to accept the offers of Peace and protection which I now make by order of General Prevost: the evils and horrors attending the event of a storm ( which cannot fail to be successful) are too evident not to induce a man of humane feelings, to do all in his power to prevent: ye may depend that every attention shall be paid, and every necessary measure be adopted to prevent disorders; and that all such inhabitants, who may not choose to receive the generous offer of peace and protection, may be received as prisoners of war, and their fate decided by the rest of the colonies. Four hours shall be allowed for an answer; after which, the detention of the bearer of this, will be deemed a positive refusal.5*

Governor Rutledge received the message through General Moultrie. He then called his Council to his home. General Moultrie asked Thomas to attend as his aide. The meeting convened with the Governor's Council. The Council consisted of Governor John Rutledge, Lieutenant Governor Thomas Bee, Colonel Charles

Pinckney, Christopher Gadsden, Roger Smith, Thomas Ferguson, John Edward, John Neufville, Col. Isaac Motte, and John Parker.

The Council considered Prevost's proposal. Laurens, Neel, Count Pulaski (newly arrived with about two hundred troops from Washington), and General Moultrie opposed the capitulation. The Governor then asked for the assessment of Moultrie's strength. He replied in the neighborhood of 2,000. The Governor and Council were alarmed at reports of up to 8,000 troops facing them. This included crack Hessians, Royal Marines, Highlanders and various Tory regiments who had joined the ranks (in truth the force was barely 3,000).

As the Council argued, Captain Dunbar of the newly reorganized Second Continental burst forth and informed Moultrie that a message had been received from Prevost which stated that he had observed the continued construction of trenches in violation of the agreement and if such action did not stop immediately his troops would march on the city. Moultrie ordered the construction to stop. Prevost waited for his answer far beyond the four hours and into the next day, the 12th. Prevost received a reply.

> *Sirs, I cannot possibly agree to so dishonorable a proposal as is contained in your favor of yesterday; but if ye will appoint an officer to confer on terms, I will send one to meet him as such time and place as ye fix on.*

Prevost refused, forcing the Council to send a second offer.

> *…To propose a neutrality during the war between Great Britain and America and the question of whether the State shall belong to Great Britain or remain one of the United States, be determined by the treaty of peace between the two.*

After a great deal of agitation and even threats of duels, the Council approved the message but could find no military to conduct it. Finally, Moultrie pressed one of his men into compliance. Col. McIntosh representing the Army and Col. Roger Smith representing the Governor met with Lieutenant Colonel Prevost in the field between the two forces.

After exchanges and clarifications back and forth, Prevost gave his reply that he would have nothing to do with the Governor, and that the garrison must surrender as prisoners of war.

When the message was returned to the Governor he replied, "Gentlemen, this is the way it stands. Do I give you up as prisoners of war?"

Some answered yes.

Moultrie with Thomas at his side turned and affirmed. "I will not deliver my forces up to be prisoners of war. We will fight it out!"

Thomas turned to Laurens. "Thank God we are on our legs again."

Moultrie then ordered a flag to be waved from the gate signifying that parleying was at an end. All day there was no reply. Finally, Moultrie sent Neel and Kinlock to address Prevost that they were sorry but the flag had waved sometime ago signaling that the conference was at an end.

All defenses were manned awaiting the attack. The next morning, the 13th, to the delight of all, there came the cry that the enemy had gone. Pulaski immediately was called with his cavalry but found that Prevost had already crossed Ashley Ferry and his forces now resided on the other side of the river.

CHAPTER 33

# Death of a Hero

General Lincoln's forces, as they retrogressed to come to the aid of Charles Town, arrived at Dorchester on May 14th, a day after Prevost made his escape across the Ashley Ferry. Prevost stayed on the south side of the Ashley and headed for the seacoast. He then took possession of Johnson Island, south of Charles Town, which is separated from the mainland by the Stono River. The river is connected to the Ashley by a canal called the Wappoo Cut. The British hoped to keep the island as a symbol of their presence and also as a base from which to forage for supplies.

In Charles Town, May was a rather pleasant time. The oppressive summer heat had not arrived and now hurricanes threatened. The Assembly purchased or offered letters of marque and reprisals to several schooners which were armed and while not able to stand up against a man of war could give warning of British intent. And besides, did not they have forts Johnson and Moultrie to defend the sea? A note of merriment sprang up as well as a round of parties to bring in the fine spring weather. The Governor hosted a ball and his wife prevailed upon Jean Neel to assist. Twins Thomas and Andrew came down from the west and upon being introduced as a part of the Neel Regiment had ample opportunity to be entertained by Charles Town's most ravishing beauties.

Thomas was dressed as a Colonel in the militia. The Neel Regiment had adopted a green uniform for occasions such as this when they would not be wearing their frontier leathers.

After the reception line and salutes to the various regiments, Thomas took Jean to the floor as the small stringed orchestra played one of the new dances called a waltz.

Jean had a green gown with a white bodice with her hair pulled back with a green ribbon. She wore white shell earrings, a gift from Running Bear. Even at her age she could steal the scene on any occasion.

"Well, fair madam, how are your sons doing in the whirl of Charles Town society?"

"Not too well. They are drug to the floor by some young maidens. They whirl a few steps and then steer them to the punch bowl. They stay there with them until relieved by some Charles Town Rice King's son, a dandy who never carried a rifle or knew a deer from a wild boar."

"My, my you are critical."

"Well, at least we have them here. Poor brother Henry and the Continentals were away for almost three years before coming home."

"Yes, he barely had time to conceive Jenny. I hear they are doing fine."

"I hope so. I suggested to Henry that he sit out the rest of the war. He lost his health in the Florida campaign and has those children of Andrew's to raise," remarked Thomas.

The ball went on until past midnight. Jean looked up to see the boys getting into a carriage with two young ladies and disappearing into the Charles Town night.

Tom turned to Jean. "I think those are the daughters of Col. Moultrie and Governor Rutledge. Don't people have to have chaperones here?"

"I wouldn't worry. Sally Rutledge will be watching them like a hawk."

"It is not the girls I am worried about. Those back country boys will be over their heads. I only wish we were flies on the wall to watch."

As they started to leave the ball, Col. Kintrock approached. "General Lincoln has ordered all regimental officers to assemble at his headquarters at seven in the morning."

Jean gasped, "Oh no, not again."

At seven the next morning, Thomas and Tom Polk walked together to the Council Chambers for a conference called by General Lincoln.

Polk commented, "I am worried about our leadership. We almost surrendered the town if not the province through the bungling of our leaders. What in the world took Lincoln so long to give up his Savannah campaign and come down to trap Colonel Prevost at Ashley Ferry?"

"I know and why did not our General Moultrie set up a more vigorous defense at the neck between the two rivers? On the other hand, he probably would have except Col. Laurens disobeyed the order to bring in the forces on the front line and retreat. His attack on General Moultrie's brother's Tory troops nearly lost our cause. Who are we serving under now?"

Polk continued. "Rumor has it that your regiment of horses will be with William Davies. Again Davies is the commander. Why can't you get a command?"

"I am a backcountry farmer. These lower state dandies can have their commands. I would rather be in the fight than take part in all of their machinations."

"I know. Your regiment is the most battle hardened. Because the Neel Rangers have remained together so long they respect you. If you had command of more regiments you would lose touch with us."

"I am obliged for the compliment, Tom. Well, here we are."

The two officers of the South Carolina militia walked into the Assembly. The

Assembly Hall still held its splendor even though it now housed the people's assembly rather than that of the Crown. The dais contained a table with chairs for General Lincoln, General Moultrie, and Governor Rutledge.

Coffee had been served and officers of the various regiments visited as they sipped their strong coffee. Thomas approached the sterling coffee service served by a Negro slave. As Thomas turned, he was spotted by General Moultrie. "Colonel Neel, a pleasure to see you. What in the world are you doing letting your young men keep my daughter and those of his Excellency the Governor out until the wee hours of the morning?" There was a smile and twinkle in his eye.

"The last time I saw young Andrew and Thomas they had been abducted by two young ladies as the boys labored near the punch bowl. Although these young officers should be court-marshaled for their lack of defense, I believe their surrender was honorable."

"I suppose. For your information, the two couples came to my home where they were well chaperoned until about three in the morning and then I threw them out—two fine young officers."

"Thank you, sir."

"By the way we are terribly short on cavalry. The Neel Rangers are assigned to Count Pulaski's regiment just sent down from General Washington."

"It will be an honor. It is good to see that the Congress has decided to help us. I have detected some lack of enthusiasm for the American cause. We must have another victory soon like Saratoga or the Tories will be active against us."

General Moultrie bid his good-bye as he had been called to the dais. The hall grew hushed as the platform officials approached. Governor Rutledge in the uniform of a South Carolina Militia Colonel, General Lincoln in the buff and tan of the Continental army and General Moultrie dressed in the same Continental army uniform took their seats. At the Governor's presence the officers all stood.

Governor Rutledge spoke, "Gentlemen, be seated. We rejoice at the restoring of our city and colony from the threat of invasion by the notorious rabble under General Prevost and his brother Col. Prevost. We are honored to have a great soldier to lead us. I now present General Lincoln who will share his plans."

"Thank you your Excellency. I now call on all of you to support our cause. I clearly was at fault in not realizing the danger to Charles Town last May of Prevost and his army. I thought his invasion of Georgia and South Carolina was a ruse to drive us from our purpose of banishing the King's troops for Florida and Georgia. I offered to resign, but I savor the support of General Moultrie and you gentlemen in helping us revenge our losses. A dagger now rests at the breast of our province. A force of General Maitland lies across the Wappoo Cut. This force acts as a base to forage among our people here in the lower regions. This force also acts as a symbol of Royal authority. We must rid our province of this cantankerous sore on the skin of our dear land. Do I have your support?"

A cheer rose from the room.

"Thank you. Now here is the plan. General Moultrie will hold the Town garrison in readiness. He will furnish each man with one hundred rounds and stand ready to cross the Ashley to James Island. I shall lead a group from the west of the John's Island composed of two battalions of light infantry under Col. Henderson on one flank and Col. Malmendy on the other. The left of the line will be supported by General Huger recovered from his injuries and four field pieces, a brigade of North and South Carolinians under General Jethro Sumner with two field pieces on the right. Col. Neel and Col. Polk's regiments of horse will join Count Pulaski's cavalry."

We will launch at daybreak on the 20th of June. None of you should disclose the strategy to anyone. Our success depends upon surprise. Please prepare your troops to be ready. You are dismissed."

As they left the building, Polk and Thomas were overtaken by Col. Laurens still limping from his wounds at the Hill. "I say Neel and Polk. Isn't it marvelous that we are on the march again? We now have our legs on. I have been assigned to General Moultrie's staff, and we are to bear the brunt of the attack across the cut. Where serve you?"

"We are with the Continental cavalry with Count Pulaski."

"Good show. You have the best mounts in the army."

Tom replied, "That is because we own them. Good luck to you, Sir." Laurens departed.

Polk turned to Tom, "Do you reckon Moultrie wants to keep an eye on him?"

"Probably. I'll bet he will be more involved in writing than fighting."

All of the preparations across the Ashley did not go unnoticed. Lieutenant Colonel Prevost on the 16th of June withdrew to Savannah taking with him the elite Sixtieth Regiment and most of the vessels which guarded the southern approaches to John's Island. The command of the British troops now evolved to Lieutenant Colonel Maitland. His forces now consisted of the first battalion of the Seventy-first regiment, part of a Hessian regiment, part of the North and South Carolina Regiments of Provincials, and some artillery.

At midnight on the 19th, General Lincoln placed his segment of the army in motion. By day break the light infantry under Lieutenant Henderson appeared before the enemy's works. At about seven o'clock Polk and Thomas mounted with their troops, heard the crackle of musket fire and knew the attack had begun.

Thomas turned to Polk and related, "I hated to give up my unmounted dragoons to another command, but I believe General Moultrie will take care of them."

"Didn't young Tom and Andrew go with the dragoons?"

"That's right. I am worried though. I didn't hear of Moultrie getting any boats. I guess he plans to swim across the Wapato."

Soon a young lieutenant came riding up. "I am looking for General Lincoln."

"His headquarters are over there. What news do you bring?" asked Tom.

"We encountered some pickets and the whole battalion fired. This alerted the Sixty-First Regiments of Scots who descended upon us. They continued fighting until all their officers were slain by those North Carolina riflemen. The enemy has retreated."

"Thank you and carry on," replied Thomas. In his heart he thought, "This is too easy." He thought that the main attack would wait for Moultrie on the west.

Tom and Polk held their mounted troops at the ready. They still heard no musketry from the pincer lead by Moultrie. Thomas slipped to Lincoln's headquarters to await orders.

Another lieutenant appeared breathless. He saluted and walked into Lincoln's tent and saluted again. Lincoln, studying his maps, looked up and said, "Report man."

"Sir, compliments from General Marion. The resistance has stiffened and our troops are in orderly withdrawal. They are being overwhelmed."

"Damn, where is Moultrie?"

"Sir, we have not seen him nor his forces."

"Col. Neel, take this order to Count Pulaski.

*Sir, ye are to immediately attack the British line with a charge of all your cavalry in order to break the British lines before General Marion.*

Thomas saluted, took the order and galloped to the hill overlooking the battlefield where Count Pulaski stood. The Count asked for a translation and then ordered all forces to charge.

Thomas returned to his command. "Neel Rangers, you have fought valiantly in every campaign for King, province and country for the past twenty years. We now lead you to rescue your brethren before the British guns. Heroes of the Snow, are you ready?"

A tumultuous roar rang out.

"Bugler, sound a cantor." The troop began an accelerated canter. Thomas raised his sword. "Rangers, charge!"

The hoofs made the ground tremble as the appropriated yells of Cherokees somehow rose in the throats of the Rangers as they charged forward. The sound would be picked up by the Confederate soldiers some seventy years later. Behind the wall, Maitland's British forces waited in good order. Suddenly the full fire of the front and rear rank of the British rang out. The smoke cleared and suddenly silence reigned except for the screaming of wounded horses and Neel's Ranger cavalry men lying on the ground. Maitland advanced, but was immediately thrown back by the regrouped forces of the newly arrived General Francis Marion, the Swamp Fox. The forces of Moultrie finally arrived after scurrying all morning for boats to cross the Wappoo cut. They too advanced on the British and threw them back. The British made an orderly withdrawal south and were allowed to escape.

Young Thomas and his twin Andrew came upon the site of the charge of the Neel Rangers. They were met by a horror. All round them lay dead horses, dead Rangers, wounded horses screaming. Some had a hoof caught in their own entrails which had been ripped from their stomachs. Rangers stood stunned by their first defeat. The unwounded were comforting their fallen comrades. As the boys approached, the familiar but drawn and tear-stained Tom Polk held a form in his arms.

"Papa," yelled Andrew as he ran toward the figures. Thomas followed.

As they approached Tom Polk, they looked down in horror at the face of their father with a massive hole on the right side of his skull. Open eyes stared at the heavens.

Polk lamented, "He is gone boys. Gone the way he would have liked, leading a charge."

Both boys knelt alongside their father. Thomas closed the eye lids of the fallen giant. They covered his body with a blanket and carried him to a boat.

Young Andrew stood in the boat and looked toward the now vacant British lines. "I swear on the altar of God, that those forces of King George shall pay for the outrages to our family. We shall fight them whereever they may be until we drive them from our sacred lands." He then embraced his twin brother Thomas and began to sob. The crewman began to row.

The news spread by the time the entourage returned to Charles Town. Jean came running down the street from the house. When she saw the form she screamed and fainted in the arms of Andrew. She was taken home. Thomas's body was taken to the undertaker.

Three days Col. Thomas's body lay in the Assembly foyer while members of the Assembly filed past, signed the memorial book and assembled for eulogies. Jean attended the wake accompanied by her sons Andrew and Thomas. She was dressed in a black dress with a white embroidered color and a veil. At the conclusion of the meeting Governor Rutledge approached Jean seated between the twins, who were dressed in militia frontier blouses. They stood as the Governor approached.

"Jean, we grieve such a great soldier. South Carolina and North Carolina are forever in your debt for the service Thomas has performed for America. Please accept this, our state Palmetto flag, as a memento of his service."

"Thank you, your Excellency, your words are most kind. Thomas died the way he would have wished in the service of his country."

An honor guard was selected to carry the body back to Bethel Church in the New Acquisition. The guard consisted of the Speaker of the Assembly and all of the Neel Ranger Regiment. The body was loaded onto a common wagon. Jean and the boys followed in the Governor's carriage, loaned for the occasion. After a week they arrived at the Bethel Church. Thomas had helped organize the church and was one of its first elders. Reverend Williamson delivered the eulogy. Messages were read from Governor Rutlege, General Lincoln, the Governor of North Carolina, and General Moultrie concerning the debt owed to Thomas. Mysteriously, a message had found its way through the lines.

> *Dear Jean:*
> *Please accept my sincerest condolences on the loss of my esteemed friend. I loved him like a brother even when opposing him in battle. I shall cherish him and grieve forever.*
> *Col. Christian Huck, lately of the King's forces.*

The pall bearers consisting of all the male members, including Tom Polk and Henry Neel, carried the coffin to the burying ground. There a prayer supplicated, a salute fired by a squad from Neel's Rangers, and the coffin lowered to the ground. Standing at a respectful distance were Running Path and Running Bear of the Catawbas and Little Carpenter, Great Peace Chief of the Cherokees. They stood in full warrior dress and stood at attention with their spears raised.

Thus ended the career of one of the Revolution's greatest fighters. His sons Andrew and Thomas never married but after the British conquered Charles Town headed militia which harassed the forces of Lord Cornwallis until their early deaths. Lord Cornwallis complained bitterly of the exploits of Andrew. Henry remained and died in the Waxhaw near Steele Creek. Many of the survivors of both families migrated to Tennessee and Kentucky.

The plantation of Thomas Neel lies under the waters of the Catawba River, which was dammed by the Duke Power Company.

# End Notes

1. Powell, William. *The War of Regulation: The Battle of Alamance, May 16.1771.* Raleigh, Division of Archives, 1971, PP. 25-26.
2. McCready, Edward. South Carolina in the American Revolution. p. 44.
3. McCready, p.35.
4. McCready, P.60.
5. McCready 364-380.

ISBN 141206689-1